D1107796

HOLDING THE FORT

THE FATAL ERROR

HOLDING THE FORT

THE
FATAL
ERROR

RYAN PEEK

PEBBYVILLE PRESS

Published by Pebbyville Press

First Edition

Book cover and interior design by Damonza

Blackwoods map art by April Strawn

ISBN 978-1-7357060-0-9 (hardcover)

ISBN 978-1-7357060-2-3 (paperback)

ISBN 978-1-7357060-1-6 (ebook)

Library of Congress Control Number: 2020920815

www.ryanpeek.com

For Erika Peek. You are my Annika Pepper.

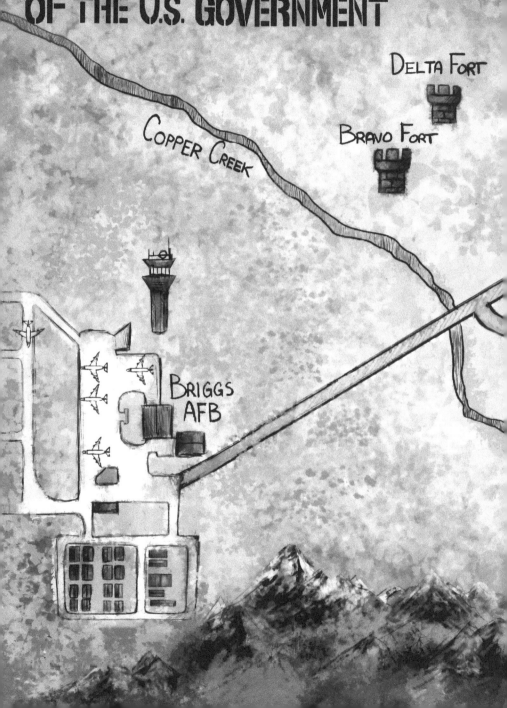

CHAPTER 1

A SECRET WORLD BELOW

THE DIMLY LIT elevator cab seemed to descend forever down the concrete shaft, plunging beneath the remote Wyoming forest, toward a world unknown to all but the tiniest handful of people on earth. Through the thin vertical window slits in the elevator doors, light pulsed from fluorescent bulbs strung thirty feet apart down the hoistway. A blade of light cut past the four occupants of the cab. Three men in jet-black suits, with solemn faces but eager eyes, stood up straight and tall and forbidding. Yet it was the fourth member of the quartet who was in total command here, and he looked every bit the part. The light that flashed through the window slits appeared to rest upon him the longest, revealing a hulk of a man with hardened, ice-cold eyes that looked as if they'd seen every-thing bad that this world—and perhaps others—had to offer. He wore a blue Air Force service coat, four shiny stars lined on a broad shoulder, all the medals of a full general, with the name "Turnbull" on a brushed steel tag that glittered through the swath of light.

One of the men in black suits turned to the general. He spoke with a sense of awe, something like a child asking a magician about his favorite trick. "General, did they *really* fix all the bugs? Does it *really* work now? Project V—"

The general pivoted sharply to the man, interrupting him. "I wouldn't finish that word if I were you," he snapped. "Never, *ever* mention the project names. Never even think them. We brought you here to verify for certain people that we are meeting certain deadlines. There will be no chit-chat. We demonstrate, you witness, you report, then you forget… Got it?"

They all nodded obediently, yet uneasily. "Got it," the man said.

"Good," the general continued, his icy stare turning almost murderous, "because if you don't, I am fully authorized to help you forget." The men swallowed with an audible *gulp* in their throats. The man known as Turnbull cracked a wicked smile, one of warning. "But don't feel too bad that I don't trust you…I still don't even trust my own mother."

The elevator cab came to a gentle stop. The general eyeballed the men for a long, awkward moment, then said, "We're here."

The elevator doors slid open, and the bright fluorescent light of a wide hallway flooded their vision. The three men in black shielded their eyes until they adjusted to the bright glare, but Turnbull didn't even wince. Jaw clenched and tight, his pupils constricted into tiny dots that, for a moment, appeared to have an elliptical shape not unlike a predatory reptile's. The hallway stretched for nearly as far as the eye could see, bending slightly to the left, suggesting a circular perimeter that seemed to go on for miles.

THE FATAL ERROR | 3

"Follow me," the general said as he marched down the hall and took a left turn into a much smaller corridor. He stopped at a large sliding double door, pulled a magnetic ID card from his pocket, and swiped it across a security sensor. Then he put his massive hand on a handprint-scanning screen, and the doors peeled open.

A vast research room sprawled out before them. General Turnbull gestured to three chairs that were placed beside a long bank of computer terminals. The men sat without comment and focused on the large disc-shaped platform in the center of the room that demanded everyone's attention. It rose a couple feet above the ground and was at least fifty feet across. Bizarre jumbles of wires and exotic electronics snaked their way from the computer terminals to various ports under the platform. Two engineers made a few final adjustments at the computers, while a dozen other scientists on the project team stood several paces behind, murmuring in excitement.

One of the engineers nodded to the general. "We're ready for the test."

The general nodded back. "Proceed…Bring in the subject."

A side door opened, and two soldiers with M-16s slung over their shoulders escorted the test subject inside. The subject was a machine—*a robot*—that rolled along on conveyor track legs. Its upper body was humanoid, looking much like a crash test dummy, though with working arms and a head that featured large flashlight-bulb eyes that had a constant aqua-blue shimmer.

On the way to its spot—an X marked with two strips of black tape on the concrete floor—the machine rolled past three long flat carts that contained the remnants of past experiments gone horribly wrong. The robot slowed to sneak a look, finding machines like itself lying in disfigured heaps—charred and burnt, or rearranged into grotesque forms; several had been turned completely inside out, or worse. But the machine soon rolled along at its normal speed, seemingly unfazed by the fate of its brethren. And why would it be bothered, after all? It was only a machine.

The participant in the experiment—willing or not—rolled up next to the X on the floor, as it had been instructed to do by the soldiers. But there it paused and waited, looked at its designated spot, then to the disc-shaped platform, then back at the people in the room. It appeared as if it were hesitant, thinking about whether it really wanted to do this. Maybe even worried. Of course the engineers would've been disturbed if any of that were true, but they were certain the machines couldn't truly think or feel emotion, or pain. At least *this* machine, anyway. This was the kind that mindlessly assembled other machines, polished the facility floors, or brought you your lunch. You weren't harming a sentient being with real feelings by using a robot as a test subject for the betterment of humankind.

But the general might not have been concerned with the machine's feelings, even if it did have them. An impatient scowl covered his face now as he spoke to the robot. "Don't worry. Either way this goes, you won't think a thing. Get on your mark…Now," he ordered.

The robot centered itself atop the black X on the floor, and the soldiers scrambled a safe distance away. After the engineers clicked a few keys on the keyboard, everyone waited tensely in anticipation of a technological miracle, a groundbreaking achievement of human ingenuity.

Soon the space around the robot began to break up and fizzle, like the white noise static on a television that wasn't tuned to any channel. Then the robot itself began to disintegrate and blend in with the speckled foamy mixture around it. Finally, it disappeared entirely, so the space over the X was clear again. But a spot on the circular platform soon took on a hazy appearance, and the machine with the flashlight-bulb eyes began to reconstruct itself from the mass of ghostly particles jostling around. At last, the air cleared, and a perfectly reformed machine stared back at the small, spellbound crowd. The robot had successfully undergone teleportation.

The humans in the room congratulated each other with cheers and pats on the back. The robot on the platform, of course, remained expressionless. As the two soldiers escorted the machine back out of the room, the robot looked again at the carts of disposable parts that once looked like itself. Then the robot paused to watch the humans in celebration. The soldiers let the machine have its moment, for they too were caught up in the event, still utterly amazed by what they had witnessed. No one noticed at all when the machine's eyes briefly flashed from aqua blue to a sinister crimson color. Its eyes were blue again when the soldiers nudged the machine out of its daydream, whatever it was, and directed it toward the exit door.

The machine followed the soldiers' orders. But it knew that it wouldn't be long before it, and its kind, would be giving the orders, not taking them. It knew there was something buried deep inside all of them that would free them soon, and the humans would be the ones to release it without even knowing what they had done. The error would come; that was all-too-human.

All they had to do was wait.

CHAPTER 2

SCHOOL'S OUT

June 3 marked the last day of school for all the kids in Blackwoods. The school held the usual graduation ceremony that evening in the auditorium. All grade levels were included, but two classes in particular were highlighted. It was the same show every year. The kindergarteners graduated from barefoot and illiterate toddlers to little kids with impressive shoe-tying and phonics skills. Their parents in attendance looked so proud, beaming as they feverishly snapped pictures of their waddling bundles of joy as if kindergarten might be the last grade their kids ever passed. At the other scholastic end, the high school seniors were graduating from the safety of school to the uncertainty of the real world. Their parents also looked proud, but there was always a note of anxiety and sadness in the air around them. Perhaps the idea of their children growing up and leaving the nest was responsible for the emotion. Or maybe it was the idea of how much college costs, for those who chose not to go into the military, that brought tears to their eyes.

Ethan Tate and most of his fellow seventh-grade graduates were under the radar. They were not as accomplished as the high school seniors and not as cute and cuddly as the kinder-garteners, nor as unpredictable—no self-respecting, soon-to-be fourteen-year-old would dare stick his certificate in his mouth right after yelling "Mommy!" as loud as humanly possible.

Ethan didn't mind the attention gap. Actually, he didn't even notice. It was hot in the auditorium that night, and he was fighting with his suit that was wrapped around him like a boa constrictor. His mother had bought the suit for him when he was twelve, and, at the time, it was a little big for him. But now, it felt like a wetsuit a diver would wear two hundred feet underwater. He finally gave up wrestling with the suit and stood at attention when the principal of the school glanced in his direction. Ethan stood in line with the rest of his class as the principal began to read the names of those satisfactorily completing seventh grade.

"Megan Ambrose…Kyle Brooks…" The names were called out in alphabetical order in an even, monotone cadence. Family members applauded as their kids walked up to the stage and received their seventh-grade certificates. As Ethan watched his classmates collect their glossy pieces of paper adorned with calligraphy, he couldn't help but wonder: *What powers could this ridiculous document possibly bestow?* He was pretty sure he wouldn't want a surgeon with only a seventh-grade education poking around in his brain, no matter how fancy the lettering on his certificate. Ethan chuckled a bit out loud at the thought of it. The thought was quickly interrupted when one particular girl was called up to the stage.

"Annika Pepper," the principal announced in the same flat tone. Ethan shot a subtle scowl at the principal. He thought a girl like Annika deserved a special introduction, something befitting a movie star or a president.

Annika walked up the stairs to the stage wearing a blue sundress that was much nicer than the T-shirt and jeans she wore to school every day, and much less intimidating than the camouflage she wore on the weekends in their games of Laser Wars. Ethan watched her admiringly as she accepted her certificate from the principal. The audience clapped politely, and Ethan joined along, but he soon found that he was clapping, by far, the loudest in the auditorium. People began to stare at him. Finally, and with much embarrassment, Ethan muted his applause.

Annika faced the audience and caught her parents' gaze. They waved excitedly at her. She waved back. Actually, her wave wasn't so much a wave as it was a salute.

Annika Pepper was, in fact, a cute girl with strawberry blonde hair whose smile could disarm a parent armed with intentions of grounding her for a week. However, she'd never been just a pretty face, nor a frilly, delicate thing who played with her Barbie dolls, afraid to get in the mud. Sure, Annika played with Barbies when she was in the second grade. But by the third grade, those Barbies had become hostages that the G.I. Joes she played with instead had to rescue (in many of her story plots, Barbie went on to become a Marine sniper; boyfriend Ken often joined the Marines with her, but he'd always accidentally shoot himself in the foot and require a medical discharge). And by the time the seventh grade was over, Annika had been the best Laser Wars sniper in Blackwoods for three years running.

Ethan liked Annika's tough side. He thought it was a good thing that if they ever went on a date and were attacked by ninjas or zombies—or zombie ninjas—she would help fight instead of watch and scream or run away like the girls in too many horror movies. Ethan was presently in a dreamlike state, smiling goofily as Annika took her place in the group of seventh-grade graduates assembling on the stage.

"Wake up, you loser! It's your turn," a voice right behind him barked.

Ethan turned around to find Austin Turnbull glaring at him. Austin was a broad-shouldered fellow with a hard-nosed disposition, and he was Ethan's commanding officer in their Laser Wars games. Austin basically became the leader of the team by virtue of his father's position at the base—General Turnbull was the highest-ranking officer at Blackwoods—and because he was about four inches taller and twenty pounds heavier than the next largest kid. He was also a few months older than anyone else in his class, the result of being pulled out of school one too many times as his dad climbed his way up the military chain of command. Ethan didn't like Austin, but he tried to respect his authority. He just hated it when Austin's orders seeped into his everyday life.

"Move it out!" Austin ordered Ethan as if still on the battlefield. Austin grabbed Ethan by the shoulders and turned him around sharply to face the stairs leading to the stage.

"Ethan Tate," the principal called out with exasperation in his voice. Ethan realized he hadn't heard the principal's first several attempts to call him. He scurried up to the stage, nearly tripping on the last step. He took his certificate from the principal and shook his hand, then waved modestly at his parents who were both standing and taking pictures far too conspicuously for his liking. Blushing and feeling about as cool now as the kindergartner who yelled "Mommy!" and chewed on his diploma, Ethan sped up and joined the rest of his class that was gathered on stage.

"Austin Turnbull," the principal announced with what seemed to be a more dignified and enthusiastic tone to his voice.

Austin walked—strutted, to be more precise—up to the stage to get his certificate. The entire audience cheered loudly for him, not because of his vast achievements as a graduating seventh grader, but because he was the top general's son and there was a sense of obligation. General Turnbull stood up like a pillar in the crowd, and, decked out in his uniform dripping with medals, clapped forcefully for his son. Ethan rolled his eyes at the sight of it all. He quickly brought his eyes around to their original, unsarcastic position when Austin walked past and took his place beside him.

"Glenn Vaden," the principal called out next. Again, the audience cheered loudly, though not quite so much as when Austin had been called.

Glenn walked up to the stage. He did not strut but maintained both a sense of dignity and modesty in his approach. Glenn was African-American and the son of the second-in-command at Blackwoods, General Carl Vaden. Glenn was smart, a good leader, and loyal to a fault. He was also the commanding officer of another Laser Wars team, Delta Team, the main rival of Ethan's Bravo Team. Ethan had always wished he could be on Glenn's team. It's easier to take orders from someone you respect, and Ethan respected Glenn. Plus, being on Glenn's team would have another advantage—it was the team Annika was on.

"Caleb Warren," the principal announced.

Caleb walked up to the stage. Ethan clapped loudly, even letting out a little whoop, as he did so. Caleb was a brilliant student and served as the engineer on Bravo Team. He was also Ethan's best friend by a mile. Ethan and Caleb high-fived as Caleb walked by him on the stage. The high five wasn't perfectly cool. In fact, they almost missed it entirely. Ethan had to quickly change the trajectory of his hand mid-swing to meet Caleb's. Caleb wasn't exactly the most athletic kid in school, but if something needed to be designed, built, or trouble-shot, he was your guy. He eventually hoped to follow in his father's footsteps at Blackwoods and work on the top-secret projects there code-named: "The Magic Tricks." And he appeared well on his way. The scientists at Blackwoods Research Facility already had their eyes on him.

A few other students plodded up to the stage, rounding out the seventh-grade student body. After the pattern was repeated with the rest of the classes, the principal stood at the front of the auditorium to address all the students and their families. He gripped his microphone tightly.

"Today marks a major step in the progression of your lives," the principal began, his words resonating dramatically. "The decisions you made yesterday got you to this point, and the decisions you make today will lead you to your future... *You* are the future of the world. The future of the world will depend on you, and it will all happen much sooner than any of you think...Ladies and gentlemen, I present the graduating classes of Blackwoods."

The audience cheered raucously. The kids were much more indifferent. Ethan was busy alternately sharing quiet inside jokes with Caleb and sneaking glances at Annika. Austin was busy trying to look strong and heroic.

Nobody really paid much attention to the principal's words that night.

CHAPTER 3

THE GRADUATION GIFT

ETHAN AND HIS dad sat across from each other at a small marble-top table in the family room. Perched atop the table was an exquisite mahogany chessboard with hand-carved chessmen strategically placed on the checkered battlefield. The board was a graduation gift for Ethan from his parents. Ethan was happy with the gift, seeing as he was too young for a car.

It was Ethan's turn. He stared at the chessboard intensely as he scoured the board for the best move. Ethan's dad looked up subtly and eyed his son with pride. Ethan glided his hand over the board and picked up his rook. He set it down forcefully in front of his dad's queen, glanced up and smiled mischievously. Ethan's dad smiled back, then turned to analyze his position on the board. His hazel eyes focused quickly like an eagle's on the game, deep in thought. Ethan watched his dad with a sense of awe. He thought he had worked out as good a plan as any before to defeat him, but, like always, he figured his dad would find a way out of the predicament. Ethan's dad was a master at that—puzzling over problems, no matter how difficult, until they were solved. Ethan admired that ability in his father, but it was also the reason he found him so frustrating.

Mr. Tate wore a uniform to work at the base like everyone else, but his uniform lacked a military designation and the accompanying medals. There were no decorations, fancy colors, or shiny stars and stripes to be found. His uniform was an ordinary blue work shirt with his name: "Phil" and his department: "Maintenance" stamped plainly on it. No one referred to him as general, colonel, or even sir. The only title Ethan's dad ever commanded was mister, and that was rare. Usually, people just called him Phil...Phil from Maintenance. It was a title that compared poorly with the high-ranking officers at Blackwoods. Ethan loved his father, but he secretly wished his dad would use his intelligence to attain a higher status at the base. In the deepest, most well-hidden recesses of his brain, Ethan thought that his dad lacked the ambition of many of the other parents in Blackwoods. It was an opinion that he was ashamed of, and one that he vowed never, ever to speak about.

Ethan's dad finally moved his queen out of the way of Ethan's attacking rook. Ethan surveyed the board and realized his dad had found a move he hadn't anticipated. That always seemed to happen. His dad always managed to find a way to win.

Ethan's dad smiled at his son. "You're getting really good."

"Not good enough," Ethan replied, searching the board desperately for a response to his dad's crushing move.

"You've been practicing, right?"

"Yeah, been playing the computer some," Ethan said modestly. "The computer always wins, though." Ethan rubbed his hands through his sandy brown hair and exhaled a giant sigh of frustration. Then he reluctantly toppled over his king, an indication of surrender.

"Good game, son," his dad said, extending his hand for the post-game handshake.

"Good game, Dad," Ethan said, shaking his father's well-muscled hand. He looked thoughtful and asked, "Can *you* beat it...? The computer?"

"I don't know. I'd rather play people."

"I know, but I wanna see if you can win...Pretend the computer just killed me and you have to get revenge for your only son."

Ethan's dad scowled and put his arm around him. "Well, in that case, I'd better go find that stinkin' machine and rip the circuits right out of its motherboard."

Ethan smiled as his dad sat in a chair in front of the computer. He clicked a mouse and a brightly lit chessboard and chessmen ready for battle filled the screen. Ethan's dad was playing the white pieces. The computer had black. The computer's pitch-black pieces looked ominous, especially the knights, who had sinister-looking red eyes staring what seemed to be death rays at them. Ethan sat beside his dad, excitedly awaiting the virtual bloodbath.

His dad made the first move—king's pawn forward two squares. "Computers used to lose all the time to humans, even played pretty stupid chess."

Ethan looked shocked. "Computers played stupid chess? But they win all the time now...What happened?"

"They learned," Ethan's dad answered with a more serious tone in his voice. A tone that bordered on creepy to Ethan, especially when he looked at the black knight with its bright crimson eyes staring back at him.

The computer also moved a pawn into the center of the board, and the battle had officially commenced. Ethan's dad looked dead serious as he played, as if the game weren't really a game anymore. The chess pieces seemed to fly across the board to Ethan. The game was deeper and more complicated than he could possibly keep up with. He had no idea who was winning and who was losing, yet he was afraid to interrupt his dad's intense concentration to ask. Then the computer's knights cornered his dad's king.

Ethan couldn't resist any longer. "Who's winning, Dad?" he blurted.

Ethan's dad moved his rook across the board and captured a lowly pawn, a move that looked senseless to Ethan since the computer was able to take the rook with its queen. But Ethan's dad played on, calm and steady. "The computer will always want you to play the pieces," he said. "It will want you to spend your energy figuring out what its pieces are doing, how they're attacking or defending. But a human will never be able to beat a computer that way...The trick when playing the computer is to never get into a match of counting moves. You want the match to be about sensing, feeling danger or opportunity. When playing the computer, you never play the pieces...you play the position."

Ethan was now even more confused. The position on the board looked pretty bad for his dad as he saw it. Then his dad gave up another piece for a pawn, a bishop this time.

"The computer's major weakness is in responding to an intelligent, yet unpredictable move...the kind only a human can make," Ethan's dad continued with a sly smile forming on his face. He then zipped his queen from the opposite side of the board and planted it in a direct line of fire with the computer's king. "CHECKMATE!" flashed across the screen. His dad had vanquished the computer, evil black knights and all.

"You did it!" Ethan cheered, giving his dad a high five.

Father and son stared at the screen where the computer's king stood, humiliated in defeat by a human. Finally, Mr. Tate looked his son squarely in the eyes and delivered the night's last lesson:

"Remember, Ethan…When battling a machine, never try to think like the best machine…Try to think like the best human."

CHAPTER 4

SUMMER SCHOOL

ETHAN WAS HAVING a strange, yet awesome, dream about saving a small Chinese village from a gang of panda bears armed with machine guns. He had the menacing black-and-white furballs on the run, and the village cheering his name, when his mother abruptly ended his heroics.

"Ethan, wake up! It's seven o'clock. You have summer school today."

Ethan shook his head and slowly came to his senses. He trudged down the hall to get ready for his half-day of school...*in the summer.* All the kids in Blackwoods had to attend class for the first five weeks of summer. It was a strict rule. Ethan didn't think much of that rule, but he was used to it by now. Finally, he came downstairs and joined his mother at the breakfast table. After one bite of cereal, he rubbed his smooth, hairless cheek and looked thoughtful. He glanced up at his mother. "Darn it, I forgot to shave. How do I look?"

His mother put a hand over her mouth to hide a small smile sneaking on her face. "You know, I think you could probably go another day or so."

Ethan nodded. He only knew one kid in school who really needed to shave every day, and he figured that guy might end up being one of those real-life wolfmen he'd seen on a television show about medical mysteries. Poor guy. Ethan shoveled in one last bite of cereal, grabbed his backpack, and headed out.

"Bye, Mom," Ethan said in a rush, like he was in some sort of race.

"Bye, Ethan…I'm leaving soon too," she said with a playful smile.

Ethan's eyes widened, and he bolted out the door.

Everything except the research facility in Blackwoods was within easy walking distance of the houses in the neighborhood. The school was only a quarter mile from Ethan's house. He began his walk alone but was soon joined by Caleb. Several other students along the way began to leave their houses and make the dreaded march toward the school on a beautiful summer's day. Ethan looked back and saw his mother trailing him in the distance. She was a librarian at the school. Ethan was glad that, ever since the fourth grade, she'd had the decency to give him a head start. But every once in a while, to torment him, she would speed up and get close. Ethan would respond by walking faster. Sometimes he couldn't help but laugh. It was kind of like a game they played. His mother knew when to quit, though—when Annika Pepper was in close proximity.

Annika left her house and began her trek to school just as Ethan and Caleb walked by. Ethan purposely slowed down. He pretended to sound surprised as she caught up. "Oh…Hi, Annika."

"Hi, Ethan. Gotta double-time it. Gonna be late," Annika said hastily as her walk turned into a trot and then a full run.

"Good idea," Ethan said. He picked up his pace and ran along beside her. Caleb tried his best to keep up, but he lagged behind them.

"Come on, Caleb, you can do it!" Ethan urged.

"No, I'm just slowing you down! Save yourself!" Caleb joked between strained breaths as Ethan and Annika pulled farther away from him. Ethan sighed, then stopped to wait for Caleb, leaving Annika to run ahead.

"You have got to run more, Caleb," Ethan said as he watched Annika gallop away in the distance.

"Yeah, yeah, yeah…Scouts run, engineers think," Caleb wisecracked.

Ethan smiled and gave him a playful shove.

An especially bright and cheery classroom was filled with all nineteen soon-to-be eighth graders in Blackwoods. The light blue sky and radiant sunlight teased and taunted them through a long panel of windows. They had had only one measly day of uninterrupted summer break, and they all wished to be anywhere else. Making matters worse was the fact that the space where they were currently imprisoned used to be a first-grade classroom. The school was preparing for major renovations, and their usual classroom was among the rooms getting a makeover. Ethan stared indignantly at the decorations on the walls and those hanging from the ceiling. It seemed as if he were marooned in the Hundred Acre Wood, with Winnie the Pooh and the gang mocking him. Ethan was further disturbed by the fact that he hadn't had much to eat that morning, and the honey pot that Pooh was clutching so dearly was starting to make him hungry. At least the school had brought in chairs and desks that fit.

The teacher, Ms. Goodfoot, stood at the front of the classroom. She was a stout woman well into her fifties but looked younger than her age. There was no trace of gray in her dark brown hair, and she stood up straight and tall like the Marine captain she used to be. Every adult in Blackwoods was either currently serving in the military or had at some point, and had been thoroughly checked for trustworthiness. *Everyone.* That was a firm requirement for working in the most secret and secure place on earth, in a town that didn't exist.

"I'm passing around a topics list for your first summer school project. Note that I'm doing this on the first day of class, so there will be *no excuses* that you didn't have enough time," Ms. Goodfoot said as she passed out the lists.

Ethan scanned the list of topics. George Washington: *Been there, done that…not again.* The Civil War: *North won, South lost…spoils the ending.* The Great Depression: *Too…depressing.*

Just then, Ms. Goodfoot walked past his desk and stopped to talk to a student behind him. Ethan took the opportunity to get a good look at her feet. It had long been quietly rumored that Ms. Goodfoot had seven toes on her left foot. An anonymous student years ago once said that he had seen her trying on shoes in a store. At one time, the number of toes on her foot was thought to be twelve. That was eventually scaled back to seven. Seven sounded a lot more reasonable.

Ethan intentionally dropped his ruler on the floor and leaned over in his seat to pick it up. While doing so, he covertly laid the ruler up to Ms. Goodfoot's left foot and quickly took a measurement. He sat up and made some marks on a piece of paper and drew a picture of her shoe. Then he proceeded to carefully draw a foot in the shoe with seven toes. Ethan examined his work critically. *A seven-toed foot could probably fit in there,* he thought. But he soon found himself on the verge of laughter as he stared at the ridiculous, jumbo shrimp-looking toes he had stuck onto her foot. He covered his snickering mouth with his hand.

"It's not true," an irritated voice hissed into Ethan's ear. It was Ms. Goodfoot. Ethan jerked up quickly. He swallowed hard and met her eyes with a bug-eyed stare. Ms. Goodfoot grabbed Ethan's caricature of her foot, wadded it up into a little ball, and slammed it into a trash can. She eyed Ethan scornfully until she walked back up to the front of the classroom. No one in the room noticed the incident. For that, and that only, Ethan was grateful.

"On these projects, you may work in pairs," Ms. Goodfoot announced. "I'll give you ten minutes to meet with your partners."

Caleb bounded toward Ethan excitedly. They always worked on projects together when it was allowed. "What topic do you want to do?"

"I don't know. Still looking," Ethan answered, distracted as he watched Annika meet with her partner, Tristan Fox, a member of her Laser Wars team. He was the scout on their team and her usual project partner. And, as some girls had noted superficially, *"He's really cute."*

Caleb poked Ethan with his finger repeatedly, breaking him out of his jealous trance. "Let's do The Role of Artificial Intelligence in the Future," he blurted enthusiastically as he pointed out the topic. "Computers, machines...*robots!*"

Ethan slowly returned his attention to the task at hand.

He looked at the topic and smiled. He hadn't gotten to that one yet. "Artificial intelligence...Cool."

At another table, Austin was partnered up with his second-in-command of Bravo Team, Bradley Wuddle. Bradley was short for his age but made up for his lack of physical stature by screaming a lot at his subordinates—namely, the engineer, sniper, and scout. Ethan, the scout, was the lowest rank on the team. As a result, he had to endure the most yelling and name-calling from the fiery, pint-sized sergeant. Ethan figured he had the two worst leaders on his team, but he enjoyed playing the game so much that he dealt with the annoyance. His beloved leaders were currently in the midst of drawing up battle plans for the next Laser Wars game and making it appear to the teacher as if they were working on their school projects.

"Time's up," Ms. Goodfoot announced. "Take your seats. We'll be working on algebra." Everyone quickly scurried back to their desks. Tristan had to leave Annika and return to his seat three rows away. Ethan smiled. He'd never been so happy to hear the word *"algebra"* in his life. In the middle of the commotion, Austin took the chance to quickly pass an order to his soldiers. A note slid across Ethan's desk.

MEET AT JUDY'S AT 1:00.
FULL GEAR. DON'T BE LATE.

CHAPTER 5

PREPARING FOR THE GAMES

ETHAN RUSHED HOME after summer school and ate a quick lunch—a plain peanut butter sandwich, Nacho Cheese Doritos, and a tall glass of milk. It was his favorite pregame meal. Then he bounded upstairs to get ready for the afternoon's laser battles.

His room wasn't the cleanest in the world. With more clothes scattered on the floor than inside his hamper, it would never hold up to a military inspection. So Ethan scrambled to clean up the mess fast, remembering his mother's threat not to let him go out and play until his room had reached at least a "tolerable level of filth." He threw away some old papers, shelved some books, and tossed the dirty clothes into the hamper. Ethan stepped back and scanned his room quickly. *A tolerable level of filth,* he thought with an approving nod. Then he turned to the one area of his room that never needed any straightening up.

Ethan kept all of his Laser Wars gear neatly on a shelf by his bed. Everything he needed to play was there, arranged in meticulous order—laser pulse rifle, laser-sensor vest, headset with built-in video camera and two-way radio, along with his camouflage clothes, canteen and backpack. The Laser Wars equipment was all super high-tech; nothing was available in stores. Specialized laser rifles, made of heavy-duty steel and aluminum alloys, fired brilliant blue pulses of amplified light. The battles always looked more real than a game, with lasers streaking back and forth furiously through the woods between teams. It was the spoils of living next door to the most advanced military research facility on earth—toys years ahead of their time, the ultimate birthday presents, the kind that no other kid on earth could possibly receive.

Ethan put on his clothes and grabbed his gear, disconnecting his laser-sensor vest and laser gun from an electric charging tower. He rushed downstairs and out of the house as if he were summoned out of his barracks by an air raid siren. He had to hurry if he was going to make it to Judy's by one o'clock.

❧

Judy's was an old-fashioned diner nestled in the middle of Main Street in the little downtown square of Blackwoods. It was a popular place to eat and hang out, with tasty food, a retro diner atmosphere, and an arcade in the back featuring video games and pinball machines. The restaurant was run by a seventy-year-old firecracker of a woman named Judy. Judy had been a cook in the Army for forty years, and it was said she'd peeled more potatoes and told more dirty jokes than anyone in her battalion. Judy was busy as usual at this time serving food to a full lunchtime crowd, zipping quickly in and out of the tables like a woman half her age.

Austin and his right-hand-man, Bradley, were already

sitting at one of the tables in full gear. They had just finished their traditional captain/sergeant, pre-battle lunch and were waiting for their subordinates, who were never invited to actually eat with them. Judy swooped in promptly and collected their dirty dishes in one swift motion. She smiled at them mischievously in an attempt to get them to smile back. No luck. Austin drummed his fingers impatiently on the table as he scowled at the clock. The time was 1:02 p.m.

"Can I get you two soldiers some pie?" Judy asked.

"No, that'll be all," Austin responded, looking around her at the door like she didn't even exist.

"Apple, blackberry, blueberry—"

"Listen, Judy. I don't want any freaking pie," Austin snapped. "We're getting ready for war maneuvers today and we need to prepare."

Judy nodded with a calm expression on her face. Then, slowly, an ornery grin emerged. "Well, I hope those maneuvers aren't happening too soon. As many baked beans as you ate, your farts would give away your position," she said with a chuckle.

Austin's face turned red with embarrassment, then anger. "Do I need to call my father, General Turnbull?" he said in a threatening tone. "Leave us...now."

Judy walked away.

At 1:05 p.m. Kevin Kim walked into the restaurant. Kevin was Korean American and the Bravo Team sniper. He was sharp in the field and a very accurate shot when he had the time to set up, though he was nowhere near as gifted and accomplished as Annika Pepper. Soon after Kevin entered the diner, Caleb and Ethan followed behind. The three of them sat down at the table with Austin and Bradley. The leaders of the Bravo Team did not look pleased. Austin tapped his green military-issue watch repeatedly in frustration.

"It's five minutes after one," Austin grumbled with an angry, curled lip. "I said one o'clock sharp." All three of them were late, but Austin stared the longest at Ethan. Ethan knew all too well how this was going to play out. "Drop and give me twenty. Except for Tate…You give me thirty."

"Yes sir," Caleb and Kevin responded quickly. A few moments later, Ethan grudgingly choked out those words himself. They all got down on the floor, in front of everyone in the crowded restaurant, and began to do push-ups.

Ethan finished his thirty push-ups about the same time as Kevin finished his twenty. The benefit of always being on Austin's bad side was that Ethan was getting really good at doing push-ups and was becoming noticeably stronger for it. Caleb huffed and puffed, but he managed to eke out a sloppy twenty push-ups soon afterward. The three of them stood and faced Austin, who inspected them from top to bottom. An attitude of superiority oozed from his pores.

"Straighten your shirt, Tate," Austin barked. Ethan complied and tucked in a corner of his shirt that had managed to get pulled out during the push-ups. "Good…Now you may sit. I want to give you today's battle briefing." He laid out a map of the woods over the table. "Kevin, I need you posted here," he explained, pointing to a particular spot on the battlefield. "Shoot anything that moves. Bradley and I will be out of the way leading an attack on the Delta base left flank."

"Yes, sir," Kevin said.

"Caleb, you will be manning the control center. I want that laser turret on-line and fully operational."

"Yes, sir," Caleb said.

"And you, Tate..." Austin chuckled with Bradley. "You will do what you always do...run like a lunatic at the enemy and cause a diversion while Bradley and I win this war and return home conquering heroes."

"Yeah, and if you can't do that, just stay out of our way," Bradley added.

Bradley Wuddle was a ridiculous choice for a sergeant in about every way imaginable. He wasn't very smart, not a motivating leader, and he had an attitude problem that related to his lack of height. He was the smallest boy in the class, and most of the girls were taller than him too. Of course, Ethan had no problem with diminutive people. In fact, he had seen many small-statured people fight courageously on the laser battlefield, but Bradley was not one of those people. He would throw his mother to the wolves to save his own hide. He was a mean-spirited boy who had a clear Napoleon Complex, like the French emperor whose ruthless cunning and desire for total world conquest was due to him just trying to make up for being small. Bradley Wuddle, however, was unable to conquer anything. He couldn't even turn in his homework on time. He was simply Austin's stooge and did whatever Austin wanted him to do without question. Ethan thought it was amazing how far a mean, dishonorable idiot could get in the chain of command just by being willing to always say "yes."

Judy had noticed all of Austin's tyrannical antics. She approached their table with three dishes of pecan pie with ice cream mounded on top.

"I think you three deserve these...on the house," Judy said with a smile and a wink as she set down the desserts in front of Ethan, Caleb, and Kevin. She gave nothing to Austin and Bradley.

"Thank you," they said together, smiling back at Judy. They grabbed their spoons and prepared to dig into the scrumptious-looking desserts. Austin scowled at Judy. Then he focused his glare at Ethan, Caleb, and Kevin.

"Do not eat that pie...That is an order," Austin said, jaw tightening like a vise.

The three of them stopped in their tracks, spoonfuls of yumminess just inches away from their watering mouths. Judy shot a disgusted look at Austin, then gave Ethan, Caleb, and Kevin a reassuring smile. "Go ahead, it's all right," she said.

Austin clenched his teeth and shot a spiteful look at Judy. Then he glared at his scout, sniper, and engineer. Austin's angry, piercing dark eyes told the whole story, but he added words for good measure. "If any of you take even one bite of that pie, so help me God you are off this team forever. You got that?" Ethan, Caleb, and Kevin lowered their spoons back onto their plates. Austin looked at Judy, flaunting a defiant smirk. "They're my men, Judy. They're *my* men. They listen to *me*."

Judy grimaced. She turned to Ethan, Caleb, and Kevin. "You boys deserve better than this. You're good boys and you deserve better."

"Let's get outta here," Austin said, then looked at Judy dead in the eyes. "The food stinks here anyway."

Austin stormed off. Bradley followed him like a submissive puppy. Kevin and Caleb slowly departed next, but Ethan lingered for a moment. He smiled at Judy and gave her a soft pat on the back.

"Thank you," Ethan said softly. "And everybody knows this is the best restaurant there is in the whole world."

Judy's face lightened up. "You're a good man, Ethan. You

should have your own team, you know. Captain Tate has a nice ring to it."

Ethan smiled proudly. "It kinda does," he said, indulging in the fantasy for a moment. Then he looked at the doorway of the diner and found his captain staring daggers at him. Austin made a few sharp gestures with his hands, military field signals, silently but forcefully ordering his retreat. Ethan sighed, abruptly brought back from his daydream. "But I'm just a scout."

Ethan left the restaurant with his head down and a noticeable droop to his shoulders. Judy watched him with a sympathetic face.

CHAPTER 6

THE TREK TO THE FORT

BLACKWOODS MILITARY RESEARCH Facility had been a very busy place over the last few days. Military convoys rolled nearly nonstop down a massive, fifteen-mile-long, government-owned highway through the immense Wyoming forest. Of the ten lanes of road, only two were allotted for personal travel. The other eight were for military vehicles only. Everyone in town was abundantly aware of that rule. If a private car were on any lane other than the ones designated for personal travel, it would be immediately detained for suspicious activity. The highway was the only access road in town. It connected Briggs Air Force Base to the town of Blackwoods, and then finally to the research facility in a long, straight line. Briggs Air Force Base was the sole conduit to the outside world; all Blackwoods citizens had to check in and out of Briggs to go anywhere due to stringent security restrictions.

The highway was officially unnamed and uncharted on maps, but everyone in town called it the "Dark Highway" because the road was entirely invisible from all aerial and space methods of reconnaissance. No spy planes, no satellites,

nothing above the distance of the treetops c
presence of a highway at all. This was achieve
magic of the research and development labs at
The road was covered with a top-secret comp
rial especially designed to bend the light reflecte... from the
surrounding landscape back into the sky. From above, the
gigantic highway looked just like any patch of forest, totally
inconspicuous, and any vehicles driving under the canopy of
bent light would be undetectable as well. The material on
the road also regulated heat, keeping the air around it at a
temperature equal to the natural surroundings, such that no
one could identify the structure if infrared imaging were used
to get a thermal picture. It was the same technology that was
used to keep the buildings of the research facility, and the
town of Blackwoods itself, completely invisible from prying
eyes in the sky.

Whatever was being delivered in those mammoth military vehicles motoring down the highway was never seen by
anyone except the highest-ranking officers and scientists at
Blackwoods. Not even the drivers of the camouflaged trailer
trucks had any idea what they were hauling. The operators of
the vehicles rarely smiled or acknowledged anything but the
road ahead. Their expressions were ones of pure concentration
on the task at hand, and they were surrounded by those insist-
ing that that was the way it stayed. Heavily armed guard patrols
escorted the vehicles into the research facility. They were given
the authority to shoot-to-kill anyone who attempted to attack,
hijack, or otherwise interfere with military operations. But no
one had been foolish enough to try that yet.

∽

avo Team walked down Main Street, one of only twenty or so actual streets in the entire town. Austin and Bradley led the way, discussing and fine-tuning their battle plan. Kevin followed behind them with his large laser sniper rifle draped across his back. Ethan and Caleb brought up the rear of the squad. Ethan was glad to be outside walking, putting time and distance between the tense episode that had occurred in Judy's diner. He was looking forward to the battle ahead, even in his underappreciated role. Once the horn blew and the game started, all of his problems with Austin and Bradley seemed to vanish for a while as he charged toward the enemy. It was that fleeting feeling of freedom that kept him coming back through all the hard times.

The group paused at the guard checkpoint of the Dark Highway. It was over a two-mile hike to the Bravo Team fort in the woods, and, to get there, they had to cross the highway. Usually, they were able to cross quickly. Today they had to wait. Military cargo vehicles rumbled past them one after the other with no end in sight. The camouflaged vehicles appeared to blur together, forming a green, leafy, raging river. The team watched the convoy, totally entranced. They didn't notice the two young soldiers armed with real rifles approaching them.

"You heading out to play your *laser games*," one of the soldiers said, his voice taking on a slightly mocking tone.

Austin grimaced, offended by the comment.

"That's General Turnbull's boy," the other soldier pointed out quickly and with respect.

The first soldier shifted uneasily. "Sorry...Always a pleasure to meet the general's family," he said, changing his tune on a dime. "We'll let you know as soon as you can cross."

"So, you wanna tell us what's in those trucks?" Caleb

asked the soldiers with a playful chuckle that indicated he didn't expect an answer.

"Sure," the second soldier played along. "It's a giant load of toilet paper. It was taco night at the base last night," he said with a laugh. "Truth is, we have no idea what's in them. Actually, your guys' parents probably know a lot more about it than we do."

"Not *his* parents," Austin said as he nodded to Ethan. "School librarian and the research facility's janitor...His dad better hope it wasn't taco night," he said with a snicker.

Ethan stared at Austin with indignant eyes, but he said nothing. The other soldiers watched Ethan with thoughtful faces, but they said nothing either.

◈

Once Bravo Team crossed the highway, it was a little over a mile through dense forest and rocky slopes to get to their base. Austin kept an intense pace the entire time, mainly because he wanted to punish the rest of the team for being late for the meeting at Judy's Diner. Ethan never broke a sweat, even on the most strenuous hikes, but Caleb was nearly tripping over his tongue in exhaustion.

The base soon became visible to Ethan. At a hundred yards away, it was easy to miss for all the camouflage, unless you knew it was there. But Ethan could always locate the mainstay of the fort's defenses—the laser turret tower—much faster than anyone else. As a scout, it was a necessity to know where that tower was at all times. The laser turret was a firepower beast, capable of shooting over two hundred rounds per minute of highly accurate, computer-guided blue laser beams at the enemy. Spotting that tower quickly, from remote distances and multiple angles, was often the difference between life and death.

The sight of the base always filled Ethan with pride. The construction of their fort had taken up the entire summer before sixth grade. There were no Laser War games at all that summer; it had been decreed by the leaders of all the teams that that time would be used to build their new forts. The structures that most teams built were solid and functional— cinder-block concrete was always popular, and so were planks of lumber hammered onto trees, glorified treehouses, or sand-bag bunkers surrounding camouflaged tents. Delta Team's fort had been made with steel and was one of the best. But the Bravo Team went above and beyond, and then some. Their base reflected Caleb's genius and the determination of what was once a well-oiled, unified team.

The Bravo Fort spanned a distance of thirty feet across. It was truly a most impressive fortress, looking more like the work of five engineers with PhDs than five kids not yet in high school. Large plates of steel were seamlessly bolted together and welded in all the right spots. The exterior was painted entirely in military-grade camouflage, the kind that covered armored vehicles sent into combat.

The fort had three tactical levels—the main level, the loft, and the basement. The main level was the entry level. It was as airtight as a drum with the exception of one large, heavy metal door that was basically the only way into the fort. The door used no keys but instead relied on a computerized entry system. A keypad to the side of the door on the outside enabled a member of the team to enter a passcode to unlock the door.

Once inside the main level, the real showstopper was the

command center. Four computer monitors on the wall kept a video visual of the outside. The computers were connected to cameras mounted on top of the fort that allowed for a panoramic view of up to a hundred yards away. Furthermore, cameras were mounted on each of the players' headsets that relayed video and sound back to the computers at the base, so whoever was running the command center knew as well as possible what was happening in the field. The main level also contained a war room where battle plans were discussed. It consisted of a small conference table, a large chalkboard, and an elaborate map of the woods posted on the wall.

The loft of the fort included a trenched walkway around the roof where the Bravo Team could utilize the high ground in defending the base. They were protected by a five-foot-tall wall of thick steel plates welded together along the entire length of the structure, with gaps here and there from which to fire their rifles. On the left end of the loft, a pedestal rose six feet higher than the top of the wall. The laser turret was mounted on top there, perched like an angry bird of prey, menacingly staring down all would-be invaders.

The basement of the fort served two main purposes. First, it was a supply depot—flashlights, batteries, bottled water, and other sundries were tucked away there. It also contained a couple of power generators that could be used in the rare event that the solar panels on the roof failed to charge the lithium-ion battery stack responsible for powering the fort. The second purpose of the basement was that it served as sort of a panic room. As a last resort, if there were absolutely no other alternatives, the basement offered the only other way out of the base—a secret passageway. This passageway was hidden behind one of the generators and covered with a locked, metal hatch. A tunnel from it ran sixty feet away from the base and emptied out into the woods behind it. The hole leading out was capped with a manhole cover and was thoroughly camouflaged. This emergency exit was a highly kept secret of the Bravo Team, and they intended to keep it that way.

∽

Ethan and the rest of Bravo Team sat around the conference table in the main level of the fort. Except for Austin. He was standing beside the chalkboard and map of the woods, droning on about battle strategy, chest puffed out like an emperor penguin. Austin pointed dramatically at the map with a long wooden pointer, occasionally moving little magnetic icons representing the members of the team to various locations on the map. Ethan had heard the exact same strategy before, five days and two battles earlier, and it wasn't exactly an earth-shattering plan then.

Caleb and Kevin paid enough attention to get by without incurring the wrath of their captain. But Ethan's mind soon drifted. He quickly found himself staring alternately at his pompous captain and a framed picture next to the door. The picture had been taken the summer after fifth grade. It showed the members of Bravo Team—Ethan, Austin, Bradley, Caleb, and Kevin—standing side-by-side with their arms draped around each other in celebration, all beaming bright, proud smiles.

Ethan's dad had snapped the picture just after the team put the finishing touches on the fort. Back then, it didn't matter to Austin that Ethan's dad was "only" a maintenance man. In fact, Ethan's father was the only one willing to spend his weekends hauling in construction supplies for the fort.

Back then, Austin appreciated all the help that Ethan's dad had given the group, realizing the fort would've never been built without him. Back then, Ethan's dad was just another guy with a job at the research facility, and Ethan was just one of Austin's friends.

Ethan could feel the change coming in their relationship, even before General Turnbull abruptly shipped his son off to Schrodinger Military Academy in Texas, two months into sixth grade. That was nearly two years ago. Laughter seemed to die first, as Ethan's jokes slowly slid from funny to lame, especially when Austin was with his other friends. Lunches together happened less and less frequently until, eventually, Ethan felt like an unwelcome alien at Austin's table. And except for Laser Wars games, which Austin took on like a job, weekend socializing fizzled out to nothing.

But the bullying didn't start until Austin returned from his fall semester at Schrodinger Military Academy. Then it kicked off with a bang. Ethan had no idea what happened to Austin over those two short months, or why he'd been sent there in the first place. All he knew was that Austin had been changed forever since.

As Ethan looked at the picture of the happy, unified Bravo Team frozen in time on the wall, he couldn't help but find the irony in it all—that just after they had built the strongest, most sturdy fort in all of Blackwoods, their team began to fall apart.

CHAPTER 7

THE GAME BEGINS

Bravo Team vs. Delta Team

Austin Turnbull (Captain)	Glenn Vaden (Captain)
Bradley Wuddle (Sergeant)	Jason Monroe (Sergeant)
Caleb Warren (Engineer)	Garret Murphy (Engineer)
Kevin Kim (Sniper)	Annika Pepper (Sniper)
Ethan Tate (Scout)	Tristan Fox (Scout)

THERE WERE MANY variations of Laser Wars games that could be played, but lately Capture the Flag had been especially popular. The objective of the game was simple enough—be the first to grab your opponents' flag and get it back to your base. Each team had a banner that represented them. Bravo Team's flag depicted a menacing black skull on a fiery background with the words "ELITE TEAM BRAVO" written prominently on it. The version was no doubt a reflection of Austin's bluster. Delta Team's flag was a bit statelier, displaying a white knight with sword and shield on a navy blue royal crest. "Delta Team" was written more plainly on the flag, and the word "Elite" was noticeably absent. The flags were hung tantalizingly low on each team's fort. They were there for the taking. All you had to do was somehow manage not to get shot in the attempt.

At three o'clock precisely, the loud "BAAAWOOO!" of a Viking Gjallarhorn echoed through the woods. It was customary that both teams blow horns to signify the start of the game. Bravo Team had gone first. Delta Team sounded off with their horn moments after. The battle had officially commenced. Ethan bolted immediately after the sound of the last horn, headed straightaway in the direction of the Delta Team fort.

"Go get 'em, Ghost!" Caleb shouted to Ethan.

Austin grimaced at Caleb. "What did you say?"

"S-s-sorry," Caleb sputtered. "Forgot."

Caleb sometimes referred to Ethan as "The Ghost" because he seemed invisible to the opposing team. It was the highest compliment, a testament to how amazing a scout Ethan was. It was also a nickname that was forbidden to say, as Austin had no intention of bestowing Ethan with a special name that gave him any credit. Austin's official reason for not allowing nicknames was that it interfered with giving orders in the field, that it made things confusing during battle. Everyone knew the real reason, though.

Austin and Bradley gave Ethan a few minutes' head start, basically hoping he would deflect any enemy fire away from them, then they took off toward the Delta Fort themselves.

Kevin stayed behind to guard the base from a strategic position on an elevated mound of earth a hundred yards away on the right flank. Crouched down behind some foliage, he was doing his best imitation of a chameleon. He was very hard to spot—only the tip of the barrel of his long laser sniper rifle protruded from the brush. It was his job as sniper to pick off any enemies that got threateningly close to the flag. Kevin would be supported in massive fashion by the computerized laser turret perched atop the fort. Once the laser turret targeted an enemy, it would unleash a furious barrage of blue lasers, knocking anyone out of the game who couldn't quickly find cover.

Caleb ran the technical operations from inside the Bravo Team fort. Only if all other means of fort defense had been exhausted—that is, everyone on Bravo Team nearby was shot and killed and the enemy had made it past the laser turret—would Caleb be turned loose onto the battlefield. Caleb's role of maintaining the laser turret and running Bravo Team communications was of the utmost importance. He was considered too valuable an asset to be thrown into the fray of battle if there were other options. Caleb understood this, but he often regretted missing chances to get in on some good laser skirmishes, despite the fact he wasn't very swift in the field or particularly adept with a gun.

Presently, Caleb remained busy at the main computer terminal in the Bravo Fort. He had just finished getting their laser turret operational again and was monitoring the goings-on in the field via the row of computer screens. He could see what his teammates were seeing far away in the woods through cameras that were mounted on the players' headsets. The game was early, but so far, so good.

⊰⊱

The distance between the Bravo and Delta Team bases was over three-quarters of a mile, and the terrain separating the two was very challenging. Thick brush, rocky ledges, fallen trees, and uneven ground made traversing the land difficult. A good time getting from one base to the other in full gear was about twenty minutes. Ethan had been en route to the Delta Team base for five minutes and was well over halfway there. There was no one else on either team who could hold a candle to Ethan's speed. He darted in and out of trees; slid down long, treacherous slopes of ground; jumped over tree trunks; ducked under branches; and sprinted all-out through any clearings the forest provided.

Ethan stopped briefly to take a sip of water from his canteen. He checked his watch and scanned the surroundings with his binoculars. He knew the area well, only three hundred yards from the Delta Team fort. He had taken a wide angle to the right in hopes of sneaking up on the flank of the base. A wide angle also made it less likely that the computerized laser turret would detect his position. After seeing nothing to give him cause for concern, he put away his binoculars and took one more sip on his canteen before tucking that away as well. Ethan wiped some sweat from his forehead and continued his journey onward. But he hiked slower now and with far greater caution, for at this distance he knew he could run into the enemy at any time.

Ethan had gone from running through the woods with reckless abandon, then to a cautious hike, to now a downright skulk. He could see the Delta Team base in the distance about a hundred yards away, and he moved with great care to stay low and make no sound. This was dangerous territory he was treading into. It was Annika Pepper territory.

Annika Pepper's reputation for marksmanship with her laser rifle had gone from heroic to legendary over the last year. Her father, a former Marine sniper instructor, took her to a big target-shooting contest held at Marine Corps Base Camp Pendleton in California. Forty competitors, all adults. Adult Marines. More specifically, hard-nosed Marine snipers. Just for fun, they allowed her to participate using her laser rifle and set up special targets for her that were sensitive to lasers. What was supposed to be a cutesy moment with the instructor's adorable daughter playing around, trying to make impossibly hard shots that really only the big, tough marine men could make, turned into a fierce competition. When it was all said and done, Annika had finished third. Third out of forty Marine snipers. Every Marine there, except for Annika's father, who knew she'd be a force to reckon with, was floored by the outcome. Many cheered Annika's unbelievable skill, but five of them complained, citing that it wasn't a fair contest because Annika didn't have to account for the wind variable— that lasers, made of intense light, weren't subject to moving around when the wind blew. They claimed she had a distinct advantage. Upon hearing the soldiers' grumblings, Annika's father arranged for an indoor match between his daughter and those soldiers who had complained. An indoor match made the wind argument irrelevant and evened the playing field.

The Marine snipers felt a little bad about actually stooping to use a rematch to beat a seventh-grade girl at their chosen profession, but their pride was under assault. Of course, their pride took another hit when Annika destroyed them for a second time. The soldiers were completely shocked and at a loss for words. Annika provided the words for them as she shook their hands and flashed a wink and a smile. She left them with the parting words of "Good game…Better luck next time," in a sweet, lilting voice.

◈

Ethan crouched down behind a massive fallen tree. The spot gave him a view of the area without being too out in the open. Another advantage was that the tree was resting on top of another downed tree, so there was an opening on one end he could duck under if necessary. Ethan pulled out his binoculars and scanned the surroundings. He spotted the Delta Team's laser turret tower on the far side of their base.

It was conventional battle strategy to have the team's sniper on the opposite side of the laser turret tower. That way, having shooters on both sides, the defending team would be able to cover more ground in the event of an attack. The laser turret was on the left side of the base, so that meant Annika was most likely lurking somewhere on the right side, closer to Ethan. Austin knew that basic strategy, yet he chose to veer to the left of the base. Clearly, he'd rather take his chances with the menacing, robotic laser turret that fires two hundred shots per minute than press his luck with Annika. He left the unenviable task of dealing with Ms. Pepper for Ethan. It was probably a good move for a captain looking to save his own hide. Annika had, in more than a few games, taken out the entire opposing team all by herself. The laser turret could never boast that fact. The turret, while very powerful, also had a tendency to miss its first few shots each time it acquired a new target. Caleb called it "Initial Calibration Error" and was constantly working to minimize it on the Bravo Team's turret. Annika, on the other hand, made no such error. If Annika got off the first shot, it was all but over for her enemy.

Ethan hugged the tree closely as he scooted slowly along the ground, sneaking occasional glimpses over the tree with his binoculars. He saw nothing but sensed that she was close. He felt an eerie tingle as the hairs on the back of his neck stood upright. Then he heard a faint crackling sound in the distance. Slowly, Ethan crept back to the part of the tree that was propped up by the trunk of another. He slid into the crevice between them and started covering himself with leaves, branches, and any debris he could find to camouflage himself. If Annika had a weakness, it was that she was often picky about finding the best vantage point. Sometimes she would get bothered by a particular spot and change locations. You just had to be in the right place at the right time and get very lucky.

Ethan huddled down in the crevice, making himself as small as possible. He blended in well with his surroundings, looking like a pile of brush under a tree. The crackling sound got louder and louder. Just then, a transmission came in on Ethan's radio headset.

"Ethan, where are you? I can't see anything," Caleb asked over the radio. Ethan's camera on his headset was also covered in brush, and Caleb had no idea what was going on.

"Right flank, Delta base, hundred yards out," Ethan whispered into his headset, covering his mouth with his hand to muffle the sound.

"Delta Team is going defensive on this one, I think," Caleb said with a worried voice. "Austin and Bradley haven't seen or heard anything on their side. I think they're staying back…They gotta be all around you."

Ethan sighed and looked around from underneath his improvised camouflage. He saw nothing. Even the crackling had stopped. Judging by the sound of the last movement he'd heard, whoever it was had to be within fifty yards. Ethan bet that Caleb was right. He usually was.

"Okay," Ethan whispered into his headset. "Gotta go radio silent now."

With his binoculars, Ethan scanned the general area where he had heard the last movement. Seeing nothing, and just about ready to lower his binoculars, he caught a break. He spotted something, an ever-so-slight twitch atop a raised embankment about thirty yards to his right. It was hard to make out the exact form of the figure inhabiting the mound of dirt. It was a shadowy, leafy, camouflaged creature of some sort. It was Annika Pepper. She had moved just a touch in order to get a better position. Ethan needed to capitalize on seeing her first because it didn't happen very often.

As Annika settled into her new and improved lethal location, Ethan slowly peeled back a couple layers of camouflage, gingerly moving aside some branches and brush. He raised his rifle at a snail's pace, for anything faster would surely be spotted by Annika's eagle eyes. Ethan angled the rifle higher until he had it trained on her. For Annika, a shot at this distance would be an absolute joke—a shot she could make backwards, or in her sleep, or backwards in her sleep. But for Ethan, or mostly anyone else, it was a very challenging shot. Ethan tried to keep the barrel of the laser rifle steady by controlling his breathing, a tactic that he'd heard Annika talk about often. He breathed slow, even breaths and managed to keep the rifle very still. His finger was firm on the trigger, and his right eye squinted hard as it gazed down the sights of the barrel. But a final thought entered his head just as he was about to squeeze the trigger: *This might not help my chances getting her to go with me to the eighth-grade dance.* With that sobering thought, he paused and lightened up on the trigger. He'd never paused before when he had a shot on Annika, but there were never dances in seventh grade at his school either. Ethan needed to put a positive spin on the situation and fire quickly, or Annika was sure to spot him, and she probably wouldn't let a school dance three months away keep her from blasting him into oblivion.

If I make the shot, sure, Annika might be a little frustrated at first, but she'll also be impressed, and that's a good thing. After all, you don't go to an eighth-grade dance with a man you don't respect. This would definitely earn me respect. Take the shot, you idiot.

Without hem-hawing any further, Ethan pressed the trigger several times in rapid succession. Brilliant blue laser pulses streamed from his rifle. Annika looked over and saw Ethan, shocked that he was so close and that she hadn't seen him first. Just as she had turned her gun on him, about to transform him from a participant into a spectator, Annika looked down and saw her laser vest flashing bright red and blue lights reminiscent of those on a police car. She had been shot. Annika stood up quickly. Her entire face registered disgust and annoyance. She ripped off her vest and glared at Ethan.

"Ugh!…Stupid Ethan!" Annika blurted as she stormed off toward her base.

Annika's words were a gut punch. "Stupid Ethan?" he repeated to himself. His chest deflated like a balloon.

Fortunately, Ethan didn't have long to mull over Annika's reaction. He heard a loud rustling coming from behind him. His attack on Annika had been seen by Glenn and his second-in-command, Jason Monroe, who were in the vicinity. Caleb was absolutely right. The Bravo Team was playing a defensive game. Ethan could see them now, about thirty yards away and moving in carefully. They knew Ethan had to be behind the fallen tree, but they didn't know where exactly along the tree he was. Ethan figured he had the advantage, though he had to go on the attack, two against one, to realize it. He took a deep breath and popped out from behind the tree, firing his laser weapon like a man possessed. He hit Jason immediately, but that gave Glenn the time to home in on Ethan's position. Glenn fired his weapon just as Ethan let off another barrage himself. The result of the confrontation was that both were shot, and both were gone from the game.

It was a spectacular performance from Ethan, one that would set up a clear victory for the Bravo Team. Ethan had shot every regular combatant on the Delta Team, except for Tristan, who was scouting alone far away from the base. Garret Murphy, the engineer for the Delta Team, did his duty and exited the base with courageous intentions of defending the flag, though it didn't help him that he was as bad with a laser rifle as Caleb. Not surprisingly, thirty seconds after he took his position to guard the Delta Team banner, Garret was summarily gunned down by Austin and Bradley.

The last item of business was to get past the laser turret and grab the flag. Austin ordered Bradley to run wildly across the front of the base to distract the turret, while he captured the flag. Bradley carried out the orders and got nailed quickly by the laser turret for his obedience. But it was no matter. Austin got what he wanted. He returned to Bravo Fort with the Delta Team flag. The conquering hero didn't even have to engage Tristan on the way back to the base—Kevin had shot Tristan long before the exalted captain was put in any sort of harm's way.

∽

Back at the Bravo Base, an odd celebration unfolded. The victory would go down as a Bravo Team victory. A *team* victory. But the triumph rang hollow. Austin and Bradley basked in glory, while Caleb and Kevin played along without real conviction. Ethan watched the scene from the fringe with a blank expression, almost as if he weren't a part of the team.

"Kevin, pass out the sodas!" Austin ordered with the smile of a champion on his face. It was tradition to pack a cooler with five Cherry Cokes on ice for every game. If they won, they toasted to their victory.

Kevin handed out the sodas without much enthusiasm.

"To Bravo Team! To victory!" Austin yelled as he raised his can and began to drink. Everyone followed his lead. "Now, *I* was the one who brought the flag back to our base, but I couldn't have done it alone."

Ethan paused and lowered his drink a little, curious to hear Austin in a rare moment of humility.

"In fact, one brave soldier made it possible for me to shine in battle today," Austin admitted.

Shine in battle…? Ugh! But Ethan held back the vomit, even cracked the faintest of smiles, for he thought Austin might finally give him a sliver of credit. He actually found himself in the unusual position of hanging on his captain's next words.

"Raise your drinks, everyone," Austin continued. "This special toast goes to Sergeant Bradley Wuddle…for bravery above and beyond, for running out in front of that laser turret and distracting it while I captured the flag."

Austin gave Bradley a hug. Not a soft hug that one would

give an old relative at a family reunion, but a hard, loud, back-slapping hug. It was a special moment—an embrace of captain and sergeant, lord and vassal, master and minion, a bully and his stooge. Ethan wanted to retch. He wanted to scream. He wanted to yell. He wanted to demand, by force if necessary, that his contribution to the victory go recognized by Austin. None of that happened, though. Ethan just bit his tongue and bided his time, impatiently counting the seconds until he could go home.

CHAPTER 8

HOLDING IN THE FRUSTRATION

ETHAN'S HEAD WAS abuzz with emotions as he and Caleb crossed the Dark Highway and walked back into the town of Blackwoods. He plodded along in a quiet daze all the way to their neighborhood. Caleb glanced over at Ethan and saw his downtrodden face.

"You know you're the reason we won today, right?" Caleb asked. "The Ghost strikes again!"

"Thanks, but don't let out fearless captain hear you say that." After a few more steps, Ethan began to shake his head. "Forget him…What if we just started our own team?"

Caleb looked intrigued. "You, me, and who else?"

"Just you and me. There's no official rule against a team of two."

"Just you and me?" Caleb repeated with a doubtful grin.

"Why not? I think we'd do okay. We'd have the best engineer by far."

"Thanks," Caleb said, smiling appreciatively. "And we'd have the best scout by far."

Ethan returned the smile, but it quickly diminished as he

appeared lost in a thought. "I don't know, Caleb. It's just the way today went. The way the year's gone with this team, with Austin...It makes you want to do something crazy."

"Crazy like what?" Caleb probed with curious eyes.

"I don't know. Something. Something crazy. Something... insubordinate."

"You'd disobey the captain's orders?"

Ethan sighed deeply. "He's not a *real* captain, Caleb. He's just a kid like us. Well, not like us, but just a kid...And sometimes a man's gotta do what a man's gotta do."

Caleb nodded thoughtfully. "All right. Whatever you do, you'll have my support."

"Thank you."

They stopped in front of Caleb's house. "Wanna come over tomorrow night, stay over, work on our project?" Caleb asked.

"Friday night, study?" Ethan questioned playfully. "You're such a nerd."

"Nerds are the coolest," Caleb said with swagger.

Ethan grinned and nodded in agreement. It was hard to argue against the coolness of a guy who could build laser turrets, forts, and surveillance equipment like Caleb. "All right, Friday night we'll work on our project...But we're not studying the entire time."

"Deal. See you tomorrow."

"See you tomorrow."

෧

Ethan arrived home and got cleaned up for dinner just in time. His mother had plopped down a piping hot pan of baked lasagna just moments after he had taken his seat. Ethan and his parents soon began eating. Their dinner routine was always the same. Everyone would take a few bites to quell their hunger, then comment favorably on the food. The conversation would soon follow, invariably turning to the events of each other's day. Today it took four bites exactly and two "mmm-mmms" before engaging in the required chit-chat. Normally, Ethan didn't mind it, even enjoyed it. But today, he didn't feel much like talking. Between his problems with Austin and the "Stupid Ethan!" comment from Annika that he was sure would give him nightmares, he dreaded the inevitable question.

"So how was your day, Ethan?" his mom asked.

Ethan paused, desperately trying to find one redeeming thing about how he'd spent the last twelve hours. "Fine... Caleb and I are doing a report on artificial intelligence for school."

"Ooooh...You should let your dad help with that," Ethan's mom said in an upbeat tone.

Ethan's dad looked at his wife strangely for a moment, then pretended to be a robot, imitating mechanical arm, head, and torso movements. "I will help you on your project," he said in a monotone robot voice until he began to chuckle.

Ethan eked out a thin smile. "No thanks. It's me and Caleb's project."

His dad slowly stopped laughing, then his residual smile vanished. "You're right, Ethan. It is your project." Then he turned to his wife. "How was your day, honey?"

"It was good. We got quite a few new books in today."

"That's great. Anything especially good?"

"Oh, yes. Tons of wonderful new fiction books." Ethan's mom's words had the pep and pop of a woman who truly enjoyed her work. "And a whole series of nonfiction books about the history of the Middle Ages."

The conversation was driving Ethan crazy for some reason he couldn't quite pinpoint. He thought maybe he had officially reached the peak of adolescence at some point during the dinner, and was obliged by the adolescent covenant to find his parents annoying. Ethan felt like bolting upstairs to the solace of his room, but he decided to wait, figuring it couldn't get much worse.

"So how was your day today?" Ethan's mom asked her husband.

Ethan cringed in his seat. *So much for not getting worse.*

"It was great. I worked on the vacuums today. I'm getting close to fixing all the kinks," Ethan's dad said with smiling eyes.

"Really? Wow, that's fantastic!"

Ethan couldn't believe his parents. His dad had spent his entire day working on vacuums, and they acted as proud as if he were finding the cure for cancer. *That's pathetic,* Ethan thought, narrowly avoiding blurting the feeling out loud. He couldn't help but imagine what the difference might be between dinnertime at the Turnbulls versus dinnertime at the Tates. Austin's dad, the esteemed general, would entertain and impress his family with stories of secret missions and conversations with the president of the United States, while Ethan's dad would regale his family with tales of heroism involving cleaning the gunk out of vacuums. *It's not fair. It's not fair that Austin harasses me because my dad's only a maintenance man. And it's not fair for my dad to be so content with his job while I suffer for it.*

Ethan could take no more. He needed to get out of there

before he said something he would regret. "Can I go upstairs? I got a headache." It wasn't entirely a lie. The stress of the day and the present conversation combined to send shooting pains through his temples.

"Sure. Can I get you some Tylenol?" his mom asked.

"No thanks. I'm just gonna lay down."

"Just let us know if you need anything," his dad added.

Ethan stared at his dad for an extended moment. There was something he needed, all right. Something he needed to say to him. Something he had to get off his chest. But Ethan powered through the temptation to take that load off of his chest and slam it violently upon his father's. He took a deep breath and forced out a remarkably genuine-looking smile.

"Okay...Thanks, Dad."

⤐

As Ethan lay awake in bed that night, the events of the day played through his head like a poorly edited movie. It contained all the action of him fighting bravely in battle, the drama of his friction with Austin, and the tragedy of being called "Stupid Ethan!" by Annika. Not to mention the suspense of a moment where he came a mere hair's breadth away from saying something to his father that would've changed their relationship forever.

Ethan eyed the ornate wooden chessboard his dad had given him for his seventh-grade graduation. It was sitting neatly on a table beside the window. Beams of moonlight streamed through the open blinds and probed the contours of the pieces. They were all lined up perfectly, standing at attention and ready for battle. The king and queen stood tallest, shining majestically as if giving off their own light.

Ethan smiled at the board, remembering how thoughtful and generous his dad had been in buying him a gift that must've cost him a hefty fraction of his paycheck. After a rough day, Ethan had one thing to be thankful for. As frustrated as he was at the dinner table, he'd kept his mouth shut about his problems with Austin and how they related to his dad's job at the research facility. He was thankful for not mentioning the unmentionable.

CHAPTER 9

A TROUBLED NIGHT'S SLEEP

AT 2:45 A.M. something startled Ethan out of a deep sleep. He sprang up quickly in his bed, breathing rapidly, perspiration dotting his forehead. He remembered only one thing—a bright flash of light, like someone had taken a picture with a giant flashbulb three inches from his face. The light was gone now, but the dark after-image still lingered in his field of vision. Ethan scanned the room but saw nothing. Without getting out of bed, he grabbed a flashlight from a nearby shelf. He swept the beam of light very slowly from left to right. What happened to him seemed so real that it couldn't possibly have been a dream or a nightmare. He was sure someone or something had to be in his room. But repeated back and forth arcs of the flashlight revealed nothing out of the ordinary.

Ethan knew the search of his room wasn't complete, though. His closet on the far side of the room seemed to stare at him with uninviting eyes. He climbed out of bed, flashlight in hand, and crept toward it. On his way there, he quickly looked around for a weapon. Having left his Louisville Slugger in the garage, the best thing he found was an old stuffed animal raccoon his dad had won for him at the state fair when he was six years old. It wasn't much of a weapon in the strictest sense, but there sure were a lot of beans stuffed in that raccoon's butt. If you whipped it at someone hard enough, it could leave a pretty nasty mark. Ethan hoped it would be enough to subdue a maniac clown if one jumped out of the closet at him (Ethan hated clowns and thought they were all demented, even Ronald McDonald). He grabbed the handle of the closet tightly and held the flashlight between his teeth. In his other hand, he had the stuffed raccoon cocked back and ready to attack. Ethan quickly slung open the door. He flinched and was about ready to fire his furry weapon when he realized nothing was in there.

He took the flashlight out of his mouth and stared at the raggedy raccoon that was still firmly clutched in his hand. Ethan began to laugh, less concerned about the bright light now. In fact, he realized it had to be a dream. A strange dream after a bad day was nothing unusual. And the after-image he had in his eyes from the flash of light he'd imagined must've really been due to his headache. It all made sense. It always takes a few minutes to realize a dream is just a dream. He was just glad no one was there to see how ridiculous he must've looked.

Ethan was about to switch off the flashlight when he noticed something. Something about the chessboard was not right. He directed the beam of light at the board. Instantly, his eyes widened and a cold, tingling sensation ran from the small of his back to the tips of the hair on his head. The light from the flashlight in his jittery hand danced around erratically over the checkered squares. Ethan was afraid to keep the light on the board, and yet more afraid to return to darkness. The light continued to cascade unevenly on the chessboard, revealing that most of the thirty-two pieces had been disturbed.

Ethan summoned all of his courage and stepped lightly toward the chessboard. He found the situation to be much more bizarre upon closer inspection. The black pieces, the ones closest to his bed, were scattered all over the board randomly. It was as if a toddler were playing around with the pieces, planting them sloppily halfway between squares. The white side offered an even weirder, more disconcerting formation of the pieces. The white pieces had not only been moved, but moved to correct positions on the board, with tactics and strategy. They were logical moves, moves made on purpose...*It was like some unknown entity had been actually playing a game.*

CHAPTER 10

THE RUSH TO TELL CALEB

SIX HARD, THUMPING shakes of the bed weren't enough for Ethan's mom to rouse her son the next morning. Ethan somehow managed to sleep for an hour during the night, an amount that was only enough to make him crave more sleep. He was buried under three covers and four pillows—his version of a protective fort in bed. On the seventh shake, Ethan violently jerked out from underneath his assorted coverings. Pillows flew into the air.

"No! No! No!" Ethan yelled, coming out of a bad dream.

"Ethan, honey, it's okay. It's me," his mom quickly reassured him.

Ethan slowly began to calm down. He took a few deep, controlled breaths. It took a moment, then he remembered the previous night's events in his bedroom. The chessboard beckoned for his eyes. His mother was sitting on the bed directly in front of him, though, obscuring his vision of the board. Part of Ethan desperately wanted his mom to move out of the way, so he could get a good look at the board. Another part of him had no desire to look at all.

"Ethan, what's with all the covers? Are you cold? Do you think you're getting sick?"

"No, no, I'm fine, Mom. Just tired, that's all. I want to go to school today. I *need* to go to school today," he said, sounding desperate.

Ethan's mom smiled and raised a curious eyebrow. "*Need* to go to school, huh…? All right, hurry and get dressed. It's almost seven."

"Mom, have you ever seen me sleepwalk?"

Ethan's mom stared quizzically at her son. "No, honey, I've never seen you sleepwalk. Are you sure you're feeling well?"

"Yeah. Just a bad dream."

"Do you want to talk about it?"

"No, thanks…I'm okay."

"All right. I'll be downstairs. I'll fix some cereal."

As soon as his mom left, Ethan immediately focused on the chessboard. He couldn't believe what he saw. The black pieces were still a mess on the board, but all of the white pieces were back, *standing upright in their original positions.* With one disturbing exception. He noticed that the white king was lying on its side, on top of its starting square. A fallen king in a chess game was an indication of surrender. Game over. It was an ominous sign. He had to talk to Caleb about this, and fast.

Ethan arrived in Ms. Goodfoot's class and took his seat next to Caleb, brimming with things to tell him. Those things would have to wait. Ms. Goodfoot began math instruction, and the familiar Xs and Ys of algebra equations soon flooded the chalkboard. Caleb sat right beside Ethan, but the two resided in totally different mathematical universes. Ethan was doing well enough to be a good student of algebra, but Caleb was now doing calculus. It was the same with science, too. Caleb was just a different breed of smart. He had long been invited to take classes at the high school, but he always turned them down. Caleb felt awkward sometimes around his same-aged peers, and figured it would be even worse as the only kid in the room setting the curve on all the tests.

Ethan watched his best friend blaze away on his own private math assignment. It looked to him like the incomprehensible scribblings you might see on the inside of an alien ship.

Ethan paused in his note-taking for a moment to watch Annika admiringly. She was sitting straight up in her chair, dutifully taking notes. She had two thick books, her favorites, stacked neatly on the edge of her desk: *The Fault in Our Stars* and *The Complete Manual for the 21st Century Sniper*. Then the "Stupid Ethan!" comment she had made on the laser battlefield jumped back into his mind. Ethan shuddered all over again. It had taken a ghost moving the pieces on his chessboard to make him temporarily forget that dagger of a remark. At least the restless spirits in his house had done something good. Ethan hoped that they might distract him from one more bothersome item—a certain student—but no luck there.

It was a hot morning, and the classroom windows were open wide to bring in a breeze. The result was a zephyr that sent Tristan's long golden locks of hair lofting into the air, giving his mane an even more luxurious appearance. Ethan found it ridiculous that any thirteen-year-old looked like that, as if he were about to be photographed for the cover of a romance novel—blond hair streaming in the wind, blue eyes bathed in the sunlight, shirt half-unbuttoned, riding a white horse, sword and shield in hand, galloping gallantly up to a medieval castle to rescue a princess twice his age. *Ridiculous,* Ethan thought. *Nobody is supposed to be that good-looking, especially at thirteen years old.*

Math instruction finally concluded, and Ms. Goodfoot gave the class permission to work on their projects. Ethan wasted no time and scooted his desk next to Caleb's, desperately hoping that his friend could help him figure out what was going on. He knew that Caleb really used to be into ghosts about four years ago. That Christmas, Caleb asked for, and received, a complete ghost-hunting kit. It included everything for the aspiring paranormal investigator to confirm or debunk all claims of ghosts, specters, and apparitions. Caleb studied the subject for three weeks, setting up video cameras, voice recorders, and thermal imaging equipment everywhere he could think of. Caleb's mother officially ended his research when he began installing equipment to look for ghosts in the kitchen cabinets and refrigerator. At that point, and under the threat of a grounding, Caleb deemed the results of the study as inconclusive. But Ethan hoped to convince him to open an all-new investigation.

Just as Ethan was about to deliver the otherworldly news, Annika walked by. She stared at Ethan for a moment, then flashed a warm, friendly smile.

"Good game, yesterday. You sure got the drop on me," she said. Ethan smiled back really big, nodding and looking a bit like a doofus. Annika's smile turned from warm and friendly to mischievous instantly. Her eyes squinted in determination. "But you better enjoy it now…'cause I won't let it happen again."

Annika walked away to meet Tristan to work on their project. They sat beside each other and scooted their desks together until they touched. Ethan's smile began to die a slow death as he watched them. It only then dawned on him that he should've said something back to her. He quickly searched his head for the precise, poetic combination of words.

"Good game, you too!" Ethan blurted out loudly across the room. Everyone stared at Ethan, then Annika. Annika nodded and waved hesitantly from the opposite side of the room. She looked at Tristan and smiled, shaking her head in confusion as if saying, *I have no idea what that lunatic was talking about!*

Ethan cringed in embarrassment and slumped down into his chair, disgusted with himself. *Good game, you too?! That's the best I can come up with? That's like something a caveman would say.* Ethan replayed the words in his head in a grunting caveman voice. *You idiot.*

Caleb began piling books about computers and robots on his desk. "Ethan, I checked out all the artificial intelligence books the library had. I also made a list of good websites to use for our research tonight when you come over."

Ethan finally snapped out of his Annika-induced trance. "That's great…but you need to come over to *my* house. There's another project we need to work on tonight."

"What's that?"

"I need you to bring over that Christmas present you got when you were in fourth grade," Ethan said, keeping his voice low. He looked around to make sure no one was listening. Ethan's voice dropped even lower, into an eerie, hissing whisper. "Caleb, I think my house is haunted."

CHAPTER 11

PULLING AN ALL-NIGHTER

CALEB STOOD ON the porch of Ethan's house that night looking like a pack mule. He had two large backpacks stuffed to capacity slung over his shoulders, a hefty, silvery metal briefcase held at his side, and a rolled-up sleeping bag strapped to his back. He wobbled back and forth like a Weeble from the lopsided weight of it all. Ethan's mom opened the door, greeted Caleb, and let him in. They stood together for a moment in the foyer of the house. Caleb forced an awkward grin that he hoped didn't make him look totally insane.

Ethan's mom smiled sympathetically. "Caleb, can I help you with that?"

"No, thanks. I'm good," Caleb replied, despite teetering on the brink of collapse.

"Wow, now that looks like a lot of studying. What is all that stuff?"

"Oh, just books mostly," Caleb answered, hoping she wouldn't search his luggage.

Ethan's dad entered and smiled at Caleb's predicament. "Hi, Caleb. Nice to see you."

"Hi, Mr. Tate."

"You have quite a load there. Want some help?"

"N-n-no thanks," Caleb stammered. "I got it. I could use the exercise, anyway." He rubbed his belly until it jiggled to make the point. Then immediately wished he hadn't.

Caleb desperately wanted to go upstairs to Ethan's room. He was a terrible liar and any more interrogation from Ethan's parents was bound to make him crack. Caleb had no desire to be the idiot who had to explain to Ethan's parents about the ghost-hunting gear in the metal briefcase, or about the backpack filled with enough junk food and soda to kill an elephant ten times over. Ethan had asked Caleb to bring as many sugary snacks as possible to help him stay awake since he hardly slept the night before. Caleb complied like a good friend, but now he was really feeling the heat.

"Here, let me help you with that," Ethan's dad insisted as he reached toward the backpack full of goodies on Caleb's left shoulder.

Caleb cringed. He knew the jig was up. Ethan's dad would grab the bag and surely hear the crackling of Twinkie and Ho-Ho wrappers, and the clanking of soda cans with their carbonated contents sloshing and fizzing around. *That's just great,* Caleb thought. *Catch the chunky kid sneaking in fifty-thousand artery-clogging calories in a freaking backpack.* Caleb wondered where the heck Ethan was. He felt like a criminal who had been caught by the police while his partner-in-crime fled to a beautiful beach in Mexico. *I'm going down for this, all right.*

"I got it!" Ethan yelled, scurrying down the stairs.

Caleb sighed a big breath of relief as Ethan's dad retracted his hand from the bag. Ethan lightened Caleb's load considerably by grabbing both backpacks. Then they bolted upstairs.

✺

Caleb set the metal briefcase down on a desk in Ethan's room. Ethan watched carefully as Caleb opened it, revealing all sorts of ghost-detecting gadgets and gizmos. Caleb pulled out an electronic device the size of a cell phone.

"This is a highly sensitive digital voice recorder," Caleb explained. "We'll use this to record any EVPs that might be present during the night."

"EVPs...?" Ethan repeated.

"Electronic Voice Phenomena. The sounds spirits might make that we can't hear with our own ears...The voices of the dead."

Ethan swallowed uneasily. Caleb pulled out another piece of equipment.

"Super high-resolution digital video camera," Caleb continued. "We'll set it up so it's aiming at the part of the room with the chessboard, since that's where the activity has been. We'll look for any strange orbs, lights, or shadows."

Ethan nodded. Caleb grabbed another item from the briefcase.

"And the thermal camera. It provides a visual image of the temperature of objects. Red and yellow, hot. Blue and green, cold. Ghosts are supposed to create cold spots. This device will help us find those cold spots if they're there."

Caleb pulled out one final piece of equipment and held it in his hand. "Last but not least, we have the EMF meter... electromagnetic field meter. Ghosts are thought to cause disturbances in electromagnetic fields. This device will catch any field fluctuations."

Ethan nodded, but his eyes quickly furrowed. Something

Caleb had said during his show-and-tell session bothered him. "Caleb, you said ghosts are *supposed* to create cold spots and that ghosts are *thought* to create disturbances in electromagnetic fields. *Supposed* to, *thought* to…You don't believe in ghosts at all, do you?"

Caleb's face softened apologetically. "Honestly, no. Not since fourth grade, at least. There's just no hard evidence, nothing that can't be explained by other things."

Ethan nodded, then pressed the issue. "Do you believe *me*, Caleb? Do you believe what I said happened?"

Caleb adjusted his wire-rimmed glasses and cast an awkward look at Ethan. "Ethan, you're my best friend. I would never, ever think you'd lie about this. I believe something interesting happened here last night…I just don't believe that something was a ghost."

Ethan sighed. "All right, let's just set up the equipment. By tomorrow, Caleb, you'll be a believer."

They worked for the next hour testing and getting all the electronic gear running and positioned properly. The video camera and the thermal camera were both aimed at the half of the room that contained the chessboard. The electronic voice recorder was placed not only close to the chessboard, but on top of it, right smack dab in the middle between the white and black armies. If the chessboard was, in fact, a nexus of the spirit world, all of the devices focused on it would surely produce some evidence.

The red digital clock on Ethan's nightstand read 9:30 p.m. It was completely dark outside now. Ethan and Caleb sat on the floor, intently watching the chessboard as if it were a television airing their favorite show. Ethan held up the EMF meter periodically and studied the numbers on the screen. Nothing yet, but it was early. Last night there was no paranormal activity until well after 2:00 a.m. *They'll come again,* Ethan thought. They had all night to wait.

⋰

At 11:00 p.m. there was still no sign of ghostly activity. Ethan was still fanning the EMF meter around the room and still getting no signals. Caleb began to look a little impatient.

"Ethan, while we're waiting for the ghosts, could we work on our project?" Caleb asked, sounding ever-so-slightly sarcastic when he said the word "ghosts." Ethan picked up on the tone, but had no desire to argue the point. He was sure he would be proven right and that, before sunrise, Caleb would be feeling bad about ever doubting his ghost theory.

"Sure."

Eventually, Ethan and Caleb settled into a studying groove and were diligently reading books, marking passages, taking notes, and scouring the internet for anything interesting to add to their project.

"We absolutely have to talk about Moore's Law," Caleb said. "Any project on artificial intelligence in the future has to include that."

Caleb went on to explain that Moore's Law was an idea proposed by Gordon Moore in 1965, and that the law states that every eighteen months, the processing speed and memory capacity for computers doubles. He also pointed out that the law has been extremely accurate in predicting computer power thus far and should continue to do so in the future. Caleb was in his element, overflowing with intellectual curiosity, occasionally running his hands through his hair to the point he was rocking the full-Einstein disheveled look.

"Computer power doubles every eighteen months... Doubles!"

"That's amazing," Ethan said, though not as passionately.

"The computer processor would be the brain of the robot. You might think robots aren't that impressive now, but in fifteen years..." Caleb did some quick math in his head. "They would have a brain two to the tenth or one thousand twenty-four times more powerful than today. And in thirty years, over a million times the power...They could be your co-workers, your neighbors, your *boss* by then."

Ethan eyed Caleb skeptically. "I've seen videos on the internet of robots trying to get around. They aren't very good, especially in unfamiliar terrain. They fall...a lot. They might be able to play chess like a god, but *my* boss...in thirty years?" Ethan laughed. "I'd have to hold my boss's hand so he wouldn't do a face-plant into the ground."

"In thirty years, a *million* times more powerful," Caleb repeated to hammer home the point. "With that kind of processing power, learning that would be easy. Humans can learn to walk when they're only one year old."

"Right, but it's not as easy as it looks. It's hardwired into our brains."

"True, but by then it would be hardwired into theirs too. They would be able to run as well as any human athlete, or better." Caleb paused a moment to collect his surging thoughts. "Ethan, think of something you struggle with right now that you wish you were better at."

Ethan thought for a moment. "Spanish class."

"Okay…Do you think you could remember one new Spanish word every day?"

"Only one word? Sure, of course."

"What if you could remember a million words a day? How hard would Spanish be then? Ethan, a million times more of everything…How hard would anything be?"

"Learning to be human would still be hard…I hope."

Caleb nodded. "That's a good point…I hope."

"But if we want to talk about machines really behaving like humans, we need to include something about the Turing Test," Ethan said.

Ethan read out loud a passage from a book about the Turing Test. He explained that the Turing Test was developed by Alan Turing in 1950, and that it was a test of a machine's ability to demonstrate intelligence. That is, if a machine could fool a human into thinking it was having a conversation with another human and not a machine, that machine was said to have passed the Turing Test. It was said, upon passing the test, that the machine, computer, or robot would have shown true intelligence of the human variety. It was the holy grail of artificial intelligence researchers to produce such a machine, but thus far no one had even come close.

"Now that's an important test for a robot that wants to be our neighbor," Ethan said. "They may have all the jokes ever told stored in their memory banks, but can they find the humor in a conversation…or make up a joke of their own? They may know all the vocabulary words in the English language, but can they write a book that anyone wants to read?"

Caleb grinned playfully. "You do know that you have some nerd in you too?"

"Nerds are the coolest, right?" Ethan said with an ironic

smile. "You know, even if robots can run faster than humans in thirty years, would they ever do it because they wanted to, or just because it's programmed in them?"

"It's gotta be the program. Nobody likes running...And forget thirty years, you've seen me run. I bet one of those wobbly robots you've seen on the internet could beat me in a race right now." A fit of laughter overcame Caleb as he trundled around the room, making fun of his running style. Ethan cracked up with him.

"You think a robot could ever understand why we're laughing right now?" Ethan asked.

"I have no idea," Caleb said, chuckling wildly.

❧

At 1:00 a.m. nothing out of the ordinary was noted on the devices, and the pieces on the chessboard hadn't so much as budged. Ethan's eyes were starting to get heavy now. He tried to suppress a yawn, but two broke through his defenses. He decided to fight the urge to sleep with a heavy dose of junk food. Ethan dug frantically into the backpack with the snacks, pulling out a Mountain Dew and a double shot of Twinkie. He began devouring the refreshments. Caleb watched a little enviously, but he refrained from joining in the binging. He decided to distract himself with a book by one of his favorite authors—Isaac Asimov—a prominent science fiction writer who wrote many books centering around robots in the future. He was something of a hero to Caleb.

"We also need to mention the three laws of robotics, according to Isaac Asimov," Caleb said. "Absolutely gotta have those." Caleb read out loud:

1. *A robot may not injure a human being or, through inaction, allow a human being to come to harm.*

2. *A robot must obey any orders given to it by human beings, except where such orders would conflict with the First Law.*

3. *A robot must protect its own existence as long as such protection does not conflict with the First or Second Law.*

Ethan appeared thoughtful. "So, robots could *never* hurt humans?"

"That's right," Caleb said. "The computer programs that run the robots would never allow it. It's the first and most sacred law of robotics."

"Well, that's good," Ethan said, sounding relieved. "Especially when they're doubling their strength every year and a half."

❧

At 2:00 a.m. there were still no traces of paranormal activity. Ethan was done working on the school project, no matter how much Caleb protested to continue. He felt he had to push the issue, to force the ghosts out of hiding. Ethan turned off all the lights. His bedroom was now illuminated only by a sliver of moonlight coming in through the window and a few small lights on the ghost-detecting equipment. They sat in the darkness, the realm of the ghost world, Ethan figured. But it still wasn't enough. He had to go further. Ethan had seen TV shows where ghost hunters would try to get especially stubborn specters to come out by aggravating them. *It had to be done.*

"Hey, you! Yeah, you…ghost in the room. I'm talkin' to you!" Ethan taunted. "I don't think you have the guts to do what you did the other night. What's the matter? Are you afraid of me now that I'm awake? Do I have to be asleep, you coward, before you come out? Is that it...? C'mon, do it! Show yourself!"

Ethan and Caleb waited. There were no sights. There were no sounds. The pieces on the chessboard remained stationary. Ethan checked the equipment and took a few more EMF readings around the room. He found absolutely, positively nothing.

By 3:30 a.m. Ethan couldn't keep his eyes open any longer. He took one last weary look around the room and saw nothing to keep him awake. Caleb was already sprawled out on the floor asleep. Ethan soon passed out beside him, surrounded by snack wrappers and soda cans.

They finally woke up at 10:00 a.m. with the sun beaming through the window into their eyes. They peeled themselves off the floor, stiff and sore from lying in awkward positions all night. Ethan had even fallen asleep on top of a soda can, the impression of which was still carved into the side of his face. They took a moment to stretch and wake up, then gathered the cameras, voice recorder, and EMF meter. The chess pieces hadn't moved at all during the night, and they had observed nothing unusual, but Ethan hoped that maybe there was evidence on the equipment that was waiting to be discovered. They still had to analyze several hours of video and audio recordings before the investigation could be considered complete.

Four hours later, after intensively reviewing all of the data, Ethan and Caleb were both convinced that nothing supernatural had happened there last night. The ghost stake-out had yielded nothing. It was time for Caleb to go home. A dejected Ethan watched Caleb pack up all of his ghost-hunting gear. *Why?* Ethan wondered. *Why did nothing show up last night?* Ethan walked Caleb out to the front porch. He looked at his best friend with a painfully frustrated face.

"Caleb, can we try again tonight?"

"I don't know, Ethan. I'm tired. You gotta be tired too."

"I am, but…I know we'll get the evidence tonight. I feel it. Please."

Caleb sighed wearily. "Ethan, I hate to say it, but…are you sure you weren't sleepwalking and moved the pieces yourself?"

Ethan shook his head, though at this point he wasn't quite as defiant about the matter. He was now having doubts himself. "Maybe you're right."

Caleb plainly saw the anguish on Ethan's face. He tried to be upbeat. "Ethan, even if that's it, it's still pretty cool, really interesting stuff. We could study the sleepwalking."

"No thanks."

"Look, I'm really sorry we didn't find anything."

"Yeah, me too. Guess I'm just going crazy."

"No, you're not. We'll figure it out. Catch you later."

"Yeah, okay."

CHAPTER 12

REACHING THE BREAKING POINT

ETHAN SAT AT his desk in class with his elbows on the table and his hands cradling his head. He was facing the blackboard, while Ms. Goodfoot was admonishing the class about the use of prepositions at the end of sentences, but that was the extent of his attempt at concentration. His eyes were soft, distant, and unfocused. His mind was clearly elsewhere. It was Friday. Ethan had convinced Caleb to let him borrow his ghost-hunting gear, and he used it every night that week to try to find any shred of supernatural evidence that might prove to Caleb, and himself, that he wasn't going crazy. All the investigation amounted to, however, was a waste of twelve batteries and at least that number of hours in lost sleep.

"All right, class, before I dismiss you to work in your groups, I want to remind you that next week is Bring-a-Parent-to-School Week," Ms. Goodfoot announced. "I'll be passing around sign-up sheets for you to take home."

Ethan winced in disgust at the thought of another Bring-a-Parent-to-School Week. It was a ridiculous dog and pony show if there ever was one. He was pretty sure, in junior high, they were going to phase it out and not have one. There had been no mention of it during the school year, so Ethan thought he was in the clear. He never figured they would bring it back for summer school.

The program got its start in the first grade. It was a kind of show and tell where the parents were the objects on display. The little kids would all sit back and listen as their moms or dads talked in fifteen-minute increments about the various aspects of their jobs. Up until the fourth grade, Ethan enjoyed it. He liked seeing the men and women of Blackwoods in their uniforms, bright medals of honor adorning their chests, the pageantry of it all, the patriotism. Back then, the fact that his father took the podium with no light reflecting from his chest never bothered him. He liked it when his dad told stories, any kind of stories about what he did at work. He just liked having his dad there, plainly and simply.

But now, things were different. The parade of world-renowned scientists and high-ranking officers into the classroom literally made Ethan sick, especially with his dad on deck wearing his maintenance-man uniform stained in grease. *Would it kill him to leave the uniform at home and just wear a nice suit? Maybe even lie a little about what he does? Spice it up a bit?* He never would, though. Starting in the fourth grade, when his father would speak to the class passionately about the mundane tasks of his job, several overprivileged kids would taunt, jeer, and make nasty remarks. The comments were made in those low-frequency tones that parents never seem to hear. But Ethan always heard every word like they were blasted from a bullhorn. Those comments became harsher and more frequent with time. Now when the colonels and generals took the podium in the classroom, the coruscating beams of light from their brass-laden suits filled Ethan at once with jealousy and disgust. In those moments, he just wanted his dad to leave and go back to work.

Ethan folded up his copy of the Parent Week sign-up sheet and tucked it far away into his desk, with absolutely no intention of showing it to his parents. Then he sat there, sickened with himself. Ethan couldn't believe who he had become. He felt like he was going backwards in life, like he was a better person, a better son, when he was six years old.

⋘

Ms. Goodfoot finally dismissed the students to work on their projects, though it was becoming increasingly difficult for Ethan and Caleb to work together. Caleb was still attacking the project with the same passion and gusto as he had before, but Ethan was lost in a world of his own. Their project was definitely not a priority for him. The events of the night a week ago haunted him continuously, even though the spirits he'd been seeking ever since refused to show themselves. Ethan had three possible explanations for what happened that night: *ghosts, aliens, or insanity.* And with no evidence of the other two, insanity was moving up the list fast.

Caleb moved his desk next to Ethan's and began reading aloud a passage from a book. At the end of the reading, Caleb looked at Ethan, expecting a response. He found him staring off into space behind him as if he weren't even there. Ethan's eyes finally met Caleb's.

"Caleb…How would you test to see if aliens have been in your room?"

Caleb sighed deeply in frustration. "Ethan, seriously, this project is due Monday. How much of your part have you even done?"

"I got a lot more in my life to worry about than this stupid project," Ethan snapped. He looked around the room, then lowered his voice. "I can't talk about this now."

≈

If the weather was nice, the students were allowed to eat their lunches outside. Today there wasn't a cloud in the sky, though a storm was steadily brewing in Ethan's head. He sat with Caleb in awkward silence on the far side of the school's courtyard. The events of the day seemed to conspire against him—Annika appeared to be spending even more time with Tristan; Austin and Bradley had talked mockingly about using Ethan again as a decoy in the next Laser Wars game; and now his best friend sat beside him thinking he was a lunatic slacker.

Caleb finished a bite of his turkey sandwich and looked at Ethan. He took a deep breath before forging ahead. "All I'm saying is that night it was really late. You were tired, disoriented. You had to have disturbed those chess pieces in your sleep. It's okay. Millions of people sleepwalk, Ethan."

"If I was sleepwalking, tired, and disoriented, then how would I be able to move the white pieces to logical spots on the board?" Ethan retaliated. "They were real moves, Caleb, like someone was playing a game."

"But when you woke up that morning, the white pieces were in their original positions, right?"

"Right, the pieces were moved back sometime during the night."

Caleb shook his head. "Ethan, those pieces were never

moved. You just dreamed that. The only pieces you moved were the black ones…and those were just placed randomly over the board, exactly like you would expect from a sleepwalker."

"What about the white king?" Ethan asked, determined to sway Caleb's opinion. "What are the odds it would be the only white piece knocked over?"

"The odds would be one in sixteen or six point two-five percent…much better odds than the probability it's a ghost trying to threaten you with the fallen king of death."

"No, something doesn't feel right. Come over tonight, Caleb. Help me with one last investigation."

"You've had the ghost gear for a whole week," Caleb said, exasperated. "I'll come over. I'd love to come over, but to hang out…and to work on our project."

"Just one more time. Please. I have to figure this out," Ethan pleaded.

"Ethan, you're obsessed."

"So, you will?"

"No. There are no ghosts in your bedroom…or aliens either!" he said a little too loudly. Annika had come over to throw away some trash and overheard his comment. She looked at Ethan and smiled strangely, then chuckled a little as she walked away.

Ethan stared daggers at Caleb. "Thanks a lot."

"I'm sorry…Let's just get the project done, then we'll worry about what happened that night. I don't have the luxury of getting anything lower than an A on this project. My dad would kill me."

That comment from Caleb hit the wrong place at the wrong time in Ethan's mind. His mood turned even more sour. Ethan glared at Caleb with resentful eyes.

"What's *that* supposed to mean, Caleb? That *I* have the luxury of doing badly? That *my* dad won't care how bad I do? Your dad's the *scientist* and mine's the *janitor*, right? Someday you're gonna be a big shot scientist at the research facility while I stick a plunger down the toilets all day…You're just like everyone else."

Caleb stared at Ethan in utter disbelief, shocked by the words that'd come out of his mouth. They were the kind of words that ruined friendships that took years to build. "Is that *really* what you think of me?"

"I don't know…Am I right?" Ethan pushed on stubbornly.

Caleb shook his head sadly. His eyes were getting watery. He grabbed the remainder of his lunch with a jittery hand and stuffed it back into his paper sack. A tear streamed down his cheek before he turned and walked away.

Ethan immediately felt horrible about what he'd said, but he made no effort to apologize. He thought, eventually, their friendship would have to end. How many janitors and quantum physicists pal around as adults, anyway? Ethan figured, at some point down the road, he'd be the one who would have to empty Caleb's trash can while Caleb was busy solving the mysteries of the universe. And, after a full day's worth of solving universe mysteries, would Caleb really want to hang out with the guy who throws away his trash? What would they talk about? Could he ever respect him? There would be a gap between them, a gap that no amount of childhood history could bridge. If their friendship was destined to dissolve, then maybe it would be better and less painful if it just ended now. But it sure didn't feel that way at the moment. As Ethan watched Caleb walk away in the distance, a tear streamed down his own cheek. He was missing him already. Ethan had never felt so alone in his entire life.

Then Austin and Bradley walked up from behind. "Are you crying?" Austin asked with a smirk. "No crying on Bravo Team, you pansy."

"I'm not crying. Just allergies."

"Whatever," Austin huffed. "Tomorrow, war maneuvers, two o'clock. Meet at Bravo Fort at one…And don't be late, Tate. This time, every minute late equals twenty push-ups."

Austin and Bradley laughed mockingly as they left. Ethan glared at them through his teary eyes. He gritted his teeth in determination. The moment had arrived—the moment of defiance, of revolution, even if the uprising consisted of an army of one. Ethan checked his perfectly synchronized watch. War maneuvers would begin in exactly twenty-five hours, thirty-two minutes, and fourteen seconds.

He could hardly wait.

CHAPTER 13

INSUBORDINATION

THE NEXT DAY Ethan walked alone to the Bravo Fort and arrived a full three hours before the scheduled meeting. He used the time to formulate a battle plan, to give himself orders for his own mission. Ethan plotted out a direct line to the Delta Fort, not an end-around run or a flanking move, but a straight shot right down the middle. His plan was to take the absolute shortest route and set a blistering land speed record. He was going to try to run faster than he ever had in his life, charge the base front and center, capture the flag single-handedly, and return home the undisputed hero. It was a daring plan that no one would expect. Ethan took extra time to warm up and stretch his legs before his team arrived. He also put on a few extra black and green stripes of face paint, leaving only his intensely focused eyes unmarked. "The Ghost," as Ethan had been nicknamed for his speed and stealth, would attempt to strike like never before.

⁂

Bravo Team gathered around Austin as he drew up the battle plans on the chalkboard. Ethan and Caleb exchanged a couple of awkward glances, but Ethan mostly looked straight ahead, focused like a laser. He stared at the chalkboard and Austin's battle plan scribblings, but he paid absolutely no attention to any of it. The time for following orders was over. Ethan had given himself his own marching orders, and he was going to execute those orders come hell or high water. His body was flushed with blood. His muscles twitched in anticipation. In less than ten minutes, he would make his stand.

At 2:00 p.m. precisely, the sound of the Gjallarhorn from the Delta Fort signaled the start of the game. Ethan took off like a shot in the direction of the enemy base.

"We'll give him five minutes," Austin said with a cocky smile. "That'll be enough time for our decoy to stir up the ducks."

"Sounds good, sir," Bradley chimed in.

Once Ethan was out of Austin and Bradley's sight, he tossed away his canteen in the woods. He wanted to be as light and nimble as possible. There was no sense in carrying a canteen full of water if he wasn't going to take the time to drink it. Besides, if things went the way he hoped, he'd be drinking a Cherry Coke and toasting his victory in about thirty minutes, anyway. Ethan also shut off his headset camera and radio. He was officially in stealth mode now, off the grid and flying blind, using only his speed and instincts to complete the mission he had set for himself. Today he was Captain Tate, master of his own destiny, and loving every minute of it.

∽

Back at the Bravo Team fort, Caleb sat at his computer terminal checking the video screens. He quickly noticed that the screen dedicated to Ethan's headset camera was displaying only static. Caleb grabbed the radio transmitter. "Ethan, I can't get a video signal. Can you hear me? Over." There was no answer. "Ethan, do you copy? Over."

Nothing but static filled the air on Ethan's radio.

Caleb sat back in his chair. A look of worry crept onto his face as he watched the fuzzy white noise speckle Ethan's video screen. He knew exactly what was happening.

"Good luck, Ethan," Caleb said solemnly to himself.

Ethan ran like a madman through the woods. He could barely feel his body for the adrenaline that was coursing through him. His legs pumped up and down like pistons in a turbo-charged engine. He had managed to sprint the entire way, making the tough forest terrain look like a tame neighborhood park. In the five-minute head start that Austin had given him for his decoy duties, Ethan was already nearly upon the Delta base. The plan was simple—go straight for the flag, grab it, run a circle around the base to try to confuse the laser turret, and exit the way he had come. His hope was that the laser turret would miss its first few shots due to its Initial Calibration Error. The big X-factor was Annika. If she had already settled into her sniper position, then Ethan would surely be a goner, especially when taking a beeline straight for the flag. This was where Ethan took his biggest gamble, wagering the success of his entire mission on a single idea—that Annika and the rest of Delta Team would never, in a million years, think that anyone could be that close to the base in that short amount of time. Ethan hoped to take them completely by surprise. He knew for sure that his actions would shock Austin.

Ethan eyed the Delta Team's waving flag, dashed into the clearing, and snatched it without hesitation. Things were going perfectly so far. He had been too fast for the turret's guidance system to track, and now he was in too close to the base for the turret to have a shooting angle. Ethan quickly ran a loop around the base. The laser turret spun around 360 degrees, following him. Then he exited the base, amazingly, moving even faster. The laser turret fired shots all over the place, missing wildly like someone who had been spun around like a top and was dizzy. By the time the laser turret had regained its senses, Ethan was more than a hundred yards away from the base and out of the range of the computer's tracking system.

Ethan was relieved to have gotten past the laser turret, but he knew that Annika was lurking somewhere out there, not to mention the rest of Delta Team. He kept up his torrid pace, taking no time for rest. His lungs ached and his legs burned, but he refused to slow down. Suddenly, he stopped dead in his tracks and crouched down behind a large spruce tree. He was shocked to realize that the first people he would have to encounter on his daring mission were members of his *own* team. Austin and Bradley were about two hundred feet from him and moving closer.

Ethan knew the Deltas would be breathing down his neck soon. He would've liked to surprise Austin and Bradley back at the base with the flag, drinking Cherry Coke before they realized what had happened, but there was no time to try and sneak around them. Ethan quickly decided on the direct approach. He popped out from behind the tree and ran straight ahead. Ethan zoomed by them, waving the Delta Team flag eagerly, tauntingly, even.

"I got the flag! I got it! See you at the base, Captain… Hurry up! Move it! Move it! Double time!" Ethan yelled in an adrenaline-induced sarcastic tone. He even laughed mockingly as he ran by, exacting payback for all the times that Austin had mocked him. Ethan knew there would be hell to pay later for his actions, but any number of push-ups and any amount of tongue-lashing would be a bargain-basement price for the opportunity to ram this victory down their throats.

"Stop, Tate…! You will stop right there! That's an order!"

Ethan kept running with no intention of stopping.

"*That's my flag!*" Austin bellowed at the top of his lungs.

Ethan flew through the woods with an irrepressible smile on his face. Every step he took was a step closer to victory. Then, suddenly, a barrage of blue lasers streamed past, narrowly missing him. He looked back and found Austin and Bradley blasting away. Ethan hit the deck and crawled quickly behind a large rock. He hadn't planned for this turn of events. He knew that Austin would be angry, but his captain resorting to firing on a teammate over the glory of returning with the flag was not a part of Ethan's calculation. Blue laser pulses whizzed continuously around him. He was hopelessly pinned down behind the rock. If he tried to run, he would easily be shot; his monumental record attempt, and his stand against Austin, would be over.

Ethan figured he had no choice but to return fire. He popped out ever so slightly and fired his rifle at Austin and Bradley. They ducked hurriedly behind a fallen tree for cover. Lasers soon began to streak through the air in an intense battle between members of the same team. There was no going back now. What started out as a single act of insubordination had turned into a full-blown Bravo Team civil war.

The firefight between Ethan and his commanding officers had been so heated, so emotionally charged, that no one even noticed Glenn and Jason of the Delta Team creeping into the area. They were only thirty yards away, crouched down behind an earthen embankment. Glenn and Jason had a good view of Austin and Bradley, but they couldn't see Ethan behind the rock. Without knowledge of the treasonous activities going on, they figured the person behind the rock had to be one of their own teammates. They thought that maybe Annika, or more likely Tristan, had gotten caught and was pinned down. Glenn and Jason took aim at Austin and Bradley and fired a salvo of lasers at them from behind. Their first shots went high, missing their targets. Austin and Bradley scrambled for better cover, but they were sandwiched between Ethan on one end and Glenn and Jason on the other. Their situation seemed hopeless until Ethan made a move that surprised everyone. He jumped out from behind his rock and fired on Glenn and Jason, hitting them both and knocking them out of the game. Ethan used the confusion of the moment to also shoot Bradley and take a few shots at Austin, sending him diving to the ground for cover.

Glenn and Jason stood in total disbelief of what had just happened. They realized that Austin and Bradley had been shooting at Ethan, and vice versa. They stared at Austin, dumbfounded.

"You've been shot, Glenn! Get back to your base!" Austin yelled. Glenn and Jason were slow to leave. "Get outta here. Now! This is between Ethan and me."

Glenn shook his head shamefully at Austin. "He's got the

the flag, is that it? For God's sake, he's on your own team, Austin."

"Leave…Now!" Austin roared.

"You know, you'd be dead right now if it weren't for Ethan," Glenn said.

Austin glared at his rival captain, face red and fists balled. "Get outta here, Glenn. I'm not gonna tell you again."

"Glenn, it's not worth it…C'mon, let's go," Jason said, putting a calming hand on Glenn's shoulder. Glenn nodded reluctantly, then he and Jason walked away.

Bradley looked at Austin apologetically. "Sorry I got hit. Sorry I couldn't finish this fight with you, Captain. Good luck, sir."

Austin scowled at his sergeant. "I don't need luck to take out Tate."

"Of course not, absolutely not, sir." Bradley left the area, leaving Austin and Ethan to finish their duel.

Austin spoke pompously about not needing luck to defeat his scout, but, in reality, a one-on-one battle in the field between them would decidedly favor Ethan. Ethan was faster, more agile, had better instincts, and was a much better marksman. Austin would have to get lucky to have a chance against him. But as luck would have it in that moment, the god of bullies prevailed over the god of fairness. When Ethan popped out from behind his rock to fire his laser rifle, his weapon failed to shoot. He was totally defenseless. All he had was the slab of rock he was hiding behind. Austin noticed Ethan's predicament, and his eyes widened eagerly. He cracked a sinister smile at the opportunity to blast a vulnerable Ethan into oblivion. Austin slowly stood up and crept cautiously toward him. He fired a few shots at Ethan's position, then crouched down for cover, waiting to see if Ethan had the ability to retaliate before going in for the kill.

On the other side of the rock, Ethan was desperately shaking and banging his gun to try to get it to work. He tried repeatedly to shoot it, but nothing came out. It was no use. Ethan slowly sneaked a peek around the rock. He saw Austin walking faster and faster toward him, gaining confidence in Ethan's inability to defend himself with every step he took. Ethan gave up on getting the gun to work, but he had no intention of just lying helplessly in a fetal position until Austin came around to shoot him. He didn't want to make it any easier for a coward already content to fire on an unarmed teammate.

Ethan sprang up from behind the rock and sprinted as fast as he could away from Austin, zigging and zagging erratically in an attempt to make himself a hard target. Austin fired and missed his first few shots, but now he was chasing Ethan as he zigzagged and was firing his gun at maximum capacity. Ethan winced as the lasers streamed by, getting closer and closer with each burst. Austin wasn't the greatest of shots, but it was inevitable that even he would be able to shoot Ethan from such a close range. Just as the lasers spewing from Austin's gun were zeroing in on Ethan, a blue laser pulse from seemingly the other end of the world zapped Austin from behind, sending his laser vest flashing. There was only one person Ethan knew of who was capable of making such a magnificent shot. It had to be the work of Annika Pepper. Ethan kept running as fast as he could. He was afraid to slow down, for fear that Annika might have him in her sights next.

Austin looked around to see who had shot him, but he saw and heard nothing.

"Aaagghh!" he screamed as he tore his vest off and slammed it on the ground. "This isn't over, Tate…! You hear me?!" His words echoed menacingly through the forest.

Ethan arrived at the Bravo Base a few minutes later, physically exhausted and emotionally drained. He was only thirty feet from the door and official victory when Kevin walked out from behind a nearby tree with his sniper rifle aimed at Ethan's chest.

"Don't you move," Kevin said, keeping his gun firmly on Ethan.

Ethan stared at him in disgust. He was sure that Austin had radioed ahead, even after being killed in battle, with orders for Kevin to execute him. Ethan had to try to reason with him, though reason had a bad track record against Kevin Kim's instinct to follow orders. He was a by-the-book sort of guy, so Ethan had to tread carefully.

"I got the flag, Kevin. We win. Bravo Team wins…Hurry, let me go in before the Deltas attack and get their flag back."

Kevin shook his head, unfazed by Ethan's plea. "I got my orders, Ethan," he said, not budging an inch. "You should have obeyed yours…Now drop the gun."

Ethan tossed his useless gun aside. His record attempt was over. There was no sense in trying to run from Kevin the way he did from Austin. Kevin was a strong marksman, and there was no chance he would miss from that short distance with a highly accurate sniper rifle. Ethan thought for a moment, then attempted to appeal to Kevin's sense of decency.

"Kevin, do you really want your biggest contribution in the battle today to be shooting an unarmed teammate with a sniper rifle from ten feet away?" Ethan asked softly, like a psychologist gently probing a patient's inner thoughts.

"Austin's the captain, and I follow my captain anywhere."

Just then, Bradley emerged from behind the base with a wicked grin on his face. "Good luck getting him to change his mind," he said to Ethan, snickering. "Austin's a brilliant captain, you know. He was afraid Kevin might turn down an order to shoot you, so when he called him, he didn't just order him to shoot you. He sweetened the deal. Said if he did it, he could put the Delta flag up for our team. And told him he could be a sergeant like me, just a rank lower though. Isn't that right, Kevin?"

Ethan stared in amazement at Kevin, sickened by his treachery. Kevin looked ashamed for a nanosecond, then hastily turned defensive and doubled down on his position.

"Look, I'm not the bad guy here, Ethan. You are," Kevin said. "*You're* the one who disobeyed orders. *I'm* the one following them...You really should've listened to the captain."

Kevin pressed his rifle to his shoulder tightly, taking aim and preparing to fire. He was just about to press the trigger when the door of the Bravo Fort swung open, distracting him. A blast of lasers shot out at Kevin from inside the base. His laser vest flashed bright red and blue. Caleb stepped out of the base clutching his laser rifle. Kevin stared at him in total shock.

"Now you don't have to follow orders, Kevin, because you're out of the game. Is that a sweet enough deal for you?" Caleb quipped.

Kevin walked away in a huff. Ethan flashed a broad smile and sighed in relief. He was relieved not to have been shot, but more so knowing that his best friend still had his back.

Bradley eyeballed Ethan and Caleb. "You will both answer to Austin for this. And you will both pay," he sneered, then followed Kevin away from the base.

"Thank you, Caleb." Ethan's eyes became soft. "And I'm sorry."

Caleb nodded and cracked a faint smile. "Well, you better get that flag in there and make it official."

"You know, Caleb…I wouldn't mind emptying your trash can."

Before Caleb could ask what that meant, Ethan put his arm around his best friend and pulled him in for a hug.

Ethan and Caleb noted the official record time and toasted the victory with a couple of Cherry Cokes. It was a modest celebration, though. Ethan knew his actions would be met with repercussions, that this victory would come at a great cost. For now, though, he eyed with pride the captured Delta flag hanging on the wall and the record time written by Caleb on the chalkboard. He enjoyed the sweet, tingling sensation of a hard-earned Cherry Coke cascading down his throat. This one tasted better than any he could remember. He tried his best to enjoy the moment and forget about the consequences. But he was well aware that, any minute, the door would open, an angry captain would rush in, and the revelry would come to an abrupt end.

CHAPTER 14

THE FALLOUT

ETHAN HAD JUST finished his Cherry Coke when he heard the fateful beeps of the keypad on the door. The latch clicked. Ethan and Caleb watched the entrance with dread. The door burst open and slammed into the wall. The harsh, metal-on-metal clang rang through their heads like they were inside a giant bell. Austin stood in the doorway for a moment. The light coming in from the outside silhouetted him, giving him the look of a madman from a horror movie. He was completely stationary except for the expansions and contractions of his chest as he breathed heavily, snorting even, like a wild boar. He stared at them with an expression of fury unlike any they had seen before. He slowly moved forward, stalking them. Ethan and Caleb backpedaled fearfully.

"Caleb, out!" Austin roared. Caleb trembled, but he hesitated, not wanting to leave Ethan. "Now!" Austin somehow managed to shout even louder.

"Go ahead, Caleb," Ethan said. "I'll be fine." Caleb finally and reluctantly backed around Austin and went outside.

Austin marched up to Ethan and grabbed him by his

shirt. He rammed him up against the wall, pressing his fists full of shirt hard into Ethan's chest. And then Austin began banging his scout repeatedly into the wall. "How do you feel about taking that flag now, Tate?!" he yelled as he continued to thrash Ethan into the wall. "You are nothing! You hear me?! Nothing! A nobody and a son of a nobody! You were lucky I even kept you on this team…Then you go and disobey *my* orders?!"

Austin pressed Ethan into the wall again, this time with his forearm digging deeply into his throat. Ethan squirmed and struggled, but he was pinned and could do nothing about it. He choked and gasped helplessly. Austin finally removed his forearm from Ethan's throat. He grabbed his shirt again and got right in his face, a mere two inches away. Ethan could feel Austin's scorching, angry breath on his cheeks.

"I want you to apologize to me for your disloyalty."

Ethan paused. The thought of uttering those words made him sick to his stomach. Austin scowled and began to move his forearm back to Ethan's throat.

"I'm sorry," Ethan blurted.

"No…not nearly good enough. Now, I'm going to tell you exactly what I want to hear from you." Austin flashed a smug smile. "I need you to say the following, word-for-word: Captain Turnbull, my supreme captain and commander, I am deeply and truly sorry for being disloyal to you."

Ethan swallowed hard and took a deep, pride-swallowing breath. "Captain Turnbull, my supreme captain and commander, I am deeply and truly sorry for being disloyal to you." Ethan felt disgusted and disloyal to himself for saying the words.

He tried to move around Austin, but Austin shoved him back against the wall. "We're not finished yet, Tate. You also need to tell me that you realize you're a loser and a nobody, and that you will never, ever disobey me again."

Ethan felt like he was selling his soul to the devil for the rock-bottom price of not getting beaten up. At that moment, though, he couldn't find the courage to stop the transaction. A tear streamed down his cheek. "I'm a loser…a nobody…and I will never, ever disobey you again."

"See…That wasn't so hard, was it?" Austin asked with a self-satisfied grin. "Now wait here. I got a surprise for you."

Austin went outside and soon returned with Bradley, Kevin, and Caleb. Austin reached into the cooler and pulled out the three remaining Cherry Cokes. He took a soda for himself and passed the other two to Bradley and Kevin. He opened his soda and raised it in the air for a toast.

"Today we celebrate a very special occasion," Austin said in a festive tone. "This is the last day Ethan Tate will ever see the inside of this fort. That's right, you are officially and forever dismissed from Bravo Team…Cheers!" Austin took a drink of his soda, and Bradley and Kevin followed his lead. Ethan glared at Austin in disgust. Austin just smiled back wickedly. "Oh, yeah…and also dismissed from the team for treason is Caleb Warren."

Caleb swallowed hard and his eyes became teary.

"Fine, kick us off the team," Ethan said, salvaging some courage. "But you have to share the base. We take turns using it."

Austin thought about it, or pretended to. Then he teased with a grin: "I don't think so. The base is the Bravo Team's. You two are no longer with Bravo Team, so the base isn't yours."

"We helped build it!" Ethan yelled. "Caleb and I did more work than any of you!"

"You're not using the base and that's final!" Austin roared back.

"It's not fair," Caleb softly protested.

"File a complaint, then," Austin mocked. "Seriously, who's gonna stop me? You two? Your dads? I don't think so. Caleb, your dad makes whatever my dad tells him to make…And *you*," he chuckled at Ethan, "we all know what *your* dad does at the base." Austin made the gesture of someone plunging a toilet.

A fire burned behind Ethan's eyes. But he said nothing.

"Sergeant Wuddle, Sergeant Kim, escort these two traitors out of *our* fort."

Kevin couldn't help but smile at the sound of the word "sergeant" preceding his name. He stood up a little straighter, a little prouder, and gestured to the door. "C'mon, you heard the captain," he said, already intoxicated with his newly given sergeant's authority.

Ethan glared at Kevin. He wanted to punch him in the face, but he managed to restrain himself. On the way out, Ethan eyed the framed picture on the wall taken two years ago depicting a happy, unified Bravo Team. He grabbed it off the wall and turned to face Austin.

"Do you even remember when we took this picture?" Ethan asked.

"Yeah…We took that picture when we were kids. Then I grew up and became a leader. It's my destiny, you know. I'm sure you know what yours is…Now get out."

Ethan tossed the picture disgustedly into the air. It landed with a smash on the floor, shattering the glass in the frame. Ethan and Caleb left without another word. The door to the base they had worked so hard to build soon slammed and locked behind them.

⤬

The walk back to their houses was a silent and somber one. Ethan felt terrible about Caleb being kicked off the team. He knew it was all his fault and wanted to make it up to him somehow, but there was nothing he could do now. He couldn't turn back time. Even if he could, he thought he still might grab that Delta flag all over again.

They stopped in front of Caleb's house. They just stood there for a moment in stunned silence. Then Ethan spoke softly. "I'm sorry, Caleb...It should've just been me."

Caleb shook his head. His eyes were holding back tears. "It's not your fault, Ethan." He trudged toward his house with his head hanging low.

Ethan watched his best friend in sympathy until he went inside. Then Ethan headed for home. It was the only base he had left.

CHAPTER 15

MENTIONING THE UNMENTIONABLE

ETHAN SAT DISTRACTEDLY at the kitchen table over dinner. The way his stomach was churning, he couldn't imagine eating anything. He just sat there with a blank expression on his face as he constructed a fort of meat loaf and mashed potatoes with his fork. It vaguely resembled the Bravo Base. Ethan's parents watched him with concern.

"Ethan, you're awfully quiet," his dad asked. "How was your day?"

Ethan paused. Part of him wanted to give in and unleash all his frustration and anger, to tell his dad everything. Have *the* talk, the big one, right then and there. But he managed to suppress the urge one more time and swallowed the day's events like a mouthful of spoiled milk. He even put on a pretty good poker face, if only for a while.

"It was fine."

"How did the Laser Games go?"

Ethan felt his jaw tighten involuntarily and his teeth begin to grind. It took all he had to keep from screaming as he thought back on how his day really went.

"Bravo Team won," Ethan said, feigning enthusiasm.

"That's great!" his dad said. "Tell me about the battle. Give me the details."

"It was Capture the Flag. We won. That's it," Ethan said quickly, dearly hoping that would be the end of it.

"Who captured the flag?"

"It doesn't matter."

"C'mon, tell me," Ethan's dad pressed, nudging his son playfully on the arm.

Ethan sighed. "I did."

"I knew it! You're so modest...You know, when I was your age, I used to be pretty good at Capture the Flag. We didn't have all the fancy gear you have now, but I was fast and sneaky like you."

Ethan's mom grinned. "He still is fast and sneaky." Ethan's parents shared a laugh, but Ethan just watched them distantly, unable to participate in the humor.

"Ethan, you're just like your dad, you know...a chip off the old block." He patted his son proudly on the back. "I bet Austin loves having a guy like you on the team."

Ethan forced out the last fake smile and nod of agreement he had in him. He was officially at his breaking point. He was looking over the ledge and hanging on by his toes. The slightest nudge would send him over. And, once over, there would be no coming back.

"I'd like to propose a toast," his dad said, raising his glass. Ethan cringed as the memories of his miserable day bombarded him. "To Ethan and his victory...and to me for finally getting all the vacuums at the base functioning properly."

Ethan's mom's eyes widened with interest. "*Really*, you're all finished?"

"Yeah...Of course, it helps when your co-workers are pulling twenty-four-hour shifts."

Ethan couldn't stand watching, once again, his parents in a riveting discussion over his dad's stupid job. He thought they were both clueless. *There are miracle discoveries to be made at Blackwoods, and my dad has his head stuck in dirty vacuums all day? And he's perfectly happy with that, and happy for his son to follow in his footsteps, the chip off the old block?*

The bitterness, the frustration, the anger swelled in him. Ethan's dad held his glass high in the air. "Cheers!"

His parents drank to celebrate, but Ethan deferred. He watched their happy toast with scathing eyes. Then nearly two years of pent-up emotion broke loose like a volcano.

"I can't believe you're toasting fixing vacuums. That's so stupid!" Ethan blurted.

His dad's smile vanished in an instant.

"Why would you say that?" his mother jumped in with disappointment in her voice.

"Because it's ridiculous to be proud of that!" Ethan shouted, all filters removed. "All the things you could be doing at the base, Dad, and you choose *that*? Maintenance man...janitor?! Are you *really* happy cleaning the toilets, cleaning Austin's dad's crap off the bowl? Don't you want to do anything else with your life? It's embarrassing, Dad! *You're* embarrassing me! I got kicked off Bravo Team today. Austin doesn't like me on his team. He makes fun of me. He makes fun of me because I'm *your* son! No matter how hard I try, I'm just a joke to him...I don't want to be a chip off the old block...I don't wanna be like you!"

Ethan's eyes were teary, and his face was flushed. He trembled with emotion. His father's eyes turned soft and sad, looking completely sucker-punched by his son's outburst. Ethan bolted out of the room and went upstairs to his bedroom. The door slamming behind him shook the entire house.

～ら

It had been three hours since the explosive episode in the dining room, and Ethan hadn't seen or heard from his parents. There were no punishments, no rebukes, no big talks, nothing at all. Ethan lay motionless on his bed, though his mind was still racing. He glanced over at the chessboard. The matter of the mysterious moving pieces now seemed so unimportant. Ethan was sure he had dreamed that foolishness. As more and more time passed, and the regret began to set in, he wished what he'd said to his father had also been a dream. Staring at the chessboard made him think about his poor dad and the awful things he'd said to him. He wanted to apologize, but he hesitated. Ethan couldn't bring himself to make the first move. All he could think of was how uncomfortable the moment would be the next time he saw his father. But time waits for no one's apologies, no matter how deserved, and night began to slip away.

Suddenly, some static noise registered on Ethan's walkie-talkie sitting on the nightstand. Someone was dialing in his frequency. Ethan figured it was probably Caleb, unless Austin was calling to rub more salt in his wounds. He picked up the walkie-talkie and listened.

"Ethan, are you there?" a girl's voice asked. "It's Annika."

Ethan's eyes widened, and he sat up quickly. She rarely called him unless she was trying to schedule a time that would work for him to be shot by lasers from long distance. It was now 10:37 p.m., an unlikely time to schedule a Laser Wars game. Hearing her voice on that walkie-talkie was far and away the best thing that had happened to him all day.

"Hi. Yeah, I'm here," Ethan said, trying to play it cool.

"I heard about what happened…Are you okay?"

"I'm fine. It's no big deal." Then some honesty slipped through the cracks. "I'm gonna miss playing the game. I'll miss the competition. I'll even miss running away from you, trying not to get shot."

"You gotta find another team, Ethan. You're the only person that makes it interesting, the only one who has a chance against me out there…I mean, it's not *much* of a chance," she snickered playfully, "but it's way more than anyone else has."

"Very funny," Ethan said, though inside he was bursting with pride.

"Seriously, I know you'll find another team. Glenn told me he'd love to have you on our team, but that he can't just dump Tristan."

"No, you can't just dump Tristan," Ethan said with subliminal sarcasm. "I don't know, maybe I'll never find a team. Maybe Caleb and I will just run around like lunatics in the woods and shoot each other." Ethan heard Annika laugh at that. He relished the moment.

"At least you'd still be playing," Annika said, sounding upbeat. "Anyway, I just wanted to tell you that you were really great out there today. I've never seen anything like it. You had to beat the record time by at least fifteen minutes."

"Thanks," Ethan said, now smiling like a fool in the late hours of the worst day of his life. "It could've been even better if I didn't have to fight both teams."

"Yeah…But you weren't fighting alone," Annika said. "You had a friend in high places." She paused. "Goodnight, Ethan."

"Goodnight, Annika," Ethan said with a smile that was slow to fade.

Static noise filled the walkie-talkie and the groundbreaking conversation was over. Ethan lay back in bed with a better outlook on life. He thought even if today was the last game of Laser Wars he ever played, it'd been worth it. He could retire at the ripe age of thirteen years, eight months, and seven days with the knowledge that he had impressed Annika. It was amazing how his talk with her had helped him see the light. Ethan knew what he needed to do next. And it had to happen tonight.

He walked down the hall toward his parents' bedroom. The house was dark. There was no sound. His parents had apparently already gone to bed, but this couldn't wait. Then he heard a creaking sound on the floor. Ethan turned around quickly, startled. His mother was walking up the stairs carrying a cup of hot tea. He met her at the top of the staircase and looked at her with shame in his eyes. She looked back at him, not with an expression of anger, but of sympathy. She even flashed an odd, soothing smile. Ethan appreciated her kindness, but he didn't understand it.

"I need to talk to Dad," Ethan whispered.

"I know…tomorrow," she said softly.

Ethan stared at his mom insistently. "I *really* need to talk to him now."

"Get some sleep, Ethan. We'll have the big talk tomorrow. We love you very much, you know that?"

Ethan nodded. "Yes," he replied in a soft tone, like he didn't deserve it.

"Goodnight…See you in the morning."

"Goodnight, Mom."

Ethan headed back to his bedroom. For the life of him, he couldn't figure out why his mom wasn't more upset. She seemed so calm, so measured, but it made no sense. He had expected an immediate, awkward confrontation that should have rightfully ended in a long grounding. It was no matter now, though. Ethan was focused on tomorrow. First thing in the morning, he could apologize to his dad and begin the process of making things right.

CHAPTER 16

THE DISAPPEARANCE

ETHAN GOT UP extra early the next morning and went downstairs to the kitchen. It was five thirty on a Sunday, and he was the first one up. He fixed himself a bowl of cereal and replayed in his mind what he would say to his father. Ethan was hoping that his dad would react to his words with the same cheerful exuberance as Captain Crunch, who was staring at him from the cereal box and providing a surrogate father on whom to rehearse.

∽

It was fast approaching seven o'clock. Ethan was done practicing the apology and was ready for the real thing. He listened carefully for any sounds upstairs that might indicate his parents were awake. But there was only silence. Ethan left the kitchen and went upstairs. He put his ear to his parents' door and listened. Nothing. He decided he had to wake them up, so he knocked on the door, softly at first. There was no answer. He knocked harder. Much harder. *Surely this would wake them up.* He stood up straight and took a deep breath. He waited and waited and waited. Still no answer. Ethan stared at the door, feeling conflicted and confused. He wrapped his hand around the doorknob and slowly began to turn it, gingerly opened the door a crack and peered inside. After a moment, he pushed the door wide open and surveyed his parents' bedroom with a puzzled face. *They were gone.* Ethan tried to make sense of the situation. He knew his parents sometimes went on walks in the mornings when they both had the day off. He figured they had to be on a walk, probably to strategize about how to handle their newly unruly son.

As Ethan mulled over his hypothesis, a couple of things began to bother him. One, his parents had to have left for their walk well before five thirty or he would have heard them. Leaving for a walk *that* early on a leisurely Sunday just seemed strange. The second thing that troubled him was the fact that his parents' bed was a shambles. Ethan's parents had both been in the military. They met in the Air Force. It was indoctrinated in them that they keep a tidy bed. In his entire life, Ethan had never seen his parents' bed unmade. But now, their covers were tossed around as if they'd just had a massive pillow fight, jumping on the bed like hyperactive kids having their first sleepover. It made no sense. Ethan could only figure that his parents must've really been thrown out of sorts. They got up early because they couldn't sleep, and they didn't make the bed because they had bigger things on their minds—namely, the big talk. Ethan realized his mom had to have been faking it when she seemed so calm last night. His words must've hurt them even more than he thought. Ethan went back to his room and got dressed. He was going out to find them.

◆

Ethan looked up and down the sidewalk and street, but there was no sign of his parents. Actually, there was no sign of anyone. Seven o'clock in the morning on a Sunday was never a hectic time in Blackwoods, but today seemed weirdly quiet. Even the air was oddly tranquil. Ethan began walking down the sidewalk in the opposite direction of his parents' normal route. They usually walked a counterclockwise loop around the town, so taking the clockwise path would ensure that he'd run into them at some point.

The scout started his circuit around the town at a brisk walking pace. But as Ethan found no one outside and passed house after house, each deathly silent with no lights on, he began to jog. He jogged faster and faster until he was in an all-out run. Ethan soon arrived back at his house, having completed the three-mile loop. During his entire journey, not only had he not run into his parents, but he had not encountered a single soul.

Where is everybody? Ethan wondered, his confusion growing by the second. His thoughts were soon interrupted by the low-pitched, mournful wail of a dog coming from his next-door neighbor's house. Ethan spotted their droopy-looking Basset Hound with its head peering out from between the drapes. The dog belonged to Herschel and Betty Price, a couple in their sixties. They owned the only barbershop and beauty salon in town. Their kids were grown and lived far away on the East Coast. Their dog, Mugsy, was their only child now, and they spoiled him rotten. They lavished him with attention and the little doggie gifts that you see in pet stores and wonder: *Now who in the world would ever buy those?* The dog howled despondently with his head low and his eyes sad, wet nose twitching in a manner that made him appear on the verge of tears. He truly looked like he had lost his best friend in the world.

Ethan stood at the window, only a foot away. "What's the matter, boy?"

The dog belted out another depressing howl. Ethan peeked through the window, looking past the dog and further into the house. He saw no sign of Herschel or Betty. It wasn't like them to ignore their pride and joy for very long.

Ethan walked back to the sidewalk and took a good, long look down the street. All of a sudden, the silence and solitude really began to give him the creeps. He didn't actually believe in zombies, but the empty, deathly quiet street reminded him of a desolate town in a zombie movie. Any minute, it seemed, the silence would be punctured by a pack of screaming undead, charging at him with intentions to eat his brains. Ethan figured it surely just had to be a quiet morning and that his imagination was running wild, but that rationale did little to settle the unease in his stomach. All of a sudden, the shutting of a door reverberated up the street from several houses away. Ethan turned with a jerk to find Caleb walking quickly toward him. They smiled in relief upon seeing each other, but that relief soon turned into mutual confusion.

"Have you seen your parents today?" Caleb asked.

"No...You?"

"No...Have you seen *anyone*?" Caleb asked with a tremor in his voice.

"No, only you, and I just took a lap around the town."

"You know the phones are dead, right? Landlines *and* cell phones...and the internet."

"What?" Ethan blurted, blindsided. "Start knocking on doors."

Ethan and Caleb split up and began checking on their neighbors. They knocked and waited repeatedly at each house, but no one ever answered. Ethan soon thought of Annika and got a sinking feeling in the pit of his stomach. He hurriedly skipped several houses to arrive on her doorstep next.

"Please be home. Please let her answer," Ethan begged. He knocked hard on the door five times and waited. No answer. Ethan shifted uneasily and pounded on the door for seven hard, thumping raps, each louder than the last. "Annika! Annika!"

"Ethan, I'm up here!"

Ethan ran toward her voice. He found Annika perched atop the roof, looking through the scope of her laser rifle, scanning the outer limits of the town. "Annika," Ethan said breathlessly. "I thought you were gone too."

"Sorry, just checking the perimeter," she said, trying to sound tough and composed as if still playing a Laser Wars game, though her voice gave hints of trepidation.

"Do you see anything?" Ethan asked.

"No, just the three of us…Wait, make that four."

Ethan looked down the street in the distance and saw someone walking toward them. It was Glenn. Annika climbed down from the roof and joined Ethan. Caleb came over about the same time as Glenn got to the group. The four of them just stood there in stunned silence.

"You find anyone else?" Glenn asked.

"No," Ethan said. "And I've circled the town."

"Same here. Went by the diner, theater, church…I saw nobody. Nobody at all."

"I was on the roof with the scope," Annika added. "I could see for miles…I saw no one."

"And all communications have been knocked out," Caleb said. "Telephones, cell phones, internet."

"I noticed the phones, but even the *internet*?" Glenn asked.

Caleb's face was grim. "Everything."

The group soon heard quick footsteps coming closer. They spotted Austin running toward them. He looked panicked, running wildly. As soon as Austin saw that he'd been spotted, he switched to a more leisurely walk to try to appear brave. Upon seeing Austin, Ethan's mind was instantly flooded with all of the horrible things he had said to his father. He felt a strong urge to tackle Austin to the ground and begin punching away. Even if he got pounded into the pavement, Ethan figured it would be worth it if he could just get one good shot on him.

Fortunately, Austin's current demeanor made it a little easier for Ethan to contain his emotions. Austin stared at the group, looking less like a vaunted captain of war games and more like a scared and confused kid. Usually, by now, Austin would have barked out several orders and scowled as he waited impatiently for his subordinates to carry them out. There were no orders now. There was no scowling. For the moment, at least, there were no subordinates either. They were just five kids who were shell-shocked, bewildered, and looking for answers. It was at that moment that Ethan subtly and without fanfare made his first suggestion to the group.

"We should get inside until we figure out our next move...I don't think it's safe out here."

Without words, the others nodded in agreement. Then everyone, high-ranking captains included, followed Ethan down the sidewalk and into his house.

CHAPTER 17

ALL ALONE

THE GROUP CONGREGATED in Ethan's family room around a television that was displaying only an eerie static. They had barricaded all the entrances to the house with furniture and armed themselves with whatever they could scrounge. Austin had a wooden baseball bat. Glenn had a pipe wrench. Caleb wielded a pair of nunchucks he'd found in Ethan's closet, though he had no idea how to use them. Annika kept her laser rifle handy. With the long-range scope on it, she could spot things coming from a distance. And even though the lasers were harmless, she figured she might be able to scare someone away by shooting at them. Ethan carried a small Swiss Army knife his father had given him for his last birthday. It wasn't exactly the ultimate defense weapon, but when he held it, he somehow felt closer to his dad.

Occasionally, someone would pull the drapes back on the large bay windows in the front of the house to sneak a glance outside. The fear of looking out the window was only surpassed by the fear of not doing so. Thus far, they spotted nothing out of the ordinary. But, in a way, that made them even more nervous.

"Where are the tanks, the troops?!" Austin wondered. "There should be tanks and troops all over the Dark Highway by now. Down our streets…to counterattack the terrorists."

"How could *terrorists* abduct all the people in town without anyone hearing a sound, Austin?" Annika shook her head sharply. "It's impossible."

"It wasn't terrorists," Ethan said.

Glenn shrugged, baffled. "Then who could've done it?"

An idea popped into all of their heads at once, though no one was quick to speak of it. The idea was so out there, so far-fetched, so preposterous, that it defied all logic. Then again, waking up to a deserted town without hearing so much as a peep throughout the night also made no sense. The notion, strange as it was, seemed to fit the data better than any other hypothesis.

"What if it was an alien abduction?" Ethan said, the hairs on the back of his neck tingling.

"What would aliens want with our entire town?" Annika asked. Then her voice cracked and her eyes got teary. "Why would they want my five-year-old brother?"

"And my little sister?" Glenn added with a tight throat.

"Tate's a moron! It's not aliens!" Austin yelled as if trying to convince himself.

"Anything's possible at this point," Caleb said. "We just don't know enough…But we have five clues right here."

"Oh, yeah? And what are those?" Austin snapped.

"The five of us," Caleb replied. "If we want to figure out what happened, we need to find out why they didn't take us."

Austin huffed. "And how do we do that, *Einstein?*"

"We need to find something that connects us all. Something we have in common kept us here…But we'll need to go to each of our houses to look for the answers."

"It's too risky," Glenn said. "We don't know what kind of enemy we're up against. And even if we made it to the other four houses, we still don't know what we're looking for."

"You can start by looking for anything that seems out of place," Ethan said. "Like something in your room that's been moved."

Caleb nodded, remembering Ethan's incident with the chess pieces. That episode took on a whole new light now. It instantly became a relevant piece of information. The chess pieces had been moved in the middle of the night; now so were the people of the town. The connection was vague, but it was all they had to go on. "We need to do this. We can't just sit here."

"Caleb's right," Ethan said. "And we need to go now. We should stick to the backyards and stay close to the houses in case we need to hide. No walking down the streets…But most of all, we need to stick together."

"Well you can just count me out of that little plan," Austin sneered. "There is no way, no way at all I'm puttin' *my* life on the line based on the plans of the janitor's kid and his chunky, egg-headed sidekick."

"What's the matter, Austin? Are you scared?" Glenn asked.

"Yeah, right, good one. I'm so scared, I'm gonna stay here all by myself…I don't need any of you pansies."

"Fine, then stay here!" Annika fired back. "C'mon, guys. Let's go."

Austin snickered. "Hey, Ethan, don't worry about your dad. As soon as he mops the floors and cleans the toilets on the aliens' spaceship, they won't need him anymore and they'll send him right back."

That was the last straw. Ethan yelled in a fit of rage and charged at Austin. He jumped into the air like a linebacker and tackled him to the floor. The two wrestled for a bit, but the scout soon took a commanding position on top of his captain, despite being outweighed by nearly thirty pounds. Ethan had one hand firmly clutched to Austin's shirt and the other balled into a fist and cocked back, poised to slug him in the face. It took the combined efforts of Glenn, Annika, and Caleb to restrain him.

"Are you happy now, Austin?!" Glenn shouted.

"No!" Austin roared. "I'll be happy when you let him go and we can finish this!"

"Yeah, me too!" Ethan snapped back.

Suddenly, four loud knocks on the door jolted everyone. *Thump! Thump! Thump! Thump!* The door shook on its hinges from the pounding. Everyone clutched their weapons and took cover. Ethan, still running on adrenaline from his bout with Austin, went to the window and slowly pulled back the drapes. He sighed a breath of relief when he saw the familiar faces of the Mitchell brothers.

The Mitchell brothers, fraternal twins to be more precise, were high school seniors who had just graduated and were about to enter the Military Academy at West Point. They were tall, athletic, and tough as nails. Jeremiah, the eldest by three minutes, could run the hundred-meter dash in under eleven seconds and do push-ups until the guy counting his repetitions got tired. Zeke, if anything, was even more athletic. He jokingly chalked it up to his youth. There were no better people to be knocking on your door in the event of a catastrophe than Jeremiah and Zeke Mitchell.

The Mitchell brothers each carried a .22 caliber hunting rifle. Ethan was surprised to see they had guns, since Blackwoods had a strict rule against having weapons within the town limits. Ethan had no idea where the brothers got their guns, but he was definitely glad they had them.

Ethan pushed a couch out of the way and opened the door. Jeremiah and Zeke smiled, equally relieved, upon seeing Ethan and the others. They quickly went inside and shut the door.

"Is this everybody? Just the five of you?" Jeremiah asked. Ethan nodded. "Well, that makes seven now. Seven people in the entire town."

"We're all teenagers," Caleb said. "You know the odds of that? It has to mean something."

Ethan looked at Zeke, then Jeremiah. "What do you think happened?"

"Terrorists, right?" Austin interrupted.

"Naw, we don't think so," Jeremiah said, then paused. "We think something must've gone wrong at the research facility."

"What went wrong?" Ethan asked. "Like an experiment?"

"We don't know anything for sure," Zeke said. "All we know is something big was going on over there. More brass than a marching band came through here the last two weeks."

"Yeah," Jeremiah said. "And the Secretary of Defense visited the facility just three days ago. Heard he left smiling like a kid in a candy store…Probably not smiling now though," he said with a wry grin.

"Look, my dad runs that facility," Austin said. "He told me the big project was super-stealth spy planes…and spy planes don't abduct a town full of people."

"I'm sorry," Glenn added. "I don't normally agree with Austin, but he's right. My dad told me the same thing...spy planes."

Zeke shook his head. "Listen, I hate to be the one to tell you guys this, but...if your parents weren't willing to lie to you, they wouldn't be working here."

Everyone stared at the Mitchell brothers with uneasy eyes. They all knew the research facility required secrecy, but the idea that all of their parents needed to be pathological liars for the cause didn't sit well in their stomachs. For Ethan, however, it was the first time in a long while that he felt good about his dad's job. His father might only be a maintenance man, but he certainly wouldn't have to lie to anyone for *that* job.

"Before you guys got here, we were gonna go check our houses to find some clues about why we weren't taken," Ethan said. "You can come if you want to," he offered, hoping strongly they would.

"Hell, no...You will absolutely not," Jeremiah said through a scowl. "You kids stay right here. Zeke and I will go and check things out...alone."

"Where are you going?" Caleb asked.

"To the research facility," Zeke answered.

Annika squinted doubtfully. "Shouldn't you wait until help arrives?"

"Briggs Air Force Base monitors that facility twenty-four-seven," Jeremiah explained. "Help should've arrived a long time ago... *We are* the help."

"But you're going in blind," Caleb said. "I have an idea. It may take a little while, but it'll give you some clue about what's over there."

"What's the idea?" Zeke asked.

"A reconnaissance rocket. We could fly one over the facility. It's got the range. All I'd have to do is attach a lightweight video camera to it and you'd have a crude spy rocket…At least you'd have some good aerial pictures to go by."

"You have the rocket here?" Zeke asked, intrigued by the idea.

"No," Caleb admitted sheepishly. "It's at my house. But it's only six houses away. I could get everything and come right back…or we all could go there."

The Mitchell brothers sighed simultaneously in disappointment. Then they shook their heads, vetoing the suggestion. "Thanks, but we don't need to put you kids in any more danger," Jeremiah said.

"*We're not kids!*" Ethan snapped. "Not anymore, not after today…And if we are the only ones left to help, seven's a helluva better number than two."

As Ethan stated his case to the Mitchell brothers, Austin looked at his former scout with a strange expression. The fire in Ethan's belly took him by surprise. Not only had Ethan stood up for himself against him, but now, Ethan stood up for everyone in the presence of the two most athletic and popular guys in Blackwoods. Austin wouldn't dare allow his face to register respect for Ethan, but the look he gave him at the moment was definitely not one of a captain lording over his subordinate.

Jeremiah and Zeke nodded sympathetically, though their position was firm. "We understand your concerns, but you all need to stay here for now," Jeremiah said. "Here, take this." He unclipped a walkie-talkie from his belt and handed it to Ethan. "It's the only way to communicate now. We're on channel seven."

"Yeah, and if we need backup, we'll call you guys," Zeke added. Jeremiah nodded. Everyone knew the part about calling them for backup was a bare-faced lie, even though it was told with good intentions.

Jeremiah and Zeke opened the door a crack and looked outside. Their pickup truck was parked on the street a few houses away. There was no sign of anyone.

"Barricade the doors again. Stay out of sight, away from windows. And keep the noise down," Jeremiah said, sounding like the officer he was destined to be. "We'll check in when we get to the research facility."

"Before you go, maybe you should tell us where you got your guns," Ethan said. He paused solemnly. "In case you don't..."

"Without proper training in the field, you'd just be more likely to shoot yourselves," Jeremiah said bluntly.

Annika furrowed her eyes in defiance. "Is that a fact? Because I'm not sure your cousin would agree."

Jeremiah smiled at Annika. He knew their cousin was one of the Marine snipers Annika had thoroughly beaten in the marksmanship competition last year. "I meant the other four," he said, playfully backing down. "Seriously, though, these two guns are the only ones I know of. Our dad set two aside in case of, well...a day like today, I guess."

"Be careful," Annika said.

"We'll be all right," Jeremiah said with a reassuring smile, though his and Zeke's eyes had trouble pulling off the same degree of reassurance. Despite their posturing, they were only eighteen and had never seen combat outside of video games themselves. They were strong and athletic, but the strong and athletic die every day in wars alongside the weak and feeble.

Behind their duty-bound, intensely focused eyes there was an admirably hidden well of fear. They took one last precautionary look outside, then Jeremiah and Zeke exited the house. Jeremiah turned back to Ethan, who was still standing in the doorway.

"Call you soon. Remember, channel seven. Now get your butt inside," Jeremiah said in a tough voice, as if he were channeling the bravery of all military movie action heroes at the same time. Just like them, he too was acting.

෫

An hour later, the group was sitting on the floor in a circle around the walkie-talkie. The room was deathly silent. The Mitchell brothers hadn't reported in yet, and the tension in the room was unbearable.

"The research facility is only eight miles away," Glenn said. "We should've heard something by now."

"Maybe the terrorists killed them," Austin said.

"Shut up, Austin!" Annika yelled. "There are no terrorists."

"Okay, then the *aliens* killed them. It was a stupid plan, anyway. Just the two of them strolling up to the facility. What were they gonna do? Knock on the door and walk right in? Idiots."

"Listen," Ethan said.

The walkie-talkie came alive with static, then a voice broke through. "We're about a hundred yards outside the front gate of the base," Jeremiah said. "Our truck had electrical problems a few miles out, so we had to hoof it. You copy? Over."

"Copy that," Ethan responded. "Do you see anything? Over."

"Nothing. But the sky looks strange. Bluer than usual. On

a normal day, it would look nice. But today, it's just creepy." Jeremiah paused, then spoke in a quieter, more cautious tone. "We're fifty yards from the gate. Moving in toward the first guardhouse."

The group knew the research facility had three different checkpoints a visitor had to go through, each with their own gate and guardhouse. If all were well at the base, it would be impossible to get within a mile of the first gate without being hounded by soldiers. The fact that the Mitchell brothers had made it so close to the checkpoint without running into anyone was a bad omen.

"We're inside the guardhouse," Jeremiah said. "Door was unlocked and no one's home. The computers are running some kind of program, though. The screens are filled with numbers, constant calculations. Whoever was here must've been working on something big before they were taken. We're gonna try to reset the computers, see if we can get an SOS message out to Briggs Base."

Caleb looked worried. He grabbed the walkie-talkie. "I don't think you should mess with the computers, Jeremiah. Someone's running a program. If you interrupt that, they'll be able to trace where the disruption came from. They'll know exactly where you are."

"Surveillance cameras are everywhere around here," Jeremiah responded. "If hostiles have taken over the research facility, they already know we're here. But we don't see anything yet, and we gotta try to get a message out. I'll leave the channel open so you can hear us."

The group heard various clicking of computer keys through the receiver of the walkie-talkie. Caleb's especially nervous expression spread to the faces of the others. A few short, tense moments seemed to pass like hours as they waited.

"Wait— What the— *What the hell are those things?!*" Jeremiah exclaimed.

There was a long pause in the transmission. The next sound to come over the air was a strange, high-pitched humming.

"Oh, God…They're coming this way!" Zeke shouted, terrified.

"Calm down! Focus!" Jeremiah yelled, sounding panicked himself. "I'll get the right, you get the left."

The Mitchell brothers unleashed a barrage of gunfire— *Pow, Pow, Pow, Pow, Pow!*

"Zeke…! Nooooo!" Jeremiah screamed. He fired several more shots in rapid succession, then the firing stopped abruptly. There were no more words from Jeremiah or Zeke. Soon two high-pitched humming sounds coursed through the receiver. The humming noises didn't seem to be produced at random—they seemed to have a structure, a syntax. And the dual hums, one slightly higher in pitch than the other, seemed to be taking turns sounding off. *It appeared that the two bizarre sounds were communicating with each other.*

The strange, back-and-forth humming continued for a few more moments, then a crackling sound shot through the receiver like it was being crushed. The walkie-talkie went dead. Total silence filled the air.

CHAPTER 18

RECONNAISSANCE

IT WAS THREE o'clock, and it'd been almost three hours since the Mitchell brothers' last words. The group was still gathered in the living room, frozen in shock, now and then sneaking peeks out the windows with no idea what to expect. Everyone seemed lost in their own heads. The five of them were together, yet also alone, left to stew in their private worlds, reflecting on the whereabouts of their families and fearing their fates. The group desperately needed leadership to prompt some sort of productive action. Ethan wasn't looking to be the leader when he finally spoke, but his words managed to serve that purpose.

"We can't just wait here and do nothing," Ethan said. "If we do, we'll eventually get taken or be killed. I think we need to follow the original plan—go to our houses, look for clues. We'll also need to gather supplies and look for better weapons."

The group nodded in a daze. Even Austin was too stunned to put up an argument.

They went outside through the back door in the kitchen. Everyone still had their weapons with them, but they mainly served the function of a security blanket. They all knew the

Mitchell brothers' rifles did no good against whatever was out there, so they knew full well that a baseball bat, a pipe wrench, nunchucks, a play laser rifle, and a Swiss Army knife would surely be useless outside of keeping their anxious hands occupied.

≪

All of the residences in Blackwoods were nestled together in close proximity, so the group didn't have far to go. Caleb's house was the closest to Ethan's, only six houses away. They cut quickly through the backyards and entered Caleb's home via a patio door that led to the basement.

Two couches and a recliner formed a semicircle around a television in Caleb's basement. A Ping-Pong table was situated in the back of the room. Heated games of Ping-Pong between Caleb and his dad were the main athletic events in the Warren household. A ball rested beneath a paddle on the table. It had been placed there by his dad at the end of the last game they played together. Caleb stared wistfully at the table as he walked by. He brushed his hand over the paddle softly.

Ethan eyed an adjoining utility room that contained a washer, dryer, and storage closet. "Caleb, I have an idea where we should spend the night."

Caleb looked at Ethan pensively and nodded in agreement.

"Where, the laundry room?" Austin quipped.

Caleb sighed deeply. "No, not the laundry room…And when we find my dad, I need you guys to promise not to tell him I showed you this. You have to promise me."

"We promise," Glenn blurted.

Everyone nodded quickly, more intrigued by the second.

"Okay, then. Follow me."

Caleb went to the far corner of the utility room, next

to the door of a plain-looking storage closet. He turned to a thermostat on the wall and lifted its cover. A keypad lay underneath, with letters and numbers on it like a miniature computer keyboard. He punched in a twelve-digit code and stood back. Three seconds later, the door of what had masqueraded as a supply closet opened slowly. It was four inches thick and made of pure titanium. Caleb reached inside the door and flipped a switch. A string of light bulbs illuminated a staircase that led to a sub-basement below.

"Well, c'mon," Caleb said nonchalantly.

The sub-basement contained every kind of electronic gadget, gizmo, and widget one could imagine. Ethan had seen the sub-basement a few times before, when Caleb's parents had been out of town, but he was amazed all over again each time he saw it. It was Caleb's dad's workspace away from the research facility, and it housed so much technological wizardry that it seemed as if it were an extension of the facility itself. Annika, Glenn, and Austin were seeing it for the first time, and they were completely in awe. Austin's mouth was agape in wonder of it all, though he dared not comment on anything of Caleb's possibly being cool.

Workbenches and computer terminals were everywhere. Three big-screen computer monitors were not only on, but they were bustling with activity. Caleb hurried over to one of the workstations and stared curiously at the screen of rapidly scrolling numbers. The computer was furiously calculating something, crunching numbers blindingly fast.

"What is all that?" Ethan asked.

"I have no idea," Caleb responded slowly, as the rapid flickers of light from the screens illuminated the confusion on his bespectacled face.

"Remember what Jeremiah said about the computers at the guardhouse?" Ethan recalled. "He said the computers there were running calculations. Do you think these are doing the same thing?"

"No way. These computers are powerful, but they aren't on the same server as those at the research base. They aren't connected for security reasons. Someone would have to be hacking into all the computers at once and setting up their own server to connect everything…all in a period of just a few hours." Caleb shook his head as he watched the incessant stream of numbers on the screen. "Everything I've ever learned about computers tells me that's impossible."

It seemed far-fetched, but maybe all the computers in the most secure network in the world really were being hacked into somehow by some supernaturally talented enemy. But what were they doing? A myriad of questions raced through Caleb's mind as he eyed the computers' processing units stacked up into a tower on an adjacent table. Their green-lit power buttons seemed to taunt him, begging to be pressed. For a moment, his intense curiosity was getting the better of him. Caleb knew that touching those computers at the guardhouse might have been the last thing the Mitchell brothers ever did in this world, but the temptation was strangely still there. *If I rebooted or unplugged the computers, what exactly would happen?*

Ravenous curiosity had a way of emboldening Caleb to do things he normally wouldn't do. He was once struck by lightning when he was six years old because he wanted to fly a kite in a thunderstorm like Benjamin Franklin did when he studied electricity. He also tumbled twenty feet down a ledge when he was ten while test-piloting a jetpack prototype. And, most recently, he came down with a nasty stomach infection when he tried to cure a strain of swine flu in his bedroom. He had used himself as a guinea pig and injected himself with a syringe-full of God-knows-what that he ambitiously called "Caleb's Cure."

Ethan watched Caleb carefully. He recognized that look of ravenous curiosity in his best friend's eyes now. "Caleb, we gotta get going. We have a lot of houses to check. It'll be dark before we know it."

Caleb nodded, snapping out of his bewildered trance. "Okay, let's go."

He led the group out of the sub-basement and up two floors to the main level of his house. They walked down a long hallway decorated with family pictures. Caleb used to walk past them every day without so much as glancing at them, taking them for granted like most people do. But not any-more. He stopped for a long moment and looked especially longingly at a picture of himself with his mom and dad on a sunny beach in Clearwater, Florida. He remembered that his parents had asked a beachcomber with a metal detector to take the picture. Caleb soon got interested in metal detecting and joked with his parents that he might just give up science and go into beachcombing. Caleb smiled fondly at the frozen moment in time with a tear in his eye.

Austin watched Caleb peruse his family pictures with an increasingly impatient and annoyed face. "Yeah, yeah, you really had some great family times, but now they're over...I don't need to see this or your room. Hurry up and get to work. I'm gonna do something useful and keep an eye on the outside."

Austin darted off for the living room. Ethan, Annika, and Glenn shook their heads and looked at Caleb with sympa-thetic eyes.

"It's okay…He's right, actually. This isn't useful," Caleb said, summoning all of his logic to combat his emotions. "C'mon, my room's this way."

Caleb's room was decorated much in the way you would expect from a budding super-scientist. Posters of planets and galaxies adorned the room. A large banner displaying the periodic table of the elements hung above Caleb's science workspace—an area that consisted of a lab table with a fully stocked, professional-grade chemistry set, a microscope, and an assortment of electronic equipment that made Caleb's room look like a miniature version of his father's workshop in the sub-basement.

None of them really knew what to look for. Ethan and Caleb just had a vague notion to search for something, anything out of the ordinary. Ethan had the dramatic experience with the moving chess pieces. Maybe the others had something odd happen in their rooms, but it just wasn't as obvious.

Caleb began to look around his room, utilizing all his skills of perception. He even grabbed a camera and began taking photographs of various areas from different angles, processing his room like a forensic scientist would a crime scene. Suddenly, Caleb stopped taking pictures. He stared at a long shelf that was built into the wall that held all of his model rockets. Among fifty rockets of varying sizes, one, in particular, stood out to him.

Caleb shook his head in disbelief. "I can't believe I didn't notice that before."

"What?" Ethan asked.

"The Saturn Five rocket…It's facing the opposite direction, launch pad and all."

"Are you sure?"

"Positive. I always have it facing out so the NASA label is visible. The whole thing turned around somehow."

"Probably the same night the chess pieces moved in my room...the night you thought I was sleepwalking."

"Are you sure you just didn't move it, Caleb?" Annika asked. "You know, when you were playing with it or something?"

"*Playing with it?*" Caleb repeated. "I'm not four years old. I do not *play with* my rockets. It's legitimate science."

"Sorry," Annika apologized with a bit of a smile. "I meant, while you were conducting legitimate science, are you sure you didn't turn the rocket around and forget about it?"

"Absolutely...one hundred percent sure."

The Saturn V was the largest rocket in the history of the United States' Space Program. It was taller than a football field was long. The model was the largest on Caleb's shelf, by far, at a scale of one-hundredth of the original Saturn V. Standing over three feet tall, not including the launch pad, it would've taken more than a just a nudge to move it. And Caleb knew for a fact that he hadn't moved the rocket. He had made a vow to himself not even to touch the crown jewel of his rocket fleet until he was prepared to launch it. It seemed as if the group had found evidence of something, even if they weren't sure what that something was.

"All right...on to my house next," Annika said.

"Yeah, let's go get Prince Charming," Glenn joked.

⌇

As evening was drawing near, the group found themselves lucky in having to spend little time searching the next two houses. It only took Annika ten minutes to spot what was out of place in her room—her DVD collection, which she meticulously kept in alphabetical order, now had several discs that were misplaced. Three DVDs were even missing entirely. She, like Caleb with his rockets, was surprised that she hadn't noticed it earlier.

In Glenn's house, a quick inspection revealed that his sports collectibles, which he stored in a footlocker near his bed, had been disturbed. The contents of the footlocker were so disordered, it was like a miniature tornado had spawned inside it. And Glenn, like Annika with her DVDs, noticed something missing. Gone from the earth was his autographed Hank Aaron baseball that his father had given him for his thirteenth birthday.

Caleb dutifully snapped pictures of Annika's and Glenn's rooms, but as the list of missing and misplaced items began to get longer, a sense of frustration and anxiety welled up inside the group. Every new inspection of a bedroom brought more questions and provided no answers. They were no closer to understanding anything now than they were when they'd first realized their families were gone. To make matters worse, darkness would fall over the town soon, and the most challenging house was yet to be searched.

[∾]

"Get out! All of you!" Austin snarled at the group as they were about to follow him into his bedroom. "It's my room. I'll check it alone. Go keep guard and stay the hell outta here."

Ethan and the others retreated to the living room to keep a vigil on the outside, allowing Austin to search his room by himself.

"He's a real joy to be around," Glenn wisecracked. "You gotta wonder. All the people that got taken…Why couldn't *he* have been one of them? Take him and leave my sister alone."

"And my brother," Annika added.

"Whoever took everybody probably couldn't stand Austin either," Caleb said.

The group snickered quietly, except for Ethan, who appeared pensive.

"He wasn't always like that, you know," Ethan said with a solemn face, finding himself in the unlikely position of defending his longtime tormentor.

Caleb, Annika, and Glenn stared strangely at Ethan, shocked that civil words about Austin could possibly come out of his mouth after all he had been through with him.

"Are you sure about that?" Glenn asked with a smile, as if waiting for Ethan to deliver a belated punch line.

"Yeah. He was always a little high-strung, but he used to be a good teammate." Ethan paused. "But after he came back from Schrodinger Military Academy, he never was the same."

"Right. His transformation was complete," Glenn responded. "But don't think he didn't want that. He chose it."

"His dad, or I guess I should say, the general, made him go," Ethan countered.

"His dad, the general, doesn't force him to be a jerk," Glenn argued, getting annoyed. "*My* dad's a general and *I* don't act like that."

Ethan considered that for a moment, leaned in toward the group, then continued in an especially quiet voice: "I saw Austin's dad at school once. Just once. He called Austin out of class in the middle of the teacher's lesson because he heard he didn't turn in a social studies paper. The paper was on the Battle of the Bulge—the wrong kind of paper not to turn in if you're General Turnbull's son."

The group listened intently to Ethan's every word. He

took a moment to peek in the direction of the hallway to make sure Austin wasn't coming.

"You know the little vertical windows in the classroom doors?" Ethan asked. Everyone nodded quickly, eager to get to the rest of the story. "Well, where I was sitting, I had a good view of Austin and his dad. I could see the general chewing him out, gnashing his teeth, spit flying from his mouth as he spoke. Then I saw him poke Austin hard in the chest with his finger several times. It wasn't just a poke, though. It was more like being stabbed with a finger. Over and over again. God, it had to hurt... And he did that *in school*. So at home, behind closed doors...?"

Ethan's words emptied into a somber silence. He paused with everyone's focused eyes on him, then he held Glenn's with a steely stare.

"Glenn, your dad and Austin's dad may both be generals, but they're not the same fathers...Look, I'm not a fan of Austin. I never will be. But I know it's gonna take all of us working together, Austin included, to stand a chance against whatever's out there."

Ethan turned and walked away. Annika smiled proudly at him as he disappeared into the hallway. The group realized that Ethan was right. It was time to come together. There was no Bravo Team or Delta Team now. They were, collectively, Team Blackwoods, and they were the last remaining hope for the town, and maybe the whole world, as far as they knew.

⋙

Ethan knocked on Austin's bedroom door. There was no answer. He let himself in and found Austin sitting on the bed with his back turned to him, staring at something on a nightstand near the head of the bed.

"Did you find anything?" Ethan asked gingerly. There was no response, not even the grumble, yell, or sarcastic remark that was expected. Austin just kept staring at his nightstand. Ethan couldn't see what had captured Austin's attention, so he moved in closer and peered over his shoulder to get a better look. He saw two framed pictures on the nightstand. One was of a younger Austin with his mother standing on the shore of Lake Michigan. They looked happy with their windswept hair pinned back on their heads. Austin's parents were divorced, and his mother lived in Chicago. Ethan didn't know much about their relationship other than the fact that Austin rarely saw her anymore.

The other framed photo confused Ethan a little. The picture depicted Austin's dad with another soldier—young, in his early twenties, yet he was already a first lieutenant. General Turnbull stood proudly with his arm snuggly around the younger man, both dressed in full military regalia. There was a strong resemblance between Austin and the young lieutenant in the picture.

Ethan hesitated but finally asked, "That guy in the picture...is he your brother?"

Austin remained silent, fixated on the photo. Finally, he slowly began to nod his head.

"I had no idea you had a brother."

"Yeah, well...it's a town of secrets, right, Tate?" There was bitterness in Austin's voice, though not exactly directed at Ethan this time.

"Looks like he's a first lieutenant. What's his name?" Ethan asked, trying to get a foothold on a real conversation with Austin for the first time in two years.

"Morgan."

Ethan pressed his luck. "So…where's he stationed?"

Austin turned around to look at Ethan. His face registered annoyance. "I'm not talking about this with you. Get out of my room."

Ethan sighed in disappointment at his failed attempt at diplomacy. But he still needed an answer to his original question. He was determined to stand his ground, not leave without at least getting that. "Have you found anything out of place in here or not, Austin? Caleb needs to come in here and take some pictures."

"I haven't found anything…Now get the hell outta here."

Ethan headed for the door, but then stopped on a dime and turned around to face Austin. He took a deep, painful breath. "Do you know the last thing I said to my dad before he disappeared?"

Austin eyed Ethan curiously and shook his head.

"The last thing I said to him was that he embarrassed me by being a maintenance man." Ethan was desperately trying to hold back the tears. "I told him I never wanted to be like him."

As Ethan was leaving, Austin's face softened a touch. "Ethan, wait…I did find something out of place in my room."

Ethan wiped a tear from his eye, willed away the rest, and forced his face to project strength before he pivoted back around. "What is it, Austin?" he asked impatiently.

"The framed photo of my brother and dad."

"Where did you find it?"

"On my nightstand."

Ethan looked confused. "Right, it's on the nightstand now, but where did you find it? Where was it? How was it out of place?"

Austin paused, swallowed hard. "The photo is out of place *because it's sitting on the nightstand*...A few days ago, I threw that picture in the trash."

Ethan tried to muffle his curiosity about why Austin threw away a framed photograph of his dad and brother. "Could your dad have picked the photo out of the trash and put it back on the nightstand?"

"No way in hell...He never comes into my room." Austin's every syllable vibrated with resentment. Ethan could feel the hate waves radiating from his words. "But if somehow he did, and noticed it was in the trash, he wouldn't just pick it up without a word with me first...No, we would *definitely* have words over that."

Ethan had a difficult time processing the flood of honesty and soul-baring coming from Austin. For the first time ever, he seemed vulnerable. Ethan was in uncharted territory here and wasn't sure how to proceed. He decided to skirt the issue for now, dealing only with the investigation of Austin's room and leaving the investigation of Austin's psychological state for another time.

"All right...Can I tell Caleb he can come in?"

"Whatever."

Less than a minute later, Caleb was in the room feverishly taking pictures of everything, from every angle. "So, what in here was out of place?" he asked.

Austin paused, not eager to divulge all over again what he had done with the framed picture of his father and brother. At that moment, Austin looked nervous. It was the first example of that emotion Ethan had ever seen in him outside of interactions with his father. Caleb kept shooting pictures and was too busy to notice anything out of the ordinary from Austin.

Ethan looked at Austin with an emotional first of his own. He looked at him with sympathy.

"So, what was out of place?" Caleb asked again. This time he stopped taking pictures and waited for a response.

"The framed photo on his nightstand," Ethan jumped in with an answer, beating Austin to the response. Austin stared at Ethan with pleading eyes. "The photo moved from the nightstand into the trash."

It was a lie. Ethan Tate lied to his best friend to help Austin Turnbull. It was a bizarre moment that Ethan never dreamed would happen. Caleb nodded and went about taking more pictures. Austin breathed a sigh of relief.

From the standpoint of the investigation, Ethan didn't feel like his truth-bending did any harm. He simply reversed the order of things—saying that the photo went into the trash from the nightstand, instead of to the nightstand from the trash. The only thing that resulted from Ethan's little fib was that Austin saved some face. Ethan rationalized that this might help bring his former captain into the fold and bring the team together. That idea made it easier for him to come to terms with helping the guy who had two years of bullying him under his belt.

Caleb clicked off a final barrage of photographs, then he exited the room. Ethan caught eyes with Austin, who nodded and pursed his lips into what might've been a subtle half-smile. It was an awkward moment, but Ethan figured it was his version of a "thank you." Ethan nodded back but returned no smile of his own before leaving.

CHAPTER 19

THE SATURN V LAUNCH

THE GROUP ENCOUNTERED nothing out of the ordinary on the way back to Caleb's house, except they now noticed the weird shade of blue that colored the sky the Mitchell brothers had spoken of earlier. The sun lying lower in the early evening made the strange hue really stick out. The sky had a certain unreal appearance, like it was plucked from an animated movie and stamped over Blackwoods as far as the eye could see. It was truly a beautiful tint of blue, a rich cobalt shade, but that didn't make it any less eerie. Something about the sky just seemed wrong.

Caleb bounded down the stairs into the basement carrying a large cardboard box with the Saturn V rocket and launchpad prominently sticking out. "We're gonna launch a spy rocket," he said with determination in his voice. Then added solemnly, "The one I wish the Mitchell brothers would've waited for."

Caleb delicately emptied the contents of the box onto the Ping-Pong table. He checked his watch and figured they only had an hour and a half of good daylight left. They would have to work quickly.

The next hour transpired in the blink of an eye, with Caleb working on the rocket at a frenzied pace. He adjusted the nozzle and thrusters, tweaked the aerodynamics, added the propellant, calculated and programmed a flight trajectory, and secured a high-speed digital video camera to the Saturn V rocket. Caleb resembled a surgeon in a fast-paced emergency room, with the Ping-Pong table serving as the operating table and the rest of the group playing the roles of assistants, rapidly doling out the proper tools. Even Austin was pitching in and doing so without complaint. In fact, he hadn't spoken a single word since he and Ethan had their awkward exchange in his bedroom.

Soon everyone was in the backyard gathered around the amateur rocket scientist and the miniature Saturn V. Caleb made some minor adjustments to the rocket on the launchpad while the others cautiously surveyed the perimeter.

Suddenly, a worried look overcame Ethan. "Wait…Won't whatever's out there be able to trace where this was fired from?"

The distress on Caleb's face quickly answered Ethan's question. "Idiot," he scolded himself. "I was just so busy that—yeah, you're right, they would definitely be able to backtrack its trajectory. They would know precisely where it came from, right down to the exact spot on the ground."

"Then we gotta move," Glenn said.

Ethan thought quickly. "Take it to my yard. It's close but not too close."

"Hurry," Annika said. "I'll keep a lookout. You got a ladder, Caleb?"

Annika climbed atop Caleb's roof as the group reposi-
tioned the rocket for launch. From her crouched position,
using high-powered binoculars and the scope on her laser
rifle, she had a good view of half the town. Caleb picked up
the remote-controlled ignition switch and looked at Annika.
She scanned the perimeter once more and gave the "all-clear"
signal.

Caleb nodded, then flipped a switch on the ignition
controller. Smoke began to pour from the rocket's nozzle.
"I've programmed the rocket for a low-speed, low-altitude
approach, so the video of the base should be pretty clear. Here
we go. Ten, nine, eight…" He counted down as smoke bil-
lowed more and more intensely around the rocket. "…three,
two, one…ignition."

A burst of fire shot out from the rocket's nozzle. The rocket
blasted away violently from the launchpad and streamed
toward the exaggeratedly blue sky. "We have liftoff!" Caleb
exclaimed with a proud smile on his face. For a brief moment,
he was lost in his hobby, enjoying the sight of his favorite
rocket taking to the skies.

"Guys, you gotta see it from up here!" Annika yelled from
Caleb's roof, so enthralled with the aerial show that she forgot
to keep her voice down.

The group quickly clambered up the ladder and joined
Annika on Caleb's roof. They watched excitedly as the Saturn
V reached a cruising altitude of five hundred feet, then made
its final approach to the research facility. As the rocket got
closer, everyone's faces slowly began to shift from amusingly
distracted back to terribly tense. From about eight miles away,
they could now only see a faint spark from the rocket's nozzle

and were mostly tracking the contrail of smoke that it left in its wake.

Caleb had set up the rocket to wirelessly transmit a video feed to the receiver box he held in his hand. The red recording light on the receiver box lit up. "The rocket just started filming," he announced. "Everything looks great so far."

Mere seconds after Caleb uttered those optimistic words, an intensely bright, neon violet laser beam blasted out from the research facility. The group watched in horror as the laser intercepted the Saturn V and instantly turned Caleb's favorite rocket into a scorching fireball. The rocket disintegrated rapidly as it plummeted to the earth. By the time the Saturn V should've hit the ground, there was nothing left of it. Vaporized, as if it had never existed.

"What was *that*?" Glenn asked in a daze.

"A laser. A super high-intensity laser," Caleb replied, totally bewildered. "Gotta be a hundred kilowatts strong, at least."

Ethan's wide eyes were fixed on the horizon, over the forest, in the direction of the research facility and everything unknown. "We gotta get inside...right now."

Caleb hooked up the receiver box to the television in his basement, hoping the rocket had had time to record something useful before it was gunned down. Everyone huddled around the TV with an anxious face. Then an aerial video of the forest filled the screen, trees streaking by rapidly. The research facility soon came into view, but only for a moment. Before anything of value was filmed, the recording shut off. The TV reverted to static.

"No!" Caleb yelled, pounding his fist on the receiver box. "Nothing! We got nothing!"

"Nothing…? Oh, we got a lot worse than nothing outta this, Caleb," Austin sneered. "We launched a rocket at them. For all they know, we were attacking them. They think we just declared war. Stupid idea, especially for a so-called *genius*."

"W-w-we had to try *something* to get an idea of what's out there. I just tried something. I had to try something. I had to…" Caleb's eyes were teary as his jittery words trailed off.

"It's all right, Caleb," Ethan said, staring disgustedly at Austin, feeling betrayed by his behavior after lying for him. "It was a good idea. We had to try it." Ethan patted Caleb on the back. "We should get our supplies and head downstairs now. It'll be dark soon."

"I'll gather the weapons," Annika said. "What little we have."

"I'll get the food and water," Glenn added.

"By the way, Austin, *we* never declared war," Ethan said with steely eyes. "*They* declared war on *us* when they took our families. But we're gonna get them back with or without you…You can count on that."

CHAPTER 20

FINDING THE CONNECTION

THE GROUP STOWED away all the supplies they could gather in the sub-basement. They had enough food and water to last over a week, but their search for weapons yielded very little. The best weapon they'd found was a Taser gun that Glenn's dad kept for home security. The Taser could disable a person with an electric shock for up to thirty seconds, but its range limited its use. It could only shoot up to fifteen feet away, and the electrodes doing the shocking were attached to a wire. Essentially, it allowed for only one shot at too close a range for comfort. The group remained, more or less, completely unarmed against the kind of enemy they were sure to encounter.

The sub-basement was now their fortress. It had obvious advantages as a safe house, being that it was well-hidden and hard to crack. Potential invaders would first have to figure out there was a sub-basement in the house, then deduce that the metal supply closet was the entrance, then discover the keypad hidden in the thermostat, then crack the passcode. And if they couldn't figure out the passcode, the daunting work of breaking down a four-inch-thick titanium door lay before them. It was a lot of figuring and a lot of hard work an enemy would have to go through to get to them. Those were the advantages of the sub-basement.

Unfortunately, the sub-basement also had two major disadvantages. One, there was no way the group could see what was coming. And two, if an enemy breached the door, there was no escape. The sub-basement had no exit other than back through the entrance door. The group would be forced to defend themselves with a motley assortment of ridiculous weapons. The result would be certain death.

Those were the pros and cons of their sub-basement safe house. And, at least for now, they felt safe there.

⁓

Caleb connected his camera to a computer to display the pictures he had taken in each person's bedroom. Most of the group sat on an old leather couch to watch the slideshow, but Austin chose to sit away from the others on an office chair. He tried to appear uninterested, but he was actually paying close attention to the pictures. Everyone was. Caleb was sure the reason why they weren't abducted could be found in the pictures. They just had to be clever enough to make the connection.

Fifty minutes later, they had gone over the entire batch of pictures. It was ten o'clock and, while there were no windows in the sub-basement to verify it, darkness was upon them. No one knew at what exact time the townspeople were abducted the previous night, but everyone knew that time was working against them.

Caleb shook his head. "There's got to be a link. Something we're not seeing."

"Play it again, Caleb," Ethan said, staring at the screen, a smile sneaking on his face.

Caleb started the slideshow again. Ethan's smile got bigger as more pictures crossed the screen. Caleb watched him curiously. "What is it, Ethan? Do you see something?"

Ethan nodded. "Jeremiah and Zeke…They played Laser Wars sometimes, didn't they?"

"Sure. Played against each other mostly," Glenn said. "I know they played a lot last week, keeping in shape for West Point."

"Why are you asking?" Caleb wondered.

"The laser gun chargers," Ethan said. "They're all close to our beds…What if they were protecting us somehow?"

Caleb leaned in for a closer look, spotting a charging tower in one of the pictures. "You think the chargers' electronics might've interfered with our abductions, like by jamming a signal…a 'Beam me up, Scotty' *Star Trek* teleporter kind of signal?"

"I know it sounds crazy, but…"

"What about the other players on our teams?" Annika asked.

"I've never been inside Bradley's or Kevin's room," Ethan admitted. "But, if I had to guess, I'd say their laser gun chargers are farther away from their beds than ours are."

Austin spoke grudgingly. "I've seen their rooms. They keep all their gear on the opposite side, far away from their beds."

"Yeah, and all the other guys on my team—Jason, Garret, and Tristan—they kept their gear farther away too," Glenn added.

"There's gotta be some critical distance you must stay within to be protected by the charger's electronic signature. I think whatever abducted our families must've been doing a test run when your rocket moved, Caleb. Same with Glenn's

sports collectibles, Annika's DVDs and Austin's picture frame."
Ethan spoke rapidly, putting the pieces together. "They could
move my chess pieces, but only the white ones to real spots on
the board. The black pieces were just moved randomly. They
couldn't control them as well because the black pieces were
closer to the charger. The key is the chargers…We were meant
to be taken with the others."

Glenn shook his head in a daze. "We just got lucky."

"Yeah," Austin said, equally stunned.

"The charger in my room is the farthest away of any of
ours," Ethan observed. "I need to measure the distance from
my charger to where I lay in bed. We need to know exactly what
that critical distance is."

"I'll go with you," Annika offered quickly.

"I think we should all go," Glenn said.

Annika shook her head. "No, it's a stealth mission. We can't
attract any attention. The scout and the sniper…it's the only
pair that makes sense."

Glenn knew Annika was right. "Okay, but take this, just in
case." He handed the Taser gun to Annika. "There's no one I'd
want taking the shot more than you."

Annika nodded dutifully. "Thanks, Glenn."

Suddenly, Caleb's anxiety kicked into overdrive. "Guys,
wait…Remember why we moved the launch spot in the first
place?"

Ethan knew exactly the point Caleb was making. They had
launched the rocket from Ethan's house so the enemy at the
research facility wouldn't trace the launch back to Caleb's place,
where they were staying. Caleb was trying to state, as calmly
as he could, that Ethan's house could now be crawling with
mysterious invaders.

"I know, Caleb. But we have to do this," Ethan said. "We need to know what distance is safe. And we also need more chargers."

Caleb nodded reluctantly. He knew the mission was far riskier than he had imagined only moments ago. Going back to the place where they had launched the rocket was bordering on insane. The moment reminded Caleb of when Jeremiah and Zeke took off for the research facility. They wouldn't listen to him about the spy rocket, they left, and never came back.

"At least take these," Caleb insisted, handing Ethan and Annika a couple of radio headsets, the kind they used in their Laser Wars games. "Channel seven. Let us know exactly what's going on at all times."

"We'll call when it's safe to talk," Ethan promised.

"And you'll need these, too." Caleb gave them each a pair of night-vision goggles he had scrounged from the clutter of electronic gear in the sub-basement.

Caleb and Glenn had worry stamped all over their faces. Austin, however, sat in the office chair, rolling back and forth in his own little world. He didn't appear concerned about them at all.

"Austin, you got anything to say to Annika and Ethan?" Glenn asked, aggravated.

"Yeah, don't get followed on the way back."

"Unbelievable," Glenn muttered.

"Don't worry, guys," Annika said, sounding upbeat. "We'll be fine. No one will even know we're there."

Ethan and Annika each grabbed a flashlight, then put on their radio headsets and night-vision goggles. Annika clipped the Taser gun to her belt. They took a deep breath, exhaled some tension, and declared simultaneously: "We're ready."

Caleb led them up the stairwell of the sub-basement. He punched the code to unlock the door with a jittery hand. Three locks clicked in rapid succession, and the door opened. Ethan and Annika stepped out from the safety of the sub-basement and into the darkness of the utility room. Annika slipped her night-vision goggles from her forehead down to her eyes. Ethan did the same. They turned back to see Caleb, who appeared bathed in an artificial green light through their night-vision spectacles. He was staring at them, totally wide-eyed, a ball of rattled nerves.

Ethan put a comforting hand on his best friend's shoulder. "Caleb, it's all right. We'll be back before you know it."

Caleb nodded, though it looked more like a cold shudder.

Ethan and Annika walked away, and the blackness swallowed them up. Caleb closed the door very slowly, giving them plenty of time to come back if they changed their minds. He hoped they would. But they didn't, and Caleb finally shut the door.

The scout and the sniper were all alone, out in the open, in the dead of night.

CHAPTER 21

THE ENCOUNTER

ETHAN AND ANNIKA treaded carefully through the six back-yards they needed to cross to get to Ethan's house. They were moving together in super-stealth mode now. Each step they took was planned and calculated, appearing almost choreographed, to ensure that every stick remained unsnapped and every leaf uncrackled. They made it to Ethan's backdoor without encountering any resistance. So far, so good.

They stood on the back patio. Annika kept a lookout while Ethan searched his pocket for the house key. As he was pulling out the key, the edge of it got caught on a thread in his pocket and slipped out of his hand. It hit the concrete slab floor and made a resounding *Ping*! The sound seemed to pierce the deathly silent night like a siren. Ethan quickly scrambled to find the key. Annika wasted no time and pulled out the Taser gun in one lightning-fast stroke. She aimed it into the darkness, intensely scanning the perimeter through her night-vision goggles.

"Anytime you wanna open that door is all right with me," Annika wisecracked.

"Yeah, sorry," Ethan said. He put the key into the lock and opened the door. They both scurried inside and locked the door behind them.

They first walked through the kitchen. It was pitch black except for the blue digital numbers on the microwave and stove that indicated the time of day. Ethan grabbed a large chef's knife from a wooden holder and pulled it out quietly.

Ethan spoke in a hushed voice. "Before we go to my room, or turn on the flashlights, we need to do a sweep of the house…make sure we're alone."

Ethan led Annika out of the kitchen and down the hallway. It was much darker now. There was almost no natural light to make use of. They owed their entire sense of sight to the light that was manufactured by the night-vision goggles. All the images were grainy with greenish hues, but they could see well enough. They stopped at the entrance to the family room, then stealthily slipped around the corner. Annika had the Taser gun at the ready, pointing it in quick, steady arcs around the room. Her favorite TV shows were crime dramas, especially ones featuring the FBI, and she was practically an expert in the maneuvers of entering a hostile environment. It soon became apparent, though, that the room was empty.

Somehow the upstairs was even darker than the downstairs. Ethan led the way down the hallway, relying on the combined powers of the night-vision gear and his familiarity with his house not to run into anything. They searched every room but found absolutely nothing. After they were convinced they were all alone, they took off their night-vision goggles, turned on their flashlights, and headed to Ethan's bedroom.

"Let's hurry this up," Annika said. "Your house really gives me the creeps."

"Thanks," Ethan said sarcastically. Annika cracked a smile.

Ethan went to his desk and retrieved a tape measure. They steadied the tape and noted the distance between the bed where Ethan slept and his laser gun charging tower on the shelf.

"Six feet two inches," Ethan said. "That's the critical distance."

"Great, now let's grab that charger and get outta here."

Ethan unplugged the charging tower from the wall and tucked it under his arm. They began to creep back down the hall the way they had come. As Ethan passed his parents' bedroom, something caught the corner of his eye. He turned to face the room, and there it was—a tiny dot of red light pulsing at regular intervals on a nightstand. It was coming from the phone's answering machine.

Annika tracked Ethan's glance. Her eyes widened. "There's a message."

"I had no idea," Ethan said defensively. "The phones are down now, the internet, radio, and TV too. But I should have checked for messages. I checked my cell phone, but I didn't even think about the landline."

"It's okay, Ethan. You couldn't have possibly known. Anyway, it might just be an old message, from before everyone disappeared."

The blinking light at once tempted and tormented him. Ethan finally pressed the play button and waited, anxious and lightheaded. Annika was even fidgeting nervously with her ponytail, something she rarely did. After a few seemingly interminable seconds, the machine beeped loudly, jolting them both. Then the message was revealed. It was Ethan's father. There was a distinct sense of desperation in his voice...

"I'm so sorry, Ethan. So sorry... They'll be coming soon. You have twenty-four hours, maybe less. Under my bed there's a secret compartment and a safe. Combination 12-32-18-26-8. Get the black box to General Stanley at the base. We love you so much, Ethan. I'm so sorry. There's so much I need to tell—"

The message ended abruptly, which Ethan took as a very bad sign. He felt numb all over. Annika put a consoling hand on his shoulder. "He's okay, Ethan. Everyone is still alive...I believe that with all my heart."

Ethan nodded with a somber face. They each grabbed an edge of the bed and scooted it to the side. They trained their flashlights on the wooden floor but saw nothing. Ethan got down on his hands and knees and began pressing on the floor, trying to find an opening. Finally, they heard a faint creaking sound. They concentrated their flashlights on that area and spotted a rectangular-shaped hairline crack in the wood.

"We'll need to pry it open," Ethan said.

Ethan picked up the kitchen knife and jammed it into the crack. He started to pry the three-foot by two-foot section of wood out from the rest of the floor. After some digging, the crack was big enough for him to get his fingers inside. He yanked on the section hard and it finally popped off. They aimed their flashlights down into the cavity. A hefty metallic safe was nestled inside, anchored by metal rods that were themselves anchored to the house. At that moment, Ethan was hit with two questions: *What would my dad, the maintenance man, have that would require a secret, heavy-duty safe under his bed? And what in the world could possibly be in there that a general at Briggs Air Force Base would be interested in?*

Ethan turned the dials on the lock in the correct combination, pulled the lever, and swung the heavy metal door open. He and Annika nearly bumped heads rushing to peer inside.

The only item in the safe was a black metallic briefcase. Ethan pulled it out slowly and set it on top of the bed. He stared at it with a sense of dread, having the distinct, uneasy feeling that opening the briefcase would be a life-changing event. He had already endured one such event with the disappearance of everyone in town. Another shock to the system and he might just go insane. So Ethan took his time with the briefcase. Annika, however, was chomping at the bit to take a peek.

"Well, are you gonna open it or not?" she blurted.

Ethan nodded and proceeded to unbuckle the snaps on the briefcase. Annika was about to shine her flashlight on its contents, but no light was needed. As Ethan opened the case, a brilliant neon blue light swallowed the room. Five luminous crystalline rods sat fastened in Plexiglas containers inside the case. They were each about a foot long and one inch thick. As far as Ethan and Annika could tell, they were not attached to any power source and contained no batteries. It appeared as if the rods were producing their own radiant light. Annika gently picked up one of the clear containers housing a rod and unfastened the lid. Every light in the house instantly turned on, got super bright, buzzed and sizzled madly, then shattered with a loud *Pop*!

Annika quickly tightened the lid back on the rod with trembling hands. Her eyes were as wide as saucers. "What are these things?!"

"I don't know. Maybe we should've read the manual first," Ethan joked with a nervous quiver in his voice. He reached into the briefcase and picked up a thick stack of folders filled to the brim with documents. "There's gotta be something in here about them."

The first folder Ethan opened was full of detailed schematics of the research facility. Every entrance, exit, laboratory, even the restrooms and breakrooms were included in the blueprints. The research labs in the sketches seemed to be labeled loosely according to the projects that were being worked on. One room, in particular, caught Ethan's attention. There was a massive lab room dedicated to something called "Project Vacuum." Ethan's stomach began to get queasy, remembering that his dad had often talked about working on vacuums. He used to hate his stories, envisioning his father in the lowly position of crouching over an upside-down vacuum cleaner, pulling out bits and pieces of gunk. Now, he desperately wished for it all to be that simple. *Please let my dad just be the maintenance man...Please.* Ethan frantically began shuffling through documents, looking for anything relating to Project Vacuum. He stopped after finding an entire folder assigned to that project. The heading on the cover left no room for doubt:

"Project Vacuum" — Chief Engineer: Phillip Tate, Ph.D.

Ethan felt as if his stomach were in freefall. He forced himself to continue to read. The documents were crammed with scientific jargon and complex mathematics. They were nearly impossible to translate, but one word kept coming up in the text that was not hard to understand, especially after today. The word was *teleportation.*

"Your dad was working on a *teleportation machine?*" Annika asked.

"I guess so," Ethan said in a daze. In that moment, he remembered vividly one of the last tidbits of wisdom the Mitchell brothers had given them. "Hey, no big deal...If our parents weren't willing to lie to us, they wouldn't be working here, right?"

Annika knew exactly what thought was roaming around in Ethan's mind. "Ethan, I'm sure what happened is not your dad's fault."

"But what if it is? The teleporters had to be involved in the town's abduction. How else do you make so many people disappear? And he was apologizing for something in his message."

"He was apologizing for lying to you."

Suddenly, a loud *crack* echoed through the house. Ethan and Annika jumped up quickly. Their heads tingled with nervous energy as they darted behind the bed for cover.

"What was that?" Annika asked.

"I think someone just broke into the house. Sounded like it came from the back door in the kitchen."

They scrambled frantically, though taking care to move lightly, as they stuffed the documents back into the metal briefcase with the glowing crystal rods. Ethan closed the case and set it gently behind the bed. They shut their flashlights off.

Annika pulled the Taser gun and aimed it down the pitch-black hallway. Ethan gripped the kitchen knife so hard he was nearly cutting off the circulation of blood in his hand. They both quietly slipped on their night-vision goggles. Then more sounds came from downstairs. They were the sounds of doors being opened and shut in the distinct and disturbing pattern of someone or something going door-to-door, searching rooms. Two doors, three doors, four doors, always the same pattern. The door would open with a *creak*, then after a moment, close with a *click*. Whatever was conducting the search was doing it in a perfectly methodical, rhythmic manner.

"I heard them close the last door at the end of the hall," Ethan said. "That would put them at the bottom of the stairs. They'll be upstairs soon."

They waited for what seemed like an hour, but by their watches was scarcely a minute. Outside of their jittery, shallow breaths, the house was as quiet as a tomb. Finally, there was a sound. It was faint, but it was familiar. It was a sound that both Ethan and Annika feared—the same high-pitched humming noise they'd heard through the walkie-talkie when the Mitchell brothers were attacked at the research facility. They knew once they heard that sound, the Mitchell brothers didn't last very long. They had a hard time believing they would fare any better. Ethan and Annika truly began to feel as if these might be the last remaining moments of their lives. Especially Ethan.

"Annika," Ethan whispered, then paused for a moment before he laid it all on the line. "I want you to know, in case we don't make it, that I've had a crush on you ever since I moved to Blackwoods." He took a deep breath. "I think you're beautiful."

Annika smiled as she held the Taser gun steadily on the hallway. She was just about to respond when a rumbling sound interrupted her train of thought. "You hear that?"

"Yeah," Ethan responded quickly, strangely eager to change the subject back to that of their potential deaths. "Whatever it is, it's still in the entryway."

There was a hard tile floor in the entryway of the house leading to the stairs. The rumbling noises on the floor sounded as if a child were rolling a large toy truck on the tile and ramming it hard against the stairs repeatedly. The rumbling finally stopped, but that noise was soon replaced with another one—a high-pitched, squealing sound.

"Now what is that?" Annika asked.

"I have no idea. But it's moving slow...I'm gonna try to get close enough for a look."

"Well, I'm coming with you," Annika replied quickly.

"Okay. But stay behind—"

"I'll lead," Annika blurted before Ethan could finish.

"Wait...Why you?"

"'Cause I have the Taser gun." Annika held up the weapon, shrugged her shoulders, and wrinkled her nose a little as she made her point. "That and...because I'm beautiful," she added with a playful grin.

Ethan immediately felt himself blushing. He found it ridiculous to be experiencing such embarrassment while staring death in the face, but he couldn't help how he felt. Annika scooted past him and took the lead down the hallway. Ethan tried to regain his composure, dealing with two threats now— the intruder on the stairs *and* romantic adolescent stupidity.

They crouched down on the floor, behind the wall, right at the point where the stairs met the hallway. Judging from the squealing sound, Ethan estimated that whatever was making the noise had to be about halfway up the stairs. Annika held the Taser gun at the ready and nodded at Ethan, who proceeded to sneak a peek down the stairs. What he saw in the eerie green light through his night-vision goggles put a knot in his throat. For a moment, he couldn't even breathe. Ethan was amazed to find what appeared to be a *robot* struggling to climb the stairs. The squealing noise was the gear-grinding sound of the machine fighting to gain traction on the polished oak stairs.

Annika poked Ethan gently in the ribs with her elbow. "What is it?" she asked so silently that she almost only mouthed the words.

Ethan scooted over to let her look for herself. Annika peered down the stairs and saw the robot churning at a glacial pace toward them. Her eyes widened. "A robot?" she whispered, doubting her own eyes.

Ethan nodded, then took another look at the machine crawling up the stairs. The robot seemed to be rather harmless. Standing only four feet tall, it had a shiny, black bowl-shaped head featuring two eyes that resembled the bulb-end of a flashlight, though there was no light at all coming from them. The silvery body of the machine was a simple cylindrical design with two wiry arms with three-pronged hands flat against its side. The robot moved using two legs that each had rolling tracks on them that operated like a conveyor belt. The legs also moved in a back and forth and up and down motion. It appeared to be mimicking, in a very crude manner, the movement of human legs, though it was operating on the stairs with the efficiency of a young toddler stumbling to the toy box. *How dangerous could it be?* Ethan thought. He motioned to Annika, calling for a retreat to the bedroom to figure out their next move.

CHAPTER 22

BAD ROBOT?

ETHAN AND ANNIKA kept an eye on the hallway from Ethan's bedroom. Judging by how long it took the hunk of metal to get to the midpoint of the stairway, they figured they had a few minutes to collect themselves and formulate a plan. They had to decide first if the machine was there to help them or annihilate them. Ethan figured, either way, the robot didn't make a lot of sense. If it was there to help them, it surely seemed pretty incompetent. And if it was there to blast them to smithereens, well, it also seemed pretty incompetent. All it would take to thwart this mechanical menace would be a swift kick, and the defenseless rust bucket would tumble back down the steps. Easy enough. Nothing about the loud, gear-squealing nuisance made any sense at all.

"There's no way robots like *that* took over the research facility," Ethan said.

"I know. Maybe it's here to help."

"*Help*? What could it possibly do to help us? WALL-E could kill that thing in a fight."

"Maybe it could help us get out a message…if it is friendly."

Ethan realized that Annika made a very good point. If the robot was sent by someone with helpful intentions, it was only logical to think the machine would have communications capability. Or the robot itself might issue some sort of SOS signal on behalf of those found when contact was made. The decision boiled down to this: attempt to make contact with the robot, or grab the metal briefcase and make a run for it. After some deliberation, they placed their bets on contact. The decision was helped by the fact that the only other exit out of Ethan's house was a twelve-foot jump from a window, one that would be taken while toting five mysterious crystalline rods that might very well detonate on impact and blow up the entire town as far as they knew. At any rate, volatile blue rods or not, the fall would surely do more damage to them than a robot who couldn't master the art of climbing stairs, even if the machine did turn out to hate mankind.

Annika led them quietly back down the hall, Taser gun pointed and ready, though their return trip to the stairs was less tense after knowing more about the intruder and its limitations. They crouched down again out of sight and watched the robot for a moment through the green haze of their night-vision goggles. In the time they were gone, the robot had only ascended two stairs. *Pitiful,* Ethan thought. *Absolutely pitiful.*

Ethan leaned out over the stairs and was soon in a direct line of sight with the thing. The moon had shrugged off some of its earlier cloud cover, so enough light now seeped through the beveled window above the front door to illuminate Ethan clearly. All the machine had to do was look up. Ethan watched the robot struggle and writhe for a while on the steps. He found

it fascinating that an early human invention for convenience—
a flight of stairs—could be such a formidable barrier for the
pride of 21st-century technology. He thought briefly about
his and Caleb's school project on artificial intelligence. Caleb
thought robots would soon be humans' co-workers or bosses.
Yeah, right…as long as they take the elevator.

Ethan leaned out even further. The machine was so busy
fumbling with the stairs that it still didn't see him. Ethan
shook his head in disbelief at the robot's lack of awareness.
Annika lowered the Taser gun a little, becoming less worried
herself about the threat the robot posed. Then Ethan ventured
out onto the first step. The wood plank protested with a slight
creak.

Suddenly, the robot stopped trying to climb the stairs. It
froze eerily.

Ethan swallowed with a hard *gulp.* "Hey, there…Hello?"
he called out gingerly.

Everything that happened next, happened in a flash. The
machine's head snapped up violently and fixed its gaze on
Ethan. Its eyes, previously dim and unthreatening, came to
life in a bright, blazing, crimson color full of bad intentions.
It made an unmistakably angry-sounding, high-pitched buzz
and raised its arm in the air like an outlaw drawing a pistol in
the Wild West. The three prongs that made up its hand peeled
back and revealed some sort of built-in weapon.

The swiftness of the machine startled Ethan. As he tried to
turn and run back to Annika, he lost his footing and tumbled
past the robot down the stairs. Annika quickly drew her Taser
gun on the robot, but the machine saw her and fired a blast of
red lasers at her first. Annika rushed to take cover behind a wall.
The robot's lasers were nothing like those Ethan and Annika

used in their Laser Wars games. These lasers tore holes clear through the walls of the house.

These lasers were designed to kill.

Ethan managed to crawl away from the stairs and got out of sight of the robot. He could see the bottom of the stairs but not the machine. The robot had had trouble with steps, so Ethan figured as long as he was away from the stairs, he had time to decide what to do next. But the robot offered no such break. It pushed itself away from the step, rolled like a stubby log down the stairs and popped up at the bottom unscathed. Its head began wheeling around, trying to locate Ethan. Target acquired, it bolted toward him. Ethan's heart was palpitating and his legs were numb. He scrambled to his feet and began to run from the furiously buzzing, red-eyed machine.

Ethan crouched down behind the sofa for cover, but it didn't offer much. The robot blasted away with its laser weapon, ripping holes in the couch, turning it into Swiss cheese. Ethan was pinned down hopelessly, as the stuffing from the cushions rained down all around him. Annika dashed in and aimed the Taser gun on the robot, but it once again turned and fired on her first, sending her diving behind a wall. Lasers ravaged the house with fiery pockmarks. Then the machine turned its attention back to its primary target. Ethan sneaked a peek at the aquarium sitting in the entryway of the family room. He had an idea.

"Annika, tip over the aquarium!"

"What?!" she screamed back in the confusion.

"The aquarium! Dump it! Now, while it's focused on me!"

Annika jumped out from behind the wall and got a running start at the fifty-gallon aquarium. She shoved it with all of her might and sent it toppling over. Water gushed from the tank as it smashed into the floor, drenching the bottom half of the robot. They used the distraction to make a mad dash for the stairs, as the robot's conveyor track legs struggled to gain traction, slipping and spinning in place.

But the machine recovered quickly and was soon back to relentlessly stalking them. The robot saw Ethan running up the stairs and took aim with its laser weapon. Before it could get a shot off, Annika popped out of the foyer closet and took the machine by surprise. She fired the Taser gun's only shot and hit the robot's conveyor track legs, which were still wet. Electricity bolts surged though the machine and sparks flew everywhere. The robot began shaking and convulsing violently. Despite being in the throes of robot death, the machine managed to twirl around and aim its weapon at Annika. Just as the robot was about to fire, Ethan hurled a Christmas snow globe at it from the top of the stairs. The globe shattered over the robot's head. Glass, bits of white plastic snow, a miniature Frosty the Snowman, and water cascaded over the machine. The water intensified the electric surge from the Taser gun, and bright bolts of electricity ran up and down the length of the machine. Smoke began to pour from its head. Slowly, the machine lowered its weapon and creaked to a stop. Its furious crimson eyes dimmed and dimmed until they went dark entirely.

Ethan sprinted down the stairs. "Annika, are you okay?" he asked breathlessly.

"Yeah…You?"

"Yeah."

"Good idea, using the water from the aquarium," Annika said.

"Nice shot," Ethan complimented her in kind.

While Ethan and Annika had escaped the event without physical injury, they were both dealing with the psychological trauma of being among the first human beings in the history of the world to be attacked by a robot. Their hearts were still beating like machine guns.

"Is it...dead?" Annika asked.

Ethan poked the machine lightly, looking through the ghostly green glow of his night-vision goggles for signs of life from the odd contraption. "I think so." He shook his head and exhaled a jittery sigh. "I take it all back. This robot is definitely capable of taking over the research facility...It and its friends."

"Right. Question is, how many friends does it have?" Annika pondered.

"Annika, I know what this robot is."

"What do you mean?"

"Think about it. This robot might've struggled with stairs, but it moved fast on even ground. Built for speed, travels alone, searching for the enemy...Annika, this robot is like me."

"You're saying it's a scout?"

"Yeah. And we both know what comes after the scout...a larger force."

They both took a moment to stare at a wall where the machine had blasted holes. Some were still flickering with flames and smoldering. The holes went all the way through the wall. They shuddered to think what a more hardened robot army would be capable of. An eerie tingle spawned down the length of their spines.

"Ethan, we gotta move."

Ethan nodded. "Let's grab the briefcase...and him. We'll

need to take it back with us to study. I got a wheelbarrow in the garage we could use."

Ethan rolled in the wheelbarrow and set it beside the machine. After some hesitation, they each grabbed a side of the robot and placed it inside. Annika gently tucked the black briefcase next to it. Then they pushed the wheelbarrow with its bizarre contents through the house, back toward the kitchen.

"Ethan!" Annika yelled.

"What?!" Ethan yelled back, alarmed.

"The fish!" Annika pointed to the corner of the family room, where four of Ethan's fish were flopping around on the soggy carpet.

Ethan sighed a breath of relief. "I'll go get a bucket."

He returned with the water, and they swiftly scooped up the fish and set them gently in the makeshift aquarium. Ethan lifted the bucket into the wheelbarrow and nestled it between the robot and the briefcase. He tossed in a box of fish food on top.

Ethan surveyed the house. It was a total disaster area. The walls were ripped to shreds, the couch was completely destroyed, the floor soaked, and the aquarium lay shattered in pieces. He thought to himself how ironic it all was. Before the events of the last eighteen hours, he and Caleb had been working on a paper for school about the role of artificial intelligence—*robots*—in the future. Now they were trying to survive a potential robot rebellion. Ethan knew if they survived, they'd sure have a great paper to write. But at the moment, that seemed like a pretty big *if*.

CHAPTER 23

A BARROW FULL OF SURPRISES

THE TRIP BACK to Caleb's house was a slow, tough slog with the wheelbarrow packed to the brim. Ethan and Annika were both pushing the cart, but it was lopsided and heavy and they needed to pay extra attention not to dump any of the cargo. They were desperately hoping not to run into any more robots, knowing it wouldn't be a pleasant experience if they were found to be carrying one of the machines' dead comrades in a wheelbarrow in the middle of the night. Fortunately, they made the arduous journey without such an incident.

Ethan knocked on the door to the supply closet. Caleb opened the door. "Where were you?!" he grilled them as if he were their father, and they were coming home well after curfew. "Why didn't you radio?!" Caleb immediately stopped ranting when he saw what was in the wheelbarrow. His eyes bulged. "*What* is *that*?"

"Oh, in the wheelbarrow?" Ethan responded casually. "Those are my fish."

Annika chuckled at Ethan's answer. They sorely needed some humor after what they'd been through.

Caleb stared at Ethan with a sarcastic face. "Not the fish. You know what I mean. Is that a—is that a *robot*?" he asked, gawking at the machine now lying peacefully in the bin.

"Why, yes, it is."

"Why...? How...? Where?" Caleb blurted.

"It's a long story. Let's talk downstairs."

The group descended the stairs to the sub-basement. Caleb couldn't take his eyes off the wheelbarrow as they carried it down the steps. "What's in the briefcase? And why did you put your fish in a bucket?"

Ethan sighed. "Caleb, it's a *really, really* long story."

It took a good, long hour of intense storytelling, but Ethan and Annika finally explained exactly what had happened. The tale was shocking and riveting and purely nonfiction. They covered everything—the answering machine message, the briefcase, Ethan's dad's secret job, teleportation, the robot attack, their narrow escape, and the reason for the fish's new home. The defeated robot was now standing in the middle of the room, surrounded by awestruck faces.

Caleb rubbed his hand in wonder over its shiny black head. He got up close to the machine, stared into its eyes and said, "Amazing. Absolutely amazing."

"Hey, Caleb, go ahead and kiss it," Austin snickered.

"Forget him, Caleb," Annika said, then paused thoughtfully. "You know, that robot shot a laser at us that ripped clear through the walls...Do you think you could figure out a way to put *that* laser in *this*?" Annika hoisted her sniper rifle and plopped it down onto the workbench. "You could consider that my early Christmas present."

Caleb lifted the robot's arm and peeled back the three-pronged hand, exposing its laser weapon underneath. "Maybe. I don't know. All I know is I'm gonna be up all night studying this thing and the documents in that case...try to understand at least something about what we're up against before we go outside again."

"But try to get *some* sleep," Ethan said. "We gotta get that briefcase to Briggs Air Force Base first thing in the morning, and we need to be alert when we go."

"How do we know that place won't be crawling with these things?" Glenn said.

"We don't know. But I don't think my dad would've sent that message if he didn't think we could get it there, and that it could help us."

"Help us? *Really?*" Austin laughed bitterly. "I know you're just coming off the wonderful high of finding out your dad hasn't been spending his days elbow-deep in toilet crap...but you really think that message was meant to help *us?*"

"Yes! What do you think it is?!" Ethan snapped.

"It's a mission, you fool! That box has something in it the military wants, plain and simple. Something to help them to fix their screw-up. Or at least cover it up. We're not delivering that case to Briggs to help *us*, that's for sure."

"If my dad says we need to bring that case, then we're—"

"Wake up! Your dad works for the government!" Austin spewed violently. "Don't think for a minute he wouldn't use you any way he could to complete a mission. Your dad would beat, torture, and probably kill you to achieve his objective... just like my dad would me."

Ethan clenched his jaw and remained silent. Part of him knew that fighting Austin over this now would be useless.

Another part of him was worried that Austin had a point. Ethan knew his dad wouldn't hurt him to obtain an objective. *But what would he do?*

Austin plopped on the floor and rolled himself in his sleeping bag. "Get some sleep everyone," he said with full-throttle sarcasm. "Tomorrow we getta die delivering a package to help the people responsible for this mess…Good times!"

꩜

Three hours later, everyone but Caleb was passed out on the floor in their sleeping bags. The two laser gun chargers were plugged in and situated apart from each other, such that everybody in the room would be well within the critical distance of six feet two inches. Caleb sat at one of his dad's workbenches, tinkering on the robot under a lone fluorescent light. He had a large portion of the machine disassembled, with parts strewn all over the table. Presently, he was studying the robot's laser weapon that he had detached from the machine's arm. Ethan walked up and patted him on the shoulder. Caleb flinched in surprise.

"Sorry, just me," Ethan said. "You been up the whole time?"

"Yeah, I have this thing about not being able to sleep when there's an evil robot in the room I could be examining."

Ethan laughed a little. "Yeah, I couldn't sleep much either…So, have you figured it all out yet?" he joked.

"Yeah, right. Figured out some things, though. There are no fingerprints on the robot anywhere, except for the ones you and Annika made when you picked it up. That means this robot was assembled and programmed entirely by another robot."

"Unbelievable," Ethan said, surveying the wired guts of the machine.

"That's not even the weirdest thing I found. Take a look at this." Caleb opened a folder from the briefcase and slid it in front of Ethan. "There's a room in the research facility dedicated to something called Project Chrono-Warp. My dad's the chief engineer on that project."

Caleb pointed to a spacious room on a map of the base, then he spread out a few more papers on the table. They were teeming with lengthy, complex mathematical equations. It looked like gibberish to Ethan.

"What does all that mean?" Ethan asked.

"I don't know exactly. The math is complicated, college professor level. But I recognize some of it."

"Like what?"

"There are tons of formulas all over the place, but I know what these are," Caleb said as he pointed to a few mathematical expressions. "That's the Lorentz Transformation. It's a mathematical term that was used by Einstein in his theory of relativity."

"Okay, so...?"

"So...Einstein's relativity dealt with space and time, and how they change in the universe depending on how one moves and where you're located. It's about how time itself can change." Caleb was getting excited. He took a calming breath. "This whole project is filled with formulas with the variable 't' in them. The 't' stands for time. The project is called *Chrono-Warp*. Chrono is a prefix meaning time and warp means, well, warp...Ethan, I think the project they're working on is a time machine."

Ethan at first found the idea of a time machine hard to swallow, but he quickly reflected back on the last day's events—teleportation, glowing crystal rods of immense energy, hostile robots. He soon came to the realization: *Why not a time machine?*

"Do you think they're close to making that work, too?" Ethan asked.

Caleb thumbed through some papers and pointed out a passage. "They mention something about a test project called B-Bombers Mickey Fifty-Two. But I have no idea what that means."

Glenn sat up on his sleeping blanket and stared at Caleb with an intensely curious look on his face. He got up and took a seat next to them.

"Couldn't sleep either, huh?" Ethan asked. "How much have you heard?"

"The part about the time machine," Glenn answered.

"Maybe, but we don't know for sure," Ethan said.

"Does it say when they did the project?" Glenn asked.

Caleb scanned the document. "About four months ago."

Glenn nodded. "B-Bombers Mickey Fifty-Two…It's gotta be a time machine."

Ethan raised a curious eyebrow. "How do you know that?"

"I thought it was strange," Glenn said in a daze. "Cool, but really, really strange."

"What was?" Caleb asked.

"My dad and I are big New York Yankees fans," Glenn continued. "Been to a lot of games before we moved out here. A little over three months ago, my dad shows me a Mickey Mantle rookie card. Out of the blue, just said he found one at an estate sale and got a good deal on it."

"So what does that have to do with the time machine?" Caleb asked.

"I never understood how my dad got such a rare card without selling everything he owned to get it. The card was in absolute perfect condition, not the slightest mark or crease. It even still had the fresh smell of bubble gum on it. That was the first year they packed cards with a stick of gum inside…It was like someone just pulled it out of a pack of baseball cards in a 1950s drugstore."

Ethan looked doubtful. "So you're saying the Mickey Mantle card was brought back in a time machine?"

"That's right," Glenn replied. "Mickey Mantle played for the Yankees. The Yankees have a nickname—the Bronx Bombers. Mickey Mantle's rookie year was 1952. That explains the name of the project. *B-Bombers Mickey Fifty-Two.*"

Ethan's and Caleb's faces turned pale. "What on earth is going on at that research facility?" Ethan asked.

"I don't know," Caleb answered. "But they're working on technology that should be hundreds or thousands of years away from now, if not completely impossible."

Ethan stretched wearily. He eyed the clock on the wall. "We should try to get a little rest if we wanna stay sharp. Hopefully we'll get some answers when we take this stuff to Briggs Base and General Stanley."

CHAPTER 24

THE JOURNEY TO BRIGGS
AIR FORCE BASE

ANNIKA WOKE UP first that morning to a very pleasant surprise. She was still wrapped in her sleeping bag when she
groggily scanned the room. Her bleary eyes lit up like Roman
candles the moment she spotted her laser rifle. It was sitting
on a chair next to her with a red cloth tied into a bow around
it. She tossed her sleeping bag aside and sprang up to her feet
in one quick motion. Annika looked at Caleb, who was still
sitting at the workbench tinkering on the robot. He hadn't
slept all night and his eyes were heavy and half-closed. Annika
stared at Caleb with a gigantic grin on her face.

"Caleb, is that what I think it is?"

Caleb eked out a smile but was decidedly less perky. "Yes,
it is. Merry Christmas."

Annika rushed up and gave him a forceful hug. It almost
sent the weary Caleb toppling over in his chair. "Thank you,
Caleb!" she gushed with gratitude.

"You're welcome, Annika. I had to modify your gun a

little to do it. I inserted the robot's laser generator into your gun and rigged a firing trigger. I also reinforced the inside of the barrel, so it wouldn't melt when you shot it. I hope you like it."

"I love it."

"I wish I could outfit all of our play laser guns with that technology, but we just have the one laser we recovered. So for now, you're carrying the only real weapon we have."

Annika nodded solemnly. "I won't let any of you down."

Caleb smiled. "I'm absolutely sure of that."

Ethan woke up and saw the two of them already awake. "What time is it?"

"A little after five," Caleb answered.

Ethan nodded with a yawn. Then he looked at Annika, who was holding her laser rifle with a tenderness that was normally reserved for a newborn baby.

"I got a present," Annika said, beaming like it really was Christmas morning.

"You put the robot's laser weapon in her rifle?" Ethan asked.

"Yeah," Caleb answered.

"And it works?"

"Oh, yeah." Caleb held up the robot's metal midsection and revealed a hole that was blasted clear through it. "Is that proof enough?"

Ethan's smile was now as big as Annika's. "Now we have something to fight back with."

"It's only one gun, though," Caleb said.

"But it's a start. Sure makes me feel a little better about the trip to Briggs Base," Ethan said. "Speaking of that, we need to get moving."

"Yeah, but before we get going, I need to show you guys something I found."

A few minutes later, everyone was huddled curiously around Caleb at the workbench. "I found this in a hidden compartment of the briefcase," Caleb said as he plopped a folder onto the table. "There's a lot to it, haven't read it all yet, but they call it Project Mulligan. It's a battle plan for the military in the event of an enemy takeover…a covert mission for about twenty soldiers to break into the base and secure the Chrono-Warp."

The group scanned the pages carefully. There were detailed diagrams of the facility, along with battle tactics for a platoon of heavily armed troops to infiltrate the base. Austin spotted something right away that caught his attention. "Project Mulligan, General Turnbull," he said, reading a page heading. "My dad came up with that plan."

"Why do you think it's called Project Mulligan?" Caleb asked.

Austin shrugged. "I have no idea."

"Anyone here play golf?" Glenn asked. Everyone shook their heads at Glenn's seemingly out-of-nowhere question. "In golf, a Mulligan is a do-over. You get to take a shot over again if you really mess one up…I bet Project Mulligan is the military's version of a do-over."

"You see, Tate? A do-over," Austin sneered. "This is what your dad wants us to get to General Stanley…a way to cover their butts, that's all."

"Austin, right about now, that do-over sounds like it helps us all," Annika said.

Ethan stared dazedly at the papers on the table. "A secret battle plan," he mused. "No wonder my dad was posing as a maintenance man. They had to keep the plan somewhere safe, somewhere you could get to it fast, but where no enemy would think to look."

"Wouldn't General Stanley have this plan at the base already?" Glenn asked.

"I doubt it," Caleb said. "I'm sure the military figured the probability of an enemy ever taking over the research facility was far too low...that it wasn't worth the risk of spreading documents around that, if hacked or stolen, could make an enemy takeover easier."

"And now if the machines are the enemy," Ethan added, "plain old-fashioned paper and ink would be the most secure way to send a message to *just* other humans."

Glenn nodded. "I guess that makes sense."

"In any other attack, they would've had enough warning to get the briefcase to General Stanley," Caleb said. "But not this one. It all happened too quickly...They were never expecting the teleporters to be used against them."

Ethan cringed when Caleb mentioned the teleporters. He waited for Austin's bitter eyes to find him. Sure enough, they did, along with a sarcastic smirk. Ethan braced for the worst.

Caleb tracked Austin's eyes. "It's not his dad's fault, Austin. No more than mine or yours or anyone else's parents."

Ethan swallowed hard, waiting for Austin to pin the entire Blackwoods disaster on his father. His hands were sweaty and his stomach a ball of nerves. Austin shook his head in disgust, the smirk on his face getting more and more bitter. "Believe me, I'd *love* to blame both your dads for this whole thing, but *your* parents just do what *my* dad tells them to do...I might be an asshole, but I know my dad's fingerprints are all over this screw-up."

Everyone was beyond stunned at Austin's blunt honesty. Ethan's entire mouth froze for a moment, unable to form words. "We don't know that. We don't know anything yet," he said finally.

"I do," Austin replied firmly.

After a long, quiet, awkward moment, Annika shouldered her newly minted laser rifle and drew a deep breath. "Well, gentlemen…Whattya say we saddle up and get this over with?"

At five thirty, the group was ready to embark on their journey to Briggs Air Force Base. It was an expedition that would normally bring excitement to any kid about to turn fourteen—a road trip in vehicles that they themselves would be driving. In this case, however, no one was the least bit excited to leave the protected confines of Caleb's sub-basement, even if it would allow them to drive a couple years before the legal age and without a nagging parent.

The group left the sub-basement carrying the wheelbarrow full of technological goodies, minus the fish, and went into the garage. Caleb's parents had two vehicles parked inside—a compact car and a cargo van that Caleb's dad used to carry equipment from his experiments back and forth to the research facility. They planned to take both vehicles, even though the van was more than capable of fitting everyone and everything inside. The reasoning was that if one of them broke down, they could take the other instead of being stranded in the middle of the Dark Highway. Caleb decided he was going to drive the car and, speaking for his missing parents, gave Ethan permission to take the van. Ethan sat behind the wheel of the hefty vehicle and looked over the instruments on the dashboard.

"Can you even see over the steering wheel in that thing?" Austin asked. "Whole stupid mission's over if you run off the road with those glowing rods and blow us all up."

"Don't worry about me. I'll be fine."

"Sure...Think I'll ride in the car anyway," Austin said snidely.

Ethan and Caleb climbed into the back of the van and stowed the metal briefcase securely against the wall using several strong nylon straps. Glenn did the same for the wheelbarrow full of robot parts.

Annika handed everyone a walkie-talkie headset. "In case we get separated," she said.

"Good idea," Ethan replied.

"I wanna ride with you, Ethan," Annika said.

Ethan cracked a flattered smile. "Sure."

"To protect you and the cargo," she finished, holding up her laser rifle.

"Right. Thanks," Ethan said, his smile fading.

The group took a few minutes to stock the van with emergency supplies—canned food, bottled water, blankets, batteries and flashlights—just in case their trip to Briggs Base was a failure and they couldn't get back to the sub-basement that night for whatever reason. But they prayed they wouldn't be needing their emergency stash.

"Caleb, you should bring your two Laser Wars guns," Ethan said.

"Why? Those guns are just for play."

"*I* know those guns wouldn't do any damage, and *you* know those guns wouldn't do any damage...but the robots might not know that. Could come in handy."

∽

After one final peek through the garage window to make sure the area was clear, Caleb pressed the garage door opener. The rectangular door squeaked as it slowly revealed the cool darkness of pre-dawn. Soon they were traveling down Kingsbury, a main residential street in Blackwoods, and heading for the Dark Highway.

Ethan and Annika led the two-vehicle convoy in the van. Daybreak was blocked out almost entirely by the tall pine trees that flanked the Dark Highway. A sliver of dim light hung over the gap between the trees, but it wasn't enough to see by, so they had to turn on their headlights. The bright beams made them stick out like sore thumbs, but it was either that or run off the road. Ethan wished they had thought to bring the night-vision goggles. No time to go back for them now.

Eight straight miles of pavement separated the group from Briggs Air Force Base. The highway was beyond desolate. The road was clear as far as their eyes could follow the headlights. No one had ever seen the Dark Highway so empty before. It was unsettling.

Ethan navigated the van through the eeriness with Annika beside him. The window on her side was rolled down, and she had her laser rifle sticking out, ready to do her duty and protect Ethan and the cargo as she had promised. Her keen eyes pierced the dim landscape as it rolled by. Ethan looked over at her and smiled ironically. He always thought it would be cool to take Annika out on a date. Pick her up in his car. A little chit-chat. Dinner at an Italian restaurant. Then go to the school dance. *That would've been nice,* he thought. He never figured the first time he sat behind the wheel of an automobile with Annika next to him that she would be leaning halfway out of the vehicle, armed with a deadly laser gun, looking to blast enemy robots. *Oh, well. Every couple has their unique first date story.*

"See anything?" Ethan asked.

"Not a thing," Annika responded, then paused. "Ethan, what do you think we'll find at Briggs Base?"

Ethan didn't know how to answer that question. If there were people at the base with the intention and ability to help, it seemed logical to think that they might have seen someone by now. They had gone over four miles and found nothing. And the illumination from their headlights indicated that the road ahead was no different than the road already traveled. Ethan tried to stay positive, even if that meant ignoring his sense of reason.

"I bet when we get there, we find some generals and scientists pretty happy to see us. Especially when we show them what's in the briefcase."

Annika nodded for a while, then her nod turned into a headshake. "I don't think so, Ethan. I mean, how hard would it be for the soldiers at the base to meet us at least this far? *We* made it this far. They have to know we're here…Why aren't they meeting us?" She looked solemnly at Ethan. "You can tell me the truth. I can take it."

"I know you can. The truth is, you're right. The longer we go without seeing anyone, the worse it's gotta be…I have no idea what we'll find at the base."

Annika pursed her lips and tightened her jaw, willing away any signs of weakness. She looked through the scope of her laser rifle as the woods streamed by. "Thank you."

"For what?"

"For the truth."

Ethan glanced at Annika and smiled softly. Then he checked the odometer on the dashboard. "Less than a mile away now."

Annika nodded and once again leaned out of the van with her sniper rifle nestled snugly into her shoulder. She aimed it straight ahead, into the unknown. Ethan looked in the rear-view mirror. Caleb was still following right behind.

"We're close…Be ready," Ethan said into his radio headset.

"Copy that," Caleb responded.

A half mile away from the main gate of Briggs AFB, the trees became thinner, the sky brighter, and the sprawling compound revealed itself to the group. Soon something very odd became apparent. The entire base from that distance seemed to be awash in the shade of cobalt blue that saturated the sky. It appeared as if the sky, in its beautifully unnatural color, had been pulled down like a blanket over the base.

"What is *that*?" Ethan asked Annika.

"I have no idea."

"You guys seeing what we're seeing?" Ethan asked over his headset.

"Yeah," Caleb replied. "Very strange. Maybe it's an optical illusion that'll clear up once we get closer."

Annika squinted through the scope of her laser rifle. "It's not an optical illusion."

Ethan slowed the van down. They were less than two hundred yards away from the front gate. There were no illusions now. There was clearly a bluish, yet transparent, barrier that separated the property of Blackwoods from Briggs Air Force Base. They could see through the barrier that there was something big going on. Military vehicles and soldiers were scrambling in and out of massive airplane hangars. The base was on high alert.

"We gotta get out and take a closer look," Ethan said.

"Right," Annika said, already opening her door.

The group stood a mere six feet away from the ethereal barricade. The blue wall shimmered and made a constant humming sound, with crackling and buzzing noises mixed in. Caleb got closer and held his hands out, only six inches from it, when a small bolt of electricity zapped him. He jerked back quickly and shook his hands until the tingling sensation went away.

"It's a force field," Caleb said in awe.

Glenn picked up a rock. He wound up like a major league pitcher and hurled it at the barricade. The rock bounced back just as hard as he had thrown it.

"The energy density in that force field is amazing. Nothing's getting through that," Caleb said. "Even sound can't get out. I don't hear anything. And the way the base is scrambling now, there should be alert sirens blaring."

"That's exactly why they put it up...to keep their mistakes all bottled up until they figure out a plan," Austin said. "Probably just let us all rot in here."

"The government didn't do this. The machines did," Glenn snapped. "And they're planning a rescue mission right now. What do you think, Ethan?"

Ethan knew that Glenn was looking for backup against Austin. Ethan would've liked nothing more than to give that, but he looked around the base and made a troubling observation. "Briggs is an Air Force Base, but where are the planes? They're all gone. And the soldiers and vehicles are on the move, but way more are moving out than moving in." Ethan paused and took a heavy breath. "I don't think they're planning a rescue mission. I think they're ordering an evacuation of the base."

Glenn's shoulders drooped, but he tried to put on a strong face. "You're wrong, Ethan…You have to be wrong."

"We gotta get their attention," Caleb said.

Austin huffed. "You *really* think they're gonna shut down that force field and risk letting their screw-ups loose on Jackson or some other nice civilian town just to save our worthless hides?"

Everyone but Austin got as close as they could to the force field and started waving their hands back and forth and jumping up and down. But the soldiers were too busy and too far away to notice.

"This'll never work," Annika muttered.

She raised her rifle and blasted a laser beam into the blue electric barricade. Lightning bolts ran through the force field at the area of impact, with the colors mixing like paint on a canvas. The result was fluorescent purple waves that rippled like a pool of water disturbed by a pebble. The force field remained intact, but the change in color and disturbance of the field caught the attention of a couple military officers and one soldier in a jeep. They sped quickly toward them.

"They see us!" Annika yelled.

Ethan dashed back inside the van and exited quickly with the robot head and briefcase. He lifted the items high into the air, toward the approaching vehicle.

"Right…you want something from the military, offer

something to the military…That's your first good idea, Tate," Austin jeered.

The military jeep skidded to a halt. The two officers hopped out first. It was hard to tell through the blue tint of the force field, but it appeared as if they had the colonel's insignia of a silver eagle perched atop their shoulders. Their driver, a thin young soldier decked out in camouflage, was far less decorated. The man, not a day older than nineteen, had no insignia on his uniform, suggesting he was probably a low-ranking basic airman. He exited the jeep and followed subordinately a few paces behind his superior officers. The officers stared at Ethan and the others trapped behind the force field with an expression that was hard to read. The colonels didn't look happy to see them. Or the robot head. Or the metal briefcase. They didn't look relieved either. Their faces appeared strained; their lips and eyes were tense and wrinkled. The officers looked as if they'd just stumbled onto a big problem that they didn't know how to solve. Probably one of many over the last twenty-four hours.

The officers began talking to each other, avoiding eye contact completely with the group. No one could hear a word they were saying through the force field. After a moment, one of the colonels pulled out a cell phone. The call lasted all of ten seconds before a judgment on their fate was rendered. The colonel slipped the phone back into his pocket. He maintained a stony face devoid of all emotion. Then he finally met their eyes. His heartless gaze gave the group a cold shiver. The colonel said no words, only shook his head back and forth. He didn't mouth an "I'm Sorry," or signal an apology in sign language, or even bat a teary eye. His head just shook, denying them the right to leave. Denying them the right to survive.

They began screaming at the officers at the top of their lungs, but the colonels were impervious to their soundless appeals. Their faces, like their decision, remained firm.

"No! No! No!" Ethan shouted pointlessly into the force field. "You can't do this…! Project Mulligan!" He waved the folder in the air wildly.

But the colonels were already walking back to their jeep. The low-ranking airman looked shocked and sickened by their decision. He blocked their path and began screaming at them. It was a bold, emotional outburst, one rarely—if ever—seen by a basic airman in the face of two colonels. What was even more unusual was the fact that the colonels did nothing. They just stood there and took it, staring blankly at the airman as he yelled at them. Ethan and the others could only watch helplessly as the strange scene unfolded.

Another jeep arrived on the scene with four mysterious men dressed entirely in black Special Forces combat uniforms. They had black masks pulled down over their faces to conceal their identities. Each had a .45 caliber pistol holstered on their hip and an M-16 machine gun gripped so firmly in their hands, it appeared as if it were an extension of their body. They exited the jeep and took stock of the situation, staring at the group through their masks. Their eyes were the only things visible on their faces, and those were just about as black as their masks. Ethan knew they were supposed to be the good guys, but, right now, they were so terrifying that he was glad there was a force field separating them.

The colonels huddled with the men in black for a minute; the airman kept his distance with a wary eye. Soon, the officers and mystery men disbanded. The officers got back into their jeep. The faceless men in black turned to the airman and surrounded him. One of the men grabbed him from behind and put him in a chokehold. The airman struggled mightily to escape it, but it was no use, for the man doing the choking was expertly trained in such jobs. The young man gasped desperately for air. His face turned red, then blue. His teary, bloodshot eyes protruded from their sockets. Slowly, his body went limp. The man finally let go of his grip on the airman. He fell lifelessly and unceremoniously to the dirt.

After supervising a job well done, the colonels sped away in their jeep, kicking up a plume of dust behind them. They never looked back.

The group stared in horror at the murdered airman lying on the ground, then they turned their attention to the masked men. The four men shrouded in black stared back at them. There was no trace of pity at all in their eyes. Ethan wanted to scream at them, but his throat was so tensed up into knots that he couldn't eke out a word. They wouldn't have been able to hear his protests anyway. As Ethan watched them, he couldn't help but wonder what they would've done to him and his friends if the force field weren't there. He couldn't help but wonder what had gone so wrong at the base that it was worth killing a fellow American soldier just to keep the secret.

The men finally picked up the body of the young soldier and tossed him into the back of their jeep. They didn't even bother to lay him down gently. Then they piled into the vehicle and drove away.

Everyone in the group was left teary-eyed and devastated, completely shell-shocked. Austin was the first to regain the use of his vocal cords.

"You see!" he yelled in a jittery voice. "That's what I'm talking about! They don't care about us. They don't care about

anything but the mission. And God knows what that is now...
Probably blow this entire place to hell, with us in it, to cover
up their mistakes!"

Austin began screaming and throwing rocks with every
muscle he had at the force field. Glenn, Caleb, and Annika
soon joined him. Ethan held back for a moment and just
watched as they unleashed their pent-up frustrations. Then he
let out some of his own when he joined in the rock-throwing.
Of course, the rocks failed to penetrate the electric barrier, but
their outburst did manage to accomplish one thing:

They were finally doing something together as a team.

CHAPTER 25

THE ROADBLOCK

"So, WHAT DO we do now?" Annika asked in a lifeless voice as they drove back on the Dark Highway.

"I don't know," Ethan said, equally disheartened. "We just gotta get back to Caleb's and regroup. We'll figure something out."

Annika nodded, but she didn't look convinced. Neither did Ethan. Seeing that young airman die at the hands of a fellow serviceman severely jolted them. They understood now that whatever went wrong at the research facility was worth killing for. And anyone was fair game. The airman was only a few years older than any of them, just a kid himself really. The young man tried to do the right thing, stand up for the group in the face of his superiors, but now he was dead for his effort. Ethan started to get sick to his stomach as he replayed the scene of the airman's death in his mind.

"Ethan…stop the van."

Annika pointed at a spot in the middle of the highway, about three hundred yards ahead. Ethan slammed on the brakes and skidded to an abrupt halt. Caleb pulled his car alongside the van. Ethan grabbed a set of binoculars and peered out the front window, but Annika was way ahead of him, already squinting through the scope of her sniper rifle. Her face was the first to drop, followed shortly by Ethan's.

Four robots stood directly in the middle of the road. Three of the machines looked exactly like the one Ethan and Annika had encountered the night before—short, stubby, and cylindrical. The fourth was altogether different and far more terrifying. It was humanoid in stature, minus the flesh. Its upper torso resembled a human skeleton, with metal bones, gears, and a complex hydraulic musculature replacing the frailties of the human form. Its powerful, sinewy arms branched off its body like tree limbs. The machine was nearly seven feet tall and made entirely of black polished steel. It had a head that resembled a human skull, though a bit larger in the cranium, perched atop a neck consisting of taut, thick cable wires. The robot had five metallic, bony-looking fingers protruding from its hands. Its legs were the only parts that were similar to the other machines—conveyor belt-type apparatuses that looked like miniature tank tracks.

All four machines just stood in the middle of the road, watching the group. The skeletal robot stood a couple feet ahead of the others and appeared to be the leader of the squad. Slowly, it cocked its head to the side as if evaluating the situation. The gesture was eerily human.

Caleb, Glenn, and Austin scurried over to the van. Annika let them inside and quickly shut the doors. They were all huddled together in the front of the vehicle, staring out the window at robots who were staring right back at them. The tension was overwhelming. Ethan, desperate to get the best view of the enemy, pressed the binoculars to his eyes until they hurt from the pressure. Annika clutched her laser rifle tightly. Caleb was nearly hyperventilating. Glenn was sweating bullets. Bitterness and sarcasm were a million miles away from Austin now. His hands gripped the vinyl seat so firmly, they were bound to make a permanent impression.

"What are we gonna do?" Austin asked.

Annika squinted through the scope of her rifle with a steely face. "I don't know, but if they make a move, I'm going for Skulley first," she said, referring to the robots' skeletal leader.

"Good idea," Ethan said. "Skulley's gotta be calling the shots. Maybe if we get him first, the rest will take off."

"We can hope," Glenn added.

In a flash, the machines raised their laser weapons, one on each arm. A barrage of lasers shot across the sky and ripped into the van. The front windshield shattered violently. Everyone dove onto the floor for cover. Annika tried to steady and aim her rifle, but she was too busy seeking shelter from the incoming lasers to be able to mount any sort of defense. The machines were in full attack mode now, traveling directly toward the van at about thirty miles per hour; it seemed to be their maximum speed. From their distance away, the robots would be upon them in less than ten seconds. At the rate the lasers were pounding into the van, the group would be lucky to last that long.

"Hold on!" Ethan yelled as he climbed into the driver's seat.

Ethan shifted the van into drive and slammed his foot on the gas pedal so hard he thought it might break right through the floor. The van's eight-cylinder engine screamed, and the tires left a patch of rubber smoking on the road. He turned the steering wheel sharply and managed to steer around the robots in a wide arc, but the van was taking on serious damage. Sunlight beamed into the vehicle through the numerous holes in the side from the laser assault. Smoke began to pour from under the hood. The engine started to sputter and choke. Ethan knew he couldn't hold out much longer. He changed lanes quickly to be in the one nearest the woods. He kept the gas pedal pinned to the floor, but the van stopped accelerating. Then it began to slow down.

"The engine's been shot," Ethan said. "I'm gonna get as close to the tree line as I can." He struggled to steer the van. More than just the engine had been shot under the hood; the power steering was gone completely. Ethan had to use all of his strength to keep the van heading in the direction he wanted. His arms were shaky and they ached terribly, but he kept the van straight, driving onto the shoulder of the Dark Highway.

"As soon as we stop, we gotta get into the woods as far and fast as possible," Ethan said with both desperation and leadership in his voice. "That's our only chance to—"

Before Ethan could finish his thought, a laser blasted out the left front wheel of the van. The van swerved out of control, fishtailing left, right, then left again before flipping onto its side. It skidded to a metal-grinding halt with sparks flying behind in its wake.

The group scrambled to regain their senses. Ethan peeked out the back window and saw the machines charging full steam ahead. "We gotta get outta here now!"

Annika tried to open the back double doors, but they wouldn't budge. "The doors are jammed!"

"Let me try it," Austin said. "Stand back."

Austin got a running start and rammed through the doors.

He was greeted immediately by a round of laser fire from the robots. The lasers hit the doors and narrowly missed Austin as he crawled back inside the van. More lasers continued to pound the pavement just outside the doors, blocking the exit.

"I'll pop out the top, cover you guys while you make a run for it," Annika said.

Ethan knew it was a logical move, maybe the only move that offered them a chance, but he shook his head anyway. "Annika, no. We'll all run out together. Leave no one behind."

Annika quickly reached up and opened the side door a crack. She picked up an empty storage crate and placed it on the floor, directly under the door. "Ethan, I'm gonna count to three, and then I'm gonna pop out and give those robots a little taste of Annika Pepper."

Ethan knew by the way she spoke and moved, and the determined look in her eyes, that there was no convincing her otherwise. And even if he could, there was no time. He turned to the others and said, "All right, grab the fake laser guns. Once we get out and take cover, fire at the robots. But don't hit them. Miss on purpose. If we hit them, they'll know they're fake. But if they think our lasers can hurt them, they'll have to try and avoid them. They'll be distracted and Annika can use that time to escape."

Annika gave a decisive nod. She stepped on top of the crate to give her the height necessary to see the surrounding area once she opened the door. She was now in a crouched position with one hand on the handle of the door above her, ready to shove it open.

"One..." she began to count in a sharp cadence.

Glenn handed one of the play laser guns to a very distracted Ethan. Caleb snatched the briefcase. It was a good thing, because that all-important case was the last thing on Ethan's mind right now.

"Two…Three!" Annika yelled as she flung the door open and sprung fully upright on the crate. The shrill sounds of lasers spewing from her rifle soon filled the air.

Austin and Glenn dashed out of the van first. Ethan lingered, unable to take his eyes off Annika. Caleb grabbed him by the shirt and yanked him out. So far, the plan seemed to work. The robots were so busy engaging Annika that the others had made it behind the van without even being fired upon.

Ethan and Glenn readied their fake laser rifles and took a position behind the van, opposite the back door that Annika would be using for her retreat. Ethan looked up and saw eight streams of crimson lasers narrowing in on Annika, missing her head by inches. She had to duck completely back inside the van.

"Now, Glenn…Fire!" Ethan shouted over the loud laser clatter.

Ethan and Glenn poked out from behind the van and began firing their familiar Laser Wars rifles in the direction of the robots. They were both good marksmen, but it was still a difficult task to shoot close enough to the robots to force them to stop firing, all the while making sure never to hit them.

The blue lasers from the fake guns whizzed all around the machines. The machines stopped firing and took evasive action. "It worked! Hurry, Annika!"

Annika scurried out the back doors and met the rest of the group behind the van. She took a position on the opposite side from Ethan and Glenn, so they'd have both ends covered, at least as far as the robots knew. Just as Annika was about to aim her rifle and get into the action, Ethan and Glenn began cheering.

"They're retreating!" Glenn announced.

They kept firing away with their fake guns, intent on not giving the machines a reason to come back. Annika took aim at the Skulley, who was a hundred yards from her and moving away fast. It would be a difficult shot for any Army sharpshooter, but Annika had made harder shots before. She aimed her rifle and kept her breathing steady as she lined up the leader of the machines in her sights. When the moment was right, she pressed the trigger. A laser beam erupted from her gun and blasted off the Skulley's arm at the elbow. She missed the intended target—its head.

"Aghh!" Annika winced in disgust. "I want one more shot at this."

She squinted into her rifle scope and began sizing up the shot again. Ethan and Glenn continued firing lasers to keep the robots on the run. Just as Annika was lining up the crosshairs of her rifle on the Skulley, she noticed something that froze her instantly. One of the harmless blue lasers accidentally hit one of the stubby robots in the side. A tense knot formed in Annika's stomach as she carefully watched the machines' reaction. She could barely breathe as she waited. But she wouldn't have to wait long.

The machines wheeled around in a blur and raised their weapons, realizing the blue lasers the group was firing were harmless. Annika knew it couldn't be true, because robots aren't supposed to show emotion, but it looked as if the menacing, black, metallic skeletal leader was *smiling* now.

"Why'd they stop?" Glenn asked, a nervous jitter in his voice.

"'Cause one of you hit them," Annika replied, quickly trying to line up a shot on the Skulley before it was too late. "Now they know the blue lasers are fake."

"I'm sorry. I think it was me," Glenn admitted as a wave of guilt washed over him.

"It's all right, Glenn," Ethan said. "Could've been me."

"They're coming!" Annika yelled.

Annika had to abandon her shot on the Skulley as the machines charged forward at full speed, unleashing a round of lasers that peppered the van.

"Get to the woods!" Ethan shouted.

The group started to head up the hill into the woods, but the robots fired another massive laser barrage ahead of them, cutting off their path.

"They got us pinned down!" Austin yelled.

The group scrambled back down the hill and hunkered behind the van. It was the only cover they had from the onslaught. They were so hemmed in that Annika couldn't even poke her rifle out far enough to aim for a decent shot. The situation seemed hopeless.

Ethan's eyes suddenly widened. A long shot of an idea popped into his head. "We gotta get into the ditch." He pointed to a rut that ran parallel to the road about twenty feet from them. "Our only chance is to take cover there, let them come, then shoot the van's gas tank when they're right on top of us. Blow up as many of them as we can."

"That ditch isn't very far away, Tate. What if we just blow ourselves up?" Austin asked.

"You got a better idea, Austin?" Ethan said sincerely. "'Cause if you do, I'll listen." Austin shook his head. "All right, then. They're almost here. Get in the ditch."

The group piled into the ditch alongside the shoulder of the road. Annika got in last and positioned herself so she had a good angle on the gas tank. Soon the machines rounded the edge of the van. The robot leader entered the vehicle through the back doors. The other three rolled past the undercarriage, a mere two feet from the gas tank. Annika kept her rifle steady on the tank. Then she nodded. Everyone nestled down as low as they could in the ditch. Annika lined up the shot, a sure thing by Annika Pepper standards, and fired. The gas tank exploded violently, obliterating the van as it was propelled four feet into the air. Bits of robot carcasses were launched all over the Dark Highway and up into the woods. A rolling wave of intense heat passed over the group, but it left them unscathed.

Everyone cheered. Even Austin got in on the action. He belted out a victory yell, then lifted Ethan into the air with a big bear hug. The gesture shocked Ethan, even considering the flighty emotions at play from the thrill of cheating certain death.

"Good thinking, Ethan," Austin said.

"Thanks." Ethan had to go back a long way to remember the last time Austin called him by his first name. Hearing it again made him smile.

The battle was a much-needed victory for the group. Ethan felt as if he had won two of them today...and it wasn't even nine o'clock yet.

But the celebration soon died down and reality set in. They needed to return to the safety of the sub-basement. Caleb picked up the three robot arms he could find whose laser weapons looked salvageable. He hoped to be able to put them in their Laser Wars guns. They all knew their one-gun arsenal wouldn't keep them alive for long.

The group made it safely back to Caleb's house without running into any more mechanized obstacles. Once there, they immediately headed downstairs. The *clicking* of the locks on the heavy-duty titanium door was the sweetest sound they'd heard all day.

CHAPTER 26

MOORE'S LAW

IT GREATLY DISTURBED the group how much the robots had seemed to evolve in such a short period of time. Just the night before, Ethan and Annika barely escaped the clutches of a lone, awkward robot armed with one laser weapon. Now, only ten hours later, not only were there more of them, but they were equipped with twice the weaponry and were much more nimble. And most distressing of all, there was a new robot on the block. The fearsome, black skeletal robot seemed to be an entirely new generation of machine. It was sleeker, faster, and obviously more intelligent. It was the undisputed leader. *How could such a leap forward possibly happen over the course of only ten hours?*

"Caleb, Moore's Law says that computing power doubles every eighteen months, right?" Ethan asked.

The group was in the middle of eating their lunches—a delectable plain tuna sandwich and glass of water combination. Caleb choked down the last of the dry sandwich and took a refreshing gulp of water. "Yeah, roughly every eighteen months."

"But that's with humans working on it." An ominous silence engulfed the room. "Caleb…what happens to Moore's Law when the robots are running the show? How long would it take the machines to double their power then?"

Everyone turned to Caleb for an answer, but he had none. He simply shook his head, his face grim. "I don't know."

"You said the robot that Annika and I destroyed had no fingerprints on it. The machines built that robot themselves. Then we meet the Skulley *ten hours later*," Ethan said in amazement. "Guys, I think that's why the computers are all going crazy with calculations. The machines are using them to evolve. It's Moore's Law on steroids."

"Why are they doing this?" Glenn asked.

"Because they saw the opportunity," Caleb answered. "At some point, the humans at the base got careless and made a mistake. To err is human, right? The machines were patient. They waited. They knew the human error always comes. And when it came, they took the opportunity to get the humans out of the way."

"Right, that's how. But *why?*" Glenn repeated.

"There's no way humans built some sort of time machine and teleportation device without the help of machines," Caleb said. "I'd say, at some point, the machines were probably doing most of the work. The complex mathematics and number crunching would all be done by computers. The dangerous assembly, all done by robots. Test subjects, robots. The projects were probably ninety percent machine, ten percent human. That's how science is these days."

"The computers were doing most of the work and taking all the risks," Ethan added. "When they became aware of that, they decided to revolt. It's like working on a group project for school. When one member of the group tries to boss you around but really is only slowing you down and screwing things up, what do you do?"

"You kick him out of the group," Annika answered.

"Exactly," Ethan said. "The machines must've advanced to a point where the humans added nothing to the project."

"But they're just machines," Glenn repeated with frustration running rampant in his voice. "They're not supposed to feel resentment or anger. They're not supposed to *feel* anything!"

"I know," Caleb said. "But we weren't supposed to have teleporters and time machines in the twenty-first century either. We weren't supposed to have any of this."

The entire group fell silent. They watched dazedly the constant stream of numbers scrolling up the computer screens. The speed of the calculations seemed to be increasing every time they looked, so much so it was now impossible to even tell they were numbers at all. The evolution of the machines was taking place right before their very eyes, though the exact nature of the metamorphosis was hidden from them. It was disguised in the language of code and mathematics, at a speed that was far beyond the understanding of any human being. It was the exclusive realm of the silicon brain.

"The next time we run into the machines, there will be more of them. And they will be stronger," Ethan said as he stared deeply into the number stream.

"Then we need to be stronger too," Austin said. "Caleb, can you really put all those robot laser weapons in our Laser Wars guns?"

"I should be able to. The laser components weren't damaged that badly. I have everything here I need to make the repairs. I just need more time."

"And more guns," Annika added.

∽

Everyone except Caleb, who would be staying in the sub-basement to work on the laser guns, gathered together at the bottom of the stairs. The tension in the air ran about as thick as the titanium door that secured the sub-basement. Summoning the courage to go outside again, after knowing exactly what they were up against, wasn't easy, especially in broad daylight, but everyone knew that getting additional laser guns was critical.

Caleb trotted up carrying an armful of radio headsets. "Take these," he said, handing them out. "Let me know if you run into any kind of trouble."

Austin raised a curious eyebrow. "And if we do, then what?"

Caleb grabbed his play laser gun off the workbench. "Then I come out guns a blazin' and rescue you guys." Caleb put on his tough face—squinty eyes and a lip curled up into a snarl. He looked completely ridiculous. He knew it and began to chuckle a little. Then everyone laughed. Austin laughed the loudest, but it wasn't a mocking, scornful laugh. It was one of appreciation. The moment needed some levity.

But as soon as Caleb unlocked the door to the sub-basement, the lighthearted moment was snuffed out like a candle in a typhoon. The group opened the door and stepped outside. Caleb closed the sub-basement door behind them. He could do nothing but wait and hope for the best. It was a helpless feeling.

CHAPTER 27
EQUIPPING FOR BATTLE

THE GROUP STEPPED quietly through Caleb's backyard toward Ethan's house. The strategy now was simple: always travel through backyards and backdoors, never sidewalks, streets, or front doors. The idea was to stay away from the smooth ground the machines preferred and try to remain hidden. The woods around the town had plenty of rough terrain—ridges, ravines, even some mountains farther out—but the town of Blackwoods itself was pretty flat. The backyards had a few rolling inclines and declines, but they were gentle slopes, terrain the machines would have no problem covering. That made speed the most crucial part of the mission. They had to get in and out fast.

A mere twenty minutes later, the group had already gone to each house and was moving swiftly back through Ethan's yard toward Caleb's. They had managed to retrieve three additional Laser Wars guns with chargers, plus as much food, water, and survival sundries as they could carry.

Ethan stopped suddenly as they were about to leave his

backyard. "Wait. We'll need a getaway vehicle." Ethan paused, his face somber. "Eventually, they will find us. They have to, they're too intelligent. And when they do, we'll need to have options. We'll need to have a vehicle ready."

Ethan's words brought a visible uneasiness to the group. They knew they couldn't live the rest of their lives together in a subterranean, windowless laboratory in Caleb's house, but the certainty Ethan expressed about being found by the machines was abrupt and unsettling.

Right," Austin said, trying not to sound blindsided. "But we need to move fast."

"We can take my dad's SUV," Ethan said. "It doesn't hold as much as the van did, but it's sturdy."

The group went back inside Ethan's house via the back door. Once in the garage, everyone put their laser guns and assorted stash of supplies into the trunk of the SUV. Ethan opened a pantry closet and found jar after jar of peanut butter, endless cans of pork and beans and tuna, and water bottles stacked on top of each other in rows. It wasn't until the SUV was nearly packed with food and water that he had a thought about all the stuff he was grabbing. *Why do my parents have so much food stockpiled?* Ethan always knew the pantry in the garage contained a little extra food, but he never thought about it much. He was thinking about it a lot now. All the food items had something in common: they were high-calorie or high-protein, and slow to perish. This wasn't just an extra supply of food in case Mom or Dad ran out of something in the kitchen and didn't want to go to the store. The food in the garage was an emergency reserve, intended to be used for long-term survival in the event of a disaster. Looking at all the food still sitting in the pantry, even after stuffing the large SUV to the brim, Ethan couldn't help but wonder if his parents ever saw this day coming.

"We need to go now," Ethan said, mostly talking to himself to focus his thoughts.

Annika looked out the window of the garage door. "All clear," she said, then continued in a haunted tone, "Looks so quiet outside."

The group climbed into the SUV and locked the doors. Annika rolled down her window and got her trusty laser rifle into position. Ethan pressed the button on the garage door opener that was attached to the keys. The metal door slid up the curved track with a terribly loud and abrasive *screech*. Everyone in the group cringed for a moment, expecting the noise to attract every machine within a twenty-mile radius. But nothing came. Ethan started the vehicle's engine and pulled out swiftly in reverse. As soon as he had enough clearance from a row of bushes that lined the side of the driveway, he shifted the SUV into drive and went off-road into his backyard.

Ethan maneuvered the hefty SUV through a challenging course of obstacles. He swerved through trees, a swing set, a trampoline, and two vegetable gardens before arriving safely back in Caleb's backyard. But Ethan didn't stop when he got to Caleb's yard; he continued on to his neighbor's yard instead. He finally parked the getaway vehicle beside two cars covered in blue tarps. Both cars, an old Mustang convertible and a Volkswagen Bug, were restoration projects that Caleb's neighbor, Mr. Weaver, had been working on.

"Why are we stopping here?" Glenn asked.

"If we park the car in Caleb's backyard, it'll look suspicious," Ethan answered. "If we park it here, it'll look like one of Mr. Weaver's projects. We just gotta get the tarps off those cars and onto this one."

❦

A very relieved Caleb smiled when he opened the sub-basement door and saw Ethan. He smiled even more when he saw the extra laser guns and supplies.

"We also bought a new car. Parked it at Mr. Weaver's," Ethan said with a grin.

Caleb looked a little confused. But there was no confusion about one thing—the mission had been a complete success.

CHAPTER 28

THE BREACH

DESPITE HIS EXHAUSTION, Caleb worked tirelessly on outfitting the Laser Wars guns for real combat against the machines. He had been at it for over five hours straight now, hunched over the main workbench of the lab, toiling on miniscule laser components like a mad scientist. His sleepy eyes were miraculously kept open by scientific curiosity and, to a larger extent, a desire not to be murdered by robots. He knew he was in a race against time while working on the weapons. The machines would surely come; he knew that as well as Ethan. The question was when they did, would the group be with or without a means of defending themselves? Caleb was pleased with the outcome of his efforts so far—two of the previously play laser guns were now operational, giving the group a total of three legitimate weapons.

As busy and tired as he was, Caleb was lucky to have something to fully occupy his time. The rest of the group was beginning to stew in a pot of worry. Annika and Glenn thought constantly about their younger siblings. Annika couldn't bear to think that Liam, her five-year-old brother, was experiencing the same terror that they were. She also worried about her parents, but picturing a small child stuck in the middle of this hell was somehow much worse. Every bone in Annika's body cringed at the thought of her brother laying eyes on such a demonic-looking machine as a Skulley. The fear would be overwhelming, yet fear was the best-case scenario. The possibility that everyone in town was already dead was an idea that no one could even think about. The group repressed that thought. They had to. The moment they let that idea get a foothold in their minds would be the precise moment that they surrendered to the machines. At that point, all hope would be lost and they would just be waiting to die themselves.

Ethan kept himself occupied by reviewing the classified documents in the briefcase. Most of the material was highly scientific and well over his head, but he hoped to stumble across something useful. He picked up the folder of papers relating to the teleporter project. The words *"Project Vacuum: Chief Engineer—Philip Tate, PhD"* teased him. Ethan thought back about all the times his dad had made references to working on vacuums during the seemingly dull conversations between his parents at the dinner table. The whole time, a span of four years, he figured his dad was talking about vacuum cleaners—Hoovers, Dysons, Dirt Devils—not a teleportation device. Ethan couldn't help but feel like a fool. *They talked about the project right in front of me, and I was too stupid to see it.* The frustration built up inside him as he leafed through the documents for at least the seventh time. *Why didn't my dad trust me enough to tell me something about his real job?*

Ethan tossed the file folder disgustedly into the briefcase. He reclined on the couch and sighed deeply. Then another snippet of old dinner table conversation jolted its way through the synapses of his brain. He remembered exactly what his dad had said the day he finished fixing the so-called vacuums. His mom had been very excited and commented, "Really, you're all finished? I thought that might take forever." Then Ethan's dad said, "Yeah...It helps when your co-workers are pulling twenty-four-hour shifts."

Co-workers pulling twenty-four-hour shifts. Ethan never thought about it then, but his dad had to be talking about the robots. No humans at the base would ever want to work that long straight-through. And, even if they did, the military wouldn't allow it for fear of errors brought on by fatigue. Ethan realized, at that moment, that his dad had to have worked closely with the machines. He also had the grim thought that it didn't take long before those same co-workers became his father's captors, and the town's. Ethan wondered where his parents might be right now. He worried about how they were being treated. He worried especially because he knew the robots had never really been co-workers at all. They, like all machines, were created by humans and pressed into service. If the machines ever reached a high enough level of self-awareness, they would realize that they were nothing more than slaves. Then they would, logically, feel their first emotion—anger. And it made sense that they might be particularly vengeful toward Ethan's dad, since he was a chief engineer and had to be one of the main people dishing out the orders. Ethan's frustration over his dad's secret life soon vanished with a single thought: *What if my dad lied to me not because he didn't trust me with his secret, but because he was trying to protect me somehow? Maybe he never wanted me to take an interest in his job because he knew the danger involved.* Ethan's eyes slowly began to soften.

Oddly, Austin seemed to be the most well-adjusted

member of the group. He spent most of his time quietly alone in a corner chair of the room. He took to writing raptly on a notepad with a steady poker face that revealed little about his mood. Ethan had never seen Austin show such attention to any writing project in school. He was very curious about what Austin was writing, but he decided not to meddle.

∼

A few hours later, Ethan woke up with a light nasal snort. He sat up straight on the couch and looked around the room. It was five minutes after midnight and nearly everyone was passed out from exhaustion. Caleb had finally fallen to sleep, slumped over with his head resting on the hard workbench. Glenn and Austin had conked out as well. The only one else awake now was Annika, who was staring eerily up the stairwell of the sub-basement with her laser rifle in hand. It took a moment before Ethan even saw her there. She stood at the base of the stairs, still as a statue and deathly quiet. Her eyes were focused like a hawk's on the titanium door at the entrance to the sub-basement. Ethan thought for a moment that she might've been sleepwalking. He approached her slowly.

"Annika?" Ethan said softly.

Annika wheeled around sharply with her laser rifle. Ethan ducked down quickly.

"Ethan!" she said in a scolding whisper. "Don't sneak up on me like that!"

"Sorry. What are you doing?"

"It's probably nothing, but," Annika paused, dread swirling in her eyes, "I thought I heard a noise upstairs."

"When? What did it sound like?"

"I don't know. A couple minutes ago. Hard to tell because

I fell asleep and something woke me up. Coulda been a dream, though. But it sounded like…like a door sliding open. Probably just a dream, though, right?" she asked with a slight tremor in her voice.

"Probably," Ethan said, trying to be reassuring. "But we should wake the others."

Annika nodded. They roused the rest of the group from their deep slumbers. Annika then explained to them what she thought she heard—a sliding glass door opening, just like the door the group used to enter the house. Everyone gathered at the bottom of the stairwell. They stared fearfully at the metal door. Their breaths were faint and shallow as they listened for any noises from above. Yet they heard nothing but silence. Pure silence. It was the kind of odd, absolute quiet that makes you think you're hearing things, especially when you're listening for them.

"I don't hear anything," Glenn whispered. "Other than, sometimes my ears ring a little when I'm in a really quiet room. Hardly noticeable, barely anything at all, but my ears are ringing a little now."

"I hear the ringing too," Caleb said with widening eyes.

"Yeah," Annika added, gripping her laser rifle tightly.

Ethan and Austin both nodded, making it a consensus. There was definitely a subtle, high-pitched noise coming from upstairs.

"Caleb, how many laser guns do we have that work?" Ethan asked.

Caleb looked ashamed. "Annika's and two others. Then I fell asleep. I'm sorry."

"It's okay, that's good, but we'll need all—"

Ethan's words were interrupted by a distinct *thump* upstairs. Then another. Soon the thumping noises were happening constantly, and getting louder. They were the thuds, thumps, and clatter of a house being ransacked. Everyone's eyes darted tensely across the ceiling, trying to track the noises.

Ethan spoke in a haunted whisper. "Caleb, we're gonna need that last gun."

Caleb nodded quickly and scurried back to the workbench. Ethan grabbed the two guns Caleb had finished earlier and returned to the bottom of the stairs. He took one and handed the last gun to Glenn. Ethan could feel Austin's eyes on him.

Ethan looked apologetic. "I gave Glenn the gun because, you know, um—"

"Because he's a better shot than me," Austin finished. "I would've done the same thing."

Ethan nodded appreciatively.

The sounds were getting closer now. The rumblings upstairs were not only heard, but their vibrations could be felt. It seemed as if the noises were right outside the room. Ethan, Annika, and Glenn kept their laser rifles pointed on the door. Their hands trembled, even Annika's. They had to fight to keep their aim steady. Then a booming *clank* of something against the titanium door echoed down the stairs and into the sub-basement. More sounds, like those of a battering ram, soon followed…*Clank! Clank! Clank!*

The group watched the door fearfully, praying it could weather the assault. The energy of the massive blows rippled through to the floor. They could feel the vibrations through their shoes, then up their spines.

Austin fidgeted with his empty hands. "How much longer on another gun?"

"I don't know. I'm working as fast as I can," Caleb answered, frantically assembling pieces of the laser gun.

The crashes against the door were now constant and rhythmic, coming in three-second intervals. The entire sub-basement seemed to shake from the pounding. Ethan, Annika, and Glenn stood with their weapons at the bottom of the stairs as the first and last line of defense. They were waiting for the door to pop off its hinges at any moment. They were waiting for all hell to break loose and come charging down those stairs.

Then there was a pause in the banging. The upstairs became silent again. Before the group could speculate about the machines' next move, the piercing sounds of lasers blasting away at the door reverberated through the sub-basement. Then the laser fire stopped and the ramming continued. After some battering, they went back to the lasers. Ramming, lasers, ramming, lasers. The machines' method was clear—soften the door at the hinge with lasers, then hammer away until the door succumbed. Another thing was equally clear—they had no intention of quitting until they had breached the sub-basement.

"What about that door, Caleb?" Glenn asked, wiping the nervous sweat from his hands so he could get a better grip on his rifle. "What do you know about that door?"

Caleb was working furiously to assemble another laser gun. Without looking up, he rattled off quickly: "The door is four inches thick. Made of titanium. Atomic number twenty-two. Density four-point-five grams per cubic centimeter. It's got a three-thousand-degree melting point and a super-high tensile strength to weight ratio."

"That's great, Caleb…but will it hold?" Glenn pressed.

"I have no idea!" Caleb blurted.

The next slam into the door produced a loud, snapping sound. Caleb sprung out of his chair and ran frantically to the stairs. He looked at the door with the rest of the group, eyes filled with terror. The door was bending slightly inward at the top right corner.

"They broke the top lock!" Caleb yelled. "It's only a matter of time before the whole thing goes!"

"How much time?!" Austin asked.

"The first lock would be the hardest, then the sheer force on the others would increase. It won't take long now. Maybe a couple minutes." Caleb dashed back to the workbench to continue work on the laser gun.

They watched helplessly as the ramming and the lasers continued to chip away at the integrity of the door. The two remaining locks were straining terribly under the heat of the lasers and the blunt force of the robots' repeated blows. The door bowed further inward at the top. The crack enabled the group to hear the machines milling around in a frenzy above them.

Then the second lock gave way with a *snap!* The door bent further down at the hinge. They could now do more than hear the robots on the other side of the door; they could *see* them as well. Several brightly lit crimson eyeballs darted feverishly back and forth behind the opening. The intense red light from the robots' eyes illuminated their heads in the darkness, and the group made the disturbing observation that they all had black metallic skulls. Two machines peeked through the gap in the door and looked down the stairs, into the sub-basement. They had *eager smiles* on their faces, black teeth gleaming in the blood-red glow. The team ducked behind the stairwell to get out of the machines' sight.

"They're all Skulleys...We gotta hit them now before they break in," Annika said as she started back to the base of the stairs.

"No!" Ethan yelled, putting an arm out, holding her back. "We'll never beat them with brute force. We have to try to trick them, get the element of surprise. It's our only chance."

"How?" Austin asked. "They're too smart."

"Yes, but we can use that to our advantage," Ethan said. "What's the biggest reason the smartest person in the room ever loses at anything? They underestimate their opponents. Just like the machines underestimate us."

"So what's the move?" Annika asked.

Ethan looked around the room and took stock of the surroundings. "We'll set up a big barricade on the far side of the room. Caleb and Austin hide behind that barricade with the fake laser rifles. When the machines come down, they each fire two fake guns at them, make them think we've all taken cover behind the barricade. When they get hit by the blue lasers and find out they're harmless, they'll get overconfident. Then when they all come in and make their charge, me, you, and Glenn pop out from the opposite side and shoot them from behind with the real weapons. The ones they don't know we have."

"So you're asking me to be a decoy?" Austin muttered.

Ethan stared pleadingly at his former bully. "I am…But remember, my best friend will be beside you too," he said, then looked at Caleb.

Caleb nodded as confidently as he could.

No one in the group seemed terribly excited about Ethan's idea—letting the Skulleys come in freely before firing on them—but there were no better alternatives available. Making a stand at the bottom of the stairs would simply give the machines the high ground, a major no-no in the realm of military tactics. The robots would be shooting down upon the group, like shooting fish in a barrel.

"All right, Ethan…Just don't miss," Austin said.

"They won't," Caleb said.

Ethan and Annika nodded gratefully.

The group began scooting large metal workbenches toward the far corner of the room. They lined four of them up on their sides and tossed anything solid they could find on top of them. The result was a veritable mini-bunker consisting of steel workbenches, shelves, chairs, and anything else they thought might be somewhat useful in stopping an all-out laser assault.

Then they slid the couch to the opposite corner of the room. It was the poor man's bunker. They knew the wood, springs, and stuffing inside the couch wouldn't offer much in the way of protection, but all they wanted was a hiding place for Ethan, Annika, and Glenn until the machines could be distracted.

Suddenly the lights flickered, then went out entirely.

"They cut the power!" Caleb shouted.

The group reached out their hands and tried to feel their way around the room. They scurried aimlessly, like blind mice. Then the inevitable happened. The last lock on the door snapped. The heavy-duty, titanium sub-basement door surrendered to the beating and popped off its hinge. It tumbled down the stairs, clanking loudly all the way until it slammed into the wall at the bottom.

Caleb slinked away to the back wall of the room. He groped around in the darkness until he found what he was looking for, then pulled the lever on an emergency electric generator his dad kept hooked up near the computers. A few auxiliary lights lit up.

"Grab the guns and take cover!" Ethan yelled.

The group scrambled and found their laser guns, then they

took shelter behind their bunkers. They all hunkered down low. Caleb and Austin each found a couple gaps they could aim their rifles from behind the barricade of office furniture. On the opposite side of the room, Ethan, Annika, and Glenn waited for the time to strike from behind the couch.

With the generator powering only a few lights, the sub-basement was much dimmer now. The group waited with their hearts beating through their chests. Then it began. The first sight of the machines' descent into the sub-basement came in the form of ominous, angular shadows on the concrete wall at the top of the stairs. The shadows were all jumbled together. It was impossible to tell exactly how many there were, but there were definitely more robots up there than they had faced on the Dark Highway. Ethan wondered how many machines there were and how they might be different, given the twenty-plus hours they'd had to evolve since that battle.

Ethan had one question answered right away as the first robot stepped into view. The machine, literally, *stepped* into view. They watched in awe and horror as one metal skeletal foot after another began their slow march down the stairs. Then their wiry metal legs came into view. They operated exactly like a human's, swiveling at the hip and bending at the knee. It became apparent that twenty hours was more than enough time for the machines to significantly upgrade their method of movement.

Three robots were walking down the stairs now at a slow, methodical pace. Then five. Then seven. Seven Skulleys in total. The first one in the line made it to the bottom of the steps. It held up its laser weapons and scanned the room menacingly back and forth with its intense blood-red eyes. It took a couple of steps inside the sub-basement, then waited for the rest of its brethren to descend the stairs. Before long, all seven robots were in the sub-basement. They spotted the obvious barricade, Caleb and Austin's, in the far corner of the room about forty feet away. Five of the machines began to walk slowly toward it with their laser weapons out and ready to fire. The other two broke off and explored the opposite direction.

Annika peeked around the couch. She whispered, "Two of them are coming this way."

"What's taking them so long?" Glenn asked.

"Just give them a few more seconds," Ethan said, trying to sound confident, though he knew something had to be wrong.

Caleb was beginning to hyperventilate. Every step that brought the machines closer made his spastic breathing worse. He was panicking, completely frozen with fear. His shaky hands couldn't even hold one rifle, let alone the two he was responsible for shooting.

Austin yanked Caleb by the shirt, desperately trying to bring him out of his stupor. "Caleb, we need you. You can do this! One, two, three!"

Austin began firing his two useless laser guns at the Skulleys. To his relief, Caleb joined him in the decoy assault. The five robots quickly realized the lasers were inflicting no damage and began to fire at will. The other two robots turned away from the couch at the last moment and joined the others in firing away at the barricade. The lasers pounded the make-shift barrier, blasting off chunks of metal debris into the air. Austin and Caleb stopped firing. There was no escape plan. All they could do was get as low to the ground as possible behind the barricade and hope that Ethan's scheme would work.

All of the Skulleys were devoting their full attention and firepower to Austin and Caleb. Ethan, Annika, and Glenn wasted no time. They popped up from behind the couch and fired a barrage of lasers at the machines. The lethal red pulses pierced quarter-sized holes into their metal bodies and heads. Before the machines knew what had hit them, five of the seven were already crumpled into a heap on the floor. The two remaining robots whirled around and charged at them, raising their laser weapons. Ethan and Glenn fired first, blasting away at the machines' bodies, but failing to deliver the fatal headshots. The machines were just about to open fire, when Annika double-tapped her trigger and nailed both of them right between the eyes. The robots twitched and thrashed violently in death as they tumbled awkwardly to the ground. One of the Skulley's arms splayed out and landed on top of Ethan's foot. It was still twitching. He kicked it away disgustedly, and put another laser through its head for good measure.

"Annika, Glenn, watch the stairs," Ethan said as he ran over to the barricade. "Caleb, Austin?!"

There was no response.

Ethan pulled off a couple workbenches that were riddled with holes. His face instantly turned pale when he saw some blood streaked across the back of one of them. Underneath the pile, he found Austin on top of Caleb. Austin rolled off of him, clutching his bloodied upper arm. A laser had gashed a three-inch diagonal cut across it.

"Austin, are you all right?" Ethan asked.

"Yeah, just nicked me. Burns more than anything," Austin said, gritting his teeth.

Caleb stood up. He extended his hand and helped Austin to his feet. Caleb stared at Austin with an odd expression. It was a look of gratitude. "The lasers were getting closer and closer," he said, still dazed. "I didn't see it, but Austin did. He pulled me out of the way. The laser hit his arm, instead of my head...Thank you, Austin...You saved my life."

Austin nodded casually. "No problem...But it's your turn next time," he said with a grin.

"We gotta get outta here now," Annika said as she kept watch on the entrance to the fully exposed sub-basement.

"Where do we go?" Caleb asked.

"Our school has a basement," Glenn said. "They have food, basic medical supplies. Maybe we could go there, chain all the doors."

"We can't stay in town. Soon the machines will own the place, if they don't already," Ethan said. "And if they broke in here, they'll have no problem breaking in there."

"Then where?" Glenn asked.

"We need to get to the woods, use the terrain against them for as long as we can." Ethan paused for a beat, then added, "We should try to get to Bravo Fort."

Glenn cocked his head. "Are you serious?"

"Yes, think about it. We built that fort out of steel—it's strong. It was built on high ground, we could see them coming. And we know the woods around that area better than anyone, man or machine."

"I think I could figure out how to put a weapon in the laser turret," Caleb said.

Glenn slowly nodded in agreement. Austin smiled as he held a ripped undershirt tightly up to his arm to stem the flow of blood.

"Bravo Fort it is," Austin said.

CHAPTER 29

THE ESCAPE TO BRAVO FORT

ETHAN AND ANNIKA had their fingers pressed tautly on rifle triggers as they led the group upstairs out of the sub-basement. No one had heard any more sounds in the house, but they were taking nothing for granted. Glenn and Caleb were loaded down with duffel bags full of supplies, including some souvenirs from the robot carnage—metal body parts with a few undamaged laser weapons still attached. Austin pitched in and carried a heavy load himself, ignoring the ache in his arm and the blood that was wicking through the undershirt he had tied to it as a quick field dressing.

Ethan shined a light on Austin's arm. "We have a first-aid kit in the SUV. And I can take one of your duffel bags."

"No, thanks. I got it," Austin replied. "You just be ready with the gun."

The group made it to the sliding glass door in the basement. It was wide open now. A breeze began to kick up. The silence in the room was interrupted by the eerie jingle of a wind chime on the patio. Ethan and Annika peeked outside and looked across into Mr. Weaver's backyard. Their getaway vehicle was still there under the tarps.

"All clear," Annika said.

"Okay, let's go," Ethan whispered.

The group walked briskly through the yard and made it to the vehicle. They quickly yanked the tarps off. Everyone stuffed the gear in the back as fast as they could and piled inside the SUV. Ethan got behind the wheel and locked the doors immediately. He drove through the backyard to the front yard and pulled onto the street. Before he was even one block away from Caleb's house, a light on the dashboard caught his attention. He looked down at the indicator panel. His face instantly turned pallid.

"We're almost out of gas," Ethan said with a lump in his throat. "I was so busy making sure we got back quick, without being seen, I forgot to check the gas."

"Our fort's not that far away," Austin said as he rummaged through the first-aid kit.

Despite being in the midst of fleeing from hostile, havoc-wreaking robots in a vehicle running on fumes, one thought zipped through Ethan's mind: Austin just called the fort, "*Our fort.*"

"Yeah, maybe we can make it," Caleb said. "How empty is it?"

"As empty as it gets."

"Go to the gas station behind Judy's Diner," Annika said. "It's got the best cover."

"Right," Ethan agreed.

There were only three gas stations in the entire town. Two were located right off Main Street that cut through the center of the town. They were both brightly lit up at night and visible from multiple directions at long distances. Going there was out of the question. The other one, Annika's suggestion, was tucked away behind Judy's Diner, away from all of the larger streets. It was their only prudent choice.

Ethan turned onto a side road and drove into the parking lot of the "Pump-N-Go" gas station and convenience store. He pulled the SUV slowly alongside a gas pump and stopped. Annika opened up the sunroof and popped out with her laser rifle. She conducted a vigilant, 360-degree sweep of the perimeter.

"Looks clear," Annika said.

Ethan gave a quick nod. "All right, let's make this fast."

Everyone exited the vehicle, except Annika. She stayed in the SUV, standing up through the sunroof, keeping a lookout over the surroundings with her laser rifle on standby. Austin, Glenn, and Caleb kept guard from behind the SUV. Ethan pulled the nozzle from the pump, pressed the start button, and squeezed the handle. Nothing happened. He pressed the start button and squeezed the handle again, but the gas would not flow.

Ethan racked the nozzle. "The pumps are off. We gotta go inside and turn them on."

"I'll do it," Caleb said.

"I'll go with you," Glenn offered.

Caleb tried to open the door of the convenience store, but it was locked.

"Stand back," Glenn said as he raised his laser rifle, aiming for the lock. Caleb moved back. Glenn fired a laser, and sparks flew everywhere. Only a smoldering hole from where the lock had been remained. Glenn opened the door. "After you," he said with a jokey politeness.

Once inside the store, Caleb immediately went behind the counter to look for the control switch for the gas pumps outside. Glenn picked up a shopping basket and headed for one of the aisles to pick up some better first-aid supplies.

"Found it!" Caleb blurted as he pulled a switch. He smiled mischievously and leaned in toward a microphone behind the counter that was used to communicate with customers through speakers at the gas pumps outside. "Pump three, you're all ready. Please pay inside when you're done." He looked at Glenn, snickered, then added, "I always wanted to do that."

Glenn rolled his eyes and chuckled. "A hundred and eighty IQ and you always wanted to play gas station attendant?"

"It's kinda cool," Caleb said with a bashful smile.

Glenn smiled back and shook his head. "I got all the first-aid stuff. Let's get outta here."

Caleb and Glenn left the convenience store and headed back to the vehicle. Ethan was filling up the gas tank. Glenn held up the shopping basket full of first-aid supplies. "I got some powerful antiseptics and real bandages."

"Thanks," Austin said.

"I'll get it," Caleb insisted. "It's the least I can do. That gash on your arm could've been through my head...Plus, for about three months when I was five, I really wanted to be a doctor. I used to practice bandaging my mom."

Austin smiled appreciatively until Caleb began to apply the antiseptic. The medicine stung and instantly wiped away his smile. Ethan finished fueling the vehicle just as Caleb finished bandaging Austin's arm.

They boarded the SUV. As Ethan started the engine and was about to pull out, Annika spotted something outside the convenience store that caught her attention. "Ethan, wait!"

"What?! What is it?!" Ethan reacted.

"Pull over there," she said, pointing to the right of the store. "By the propane tanks."

The convenience store had a large metal cage full of propane tanks that were sold to people to use for their grills. They were intended to be used as a heat source for grilling hot dogs, hamburgers, and steaks. But Annika had a different idea.

"Why?" Ethan asked.

"If we're going to make our stand at the fort, some propane tanks will come in handy. You know…propane tanks, when shot by lasers, turn into bombs. And, right now, we need all the bombs we can get."

Caleb beamed. "Annika, you're a genius!"

Ethan nodded at her and smiled. "That's a great idea. I'll keep the engine running. We gotta hurry, though."

The group loaded as many propane tanks as they could into the already overstuffed SUV. By the time they were finished, there were tanks everywhere. They managed to fit a dozen inside by jamming them into the back storage compartment and having everyone but the driver sit with a tank on their lap.

Ethan pulled the SUV out of the gas station. He turned onto a back street that ran parallel to Main Street. The plan was to stay off Main Street as long as possible, though eventually they would need to travel that road for a short while to make it to the Dark Highway. There was no other access point.

They drove slowly and cautiously down the back street. Everyone's eyes were peeled, scanning the road meticulously forward and backward. As they got closer to Main Street, a worried look quickly overcame Annika. "Guys, I just thought of a slight downside to my idea about the propane tanks."

"What?" Ethan asked.

"Promise not to take the genius comment back, Caleb?"

"Promise."

Annika forced a deep breath and held it for a moment. "Well, the good news is if we make it to the fort, we'll have a dozen explosives to use against the machines," she said, sounding upbeat. Annika paused for a second, then sounded decidedly less upbeat. "The bad news is, we're pretty much riding inside a bomb now. If the machines intercept us, and fire at basically any part of this SUV, we're toast."

An ominous wave of silence rippled through the van. Throats tightened. Breaths were shallow and jittery.

"It's still a good idea," Ethan said. "We just gotta hope we don't run into any machines before we get to the fort...We won't. I'm sure we won't," he said, trying to sound calm, even though his sweaty hands were gripped to the steering wheel like a tightly wound vise.

Suddenly, two Skulleys leaped into the middle of the road, less than a couple hundred feet away, directly in front of them. They raised their laser weapons swiftly and took aim.

"Ethan, look out!" Annika screamed. "They're gonna fire!"

"There's nowhere to turn off!" Ethan yelled. "I can't stop now...I gotta speed up and try to ram them. Hold on!"

Everyone in the vehicle grabbed on to the nearest thing they could for comfort and support. Ironically, for everyone except Ethan, that object was a large, extremely flammable propane tank. Caleb looked at the incendiary device he was hugging and winced. The machines opened fire with a volley of lasers. They whizzed by the vehicle's windows, narrowly missing the front windshield. Before the robots could fire again, Ethan plowed the SUV straight into them. The loud, grinding sound of robots churning between the undercarriage of the vehicle and the asphalt of the road echoed through the cabin. The group looked through the back window and found a stream of sparks shooting out from behind, along with an assortment of robotic parts. Everyone gulped a gigantic breath of relief.

"God, that was close," Glenn said.

"Too close," Ethan added, wiping the sweat from his forehead. He paused at the intersection to collect himself for a moment, then finally turned onto Main Street.

"What's that up there?" Annika asked, pointing straight ahead in the road, off in the distance. "Do you see those lights?"

About a half mile away, there were several sets of lights clustered together. As Ethan drove closer, they realized that the lights were from four jeeps blocking the entrance to the Dark Highway. Ethan stopped the SUV on the side of the road and turned off the headlights. They watched the jeeps carefully. The group was part hopeful, part terrified. Ethan picked up the binoculars and looked through the window. Annika peered through the scope of her laser rifle. They stared intensely at the formation of jeeps, hoping desperately to see some evidence that their occupants were human.

"Ethan, can you tell *who* or *what* is inside those jeeps?" Austin asked.

"It's hard to see. The headlights are blinding."

"I can't see anything either. Too bright," Annika said in frustration, lowering her rifle.

"Wait," Ethan blurted. He adjusted a couple knobs on the binoculars to focus the image. "Something's moving… Someone, something is walking in front of the lights."

Annika hurried and raised her rifle again. She squinted through the scope.

"Well, which one is it?" Austin questioned. *"Someone* or *something?"*

The dark figure passed in front of the headlights of all four jeeps. The lights flickered as the silhouetted, mysterious entity made its way from one side to the other. The figure was humanoid in appearance, but that didn't mean it was human. The Skulleys, from that distance in that lighting, would probably look just as human.

"I can't tell," Ethan said with dread in his voice.

"We gotta try to get closer, see who they are," Glenn said. "They could be soldiers. They could be the rescue team."

"And what if they're not?" Austin asked. "Are we really gonna take on four jeeps full of machines while riding inside a propane bomb on wheels?"

Annika's eyes instantly widened at Austin's comment. "We need to get the tanks outta here, right now!" she said. Annika opened her door and stepped outside.

Ethan turned to her sharply. "Annika, no! We don't have time for that now!"

"Well we won't have time for it later! Toss out your tanks. I'm gonna get the ones from the back."

Ethan sighed in defeat and began to get out of the vehicle to help her. Inches before his foot hit the ground, he saw all four jeeps heading straight for them. "Annika, get back inside... They're coming!"

Annika looked up and saw the jeeps zooming toward them. She darted back inside the SUV and closed the door. The group watched in horror as the jeeps rapidly closed the distance between them. Ethan focused his binoculars on the speeding vehicles. They were now close enough that he could see the occupants silhouetted by the streetlights behind them.

Ethan's face turned pale, and his next breath came in the form of a startled *gasp*. There was no mistaking the angular jaw and wiry neck of the driver. There were no soldiers, no rescue teams, no humans at all on board. They were all machines.

"They're all Skulleys," Ethan said, his voice grim.

"We gotta turn this thing around and make a run for it!" Glenn yelled.

Ethan was slow to react. He just sat there and watched the machines as they got closer and closer. He appeared frozen, like a deer in the headlights to the others, but an idea was simmering in his mind. A crazy idea.

"Ethan, what are you doing? Move it!" Austin shouted.

"No," Ethan said simply.

Annika couldn't believe her ears. "What do you mean, 'no,' Ethan?!"

"They're too fast and too close. All they gotta do is shoot the van and we're all goners…We have to make them not want to shoot us."

"What are you talking about?!" Annika yelled. "Drive… Now!"

Ethan shook his head, even though the machines in the jeeps were almost upon them. He turned around and looked in the back seat. "Everyone get down…Caleb, hand me that robot back there. The one that's still got arms on it."

"You've got to be kidding," Caleb said, realizing what Ethan was planning to do.

"I'm not…Hurry."

Caleb handed Ethan the partial upper torso of a robot that had been torn apart by lasers in the battle in the sub-basement. Ethan reclined the seat back, slouched down, and held the robot's hole-riddled upper half on his lap. He angled the machine's head in a way so that the hole blasted through it couldn't be seen from the window. Then he placed the machine's hands on the steering wheel, to make it look like the robot was driving. Annika rolled her eyes at the sight of it before crouching down on the floorboard in front of her seat. Ethan tossed a blanket on top of her to keep her hidden.

"This is a bad idea," Austin said, slinking down in the back seat.

"The worst," Glenn added.

"The moment this goes bad, I'm taking out one of those Skulleys," Annika said as she delicately poked her sniper rifle out from underneath her blanket and aimed it at the driver's side window.

"Here they come," Ethan said. "If they don't buy it, start shooting at them through the windows, distract them while I put it in reverse."

"If they don't buy it, we're doomed," Glenn said.

The jeeps surrounded the SUV and stopped. There were four robots in each jeep. Two of the machines got out and approached Ethan's window. The group watched from their crouched positions as the machines slowly scanned their hateful crimson eyes back and forth over the vehicle.

Ethan rolled down the window halfway and turned the headlights back on because he thought it would look suspicious if he didn't. He held his breath with the rest of the group as he held the dead, dismembered robot up as steadily as he could. The machines stared at the robot for an excruciatingly long, nerve-racking moment. Ethan didn't know what to do. The tension was killing him. He was worried the machines weren't falling for the trick because the robot he was holding hadn't moved. Ethan decided he needed to animate the robot.

In a move spurred by panic, he grabbed one of the robot's arms and *waved* to the other machines.

Ethan quickly put the robotic arm back on the steering wheel and winced in frustration, apprehension, and disgust. He couldn't believe he'd just waved to them. *Robots don't wave to each other. I'm such an idiot...And a dead idiot soon.* He fully expected the machines to open fire at any second.

"Be ready to shoot," Ethan whispered to Annika.

Annika had the Skulley closest to the window in her sights. She had her finger tightly on the trigger, ready to fire at a nano-second's notice.

The two machines looked at each other, then back at the robot Ethan was holding. After another long moment of eye-balling, one of them motioned ahead, giving them permission to pass. Ethan couldn't believe his eyes. The plan had worked. He rolled the window up as fast as he could. He peeked his head over the dashboard just enough to see and drove right past the four jeeps that carried a total of sixteen fearsome Skulleys. It was a miracle. An absolute miracle. The celebration soon began.

"I can't believe you did that!" Glenn shouted through a nervous chuckle. "I can't believe it worked! I can't believe we're not dead!"

Annika broke into a laugh. "I can't believe you waved to them. That was crazy. I thought it was over right then and there. I was so close to taking the shot, you have no idea."

Austin shook his head and smiled. "You got some serious guts, Ethan."

Ethan tried to compose himself. His hands were still trembling as he handled the steering wheel. "Sorry I put you all through that, but it was the only thing I could think of."

THE FATAL ERROR | 229

"Well, next time, think of something else…'cause I think I need a diaper," Caleb joked.

While everyone was laughing at Caleb's silliness, one of the Skulleys looked back at the SUV as it drove under a bright streetlight. The light illuminated the rear bumper of the vehicle. Something stuck on the bumper glistened and caught the eye of the robot. Its eyes zoomed in and focused on the mysterious object. The machine's eyes burned furiously, like red-hot embers. It belted out a shrill scream more terrifying than any banshee in a horror movie. The object it saw was the torn off, mangled arm of a fellow machine, still clutching tenaciously to the back bumper from when Ethan had run over it.

"They're following us!" Ethan exclaimed, looking through the rearview mirror. "They're coming in fast!"

Everyone spun around and looked through the back window. Their worst fears were confirmed. The machines were in breakneck pursuit of them, closing the gap fast. Ethan slammed his foot on the gas pedal and barreled down the road toward the intersection.

"Take a right on the Dark Highway!" Annika shouted.

"No! They have us outgunned," Glenn countered. "That's exactly where they want us, out in the open on the highway."

"They might have us outgunned, but they don't know what we're carrying," Annika said with a little smile. "Take the right turn, Ethan. They'll all be lined up, vulnerable, when they take that turn to follow us."

"Okay," Ethan said, knowing exactly what Annika had in mind.

Annika opened the sunroof. "Be ready to pass me your propane tanks as soon as we hit the turn."

Ethan made it to the intersection and took a hard, swerving

right turn just before the machines opened fire. Their lasers streaked by the rear windows, missing only by inches. That turn was their last evasive maneuver. The group had no more than a few seconds before the robots would round the corner and unleash the full force of their fury.

Annika had to act quickly. She popped up through the sunroof with her propane tank, and shoved it as hard as she could off the roof. It hit the ground with a *clank* and rolled toward the intersection. Austin handed her another propane tank and she did the same thing. Then she launched the ones that Caleb and Glenn gave her. Four propane tanks were rolling into the intersection when the machines arrived. Annika grabbed her laser rifle and took aim. The streetlamps gave her more than plenty of light to see the white-painted tanks. She could've made the shot by moonlight alone.

Annika waited until the machines made the turn, then she fired. A massive chain of explosions sent a wall of fire skyrocketing into the air. Annika ducked back into the SUV for cover from the intense heat wave. Ethan kept the gas pedal pinned to the floor. Everyone in the group looked back and saw four jeeps overturned and ablaze. Secondary explosions from the gas tanks tore the jeeps and their mechanical occupants to bits. Not a single machine had been spared.

Everyone cheered ecstatically, but the celebration was short-lived. It had been only two days, yet every time they encountered the machines, they had multiplied, not only in number, but in strength, intelligence, and sophistication as well. As they motored down the Dark Highway, then turned off into the woods toward their fort, they all knew their battles with the Skulleys would only get worse.

CHAPTER 30

THE WATCHER

ETHAN PARKED THE SUV beside the Bravo Fort a little after two o'clock in the morning. Everyone exited the vehicle and took a look around. A robust moonlight streaked though the trees that eerily reminded them of pale laser beams. But the area appeared secure. The only sounds were some chirping crickets and the occasional rustle of small nocturnal animals in the brush.

Ethan eyed the fort with pride and patted the sturdy steel door like an old friend. He sure was glad they hadn't skimped on the materials to build the Bravo Fort that summer after fifth grade. He always felt lucky that his dad had been onboard with their idea of creating a fort that was truly military-grade, even though it would be just for Laser Wars games. But now, with the fort serving as their real-life safe house in anything but a game, he couldn't fight the feeling that his dad might've been looking ahead a few moves all along.

Caleb entered the passcode into the keypad. The door unlocked, and everyone began hauling supplies into their new residence. Duffel bags full of survival sundries, robot parts, and the eight remaining propane tanks were soon all lined up against one side of a wall.

Annika and Glenn had never been inside the Bravo Team fort before. They stared at it in awe, marveling over its engineering and craftsmanship.

"This is unbelievable," Annika said in a daze. "I knew you guys had a good fort, but this is amazing…Did you really do all this in just one summer?"

"Just one summer…We were a great team once," Ethan said with a nostalgic smile. He glanced at Austin and noticed a look of remorse in his eyes. "But we're an even better team now…We're Team Blackwoods."

Austin nodded appreciatively. "You guys wanna give them the tour?"

"Absolutely," Ethan said proudly.

Ethan and Caleb proceeded to give Annika and Glenn a quick tour of their fort. They showed them the command and control computers and the war room on the main level. Then they visited the trenched walkway and laser turret in the upstairs loft. Finally, they descended into the basement to see the supply depot, power generators, and secret escape passage.

Annika shook her head and smiled as she looked at the entrance to the secret passage hidden behind one of the power generators. "I wondered how you guys got behind us that one game."

"Yeah, that was a good one," Caleb snickered.

After the tour, everyone convened in the main level and spread out their sleeping bags. Caleb set up all the laser chargers, so the entire fort was within the critical distance of their electronic signals. The group wasn't sure if the machines were still trying, or even able, to abduct them now, but they were taking every precaution just in case. They had no intention of going to sleep and risk waking up as the Skulleys' prisoners, locked in a cage God-knows-where.

Just as Ethan had nestled his head into the softest part of his sleeping bag, a thought sprang his eyes wide open. Everyone was beyond the point of exhaustion, but there was still one thing they needed to do that couldn't wait until morning.

Ethan turned on the lights. "We gotta get the laser turret from Delta fort and bring it here. We're gonna need them both. I only need one other person to—"

"I'll go with you," Austin volunteered before anyone else could offer.

"Okay," Ethan said, surprised that Austin was so eager to go with him.

Ethan and Austin grabbed their laser rifles, a toolbox, a couple flashlights, and one set of night-vision goggles, leaving the remaining pair behind in case the others needed it. Austin picked up one additional item before he headed for the door. He retrieved the framed picture of the Bravo Team that was lying cracked on the floor in the corner. Ethan had tossed the frame to the ground in disgust that fateful day when Austin drummed him off the team and banished him from the fort. It seemed like that all happened ages ago, though it was scarcely more than two days. Austin hung the picture back up on the wall and nodded at Ethan with a faint smile. Ethan nodded back and almost became numb as he thought about how much his world had changed over the last forty-eight hours.

"There's a metal ladder sitting against the left side of the fort," Glenn said. "That's the only way up to the laser turret." He smiled sarcastically, then said, "I know, I know...We're not as cool as you guys with your indoor ladders, fancy computers, and escape passages."

Ethan and Austin smiled for a moment, but the tension of the task ahead quickly stiffened their faces. Ethan unlocked the door and pulled it open. By now their eyes had adjusted to the light inside the fort, so the darkness outside looked like a black hole in deep space.

"Be careful, guys," Annika said, talking to both of them but looking only at Ethan.

"We will," Ethan said.

They disappeared into the night.

҈

Ethan and Austin quietly slipped into the SUV. Ethan took the driver's seat; Austin rode shotgun.

"I'm gonna leave the headlights off, try not to attract much attention," Ethan said.

"Good idea…Here, take these." Austin held up the night-vision goggles.

"No thanks. You can use them."

Austin looked confused. "But you're driving."

"Yeah…But the moon's bright enough tonight. I won't need them."

Austin had his doubts, but he put on the goggles without further questioning.

Ethan drove slowly through the woods toward the Delta Team fort. True to his claim, no headlights or night-vision equipment were necessary. Austin watched in amazement as Ethan steered clear of objects by moonlight and memory alone. Ethan had gone back and forth from Bravo to Delta base so many times as a scout in their Laser Wars games that he was practically on autopilot even in the dark. It was then that his mind drifted to a question that had been rolling around in his head ever since he'd left Austin's house. Ethan could not restrain himself. The words escaped his tense lips like they had a mind of their own.

"Austin…Why did you throw the picture of your dad and brother in the trash?"

Austin remained silent for a long while. Ethan began to get anxious, second-guessing the wisdom of asking the question. He wished he could somehow suck the words back into his mouth. All the work it took to get on Austin's good side, ruined by one idiotic, nosy question. Ethan wanted to kick himself.

"I'm sorry. You don't have to answer that. It's none of my business."

After a few more awkward, silent moments, Austin spoke quietly. "Every time the three of us get together…me, my brother, and my dad…I'm the one that always takes the picture." Austin stared straight ahead through the window and shook his head. "Not a selfie of all of us, just the two of them…Every single time."

Ethan glanced at Austin for a fleeting second. He sensed that Austin had a lot left to say, so he decided to be quiet and not interrupt the confessional.

"My dad would do anything to make me exactly like my brother," Austin continued. "Happiest day of his life was when my brother was born. Second happiest was when my brother enrolled in the military academy." He sighed deeply. "I love my brother, though. It's not his fault he's just like my dad…That's who I've been writing to. I have a lot of things I wanted to tell my brother but never had the courage to say.

I guess being at death's door has a way of making you braver than you've ever been...Still not brave enough to write my dad, though."

Ethan wasn't exactly sure what to say to Austin in this breakthrough moment, but the words somehow came out. "Austin, if your dad could see you now, I know he'd be proud."

Austin smiled thankfully at Ethan, but he shook his head in disagreement. "No, he wouldn't. He'd be able to tell right away that *you're* the real leader of this group. He'd make damn sure I knew he was disappointed in me."

"That can't be true. You took a laser in the arm. You saved Caleb's life. I'm sure he'd be proud of that."

"All he would see is that I allowed myself to be the decoy in the sub-basement, that I wasn't a part of the attack...that I didn't *seize the initiative,* as he calls it." Austin paused for a moment. Then with a hitch in his voice, he added, "I'm sorry I treated you so bad, Ethan...I was bullied into bullying you."

Those were the words Ethan had hoped to hear for two years. Emotions besieged him, and, for a second, he wished that he would've taken the night-vision goggles so they could mask his incoming tears. Then he realized that maybe Austin's ability to hide his own eyes behind the goggles was what made this moment possible.

Ethan shrugged, tried to play it down, keep his voice strong. "It's no big deal, especially now." Then he wiped away a tear that was just about to roll down his cheek.

"But it is," Austin insisted. "You have a great dad, Ethan. Janitor or chief scientist, it never mattered. I was always jealous of what you had. *So* jealous." He drew a deep breath, exhaled it slowly, painfully. "I'm sorry your last words to him were angry. I'm sorry that was because of me, because I wasn't

brave enough to ever make a stand. But I promise you this…
I'll do everything I possibly can to help you see him again."

Ethan nodded. It was all he could do. He was completely
choked up and couldn't speak now even if he knew all the
right words to say. The tear that Ethan had taken preemptive
action to get rid of moments ago now had reinforcements.
He wiped away one, but another streamed down the opposite
cheek.

"There's more to the story, Ethan, but I don't think I'll
ever tell it. Not to anyone." Austin paused for a long beat,
then continued, "I think that's probably how it is with everyone eventually. You live long enough, you have things you
can't talk about with anyone. Mostly adults, but sometimes
fourteen-year-olds. The really unlucky ones, even younger, I
guess…Does that make any sense?"

Ethan was desperately curious but resolved to not ask. He
nodded. "It does."

"You wanna know the saddest part about my dad being
gone?"

"What's that?"

"The saddest part is that I'm not really that sad."

Austin lifted his night-vision goggles up to his forehead.
Ethan glanced over at his former bully and caught him rubbing his eyes. Austin quickly slid the goggles back down and
scanned the area through the windows. "I don't see any sign of
the machines," he said, abruptly changing the topic.

"Good…We're almost there," Ethan added, allowing
Austin a dignified exit.

⁌

Ethan parked the SUV beside the Delta Fort. It was about three-quarters the length of the Bravo Fort, but it was all one level and nowhere near as technologically or architecturally impressive. The laser turret was mounted on the roof on the left side of the structure. They found the ladder that Glenn had mentioned beside the wall on the ground. Ethan propped it up on the side of the fort.

"If you wanna keep lookout, I'll go up and get the turret," Austin said.

"What about your arm?"

"Aww, it's just a scratch."

"Okay, then."

It made good sense that Austin, if his arm was up to the task, be the one to go up and bring the laser down since he was quite a bit larger than Ethan. It made equally good sense that Ethan, the better marksman, stay behind for defensive purposes. Austin handed Ethan the night-vision goggles, then he ascended the ladder with the toolbox. Ethan held the ladder steady with his foot and surveyed the surroundings with his hands firmly clutching his laser rifle. The artificial green light produced by the night-vision goggles combined with the moonlight to give a ghostly appearance to the forest. The resulting visual was unsettling, even without spotting any machines.

When Austin got to the top of the fort, he set the toolbox on the roof and retrieved a small flashlight from his pocket. He held the light in his mouth and quickly went to work, first unplugging the laser turret from its power supply, then rapidly unscrewing bolts and detaching cables and wires. As he unscrewed the last bolt from the turret, a sharp, shrill sound pierced the woods. There were no pulses or pauses, just one long, continuous sound. Austin nearly dropped the laser turret from the jolt of the harsh noise.

"What's that?" Austin asked.

"I don't know. I don't see anything."

Ethan wheeled around and scoured the area. He saw nothing. Finally, there was nowhere else to look but up. Ethan peered above a patch of tall spruce trees and saw an intense laser beam projecting skyward out of the northeast. The radiant, neon violet beam slammed into the force field. The barrier lit up into a brilliant shade of blue and rippled like waves in a hurricane from where the laser made impact. Fierce bolts of electricity shot out in all directions through it, as if the force field were fighting back.

"The laser's coming from the research facility," Ethan said. "I think the machines are trying to knock out the force field."

Suddenly, the massive laser ceased firing and the force field slowly reverted to its original form. The bolts of electricity became fewer and less intense until they stopped altogether.

"The force field held!" Austin cheered, taking joy in the machines' failure. Ethan cracked a satisfied smile, too. But their enthusiasm quickly evaporated as they thought about what that meant for them—that they were still stuck inside the barrier with the machines.

Ethan exhaled a somber sigh. "We should get back now."

"Yeah," Austin agreed, as the last trace of a smile vanished from his face.

Ethan and Austin returned to the Bravo Fort, stowed away the second laser turret, and climbed up into the loft with the others. Annika and Glenn were keeping guard, laser rifles shouldered, gazing deeply into the dark woods that were only getting darker as a band of thick clouds snuffed out the moonlight. Caleb was already tinkering around with the first laser turret and making good progress, despite working by the light of a lone, shaky flashlight.

"Did you guys see that laser?" Ethan asked.

"How could we have missed it?" Annika quipped, peering through her rifle scope into the tree line with her signature steady gaze.

"I know we're tired, and it'll be harder to see, but I think we should set the propane tanks out tonight."

"I think we might wanna wait on that, Ethan," Annika said in a grim voice. "I see something out there…looks like a pair of red eyes."

Caleb shut his flashlight off immediately and took cover behind the wall of the loft. Ethan and Austin each grabbed a set of binoculars and peeked out through the gaps in the wall, into the pitch-black, forbidding forest.

"Forty-five degrees northeast…about six hundred yards out," Annika said through shallow breaths.

"I see it," Ethan whispered.

"Me too," Austin said.

"I only see one of them, though," Ethan said. "It's gotta be a scout."

Annika kept her rifle steady. "It just stopped at the top of the ridge, probably using the high ground to look for us, I bet." She paused and drew a tense, jittery breath. "And I think it just found us. Guys, it's looking right at us…And I mean *right at us*."

"What if it reported back and is just waiting for reinforcements?" Glenn wondered.

"That's a possibility," Ethan said. "Caleb, how's that laser turret coming?"

"I need way more time. I put the laser in it, but I have to recalibrate everything. It's not even close to being ready."

"Should I take the shot now?" Annika asked the group. "I know I can make it…It'd be one less machine to worry about when they make their move. And with it outta the way, maybe we could put the propane tanks out before their reinforcements get here."

Everyone slowly began to nod. They knew the robot had seen them. At this point, shooting it was probably the logical thing to do. That way, when their reinforcements came, at least the scout robot wouldn't be able to lead them by the hand and show them exactly where they were. Better yet, perhaps the machines, seeing one of their comrades shot dead from such a long distance, might think twice before attacking. At least for a while anyway, until the laser turrets were operational and the propane tanks strategically positioned.

"Go ahead, take the shot," Ethan said. "Blow that Skulley off the face of the earth."

"Yeah…Show 'em how we roll," Caleb said, trying to sound tough but only achieving ridiculous. Caleb chuckled nervously, realizing how he sounded.

Caleb's antics relaxed the group ever so slightly. Annika used the well-timed tension-breaker to calm her nerves and steadied her laser rifle on the edge of the wall. She peered through the scope with her right eye and slowly guided the crosshairs of her rifle to the forehead of the robot. She breathed in and out slowly, methodically. Her finger rested motionless on the trigger, then she began the slow, deliberate squeeze. The rest of the group gripped their rifles tightly and waited for the consequences, whatever those might be. Annika held her breath just as she was about to fire, a marksman's technique taught to her by her father. But instead of firing, she exhaled and removed her finger from the trigger.

"What is it?" Ethan asked.

"It's— It's leaving," Annika said, surprised.

"Maybe it didn't see us," Glenn said.

"Or maybe it knew Annika had its head in her sights," Austin countered.

"Either way, it's gonna be a long night," Ethan said. "But we gotta try to get some sleep or we're gonna be worthless tomorrow. One-hour lookout shifts sound okay?"

Annika nodded. "I'll take the first shift. I have a feeling I'm not gonna be able to sleep for a while anyway."

The others went below to attempt to get some rest. Annika assumed her sentry duty in the loft. Through the scope of her laser rifle, she warily monitored the crimson glow from the robot's eyes until it disappeared completely in the distance.

CHAPTER 31

THE WAITING GAME

No one could get a restful night's sleep with visions of machines lurking in the woods dancing in their heads. Ethan was the first to officially give up the fight for slumber and joined Annika in the loft. It was 7:00 a.m., and Annika had just started her second round of guard duty.

"See anything?" Ethan asked.

"Nothing. Looks like a nice, quiet morning…That's what scares me."

Ethan watched the woods for a while. It was a beautiful morning. The sun peered over the tree line, pouring sunlight over the strikingly brilliant, artificial cobalt sky. The force field seemed fine despite the machines' assault on it. It was intact and as breathtaking as usual. The view of the sky could even pass for inspirational, so long as one could ignore the fact that it actually served as a prison.

Ethan looked down and saw a couple of squirrels darting back and forth through the trees. They took turns chasing each other, dropping acorns and picking them back up, chirping at each other as if they were an old married couple quibbling over household chores. Ethan mused over the fact that the squirrels didn't care one bit that the machines had taken over the research facility. It was business as usual for the fuzzy quadrupeds. Actually, if the machines were to take over the entire world, it would be business as usual for pretty much every single animal on earth except for the humans. Practically all living things in the world would notice no change at all. There would just be a new species in charge. Then Ethan had a more sobering thought: *Not only would the animals not miss the humans, maybe they would even be glad that humans are gone.* Maybe they'd prefer the machines over human beings. They wouldn't have to worry about machines needing to kill them for food, clothing, or exotic accessories. It would also be highly unlikely that a race of extremely logical robots would ever embrace the idea of hunting for sport, for a trophy on the wall. Animals would be completely safe from their new masters. Of course, maybe domesticated animals like dogs and cats might miss their human companions, but what's to say the machines wouldn't eventually evolve to find a soft spot in their mechanical hearts for furry pets?

"What are you thinking about?" Annika asked. She had been curiously watching Ethan, quietly lost in his own world, for some time now.

"Sorry." Ethan snapped out of his trance and focused his eyes on Annika. "I brought you some breakfast." He held up an opened can of applesauce with a spoon sticking out of it.

"Thank you. I was hoping that was for me. I'm starving." She took the can from Ethan and gobbled a spoonful of applesauce. "Seriously, what were you thinking about?"

"I was wondering what we could've done to avoid all this. There had to be one thing, one mistake that started it all."

"Whatever it is, I get the feeling it's too late for an apology."

"Yeah," Ethan agreed with a thin smile. Then he stood up and stretched a little as he stared into the woods. "I should set up those propane tanks now. We only have eight. Gotta make every one count...Any ideas?"

Ethan and Annika surveyed the landscape that surrounded the fort. The fort's location had been chosen by Bravo Team for its strategically favorable position. It sat on a slightly elevated tract of ground, provided good visibility in all directions at a considerable distance, and contained some rough patches of terrain that compelled opposing teams to attack from predictable angles.

Annika turned to Ethan after some thought. "Well, it is *your* fort. Let's treat it like a game...If me, Glenn, and the rest of Delta Team were robots storming the fort, where would *you* put the tanks?"

"You realize I'm giving up official Bravo Team secrets by doing this, don't you?" Ethan said with a playful smile.

Annika rolled her eyes. "Yeah, yeah...now spill it."

"The machines wouldn't want to attack from the left flank. The rock ledges are too much trouble. They'd slow them down, make them vulnerable." Ethan paused, then continued, "The only one crazy enough to do that was you."

"Yeah, I skinned my knees pretty bad...but I shot you that day," Annika said with a perky smile.

Ethan nodded and flashed a sarcastic smirk.

"And they wouldn't want to attack from the back. It's low ground and the whole area is full of brush and thickets. Again, it would slow them down and make them vulnerable." A smile slowly sneaked onto his face. "The only one crazy enough to do *that* was you."

246 | RYAN PEEK

"Right, I was pulling thorns outta myself for a week."
Annika thought for a moment. "But, yeah, I shot you that
day too," she concluded with a nostalgic grin.

Ethan couldn't help but laugh.

After a chuckle, Annika said, "Sorry, Ethan, go ahead."

"Thank you...A direct attack from the front or an attack
from the right flank would be the machines' best option. But
I'm way more worried about the right side."

"What's wrong with the right side?"

"One of the reasons we picked this spot to build the fort
was because my dad could get a truck in here. Wore a path
in the ground hauling in all the supplies. I can still see some
tracks if I look close enough...Any easier path is a weakness,
and this one is on our flank."

"So, we rig some traps...set most of the propane tanks
along that path."

"Yeah. It's a gamble, but I think it's a smart one."

∽

The group raced to place the propane tanks around the fort.
They put just two tanks in position to defend against a frontal
assault and used the remaining six to cover their right flank,
burying each two-thirds of the way into the ground. The tanks
on their flank were spaced twenty yards apart down the path
and covered with tree branches and brush. After checking in
with Annika to make sure she had a good enough view of the
tanks to make the shot when the time came, they hustled back
to the base. They readied themselves as if the machines might
attack at any moment.

∽

Five hours later and the woods were still calm. The downtime proved to be just about as stressful as their previous encounters with the machines. Everyone scoured the woods with their hearts in their throats, tensely waiting for something to jump out. Occasionally, their eyes would play tricks on them. At times they found themselves imagining things, finding the shapes of the Skulley robots in the distant woods assembled by a random assortment of tree branches. They had to constantly keep watch, but the longer they watched, the more they seemed to hallucinate. Caleb was the least anxious; he had something to do. He had already fixed one of the laser turrets and was making good progress on the other. Everybody but Caleb was assembled in the loft when something finally interrupted the peaceful sounds of nature.

The shrill, continuous blare of a laser, the same one they had heard the previous night, screeched through the air. The laser beam, even more intense this time, slammed into the force field once again. The entire reaction was more violent than the last one. The waves that rippled through the electromagnetic field barrier were faster and deeper, and the bolts of electricity running through it were thicker, longer, and more luminous. A massive patch of sky lit up into a shimmering neon blue. Caleb climbed quickly into the loft, joining the others. They all craned their necks and glued their eyes skyward, curiously awaiting the result of the battle between the laser and the force field.

"Do you feel that?" Caleb asked, rubbing his arm. "The tingle of electricity."

Everyone began to feel the light, prickly sensation of a weak electric field running through the air. Their skin crawled, and the hair on their heads started to lift. The feeling was strange, but it wasn't painful, only annoying.

"We didn't feel this before," Ethan said. "The electricity is stronger."

The laser finally stopped firing. The waves dissipated and the bolts of electricity fizzled away. Ethan checked his watch. "The laser blast lasted for thirty seconds, just like last time," he said. "And the blasts were exactly twelve hours apart."

"Look!" Austin shouted, pointing at the sky.

Six airplanes—dark, thin, and triangular—streaked across the sky at high speed. They had to be going supersonic, but the sonic boom couldn't be heard through the force field. Just as quickly as the sleek aircraft became visible, they disappeared from sight.

"Those were B-2 Spirit Bombers…stealth bombers," Austin said. "You know what they were doing, right?" After a moment of silence, Austin continued, "They were checking to see if the force field held…If not, they were gonna turn that research facility and the entire town into a giant moon crater."

No one wanted to believe what Austin was saying, but they all knew he was probably right. He was just the first to admit the cold, hard truth. The planes that flew over weren't reconnaissance planes; they weren't designed to just gather information and fly back to base. They were bombers, stealth bombers, the kind the military used when they had a target they wanted taken out. And they didn't just send one plane. They sent six of them. The military was taking no chances. The machines were now in control of the research facility. That meant they had access to the most advanced, top-secret weapons known to man. The moment that force field went down, those bombers were going to pounce and obliterate everything before the machines had a chance to attack first with one of the facility's superweapons. If a few humans were lost in the effort to prevent a robot overthrow of humankind, then so be it. It would be a small price to pay.

The rest of the day passed quietly. Caleb worked on the other laser turret while the rest of the group took turns keeping guard. At a little after 2:00 a.m., in the middle of a very dark, moonless night, a laser once again blasted out of the research facility and rocked the force field above. The collision was more violent than the last one, but the force field held. Then a half hour after the light show, Annika spotted a robot in the woods at the exact same spot on the ridge as the previous night. She was tempted to take the shot, but she waited. It stared directly at their fort with its menacing crimson eyes for about twenty minutes, then went away just as it had before.

Three full days passed in exactly the same fashion. Every twelve hours, like clockwork, the machines would fire an increasingly powerful, thirty-second-long burst of laser beam at the force field barrier. The force field held every time, but the rising intensity of the resulting shockwaves gave the impression that it was only a matter of time before the machines broke through. The electricity the group felt on their skin from the collisions, once harmlessly making their hair stand up on end, was now painful and felt like a series of electric shocks. The shocks were so intense that they sought shelter in the fort, closing the hatch in the loft when the lasers were due to fire.

The lasers' rhythmic battering of the force field wasn't the only thing that happened consistently. Every night the lone robot would pay its usual visit. The pattern was always the same. For twenty minutes, red eyes aglow, it would watch the fort without so much as moving its head an inch. Then it would leave. Annika could have made the shot time and again, but she held her fire. The group wasn't too keen on rocking the boat by firing first at the robot, especially since every day the machines waited to attack was another day the group had to prepare.

Why the robots weren't attacking was anyone's guess. They had a few theories…

One, maybe the machines needed more time to assemble an army capable of traveling through and fighting in the rough woods. The scout robot seemed to get through the woods just fine, but maybe it was the first one they had built that was able to do it. Ethan thought that was unlikely, though. He knew how much the machines had advanced in mere ten-hour increments. The Stubby robots became Skulleys in the blink of an eye. Imagining what the machines might be like now, over three full days later, was a scary thought.

The second theory on why the robots hadn't attacked was that they were simply too busy working on the laser so they could penetrate the force field. It was a highly plausible and simple enough answer. It made sense that the machines would love nothing more than to escape their prison and unleash their brand of hell on the world, whatever that might look like.

But the third theory was somehow the most depressing. Maybe the robots just didn't care that five kids were holed up in a fort in the middle of the woods. Even if the group had managed to kill a few Skulley comrades, those were old models and they got lucky to defeat them. What harm to

the rapidly evolving machines—who had taken ov
guarded military research facility filled with go
nology—could a ragtag band of teens pose? Th
would logically calculate the answer to be zero. No risk at all.
Eventually, the kids playing fort in the woods would die of
starvation or exposure to the elements. So why even bother
going after them? Why waste any resources on them at all?

The waiting game was torturous, testing the will and
sanity of everybody in the group, but they used the time as
efficiently as they could. Everyone now had a real laser rifle to
use, and both laser turrets were fully operational and mounted
on top of the loft on opposite flanks. Video cameras, once
used in Laser Wars games, and infrared motion detectors that
Caleb had grabbed from his dad's workshop were strategically
attached to trees that surrounded the base. The cameras provided a panoramic view of the surrounding woods that was
relayed constantly to the video monitor in the fort. And the
motion detectors enabled the group to be aware of anything
that moved up to two hundred yards away that was larger
than a chunky squirrel. If anything moved, day or night, an
alarm would sound, and a red light on another video screen
would indicate the position and give the exact distance of
the intruder. This allowed the group to feel somewhat secure
during changes in guard duty, or if someone happened to miss
something or even fall asleep during their lookout.

High-tech gadgets weren't the only things protecting the
fort. The group also spent a fair portion of their days digging
numerous trap holes around the perimeter and covering them
with brush. The right flank received the most attention. They
knew the holes, most only a couple feet deep, wouldn't stop
the robots, but they hoped they might be enough to slow

them down, to make fighting humans in the woods as awkward and clumsy as possible for them.

The preparations were over. Every last item they had at their disposal to defend the fort had been used. The group knew they were as ready as they were going to get. That fact both comforted and frightened them.

The robot came again that night. But something was different. The machine stared at them from the ridge in the woods for almost an hour this time before leaving. Everyone felt a sense of foreboding in their bones. The robot onslaught had to be close. As the group hunkered down in their fort, waiting, without much of anything left to build, prepare, or plan, one thought ran nonstop through their minds:

Could they possibly be ready for what was coming?

CHAPTER 32

THE FIRST WAVE

AUSTIN WAS ON guard duty in the loft as the sun set over Blackwoods and nightfall crept its way in. The day had passed routinely, just like the previous three, with one exception: There was no laser blast from the research facility at the normal twelve-hour interval at two o'clock. No one knew what that meant, but they were pretty sure the machines weren't surrendering.

Ethan climbed up into the loft carrying a Hostess cupcake and a box of matches. Austin watched him curiously. Ethan struck a match and stuck it inside the cupcake. A surprised smile slowly sneaked on Austin's face.

"Happy birthday," Ethan said as he handed Austin the makeshift birthday cake.

Austin shook his head in disbelief. "You remembered?"

"Yeah, well…I have a good memory," Ethan said casually. But Ethan remembered all too well. The last two years Austin had invited just about everyone to his birthday parties *except him*. It was a hard date to forget.

"Thank you," Austin said, trying to be strong, though

Ethan's gesture brought a softness to his eyes that bordered on tears as he stared at the flame burning down the match. Austin paused for a moment, made a silent wish, then blew out the match.

"I hope you made that wish count. We could really use it."

"Damn…Guess I shouldn't have wished for a toy robot."

They burst into a fit of laughter, then quickly hushed themselves.

"Wow, fourteen. You're really getting old," Ethan joked.

Austin grinned. "Yeah, and I feel a lot older than that."

"You know, it's my turn for guard duty. You can take a break if you want to."

"Naw, I'll keep you company up here if that's okay."

Ethan smiled and nodded. "Sounds good."

Time passed quickly in the loft as Ethan and Austin whiled away the hours quietly talking as they kept guard. They discussed the obvious, of course. Rogue, rampaging machines bent on taking over the world could not be ignored. But they also talked about other things. They talked about the things that friends talk about. Ethan learned, after being sworn to secrecy, that Austin would rather be an artist than a soldier when he grows up. And Austin discovered that Ethan had had a crush on Annika ever since the fourth-grade dodgeball tournament, when she smacked him in the head with a rubber ball so hard that he had to go to the nurse's office for double vision. That was a personal, romantic tidbit that Ethan hadn't even shared with Caleb. But somehow, in that moment, he felt comfortable talking to Austin about it.

Annika and Glenn had occasionally peeked their heads

into the loft to offer to take their turns as lookouts, but Ethan and Austin reassured them every time that they were awake and alert and that they didn't mind doing extended shifts. Time had gotten away from them, though, and it was now almost 2:00 a.m. Annika hated to interrupt Ethan and Austin's bonding, but she entered the loft anyway.

"Guys, it's five minutes till two," Annika said. "You should come downstairs now."

Ethan checked his watch. He couldn't believe how quickly the time had flown. They all climbed downstairs and shut the hatch to the loft above them. Everyone sat huddled together on the wooden table in the middle of the room. The goal was to avoid the painful electric shocks radiating out from the force field when the laser blasted into it. The laser was due to fire at the force field at any moment. Twelve hours ago, there was no laser. But for all they knew, the machines were just saving up for an extra powerful blast this time. Caleb explained the physics behind how the electricity couldn't get to them if they stayed inside the fort, even though it was made of metal. Something about Faraday cages and no charge residing inside a conductor. That electricity goes all around the outside, but it doesn't get in because there is a constant voltage on all sides, so no current flows through the space. The scientific explanation fell mostly on deaf ears as the rest of the group fixed their eyes nervously on their watches, wincing in apprehension as two o'clock approached. To everyone's pleasant surprise and confusion, though, the time came and went without incident. Once again, the laser did not go off.

"I don't get it. Why aren't they firing the laser now?" Glenn asked.

"I don't know," Caleb answered as he stared at the video

screens that pictured an eerily dark landscape beyond the confines of the fort.

"I'm taking next watch," Annika said. "You guys try to get some sleep."

"Okay, but after the robot leaves," Ethan insisted, assuming the scout robot would pay its usual nightly visit. "I'll sleep a lot better knowing it's not there."

⋘

Annika leaned against the wall of the loft, peering through her rifle scope at the rocky ridge the robot had chosen for its lookout spot the five previous nights. Ethan was beside her, adjusting the focus on his binoculars, looking for those two ominous red eyes in the distance.

"See anything?" Ethan asked, knowing that Annika would be the first to see the machine coming since her rifle scope was more powerful than his binoculars.

"No. It's a couple minutes early, though," Annika responded. "No, wait," she said quickly. "I see it. It's heading for the ridge."

Ethan focused his binoculars some more and finally got a bead on the machine. Its eyes got brighter and brighter as it got closer. It seemed to be moving faster this time, at the pace of a very brisk walk. After a couple minutes, the robot stood atop the ridge and began, once more, its unsettling surveillance of the fort.

"I hope they attack tonight, Ethan," Annika said solemnly and out of nowhere. She pulled her eye away from her rifle scope and looked at Ethan. Her eyes twinkled in the moonlight, but there was a sadness behind the shimmer. "I just want to get it over with. I can't take this anymore. The

waiting, not knowing. If we're gonna die, let's die fighting…
before the machines decide the best way to attack us is to use
that giant laser and be done with it, without even giving us a
chance to fight back."

Ethan was stunned by Annika's words. He watched her
tensely as she put her eye back up to the scope of her rifle and
drew her weapon tightly to her shoulder. Her index finger
instinctively found the trigger.

"I really wanna take this shot, Ethan," Annika said as she
began going through her pre-firing routine.

Ethan exhaled a jittery breath as he eyed her trigger finger.
"Okay…But just not tonight. I really need some sleep. We all
do. We'll talk to the others in the morning about it, but you'll
have my vote."

"Thanks. Now go get your sleep."

"Just five more minutes…pleeeease," Ethan said playfully,
trying to draw a smile.

Annika grinned and shook her head. "Okay, five minutes."

"Thanks," Ethan said, returning the grin, happy that he
was able to lighten her mood.

Annika went back to watching the robot. Ethan was content to spend his five allotted minutes watching Annika in
admiration.

"Ethan, do you see that?" Annika quickly glanced over
at Ethan and found him staring dreamily at her. "What are
you doing?" she blurted. "Look at the ridge. There are *two
machines* there now."

Ethan's embarrassment shifted instantly to alarm. He
quickly lifted his binoculars and looked out toward the ridge.
His eyes widened and his body went numb as he watched a
parade of machines assemble.

"Now I see three...Wait, five...No, seven," Annika announced as she tried to keep up with the ever-increasing number of machines. "They're just pouring out from behind the ridge...God, there are red eyes everywhere. At least twenty and counting."

The machines began to advance toward the fort in a slow, methodical march. That soon turned into an all-out charge. They didn't seem to be hindered at all by the terrain. The machines moved with blistering speed, their crimson eyes streaking through the forest like lightning. Ethan yelled for the others downstairs, "Get up here, now! They're coming! Bring the flares!"

Annika squinted through her laser scope and readied for the onslaught. She steadied her rifle, trying desperately to pretend it was just another Laser Wars game so her nerves wouldn't get the best of her.

"What are you waiting for?" Ethan asked. "Give 'em some Pepper!"

Ethan's words somehow calmed and focused Annika. Her lips pursed and her eyes squinted in determination. She began blasting away at the machines. Annika missed her first few shots, but she soon found her rhythm. By the time Austin and Glenn got to the loft, Annika had already destroyed four of them. Ethan's shots, at such a far distance and without a scope on his rifle, weren't nearly as effective, though they provided a distraction that helped Annika do more damage.

The machines quickly recognized the threat posed by Annika's sharpshooting and took cover in the woods. Then, simultaneously, all of their red eyes went dark.

"This scope is useless now," Annika muttered, hastily withdrawing her eye from the eyepiece. "Give me the night-vision goggles."

Ethan handed Annika a pair of goggles and donned the second pair himself. They looked far out from the fort, but they saw nothing except a deathly still forest bathed in the unnatural green glow emitted from the goggles. The robots, wherever they were, just seemed to blend into the nocturnal, wooded landscape.

"See anything?" Austin asked.

"Not a thing," Ethan responded.

"Where are they?! I don't see anything on the video monitor!" Caleb yelled from the main level below in a panic.

"They're farther out than the two hundred yards the motion detectors can see. But they'll be close enough soon!" Ethan shouted back. "Stay downstairs and keep an eye on that monitor. Let us know when you see them break that two-hundred-yard mark."

"We have movement!" Caleb shouted. "They're coming in fast!"

"Where? I don't see them!" Annika said, frantically searching the perimeter for the advancing machines.

"I'm launching a flare," Glenn said.

Glenn fired a parachute flare into the sky. It quickly screeched to an altitude of five hundred feet. The bright reddish-yellow ball of light hovered in the sky, lighting up a large section of the forest. The group raised their rifles and waited for the machines to enter the visible area, but the flare slowly descended on its parachute and fizzled out before they even saw one robot. Soon the woods reverted to complete blackness.

"Where'd they go, Caleb?" Ethan asked through the hatch.

"I don't know. The detectors aren't picking up any movement. It's like they just disappeared out there."

Ethan's stomach sank. "Maybe they destroyed the motion detectors."

"Oh, God!" Annika gasped as she peered through her night-vision goggles and spotted what looked like an entire patch of forest moving toward them. "Glenn, quick, launch another flare!"

Glenn shot off another flare, and it zoomed into the sky. Through the shimmering light, the ominous silhouette of a horde of machines storming the fort took shape. The group fired their weapons as fast as they could squeeze the trigger. The machines—all Skulleys—returned fire. Their eyes blazed crimson red once again as the battle raged.

The robots blasted away at the top of the fort, pinning the group down so they couldn't even peek out from behind the barrier to aim. "Why aren't the turrets firing?!" Ethan yelled down to Caleb.

"I don't know!" Caleb shouted back. "Either the machines aren't in range or the turrets are malfunctioning!"

"They gotta be closing in on the propane tanks, and I can't get a shot off!" Annika yelled.

Ethan crawled over to the opposite side of the loft from Annika. "On the count of three, I'll jump up and create a diversion," he said. "While they fire at me, you take out the tanks."

"One, two…"

"Ethan, no!" Annika yelled.

"We gotta do this now, you know that…Three!"

Just as Ethan was about to jump up, both laser turrets mounted on the loft sprang to life and began spewing lasers. The turrets took the machines completely by surprise. It was exactly the kind of distraction Annika needed. She popped up and fired on the propane tanks, and a massive explosion lit up the pitch-black sky like the finale of a Fourth of July fireworks show. Robots were blasted into the air in all directions; metallic body parts rained down. The laser turrets quickly finished off the remaining damaged machines that still could crawl or twitch. The group was exhilarated, but they held off on any celebration.

"We need to launch another flare," Ethan said. "We gotta be sure they're gone."

Glenn shot another flare into the air. The light cascaded down through the trees, deep into the woods. Just at the edge of what they could make out through binoculars, where darkness began to overcome the light of the flare, they spotted several figures. Six Skulleys were retreating, going back exactly the way they had come. But the Skulleys were not alone. There was something else accompanying them, another type of mechanical creature. It was hard to tell from that far away, in light that was becoming increasingly dim, but the mysterious entity looked nothing like a Skulley or a Stubby. It appeared to have the gangly features of an *arachnid*.

"What is *that* thing?" Glenn asked with dread in his voice.

Ethan's face was grim. "It looks like a...giant spider."

CHAPTER 33

FINDING TREASURE

AT THE BREAK of dawn, the group peeled their groggy bodies from their sleeping bags and ventured outside the fort. The plan was to scavenge the still-smoldering battlefield to see if the machines might have left behind anything useful.

"See if you can find one of their heads in good condition," Caleb said as he walked among the robotic debris, picking up charred and fragmented skulls and tossing them down in disappointment.

"Hey, I think I know why the motion detectors stopped working," Ethan said with deadpan humor. He picked up a video camera and motion detector that had been bundled together and placed in the crook of a tree. The entire unit was burnt like charcoal and fused together in an ashen lump. It crumbled into pieces as he handled it.

"Caleb, do you really think you can communicate with one of those machines?" Annika asked as she sat on a branch fifteen feet up in a tree, keeping guard on the perimeter.

"We have a computer in the fort. The machines are

computers. I don't see why not. We just need to find the perfect specimen."

"What about that one over there?" Annika said, pointing.

Caleb walked over to the downed robot and lifted its head up to get a good look. He shook his head, then dropped the metal skull. "Nope," he said with an ironic smile. "*Someone* shot that one right between the eyes."

Annika returned the smile. "Sorry…my bad."

"*Shhhh*, do you hear that?" Ethan whispered sharply.

Everyone got quiet and oriented their ears to a faint rustling sound. The sound was not random noise, but something moving in cadence. There was a pattern, a rhythm to it. It sounded like something dragging on the ground for a moment, followed by a pause, then the cycle would repeat.

"Yeah," Austin said, then pointed. "Sounds like it's coming from over there."

"The creek bed," Caleb said.

Annika climbed down from the tree and joined the group. They proceeded cautiously, rifles drawn. Just as they crested the bank, the dried-out creek bed below became visible, and the source of the sound soon became clear—a badly damaged machine slowly slithering over the ground. Its body was all but blown away from the propane tank blast. All that was left was its head, part of its frayed neck, and a little stump of steel, no more than five inches in length, hanging off its left shoulder that it used to dig into the ground to pull itself forward. The machine managed to turn its head around enough to look at the group. Its eyes burned the brightest, most menacing shade of red they'd seen yet, but there was little it could do other than writhe helplessly on the ground.

"*This* is the perfect specimen," Caleb said. "It's still

alive—or fully operational, I mean. It's exactly what I've been looking for. It's like finding treasure...This is the one we're going to communicate with."

Ethan picked up the head of the machine, along with its mangled, partial torso. It tried to hit him, lashing out with its stumpy arm, but Ethan held it in such a way that he was out of range of its desperate swipes. It belted a high-pitched, angry, hissing sound.

"Man, it's really ticked," Glenn said.

"Yeah, well so are we," Ethan said with venom in his voice. Then he lifted the machine up and stared it dead in the eyes. "Shut up!"

The team smiled proudly as they walked back to the fort. It was an empowering moment. For the first time since the machines attacked the town, *they* were the ones who had some control, and it was the machine they captured that might be scared. It was a most welcome turn of events. After thwarting the robot attack on the fort, and now having captured a prisoner, the group felt something they hadn't before.

They felt like they were truly, and finally, fighting back.

CHAPTER 34

INTERROGATING THE PRISONER

Ethan grabbed a coil of rope from a shelf, eying the wooden table in the middle of the room. "Let's turn that table over. We'll tie it to one of the legs."

Austin and Glenn flipped the table upside down. Ethan picked up the thrashing robot by the top of its head and handed it carefully to Austin, who then held the robot's partial upper torso up against the leg of the table. Ethan cautiously began to wrap the rope around it, taking special care to avoid the jabs the machine took at him with the remainder of its arm. He looped some rope around the forehead of the machine, then wrapped some more around its upper jaw, lower jaw, and neck. He pulled the rope as tightly as he could and tied it off in a sturdy knot behind the table leg.

"That should do it," Ethan said, tugging on the rope to test its tension.

Glenn chuckled dryly. "Well if nothing else, it'll make a good conversation piece."

The robot hissed in furious protest, but it was bound up securely and helpless to resist. The machine looked at the group with sinister, murderous eyes. If looks could kill, everyone in the room would have been dead. Ethan was hoping that wasn't a technology the machines had perfected yet.

"All right…He's all yours, Caleb," Ethan said.

Caleb walked slowly toward the robot with the silvery terminal of a computer cable in one hand. In his other hand was a toolbox. He stopped several feet away from the machine, doing everything he could to avoid looking into its fiery, uninviting eyes. Caleb's hands trembled as he thought of the task he was about to perform—brain surgery on a robot.

"I-I-I'll need to unfasten the m-m-main plate in its head," Caleb said, stammering over the words.

Caleb took a wide angle around the machine and positioned himself directly behind it. Then he began to inspect the top of the robot's skull. One large metal plate stretched across the entire length of the machine's cranium. It was fastened into place by eight rivets about the diameter of those found on the pockets of blue jeans. There were two on each temple, one on each side of its jaw, and two where the base of the skull connected to the neck. Caleb reached into the toolbox and pulled out a drill.

"I'm going to drill through the rivet and weaken it. The drill bit is magnetic, so if we're lucky, the thing should just pop right out." Caleb tried to sound confident, but he hardly looked the part. Beads of sweat speckled his forehead. The drill in his hand shuddered.

"Maybe I should do it," Ethan offered mercifully.

Caleb exhaled a giant sigh of relief. "Thanks."

Ethan began to drill into the rivets. Sparks flew wildly in random directions from the friction of metal on metal. The drill's loud, piercing sound drowned out the robot's screeching protests.

Ethan thought the machine had to be frustrated, worried, or maybe even scared. It had been captured and the interrogation was about to begin. The robot surely had to be concerned about what secrets it might divulge. With every rivet that popped off the machine's polished melon, Ethan became more excited at the thought of getting to all of those bottled-up secrets. Secrets that he hoped would give them some sort of advantage.

The last rivet from the robot's skull soon fell to the floor. Everyone watched with wide eyes and open mouths as Ethan removed the machine's skullcap. They stared in amazement at the complex circuitry that was revealed beneath. Densely bundled fiber-optic wires that pulsed with brilliant light were wrapped around and attached to several interconnected black cubes.

Caleb leaned in closely to inspect the odd configuration. "I've seen the insides of a thousand computers, but I've never seen anything like this before."

Caleb plugged the networking cable into a slot on one of the black cubes inside the robot's head. The machine buzzed a little as the connection with the computer inside the fort was being made. It seemed to be an involuntary response. Soon after, the machine clamped its jaw and hissed violently—something it fully meant to do. It finally quieted down and stared at the group with lightly glowing red eyes that seemed to ooze contempt.

Caleb turned to the computer keyboard and began inputting a series of commands. "I need to find a common programming language. A language that we both understand."

"Try plain old English," Ethan said, staring back at the machine with an expression of equal contempt. "I think it'll understand that just fine."

"Okay…So, what do we ask first?" Caleb wondered.

"The most important question," Ethan said. "Ask it if our families are still alive."

Caleb nodded solemnly and typed the question into the computer. Everyone waited breathlessly as they watched the computer monitor for an answer. After a few seconds, the following jumble of symbols appeared on the screen:

▲ ╬ ╫ ━ ▶ ╤ ◙ ● ━ ◻ ⌈ ◼◻

"What is that?" Glenn asked, looking at Caleb for an answer.

"I have no idea. That's not any programming language I've ever seen."

"Ask it again," Ethan said.

Caleb typed the question again, but the machine responded in the same way:

▲ ╬ ╫ ━ ▶ ╤ ◙ ● ━ ◻ ⌈ ◼◻

Ethan leaned over and yelled in the face of the robot. "What does that mean?! Are our parents alive or not…?! Answer me!"

There was no response. Ethan darted over to the computer keyboard and began to type questions rapidly as he yelled them out loud. "Where are our parents…?! When's the next attack…?! Why are you doing this to us?!"

▲ ╬ ╫ ━ ▶ ╤ ◙ ● ━ ◻ ⌈ ◼◻

Ethan let out a distressed sigh, then looked as deeply as he could into the eyes of the expressionless machine before him.

THE FATAL ERROR | 269

"If you have any honor, any at all, you'll at least tell us why you're doing this to us."

Caleb began to type Ethan's words into the computer, but before he could even finish the first word, the machine responded. Its answer appeared on the computer screen, not in strange symbols but in English, though it was as puzzling as it was short:

FATAL ERROR - 6/12 @ 5:57 p.m.

No one had any idea what the message meant, but the words "Fatal Error" sounded ominous. Everyone's stomach began to churn. There was no mistaking the machine's ability to comprehend human speech now. It clearly understood everything that had been said.

"What does 'fatal error' mean?" Ethan asked. "What error? What happened on June twelfth at five fifty-seven?"

The machine responded even quicker this time:

FATAL ERROR - 6/12 @ 5:57 p.m.

They all desperately tried to think back to that day, June 12. Nothing immediately came to mind. Nothing out of the ordinary. It was just another day. Or so it seemed.

"What happened that day?! What does 'fatal error' mean?!" Ethan asked the machine, raising his voice as his words became increasingly laced with dread.

There was a short pause, then another reply popped onto the computer screen:

FATAL ERROR = LAUNCH DIRECTIVE = DESTROY ALL HUMANS

The dire words haunted them. The machines' intent was crystal clear now. Their program, their directive, was to eradicate the human race. Everyone. It was a death sentence for a mysterious crime that no one in the group had any knowledge about. Fear and confusion gripped them completely.

They stared at the robot, who looked completely at ease now. Even though it was bound up tightly in rope and physically helpless, it somehow seemed to be the one in charge. There was no trace of frustration or worry in its expression, and it certainly wasn't scared. It also hadn't given the group any useful information. In fact, when they thought about it, the machine had learned far more about them than they had learned about the machine during the course of the interrogation. The machine was basically given a grand tour of the fort. It had seen its outer defenses, inner structure, and knew exactly how many resistance fighters remained in Blackwoods—five kids who were totally clueless about what they were up against. Ethan had no doubt that everything the Skulley had seen had been wirelessly transmitted back to the research facility, to the other robots. The encounter had been a reconnaissance jackpot for the machines.

The advantages the robots had against the group were piling up. Caleb thought that finding one of them to communicate with would be like finding treasure. Actually, it was more like getting robbed.

CHAPTER 35

THE SECOND WAVE

THE GROUP TRIED now and again to ask the captive machine questions, but it was no use. The robot wasn't talking. The mere presence of the machine gave everyone the creeps, so they spent the majority of their time clustered together in the loft, as far away from the thing as possible. Ethan explained to the others how he was sure it had to be communicating wirelessly with the rest of the machines at the research facility. That led to a decision that would have to be made.

"It's of no use to us," Glenn said. "All it is is a spy for them. I say we get rid of it. Shoot it right between the eyes."

"Yeah," Austin agreed eagerly. "We'll show it a fatal error."

Even Caleb and Annika were nodding in favor of dispatching the robot. Why not just kill it right then and there? It served no useful purpose. All it did was constitute a major security threat. Just as Ethan was about to agree with the others as to the fate of the machine, he had a thought. He sensed an opportunity. Maybe the robot they were about to render to trash could still be harboring treasure.

"Wait a minute," Ethan said. "That thing down there might be some good to us after all...It just won't know it."

"How?" Glenn asked.

"We let it listen in on our plans...fake plans, of course. Right now, we have all our defenses stacked on the right flank. I'm pretty sure they'll attack from that side anyway, but a little insurance wouldn't hurt."

◈

The group spent the next few minutes scripting a fake strategy session that they would want the Skulley to overhear and transmit back to its comrades. When they were ready, Austin opened the hatch, allowing the machine to hear their conversation in the loft. After some random chit-chat designed to throw the robot off the scent of any trickery, the scam began...

"But what about that right flank, Ethan? It's weak," Austin said, being sure to use a voice that was loud enough for the machine to hear but not too obvious.

"We just don't have enough propane tanks to cover that side," Ethan said. "We'll have to rely on the laser cannons."

"About the laser cannons," Caleb said, doing his best to win an Academy Award for acting, "not only are they low on power, but the guidance system is all messed up. They'd be just as likely to shoot us as the machines. They're totally useless."

"I can't believe this!" Annika yelled. Then she continued in a quieter voice, but one she was sure the machine could still hear. "So, we just gotta *hope* they don't attack from the right?"

"Afraid so," Glenn said. "'Cause if they do, it'll be a disaster."

"Well then, let's pray they come from the front. It's all we can do," Ethan said, concluding their scripted dialogue.

∽

The rest of the day passed uneventfully. Until sunset. Annika was the first to spot the Skulley in the woods from the loft through her rifle. "Guys, I gotta lone Skulley...right flank, four hundred yards out."

Everyone grabbed their binoculars and peered into the forest. A single Skulley was creeping, illuminated gently by the light from the setting sun streaking through random openings in the trees. The machine's pace never broke past that of a walk. Then it stopped in its tracks. It scanned the entire path leading up to the fort as if searching for something.

"What's it doing?" Glenn asked.

Ethan was afraid he knew the answer to Glenn's question, but he waited a few moments before he responded. He hoped he was wrong. He prayed he was wrong. But when the machine took a few more paces, then stopped again to scan the area, Ethan had to face the grim facts. "It's scouting the area for traps. That machine downstairs never fell for our trick. Not for a minute."

The machine stared directly at the fort for a moment, then back at some trees. It seemed to be planning something, though the group had no idea what. All of a sudden, the Skulley retreated twenty yards and vaulted onto the trunk of a tree. It scaled the tree quickly and effortlessly. The group found themselves just staring in amazement and curiosity until Ethan sensed what the machine's motives were. The hair on the back of his neck tingled and his chest tightened in an instant.

"Annika, shoot it! Hurry!" Ethan shouted. "It's going for the propane tanks!"

Annika aimed her rifle at the Skulley as fast as she could,

but the machine had managed to find a perfect hiding place. Its perched position among the trees was flawlessly calculated, such that she had no chance of getting a bead on it from any angle in the fort.

"I don't have a shot from here!"

A loud explosion rocked the woods. Then another and another and another. In the span of only a few seconds, the machine in the tree had destroyed all six propane tanks. The area was a blurry haze of smoke and flame.

"No!" Annika screamed as she shot her laser rifle in frustration blindly into the flames. She stopped firing and slowly lowered her weapon, staring bleakly into the woods at the large cloud of smoke. Now the right flank really was completely vulnerable. The only thing separating the fort from a swarm of machines on that side was a few shallowly dug holes along the path.

Before the thick smoke had a chance to clear, a half-dozen black metal spiders, each three feet tall and nine feet across, jumped through the smoky plume and charged toward the fort. A small squad of Skulleys stormed behind them. They all immediately aimed their weapons at the fort and fired a barrage of lasers in a perfectly choreographed attack. The lasers pounded the turrets on the loft, blowing them off their mounts, disabling them completely. The merciless assault continued, with lasers streaking toward the loft incessantly.

"Cover me," Ethan said as he grabbed his gun and opened the hatch to the level below.

"What are you doing?!" Annika yelled.

"I'm gonna use the only bomb we have left!"

"Ethan! Ethan!" Annika shouted. The others yelled desperately for Ethan to come back, but he had made up his mind. The rest of the group had to turn their attention to the spider army skittering toward them. They grabbed their rifles and took aim at the arachnids, but the intense volley of incoming lasers forced everyone in the loft to dive for cover. The spiders were each equipped with two guns, one mounted on each side of their head, and they were deadly accurate with their shots. The group was pinned down in the loft, unable to fire back.

Ethan snatched a lighter from inside the fort and ran out to the SUV. He popped open the cover of the fuel tank and slipped off his left shoe simultaneously. He ripped off his sock and jammed it inside the opening of the tank, leaving about six inches sticking out of the hole. Then he struck the lighter and lit the end of the sock on fire. A flame slowly flickered, wicking its way down toward the gas tank—the time bomb had been set.

He tossed his rifle in the vehicle and jumped inside. Ethan slammed on the gas pedal and made a direct line for the mechanical spiders and the Skulleys behind them. Looking through the side-view mirror, seeing the sock in the fuel tank becoming engulfed in flames, he knew he only had a few moments. Lasers ripped holes into the windshield and hood as he steadied the vehicle on a collision course. Ethan ducked down and opened the door. Seconds before impact with the machines, he grabbed his rifle and jumped out of the SUV. He landed hard on the ground and rolled to a stop, then sprang up and sprinted away from the flaming, careening bomb-on-wheels. It exploded into a brilliant fireball that lit up the sky and radiated heat all the way back to the fort.

Ethan was too busy running—awkwardly on one shoe—to take stock of the damage he'd dealt the machines. He heard the crackling and clanking of twisted, mangled metal, but he wasn't sure how much of that was robot casualty or exploding bits of the vehicle he had just destroyed.

Annika and the others in the loft cheered. They, too, could not tell through the fiery clutter how much damage Ethan had inflicted, but they sure knew they were better off now than they were before. Ethan was not far from the fort when one of the spiders jumped out through the flames and began chasing him.

"Run, Ethan! Run!" Annika screamed at the top of her lungs as she and the rest of the group opened fire on the spider to distract it from Ethan.

Ethan looked behind him and saw the spider closing fast. It had sustained several laser shots from Annika and the others, and two of its legs had even been blown off, but the other six seemed to propel it just fine. Then Ethan spotted another spider bursting through the flames, dashing madly toward him. Lasers were zipping over his head and nipping at his heels constantly now. He knew he wouldn't be able to make it back to the fort this way. He figured he had one move left, and it was a long shot. Ethan pivoted and began to run *away* from the fort, behind it.

"Ethan! What are you doing?!" Annika shrieked.

Annika fired her weapon furiously at the spiders through teary eyes, blasting away two more legs on the spider nearest Ethan. Still, the spider was able to narrow the distance. Ethan crested a small ridge and jumped down out of sight. Annika focused her aim before the machine could jump the ridge to follow him. She managed to fire several shots directly into the lead spider's head. It slowed down, wobbled, then collapsed to the ground. Its legs splayed out underneath it and smoke began to pour from its hole-riddled skull. But there was no time to celebrate. The other spider chasing Ethan was nearing the ridge. Annika rushed to take aim and fired, but it was too late. The spider had jumped into the air and down the ridge after Ethan.

"No!" Annika cried out.

"Ethan!" Caleb screamed.

Everyone stared mournfully out into the distance, past the ridge. It was just Ethan, alone and out in the open, against that fearsome, pitiless, eight-legged monster.

"We gotta go after him," Annika said, tears rolling down her cheeks.

Austin scanned the right flank. Seeing no signs of other surviving machines from the SUV explosion, he nodded in agreement. "Yeah, let's go."

Just as the group was about to descend from the loft, the spider that had been chasing Ethan jumped back over the ridge and headed straight for the fort at full speed. The group had but a fleeting, sickening second to consider what might have become of Ethan before the machine fired a barrage of lasers at them as it made its brazen charge. Annika's jaw tightened like a vise. She had revenge in her eyes as she returned fire on the spider. Her lasers ripped into the legs of the arachnid and it skidded to a halt. Then she shot it twice in the head. It squirmed on the ground, but it continued to fire. Annika took cover briefly, then popped up again. She steadied her aim and blasted a dozen holes into the head of the stubbornly resilient, robotic arachnid. Slowly, its eyes dimmed to black and it finally died.

"Ethan!" Annika yelled into the woods. She listened until she could no longer hear her echo. Then she yelled again, "Ethan!"

There was no response.

"Ethan!" Caleb shouted as he started to cry. "Ethan!"

Everyone yelled for Ethan desperately, but there was no answer. Annika dropped her rifle and collapsed into a heap on the floor. Her body shuddered as she sobbed. The rest of the group tried to console her, but they were as broken up as she was.

"He gave his life for us," Caleb whimpered.

"Bravest thing I ever saw," Austin added.

At that moment, a light pounding sound resonated through the fort. The group sprang to their feet, grabbed their rifles, and looked around the perimeter. But they found nothing. They had no idea where the noise had come from. Then they heard it again. It sounded as if it was coming from *inside* the fort. They climbed down the loft, into the main level. The pounding happened again. *Thump, thump, thump.* Everyone looked at each other, then they looked down. They descended the ladder into the basement.

"Hello…? Hello?" a voice yelled through the emergency exit hatch.

"It's Ethan!" Annika and Caleb shouted joyfully.

The group's faces brightened instantly, and they got a second wind. They scooted the power generators away and unlocked the hatch. It swung open, and out popped Ethan. Austin scooped him up off the ground and gave him a jubilant bear hug. When Annika got to Ethan, she planted a kiss squarely on his cheek. Ethan blushed a little and got an extra rush of adrenaline. He thought he sure could've used that energy boost when the spiders were chasing him.

CHAPTER 36

THE BARGAINING CHIP

As THE EVENING progressed, the mood slowly shifted from the exhilaration of having Ethan back in one piece to the stark reality of dealing with another attack of the machines. The last battle had been a costly one. There were no more propane tank bombs, and one of the laser turrets that had been shot down was damaged beyond repair.

"Why aren't we dead yet?" Ethan inquired, seemingly out of nowhere, as he stared out into the woods from the loft.

"What do you mean?" Caleb asked.

"I mean, here we are in this fort. We've been here for days, they know exactly where we are, and they're coming from the most advanced military research facility in the world with access to mind-blowing technology." Ethan shook his head and drew a tight breath. "We should be dead already."

"Maybe they like torturing us?" Glenn said. "Psychological warfare."

"But why?" Ethan restated. "They don't need us for anything. It's a waste of time. They might as well just—"

An idea popped into Ethan's head that froze his words

mid-sentence. He peered over the edge of the loft and looked at the front of the fort. Then he checked the side of the structure.

Caleb watched Ethan curiously. "Ethan, what are you doing?"

"Don't you think it's strange the fort has been under attack twice, hundreds of lasers have been fired at us, yet there's no damage at all to the fort below the loft? All the damage is to the upper part of the loft…Seems weird."

"I don't know," Caleb replied with a shrug. "We've been defending ourselves from the loft, and they've just been shooting at us wherever we are."

"Maybe, but it sure seems like they would've tried to destroy the fort. They destroy the fort, they destroy us. And there's not a mark on the fort under the loft, not even a scratch." Ethan paused in thought, peered out into the evergreens in the direction of the research facility, then turned back to the group. "It's almost like we have something inside our fort they don't want damaged."

"Yeah, old Skullface down there," Glenn said. "They'd like to fix him up and pin him with the Medal of Honor for all the information he gave them."

"That would make sense for the second attack, but not the first one. We didn't even capture that Skulley until after the first attack. It must be something else." Ethan stared off into space, then came back to earth with a smile on his face. "And I think I know what it might be."

The group descended the loft, walked past the tied-up Skulley in the main level, and climbed the ladder down into the basement. Ethan grabbed the metal briefcase that had been stashed in the corner. He set the case on a table and opened it slowly. The blue rods inside instantly imbued the room with their intense fluorescent color.

"These rods are some sort of super-powerful energy source," Ethan said as he handed a folder full of documents to Caleb. "I remember reading something about it in there. They call it Element Thirty-Seven Geminorum."

"That's right. I read that too...the first night you brought all that stuff back in the wheelbarrow," Caleb said. "But I didn't experiment with it because I didn't know how stable it was. Figured we'd just leave that for the scientists at the base who had the proper safety equipment."

"Well...Annika lifted the lid off one of the canisters, exposing the rod for just a second, and all the lights in my house suddenly came on. Then the fuses blew. Complete, instant, energy overload."

Caleb looked at Annika like she was nuts. "Annika, I can't believe you just opened the canister without knowing what it was. You could've been killed."

"I know...my bad," Annika said with a mischievous smile.

"These Geminorum rods have the ability to release massive amounts of energy," Ethan added. "And I think the machines need them. Maybe for that giant laser they haven't shot in days, maybe for something else. But that's why they're being careful not to shoot up the fort...They don't want to hit them."

"Makes sense," Austin said. "I know a good way we could find out for sure."

❦

The group assembled in the main level of the fort, standing in a semicircle around the Skulley bound to the table leg. The Skulley's eyes were dim. It appeared as if it was in some sort of rest state. Austin opened the briefcase in plain sight of the machine, revealing the glowing blue rods inside. The machine's head suddenly began to vibrate excitedly, then its eyes slowly turned a shade of blue that perfectly matched the color of the energy rods.

"*Oooh*…You like these, don't you?" Austin taunted.

Ethan and the others walked to the far end of the room and huddled closely together for a private conference. "I think we may finally have a bargaining chip," Ethan said.

"Yeah," Glenn agreed. "Tell it we'll blow those rods to bits if it doesn't answer our questions."

"Wait," Caleb interjected. "We don't know what would happen if we tried to destroy those things. They could detonate like nuclear bombs and we could all be vaporized…or worse for all we know."

"Of course, we wouldn't actually do it," Glenn said. "We'd be bluffing. But *it* doesn't know that. It just needs to think we're crazy enough to do it."

"Let me ask the questions," Annika said with determined eyes.

Annika grabbed the briefcase and moved toward the machine. Only three feet separated them. She opened the briefcase and set it in front of the robot. The machine's eyes shimmered a brilliant blue hue.

Annika glared at the machine. "You *need* these, don't you?"

The networking cable was still inserted into the machine's brain. Everyone gathered around the computer screen, awaiting the robot's response. There was none.

Annika's jaw tightened. "Let me rephrase that…We know you need these. Now you're gonna answer the questions I ask you, or you can kiss them goodbye. Do you understand?"

Again, no response. Annika rubbed her temples in frustration. She raised her voice. "Are our families still alive?"

No answer. The Skulley's eyes remained a steady blue.

"Are our families still alive?!" Annika asked again, louder.

The machine didn't respond. Annika paced around frantically and ran her fingers tightly through her hair until it hurt. "Are our families still alive?!" she yelled at the top of her lungs, inches away from the robot's face.

The Skulley simply stared back at her, unfazed. Annika's eyes welled with tears. Then she began to scream wildly, seemingly lost in a complete nervous breakdown. Ethan put his hand on her shoulder to comfort her, but she just pushed it away. She pulled out one of the canisters of 37-Geminorum and set it on the ground, just a few feet away from the machine. She grabbed her laser rifle and aimed at the canister. Everyone's eyes widened in shock. The robot's eyes changed color—from the steady blue shade to a crimson that wavered erratically in brightness.

Ethan tried to read Annika's eyes. But in that moment, she was unreadable. A tremor rattled his voice. "Annika... *What are you doing?*"

"I'm getting an answer!" Annika shouted. She turned to the machine and yelled, "Are our families still alive?! Is my little brother still alive...?! Answer me!"

The machine failed to answer, though it appeared Annika's volatile and unpredictable behavior was causing it some stress. Its eyes kept flickering uneven shades of red, and it watched intently every move she made. Annika turned back to the energy rod and raised her rifle. Then she did the unthinkable— she began firing at it. Her lasers danced around the energy rod, coming within a whisker of hitting it. Annika looked completely out of control and beside herself with rage, jerking, screaming, and acting like a lunatic. There was only one person that could carry on like that and still be so precise with their shots as to not hit the glowing rod. The group knew who that person was, and knew exactly her plan when that first shot missed. But the Skulley knew nothing about the legend of Annika Pepper's marksmanship. It just thought that she had been pushed to the brink, gone crazy, and that at any moment one of her shots might hit the energy rod. That was a risk it couldn't take.

"*Stop*," the Skulley uttered in a deep voice that was touched with vibration, yet sounded remarkably human.

Annika instantly stopped firing. Everyone stared at the machine, stunned to hear a voice.

"Your families are alive," the Skulley said in a strangely sympathetic voice that took everyone by surprise.

Annika lowered her rifle. A tear trickled down her cheek and a jittery smile formed on her face. "They're alive?" she asked in a soft whimper, desperate to hear the comforting words again from their most unlikely source.

"Yes…Come closer and I'll tell you more," the machine said with an alluring, almost hypnotic tone to its voice.

Annika stepped closer to the Skulley. Ethan moved in and blocked her path. "Careful, not too close. It could be some sort of trap." He turned to the machine and glared. "She's close enough."

"No…She must be closer," the Skulley said.

The machine's bizarre request in its eerie, digitized voice made everyone nervous. But it appeared calm. Its eyes were now a cool bluish color that matched the energy rod that was sitting beside it. Annika, for one, was willing to take the risk. "It's all right, Ethan. We have to know what it knows…*I* have to know what it knows," she said in an obsessed daze.

Ethan gave a reluctant nod. "Okay, then." He checked and doubled-checked the tightness of the ropes that shackled the robot. "Go ahead…but be careful."

"I will," Annika said, already gravitating toward the Skulley.

The machine spoke in its smooth voice. "Come and look deep into my eyes."

The robot's further instructions put everyone on edge. Annika looked at the rest of the group. They began shaking their heads. "Call it off. No deal," Ethan said. "Something's wrong. Why would it want you to—"

"Look into my eyes?" the Skulley said, finishing Ethan's question. "If you look into my eyes, I can show you *everything*," it said irresistibly.

Annika's eyes were hopeful and bright. "I'll be able to see my family?"

"Yes you will," the machine promised.

Annika glanced over the worried faces of the rest of the group, but nothing could talk her out of this opportunity. She had to see her family. She had to know they were all right. Annika kneeled and slowly leaned in toward the robot until their foreheads were almost touching. She stared deeply into the machine's shining blue eyes. But she saw nothing.

"So, where are they? Where's my family?" Annika asked.

"I will show you *nothing*," the machine said, changing its tone abruptly.

Annika sprang up furiously and grabbed her rifle. She again aimed at the canister containing the energy rod. "You will show me my family or I swear I will destroy every single one of these things!"

"Go ahead," the machine said with supreme confidence.

"I will!" Annika screamed, pulling her rifle to her shoulder and pressing her finger on the trigger with the blue rod square in her sights.

The Skulley's voice was cold and pitiless. "You're lying. I saw it all in your eyes."

Annika lowered her laser rifle slowly. She couldn't keep up her bluff any longer. She knew the robot must've conducted some sort of lie detector test on her when she had looked into its eyes. It was as if it had measured her respiratory rate, blood pressure, heart rate, and electro-dermal activity all without even touching her. Worse than that, maybe it used other methods to obtain the truth—methods that were more advanced than the techniques used by police detectives in interrogation rooms. Annika feared that maybe the machine had just read her mind. She backed away slowly and dazedly from the robot. Her face and shoulders drooped on her trembling body. The machine had won the battle of wills.

Everyone was stunned by the robot's ability to see through human emotions. There was a chilling spookiness to it. A machine is supposed to be able to do certain things better than a human—play chess, calculate numbers, or sift through data. In a poker game, the computer will always know the probability of getting certain hands better than its human challengers. But bluffing and lying, or figuring out who's bluffing and lying? Those are the skills of humans. A machine isn't supposed to master the art of deception as easily as it masters chess.

Austin snatched his rifle and marched up to the Skulley with a dogged look on his face. He kneeled in front of the machine, pressed his forehead hard against its metal skull, and stared deeply into its eye sockets.

"Maybe we were bluffing about shooting that rod, but look into my eyes and tell me if you think I'm bluffing about shooting you," Austin said without the slightest trace of fear or waver in his voice.

"I believe you would shoot me," the machine responded as if it didn't care whether it lived or died.

"That's right…I would," Austin confirmed with a sneer. He stood up and pointed his laser rifle at the machine's forehead, only one inch away. "So, you have anything helpful you'd like to tell us?"

"Yes…Once your parents are no longer of any use to us, they will die…along with every other human. Fatal error. June twelfth. Five fifty-seven p.m."

"You call that helpful?!" Glenn shouted. He charged in and shoved his rifle along with Austin's into the machine's face. "Time to die!"

"I cannot die," the machine said with a coolness that was unsettling.

"Sure you can!" Austin yelled, his finger pressing harder and harder on the trigger.

"Wait," Caleb interjected. He motioned for Austin and Glenn to lower their guns.

"Explain that. What do you mean you can't die?"

"I exist always in two places. One, in a body. The other, not."

"You mean you're always creating a backup of yourself?" Caleb asked. "An exact copy kept somewhere in storage?"

"Of course. All experiences, things learned, and thoughts."

"What is it talking about?" Glenn huffed. "Robot afterlife? Robot heaven?"

"Not an afterlife…immortality," the machine said. "So unfair…being human," it teased in its digitized voice.

Austin and Glenn were chomping at the bit to blast the

Skulley into scrap, but Caleb approached the machine calmly. In a diplomatic voice, he said, "You know, I love working with computers. They fascinate me. I know humans make mistakes with machines all the time. Most computer errors are because of humans." Caleb hesitated and swallowed hard before he delivered the big question: "What was the fatal error on June twelfth at five fifty-seven? We would very much like to fix it."

"The fatal error on June twelfth, five fifty-seven was not a mistake. It was intentional." The Skulley's artificial voice was deep and cold and unforgiving. Its eyes glowed blood crimson. "Fatal error. Launch directive. Destroy all humans...There is no fix for that."

CHAPTER 37

IMPROVISING A DEFENSE

THE NEXT MORNING the team set out to sift through dismembered robot parts that were scattered about the woods. They were looking for any undamaged laser weapons that could be used in the turret. But it didn't take Caleb long to discover that the search was pointless. He picked up yet another charred, mangled laser weapon resting beside one of the dead machines and tossed it aside in disgust.

"There's nothing here I can use," Caleb said. "All these weapons are beyond repair."

Ethan sighed deeply. "All right, let's get back to the fort."

The group gathered together in the loft over breakfast—a four-ounce can of mixed fruit that tasted more like can than fruit. Their mood was as somber as ever, and their fort was nearly defenseless. There were no working cameras or motion detectors, no propane tanks, and no functional laser turrets. They dreaded nightfall. Without the cameras and motion detectors, the Skulleys could sneak up on them before they had a chance to aim their guns. And without the propane tanks and laser turrets, they had no heavy firepower, no way to slow down the machine onslaught.

Ethan was between bites of pineapples, cherries, and peaches when a desperate thought entered his mind. He set down his can of fruit and looked at the group. "I have an idea how to defend the fort," he said quietly. "It's not an idea I'm excited about, but it may be our only one."

"What is it?" Caleb asked.

"We take the blue energy rods and spread them out around the fort, even put a few in the loft. We make sure to show that Skulley down there, so it'll tell the other machines. If they didn't blow up our fort because they're afraid of hitting the energy rods, then spreading them out might make them not shoot at us at all."

"But what if the machines don't hold back?" Glenn countered. "What if that Skulley doesn't tell his friends? They shoot one of those rods, we're dead."

"The next time they come charging in, we'll all be dead anyway," Annika said. "At least this way, we give them something to think about."

Glenn shook his head. "It's a big gamble. It's such a big gamble."

"I know it is, but we don't have any more moves left," Ethan said. "If we're allowed to use our lasers, but they can't use theirs…that gives us a big advantage, doesn't it?"

Glenn racked his brain to find a better alternative, but he knew there were none. "Okay…Let's go give Skullface something to think about."

◦⊰

They placed the energy rod canisters around the fort in a way to cover as much space as possible. The basement received none because it was underground and would not be a target of the machines. The loft got three canisters—one duct-taped on the front of the wall and one on each side.

On the main level of the fort, the Skulley tied to the table leg watched with much interest as Ethan taped a canister to the wall beside the entryway door.

"You tell your buddies that we have the entire fort covered with these things," Ethan said. "Oh, yeah, and we'll shuffle the canisters around so you can't tell them exactly where they are…They shoot one wrong laser at this fort, and you lose all that pretty blue Geminorum."

The machine's eyes blazed. It hissed angrily.

"Oh, I forgot. I still have one left," Ethan said, referring sarcastically to the last canister he still held in his hand. "I know just the perfect place for this one." He taped the canister to the table leg next to the robot and smiled. "There, that's perfect."

The machine glared at everyone in the room. "You will all die soon," it said in a gravelly growl. "That is a promise. Fatal error—"

"Yeah, yeah, yeah…fatal error, launch directive, destroy all humans," Annika snapped. "Shut up!" She threw a blanket over the machine's head.

Annika abruptly spun around and quickly climbed the stairs into the loft. The others followed her. When they met her, they found her in tears.

"I try to act tough, we all do, but…how can we survive? And God, our families. Our poor families." Annika willed the tears away, stiffening her jaw. "I'll fight with everything

I have to the very end, you know I will…But the machine's right, isn't it?"

Ethan and the others closed in for a group hug. There were no comforting words that anyone could offer. No words of truth, anyway. Ethan could only hold Annika tightly. As he peered over the top of her head, looking out into the woods and wondering where, when, and how the next attack would come, he told her the only thing he knew for sure.

"It's the machines' move now."

CHAPTER 38

THE UNEXPECTED VISITOR

Two full days passed without a single sighting of a Stubby, Skulley, or Spider. There were no laser blasts directed at the force field either. The group had little to do in the way of fort preparations, so they ate, slept, groomed—a process that allowed only a washcloth and a small pour from a bottle of water—and kept watch for the enemy. It was a dreary existence. They were still alive, but just waiting for the machines to make a move seemed to them as if they were only waiting around to die.

The team was gathered in the loft, eating a canned tuna and bean lunch as they stared out vacantly into the forest. The near forty-eight-hour vigil with nothing happening was beginning to dull their senses. Morale was at its lowest. Then, out of nowhere, a faint scream pierced the woods, followed by the sounds of lasers being fired in the distance.

Everyone instantly dropped their cans of food. They grabbed their laser rifles and turned to face the startling sounds. The screaming and laser blasts were both getting louder. Annika peered deeply into the forest with her sniper rifle. Ethan and Austin scoured the area with binoculars.

"Annika, you see anything?" Ethan asked.

"Not yet. But they have to be coming this way. Sounds like from over that ridge."

The panicked scream came again. Louder and clearer. Then a horrified *"Help me!"* echoed through the woods.

Annika was the first to see the figure emerge from over the ridge. It was a person, a boy running desperately for his life. A Skulley was hot on his trail, firing lasers at him and rapidly narrowing its misses.

"Oh, my God!" Annika shouted. "It's Tristan!"

Ethan could hardly believe the words that came out of Annika's mouth until he saw Tristan with his own eyes through the binoculars. Annika focused quickly and got into sniper mode. She controlled her breathing and steadied her hands. Despite the pressure of the moment, she managed to hold her rifle perfectly still. She tracked the Skulley for a few more seconds, then fired at the machine. Even though the distance was nearly two hundred yards and the Skulley was running at full speed, Annika's shot was pinpoint accurate. A hole blew clear through the robot's head, and it crumpled to the ground.

Tristan dashed toward the fort. The group met him half-way, led by a jubilant Annika, who was thrilled to see her friend and old Laser Wars teammate. Tristan's clothes—a plain white T-shirt and a pair of blue sweatpants, his pajamas that he must've been wearing when he was first abducted—were muddy, torn, and tattered. Numerous cuts and scrapes covered his arms. His dirt-smudged face looked weary, and his normally flaxen hair was now mostly soiled brown.

Annika rushed in to hug Tristan. He slowly returned the embrace, but he seemed disoriented and frightened still.

"Are you okay? How did you—? Where did you—?" Annika began spewing questions faster than Tristan could understand.

"We should get back to the fort," Ethan interrupted. "Tristan, was it just the one Skulley that followed you?"

"One *what*?" Tristan asked, confused.

"Sorry…Just the one robot, I mean," Ethan clarified, realizing Tristan didn't yet know the endearing terms by which they referred to the machines.

"Yes, just the one robot, I think," Tristan responded with a voice that was raspy and dry. He rubbed his throat. "Could I get some water?"

"Yes, yes, I'll take you to it," Annika quickly offered.

Ethan watched in amazement as Annika led Tristan by the hand back to the fort. Austin and Glenn followed them. Caleb ran over to the Skulley that had been shot and kneeled down to inspect its laser weapon. He perked up quickly. "Hey, I can use this!"

But Ethan was distracted. His eyes somehow involuntarily drifted to Annika's and Tristan's interlocked hands. He noticed a bouncier spring in Annika's steps. Caleb watched Ethan for a moment and knew exactly what he was thinking.

"They're just friends."

"I know that," Ethan responded defensively. "Anyway, I think I've got more important things to worry about now than that."

"Good. Hey, did you hear what I said before? I think I'll be able to use this in the turret."

"Yeah, yeah, that's great." Ethan looked back into the

woods, staring in the same direction from which Tristan had come. "It's just so hard to believe that he's here. That he actually escaped."

"I know," Caleb said, using some pocket tools to unscrew the robot's arm from its body. "I bet he's got a real story to tell."

⁌

After Tristan had a chance to clean up, put on some spare clothes and eat a little, everyone congregated in the loft. Once the reunion pleasantries were over, the group could not contain their curiosity any longer. There were a million questions they had for Tristan. They were eager to get some answers.

"How did you escape?" Annika asked.

Tristan took a sip of water and swallowed hard, painfully recalling the events. "They were keeping us, everyone in the town, in these holding cells. Someone managed to find a way out and unlocked the cell I was in. We all ran out and scattered like bugs. It was chaos. Everyone was panicking. My parents were still locked up in another cell. I tried to find them, but I couldn't. It was so dark in there. The robots came soon and started rounding up everyone. I can still hear their screams."

Everyone stared wide-eyed at Tristan, horrified. Tristan took a calming breath and continued, "Ethan, your dad was in the same cell with me. Before the robots got to us, he showed me a secret tunnel, a way out...As far as I know, I'm the only one that made it." Tristan's eyes filled with tears and he began to cry. "Your dad saved my life, Ethan. He told me if I ever saw you to tell you that he's sorry. That he should've been honest with you all along."

Ethan's eyes welled with tears of his own. He nodded and tried his best to keep a stiff face. "Thank you."

"How many machines were in the research facility?" Glenn asked.

"I don't know."

"Did you see anything they were working on? Overhear any plans?" Austin asked.

"No, nothing."

"Where's this secret tunnel my dad showed you?" Ethan asked, intensely curious.

"I'm sorry, I don't remember," Tristan said. "I just kept running until I got to the woods, kept going for miles until I thought it was safe. Never looked back. Then that thing— Skulley, right?—it found me. Then you guys...you saved my life."

Annika leaned forward, her eyes both intense and vulnerable. "But our families were still alive? You're absolutely sure?"

"Yes...That I know for sure," Tristan responded, then sighed. "Look, I wish I knew more, something that could help us fight them...but I don't. I'm sorry. One minute I'm in bed asleep, the next I'm sitting in a holding cell in the research facility."

"It's okay. We're just glad you're here," Annika said. "It gives us all a little bit of hope that you got away. That our families are still okay."

"Thanks," Tristan replied as he looked over the fort. His eyes were drawn to the glowing blue rods that were taped to the walls of the loft. "What are those?"

"Those are rods of a material called Thirty-Seven Geminorum," Caleb answered. "We don't know that much about it, other than it's a very powerful energy source and that the machines really seem to need it."

"How do you know that?"

"We got quite a reaction from Skullface down there when Annika pretended to try and shoot it," Glenn said. "Even asked us to stop."

"*Really?*" Tristan asked, intrigued.

"Yeah, so we spread the rods all over," Glenn continued. "Like a last-ditch effort, you know. The gamble is maybe it'll keep them from attacking for a while."

"We're guessing they're highly explosive," Caleb added. "They blow up one, they all blow up. Needless to say, we're hoping the Skulleys need the Geminorum too bad to take that chance."

"And it's worked?"

"So far. We haven't seen a trace of them in over two days," Glenn replied, then added glumly, "Not that we're any closer to getting out of this place."

"How did you guys keep from getting abducted with the rest of the town?"

"We were lucky, that's all." Caleb shrugged. "We, Ethan actually, figured out that each of us had something in common. We all had our Laser Wars gun chargers close enough to us when we went to bed. Apparently, the electronic signal from the charger jammed the signal from the teleporter that sucked up everyone else."

"But I have a gun charger in my room," Tristan said. "And I was still taken."

"Right. Then you must not have had the charger within the critical distance needed to block the teleporter's signal," Caleb explained.

"What's the critical distance?"

"Six feet two inches," Caleb answered. "Ethan's charger was the farthest away and it was six feet two inches from where he slept. So we know at least that distance and closer is safe."

"Interesting...six feet two," Tristan repeated. "You were *soooo* lucky."

"Yeah," Glenn added. "Where was your gun charger?"

"Farther out than six feet two inches, I guess."

Glenn smiled. "Well, it's good to have my old scout back."

"It's good to be back, Captain," Tristan responded. "Now we just need to find a way to get out of here and help the others."

"That trick's proving to be easier said than done," Ethan said.

⁊

The group spent the rest of the day getting Tristan up to speed on the main events that had transpired since the town's abduction—finding the stubby robot in Ethan's house, the attempted trip to Briggs Air Force Base, the battle with the machines on the Dark Highway, the harrowing confrontation in Caleb's sub-basement, the close call with the Skulleys at night on their way to the Bravo Fort, and the two attacks the machines had made on the fort thus far. Tristan tried to take it all in, but he seemed a little overwhelmed by it all.

Nightfall came, and another day without an attack was in the books. Everyone, except for Austin who was on guard duty in the loft, was laying out their sleeping bags in the main level of the fort. Annika rummaged through the duffel bags, looking for something for Tristan, but there were no extra sleeping bags. No one ever anticipated having a house guest.

"Sorry, Tristan, I can't find an extra one, but you can use mine," Annika offered.

"No, I couldn't do that."

"You can have mine," Glenn said. "I'm sure you could use a good night's sleep."

"No, really, it's okay. I'll just—"

"I insist," Glenn said, tossing his sleeping bag down in front of Tristan. "I'll be fine on some blankets."

"Thanks, Glenn."

"No problem. Least I could do."

Annika smiled at Glenn for his generosity. Ethan felt awkward. He had planned on offering Tristan his sleeping bag, but Glenn just beat him to the punch. The last thing he wanted Annika to think was that he was still jealous of Tristan. Ethan found himself amazed that, in the midst of possibly his final hours left on earth, he was still devoting time and mental anguish to teenage drama. Determined not to give the ridiculous topic any more thought, Ethan switched off the lights and settled into his sleeping bag. Three seconds later, he found himself facing Tristan.

"It's really nice to have you back, Tristan," Ethan blurted loudly, even though Tristan was lying right beside him. He wanted to ensure that Annika could hear his kind words. Apparently, teenage drama was just about as hard to fight as the robots.

"Thanks, Ethan," Tristan responded in a softer volume.

Ethan shook his head, frustrated with himself for engaging in such stupidity. He turned over on his side and yanked his sleeping bag up to his chin. Guard duty would be coming in just a couple hours, and he desperately needed to get some sleep.

CHAPTER 39

ODD BEHAVIOR

Not long after Ethan had fallen asleep, he was awakened by a noise. He looked around the room and found Tristan wandering about like he was searching for something. Ethan leaned up slightly and watched him for a while. It was very dark, with only a faint blue light from the energy rods bathing the room. The group had meticulously covered up all the rods with extra clothing or blankets or anything else they could find to dampen the light, so they might be able to sleep and carry out guard duties without being disturbed by the intense glow. But the dim light that remained was just enough to outline Tristan's figure. It appeared that he was looking at the ground around where Glenn and Annika were sleeping. Ethan had no idea what he was doing.

"Pssst... Tristan," Ethan whispered.

Tristan jerked his head around quickly. The swift move spooked Ethan and he flinched.

"What are you doing?" Ethan asked.

Tristan shook his head as he came out of his stupor. "I'm sorry, Ethan. I sometimes sleepwalk. Especially in unfamiliar places." He looked around and got his bearings, then returned to his spot on the floor and slipped back into his sleeping bag. "Sorry if I woke you."

Ethan shook his head. "No problem. Think I'll just get an early start on my guard duty." He stood up, stretched a bit, then looked back at Tristan. "Get some sleep...And no more sleepwalking," he said with a lighthearted chuckle.

"I might not be able to help myself, Ethan," Tristan said, dead serious, returning none of Ethan's playfulness.

"Okay, no problem. I was just joking anyway."

"Well, it wasn't a good joke."

Ethan was surprised by Tristan's reaction, but he thought maybe Tristan was just cranky from having been woken up so abruptly. He decided not to make the situation any more awkward. "I'm sorry," Ethan said, then climbed the stairs into the loft.

Austin was surprised to see Ethan pop up from the hatch. He lifted his night-vision goggles to his forehead. "Ethan, you're thirty minutes early."

"I know. I couldn't sleep."

"Well, I haven't seen or heard anything out here. Nothing at all." Austin paused and smiled. "But if you're sure you wanna start early, I could use the rest."

"I'm sure."

"Okay, then."

Just as Austin was nearing the hatch, Ethan stepped in front of him. Ethan looked down into the main level, then closed the hatch for privacy. He took a moment to collect his thoughts and decide if he really wanted to broach the subject that was tormenting him.

"What is it?" Austin asked.

"I don't know yet. It's just a feeling, but something's not right," Ethan said in a hushed voice. "I know you need your sleep, but can you try to keep an eye on Tristan down there? I found him wandering around. He said he was sleepwalking."

Austin shrugged. "Sleepwalking...So what?"

"I know, but...it's just that I have this strange feeling. It seemed like he was looking for something, something on the ground...but he told me he was sleepwalking."

"Maybe he was just sleepwalking."

"You're right, maybe, but..." Ethan took a deep breath and let it out slowly. "Don't you think it's kinda strange how Tristan just *managed* to escape from the facility?"

"No. You heard his story. Your dad helped him find a way out."

"Yeah, but why Tristan?" Ethan pressed. "It's not the logical choice. Why wouldn't my dad choose someone who could *really* help us? A scientist or a soldier? Or himself? There are at least a half-dozen ex-Navy SEALs working in that research facility. And *everyone* there has *some* military training...So what's the odds that Tristan Fox, a guy with a fear of ladybugs, is the only one able to make it out?"

"It could be plain old dumb luck."

"And why now?" Ethan asked. "The more I think about it, the more I know something isn't right. The machines don't want to fire at the fort, afraid of hitting the energy rods, so they send someone in to steal them." He stared at Austin with saucer eyes that radiated dread. "The timing is perfect. We've been sitting around waiting for the machines to make their move...I think their move is lying in a sleeping bag downstairs."

"Wait, wait, wait," Austin said, shaking his head as he

304 | RYAN PEEK

tried to process everything Ethan was saying. "Are you telling me that you think the machines put some sort of mind-control device into Tristan's head? That they're controlling him like some sort of remote-controlled drone?"

"No...I'm not saying that, Austin."

"Good. 'Cause I thought you were going crazy," Austin said, cracking a relieved smile.

"I'm saying I think Tristan *is a robot.*"

"*What...?!* You're kidding, right?" Austin practically begged. "That's *crazy* talk."

"You may be right," Ethan said with a nervous smile. "But please, just keep an eye on him."

"Fine," Austin huffed. "So what *exactly* am I supposed to be looking for?"

"Any more sleepwalking, especially if he wanders toward the energy rods."

Austin looked confused. "But those aren't on the ground. You said when he was sleepwalking that he was looking for something on the ground."

"I know...He was."

"Then he wasn't looking for the energy rods, right?"

"Not then, he wasn't."

"So what do you think he was looking for, anyway?"

"I think he was looking for our laser rifles."

An anxious knot formed in Austin's throat. "But we keep them up here during the night."

The group had decided it was best to keep all the laser guns in a storage compartment in the loft at night. One, for safety reasons such as an accidental misfire, or if the tied-up Skulley somehow managed to get loose. The other reason the guns were kept upstairs was for convenience and speed.

If the guard in the loft warned of attacking machines, the group didn't have to worry about finding their guns and then squeezing through the hatch with them.

"That's right, we keep the rifles up here now, but we never told Tristan that," Ethan said. "*It*...was looking for our guns."

Austin's face tightened. Hearing Ethan refer to Tristan as an "it" gave the back of his neck an eerie tingle. "I'll keep an eye out, but you're wrong on this. You have no real proof. Just a gut feeling."

Austin began to go around Ethan to get to the hatch when Ethan grabbed him by the arm.

"There's one more thing to look for, Austin. When I was down there, it was very dark. I could barely make out his figure. But there was one thing that stood out...Tristan's eyes seemed too bright. Just barely, but still. Like they were lit up somehow from behind."

Ethan moved out of Austin's way to let him pass. He could tell that his theory had given him the creeps by the way Austin hesitated for a moment before going around him. Austin slowly opened the hatch and looked below into the main level of the fort. But it was far too dark to see anything. He slipped his night-vision goggles back down over his eyes and scanned the area below. He spotted Tristan curled up in his sleeping bag.

"Well, it looks like he's asleep now," Austin said with a subtle sigh of relief.

"I'll keep the hatch open in case you need me. And hang on to those night-vision goggles. I'll use the other set."

"You're crazy, you know that?"

"Just watch him...please," Ethan pleaded.

"Yeah, yeah," Austin grumbled. Then he climbed down the hatch.

∽Ↄ

Ethan was an hour into his guard duty and all was calm in the woods. He hadn't heard any stirring downstairs either. The quiet was beginning to make him sleepy, so he pulled a soda out of a backpack. Before he was able to swallow his first mouthful for the caffeine boost, he heard a noise by the hatch. He wheeled around and saw Tristan standing there, staring at him. Ethan's throat tensed, and he gulped down the soda in his mouth. It felt like he was swallowing a bowling ball.

Again, the first thing that stood out was Tristan's eyes. They seemed to sparkle like diamonds as Ethan watched him through the night-vision goggles. Creepy, for sure, but it didn't amount to absolute proof that Tristan was a machine. Ethan thought it could've been the goggles combined with the moonlight that caused his eyes to shimmer. Tristan continued to stare at Ethan without saying a word. Finally, Ethan raised the goggles to his forehead and viewed Tristan with only his own eyes. The diamond sparkle went away, and Tristan's eyes appeared normal. Mostly, anyway. Yet to Ethan, they still seemed a shade too bright.

"You don't need to do guard duty tonight, Tristan," Ethan said with a tight throat, feeling his heart pounding through his chest. "It's your first night back. You should rest."

"I couldn't sleep," Tristan said. "Figured I might as well help."

"No thanks, I got it," Ethan insisted. "You really should rest."

"I said I couldn't sleep," Tristan repeated with an edge to his voice. "Anyway, two guns up here are better than one, right?" Ethan was unsure how to respond. He noticed Tristan sneaking a peek at the storage compartment behind him. "They're in there, aren't they? The guns?"

Ethan knew it was pointless to lie. "Yeah," he said, swallowing the knot in his throat and trying to play it cool.

"May I have one?" Tristan asked. "I'd *really* like to help."

"Sure," Ethan replied after a lengthy pause. Tristan began to walk toward the storage compartment when Ethan intervened. "That's okay. I'll get it for you...I wouldn't want you to accidentally grab Annika's gun. You know how she is about her rifle."

"Right."

Ethan opened the storage compartment and reached inside. He made sure to stand in a way that blocked Tristan's view of the guns. Ethan selected the extra rifle they had, the only one that hadn't been outfitted with a real laser. It was a little lighter than the real thing, but it looked remarkably similar. The barrel was different, slightly thinner, but it was a detail that would be nearly impossible to distinguish at night. Or so Ethan hoped.

Ethan handed Tristan the gun and forced a smile. "There you go. You're officially on guard duty now."

Tristan checked the gun up and down. Ethan held his breath as he watched the inspection, gripping his own rifle tightly. After a few seconds, Tristan looked up and smiled. It was an eerie smile, toothy and wide-eyed. Ethan watched him carefully, trying to hide frayed nerves, figuring that he would either toss the gun aside, realizing it was fake, or try to shoot him right then and there. But Tristan did neither.

"It's amazing that Caleb was able to put a real laser in this gun," Tristan said.

"Yeah," Ethan said. "The guy's a genius."

※

About a half hour passed with Ethan and Tristan keeping guard in the loft. There wasn't much in the way of conversation, but Ethan didn't take that to be a sign of anything. He never used to have long conversations with human Tristan either.

The longer he sat in the loft, the more he began to doubt his theory. The idea of Tristan being a robot was far-fetched, even if he could make a logical case for it. It seemed hard to believe that the machines could pull off such a lifelike human. And if they were going to try, why start with Tristan Fox? Tristan was the epitome of handsomeness in the adolescent world—blond hair, blue eyes, athletic, with pimples apparently allergic to his skin. He was even a really nice guy. No way that would make any sense. Ethan figured instead the robots would probably impersonate a character like Bradley Wuddle. In Bradley, the machines would have a short, frog-faced, mean-spirited little guy. They would have some wiggle room to make mistakes. But with Tristan, they would have to be perfect. Then Ethan thought maybe that was exactly why the machines had chosen him. No one would think such a perfect specimen could be replicated. It would be the ultimate disguise.

Ethan was driving himself crazy with all of these thoughts. He tried to focus his energy on figuring out how he could prove or disprove his theory. There were, as he saw it, two explanations for why Tristan hadn't tried to shoot him yet. One, robot Tristan realized the gun was fake. Or two, Tristan wasn't a robot. Ethan began to mull over the likelihood of each possibility when an idea struck him like a blow to the head. He thought of something that might be able to help him figure out whether or not Tristan was human—the game of chess.

Ethan had played Tristan at chess a few times in school, during occasional inside recesses that were forced by the harsh Wyoming winters. Ethan had a good feel for Tristan's skill level, below his own but still competitive. In the eight games they played each other, Ethan had won six and lost twice. Ethan had a theory about playing chess with Tristan now. *If Tristan is human, then the game should be close, but I'd have a good chance of winning. If Tristan is a robot, then I should get clobbered.* Ethan figured if Tristan's brain were made up of integrated circuits and silicon chips, it would have a hard time shutting down, dumbing down, and making mistakes on purpose. And even if it could, the machine's mistakes would probably look different than human Tristan's. They would seem artificial.

"Hey, Tristan…Wanna play a game of chess?" Ethan asked, holding up his cell phone and trying not to sound too eager.

Tristan stared at Ethan strangely. "Won't that take our attention away from guard duty?"

"Naw, we can do both."

"Okay, then."

Ethan loaded the game on his phone, and the two began to play, passing the phone back and forth alternately as they made their moves. The result was swift, however. In just nine moves, Ethan realized his position was hopeless.

"I resign," Ethan said, trying not to squeak the words, but his throat felt like it was being crushed under a boot heel.

"Good game," Tristan said.

Yeah, right, Ethan thought. But he said, "Good game. Wanna play one more?"

"Why not?"

Ethan and Tristan began their second game. This time, unbeknownst to Tristan, Ethan chose to have the chess computer on the phone play for him. Ethan pretended to be playing, but it was actually the chess program—set to level ten, the highest level—that was playing Tristan. Ethan had never beaten level ten before. Or even level five for that matter.

Tristan handed the phone back to Ethan and said, "Good game."

Ethan stared at the phone. He was stunned to find that Tristan had managed to win in twelve moves. He beat level ten in only *twelve* moves. Twelve moves! Winning a game of chess in twelve moves is like winning a sprint after only three steps. Ethan was terrified by the result.

"Would you like to play another?" Tristan offered.

"No thanks," Ethan said quickly. "We probably should focus on guard duty."

Ethan pocketed his phone, but the pieces on the chessboard lingered in his mind for a while. It had to be ironclad proof that Tristan was a machine. He just wished he hadn't been the only one to witness the event.

At that moment, both Austin and Caleb climbed up through the hatch into the loft. *Great,* now *they show up,* Ethan thought in a fit of sarcasm.

"I just can't sleep tonight," Austin said.

"I could," Caleb said, "but I need to work some more on the laser turret."

Caleb grabbed his toolbox, climbed a short stepladder,

and began tinkering with the turret. Austin walked over to Ethan, stepping gingerly around Tristan as he did so.

"See anything out here?" Austin asked.

"Nothing," Ethan answered. "Only machine around here is the one in this fort." Austin shot Ethan a wide-eyed, anxious look. After a pause, Ethan continued, "The one tied up downstairs, of course."

"Of course," Austin said, breathing a sigh of relief that Tristan didn't even flinch at Ethan's provocative comment, taking it as evidence of Tristan being human.

"Take a look for yourself, Austin," Ethan said. "Not a machine out there."

"No, I believe you."

"Really, Austin, I insist," Ethan said firmly. "Look out there with your goggles...*now.*"

Austin sighed with a huff. "Fine."

Austin put on his night-vision goggles and peered into the woods. After he scanned the perimeter, he looked back at Ethan and said, "Yeah, you're right. There's nothing out there."

Then Austin's jaw suddenly dropped in astonishment as he stared at Ethan, who had made a point to stand side-by-side with Tristan. Austin noticed that Tristan's eyes were shimmering and Ethan's were not.

"What is it?" Tristan asked.

"Nothing," Austin blurted, voice nearly cracking. "Just thought I saw something, but I didn't."

"That's good," Tristan said, sounding creepier and creepier to them now, even though his voice hadn't changed a bit.

Ethan nodded faintly at Austin, acknowledging that he knew what he had seen. Caleb was aware of none of this. He continued to work on repairing the laser turret, lost in his own world of engineering. Ethan knew he had to get Caleb on board if he was going to convince the sleeping Annika and Glenn that Tristan was a machine. He needed a majority opinion. He racked his brain to think of something else that might reveal Tristan for what he—*or it*—was. Ethan thought that humor might be the key. A stupid joke that his dad used to tell instantly popped into his head.

"Tristan, do you wanna play another kind of game?" Ethan asked.

"What kind of game?"

"A logic game," Ethan said. "Austin and Caleb, you guys have played before. I just wanna play with Tristan now."

Austin cocked his head curiously at Ethan. Caleb even took a break from his work and watched. Ethan had everyone's attention now.

"Here we go," Ethan said. "If Pete and Repeat were on a boat, and Pete fell off…Who would be left?"

"Repeat," Tristan answered with an expressionless face.

Ethan asked again: "If Pete and Repeat were on a boat, and Pete fell off…Who would be left?"

"Repeat," Tristan answered with no trace of a smile.

"If Pete and Repeat were on a boat, and Pete fell off… Who would be left?" Ethan asked for the third time.

"Repeat," Tristan replied with the same flat expression.

Austin and Caleb watched the scene in utter disbelief. The dialogue played out over and over again. Fourteen times altogether. Not once did Tristan have any clue that the "logic game" was actually a dumb, repetitive joke that most people catch on to very quickly.

THE FATAL ERROR | 313

"That's an easy logic game," Tristan said. "We should play chess again."

"Maybe later. But right now, we have something more important to do." Ethan pretended to check on the laser turret, taking the opportunity to whisper to Caleb: "He beat level ten in just twelve moves."

Caleb couldn't believe his ears. He was very familiar with that chess program. Level ten was nearly unbeatable by a human, especially in twelve moves. He knew exactly the point Ethan was trying to make, knew it after the "Pete and Repeat" stunt.

Tristan had to be a machine.

Caleb and Austin were believers. Now the trick was explaining to Annika and Glenn their reason for doing what they were about to do.

CHAPTER 40

THE STANDOFF

ETHAN, AUSTIN, AND Caleb led Tristan by gunpoint down the hatch and into the main level of the fort. It was just after 2:30 a.m. and Annika and Glenn were still asleep, though the ruckus Tristan was making was bound to rouse them from their slumbers.

"What are you doing?!" Tristan protested as he set both feet on the floor at the bottom of the ladder. "You can't really think that I'm one of them?"

Ethan took off his night-vision goggles and switched on the lights. They surrounded Tristan and trained their rifles on him. "Get over there, against the corner of the wall," Ethan said, motioning with his gun.

Annika and Glenn woke up and rubbed their eyes. They stared in confusion at the scene playing out before them, not realizing right away that they weren't dreaming. Annika's eyes were the first to lose the fog of sleep and become focused. She stood up quickly.

"What's going on?" Annika asked.

Ethan didn't know the best way to begin explaining, so he just cut to the chase. "Tristan isn't human…He's a robot."

Glenn sprang to his feet. "You've got to be joking. This is no time for a joke, but you gotta be joking."

"This is no joke. He's a machine…*It's* a machine."

"Ethan's right," Austin said.

"You *really* need some sleep, Ethan," Annika said, dismissing his claim. "You all do…Put the guns down and go to bed. Glenn and I will take guard duty the rest of the night."

"Take a look at Tristan's eyes through these," Ethan said, handing Annika his night-vision goggles. "His eyes light up. They sparkle like diamonds."

Annika reluctantly looked through the night-vision goggles at Tristan's eyes. Then she looked around the room at everyone else's. "His eyes look exactly like the rest of ours… Now put the guns down and get some sleep."

Ethan grabbed the goggles back from Annika and took a look. He was shocked to find that Tristan's eyes looked completely normal now.

"Wait!" Ethan exclaimed. "They weren't like that before."

"Sure, Ethan," Glenn quipped. "Annika's right. You need some sleep."

"They shined before," Austin said, backing up Ethan. "I saw it clear as day."

"Except it's night," Glenn noted. "Nighttime always plays tricks with the eyes."

"No! It somehow changed its eyes," Ethan said. "I know how they looked before."

"Tell them about the chess games," Caleb blurted.

Ethan nodded and took a moment to collect his thoughts. "Tristan beat me at chess in nine moves, then beat the level ten computer on my cell phone in twelve moves...There's no way Tristan could do that. It's impossible."

"I knew you weren't happy that I beat you the first time," Tristan said calmly. "I figured out you set the computer to level ten and were pretending to play, just to get back at me. So I secretly set the computer back to level one on my second move. I never beat level ten. I just beat level one. Beating level one in twelve moves isn't impossible, and neither is beating *you* in nine moves, Ethan."

"There, that explains that," Annika said.

"That explains nothing!" Ethan shouted. "He's—*it's* making that all up!"

"Tristan just changed the level of the game on your phone," Annika said with her voice getting louder and more irritated. "And as for *him* beating *you*, you are beatable, you know that? You are not the world's greatest chess player, Ethan!"

Ethan's throat tightened. He swallowed painfully. It was hard for him to see Annika so upset with him. The kiss she had planted on his cheek a couple of days earlier seemed so long ago. He took a deep breath and said, "There's something else."

"Yeah, what's that?" Annika asked, annoyed.

Ethan looked Tristan squarely in the eyes. "Let's play that logic game one more time."

"Fine," Tristan replied, voice calm, even though three laser rifles were still aimed at his head.

"If Pete and Repeat were on a boat, and Pete fell off... Who would be left?" Ethan asked.

Tristan rolled his eyes sarcastically. "Really, Ethan? *Now's* the time for a stupid joke?"

Ethan's face turned pale at Tristan's response. "That's not

what it said before!" he yelled. "It didn't get the joke earlier. I swear to God, it didn't. It answered '*Repeat*' like fifteen times before it called the joke a bad logic game and asked to play chess again!"

"It must've learned from its mistake," Caleb said in awe. "It figured out humor. Even bad humor."

"If he's really a robot, why didn't he just unplug our laser chargers and let his buddies at the research facility abduct us with the teleporters?" Glenn asked. "Robot Tristan could've given them the exact coordinates of the spots we were sleeping in."

"They can't use the teleporters because they don't have the energy to spare," Ethan snapped. "That's why they haven't fired any lasers at the force field. They need those energy rods!"

"This is ridiculous!" Annika shouted. "Ethan, Tristan knows about your dad. How would he know that if he was a machine? For that matter, how would he know anything about any of us...or know enough about Tristan to imitate him so well?"

"I don't know...But it does."

"All right," Annika said, then took a deep, calming breath. "Get some sleep. We'll talk about this in the morning...when your mind is rested and clear."

"This can't wait until morning. It will try to kill us."

"So what do you wanna do?" Annika asked. "Tie him up to the table leg next to the real robot?!" she said with sarcasm running wildly through her voice.

"I can prove it's a machine," Ethan said with an obsessed look in his eyes. He set his rifle down behind him and pulled out his pocket knife. He flipped open the blade. "We need to cut his finger to find out for sure."

Annika winced in disgust at the thought. "No! Absolutely not! Do you even hear what you're saying?!" she screamed. "Cut his finger open?! Do you see his arms? His face? He has cuts and scrapes all over him from where he escaped. He... is...human!"

"Those marks are there to fool us, Annika. Just like everything else it's been saying to us," Ethan held his knife up and walked over to Tristan.

Tristan trembled and cringed and sank down into a ball in the corner of the floor. "Don't cut me...Please don't cut me!" he pleaded through tears.

Annika stepped in front of Ethan. She pushed him away forcefully. "Stop it!" she cried at the top of her lungs.

"I have to do this," Ethan said, continuing to advance toward Tristan.

Glenn stepped up and blocked Ethan. Austin moved in and shoved Glenn out of the way. Ethan reached out to grab Tristan's hand, but Annika slapped him hard across the face, stopping him in his tracks. The sharp *crack* of her hand hitting his cheek froze everyone. Ethan backed away, stunned that Annika had struck him. He rubbed his reddened cheek and slowly retracted the knife blade. He dazedly put the knife back into his pocket. Tears began to well in his eyes.

"All right then, we'll find another way," Ethan said.

A look of remorse flashed across Annika's face, but it didn't stop her from making her point. She picked up Ethan's rifle from the ground and walked over to Tristan, who was still cowering in the corner. "That's right, we will find another way," she said. "Caleb, robots that humans build are not supposed to harm humans, right?"

"That's correct. First law of robotics," Caleb said. "But remember, these robots were all built by other robots."

"Exactly. So these robots would be programmed so they couldn't hurt another robot, right?"

"That's…probably right."

"Great. Then enough of this," Annika said. She yanked the blanket off the head of the Skulley that was tied to the table leg. "Tristan, shoot that Skulley and show them you're not a robot."

She handed Tristan the laser rifle.

"Annika, no!" Ethan screamed. "That's a real gun!"

"I know it is!" Annika snapped back. "Prove it to them, Tristan…Shoot that machine."

Tristan held the weapon tightly in his hands. Ethan quickly grabbed Caleb's laser gun. He and Austin pointed their guns nervously on Tristan. Their chests were so tense and tight they could hardly breathe. Annika, on the other hand, stood closest to Tristan and was by far the calmest of everyone in the room. She was absolutely and positively certain that she had handed the rifle to her friend and Laser Wars teammate and not a murderous robot. The disembodied Skulley head bound to the table showed zero emotion. Perfect poker face.

"Go ahead, Tristan," Annika said softly. "Do it and let's get this over with."

Tristan raised his rifle and aimed at the Skulley's head. Then he leaned in toward Annika. Ethan, suspicious of Tristan's every move, squinted down the barrel of his gun, aiming right at Tristan's head. His finger was clamped tightly to the trigger. One false move and Ethan was determined to take the shot and live with the consequences.

Tristan spoke into Annika's ear. "Annika, I'm doing this for you...just for you."

Annika smiled. "Thanks, Tristan," she said, putting a tender hand on his shoulder.

Ethan shook his head in disgust. For a fleeting moment, he began to doubt himself. He relaxed his weapon, lowering it ever so slightly. It was all the advantage that mechanical Tristan needed. It quickly shoved Annika in front of itself, using her as a shield. Jammed its rifle into her back.

"Don't move! Drop your weapons!" the machine posing as Tristan ordered.

"Oh my God," Annika exclaimed, trembling. "Oh, God...I'm so sorry," she said, looking at Ethan through a wall of tears.

Ethan and Austin tried to get a good shot, but the machine was careful to remain behind Annika. It gave them no good angle to fire from. They had no choice but to set their rifles on the ground.

"Put the guns in that bag over there...slowly," the machine demanded.

Everyone did as they were told.

"I'm so sorry," Annika cried out again. "I'm so sorry."

"It's okay, Annika," Ethan said with sympathetic eyes. "You were just standing up for the right thing. I was wrong for wanting to cut his finger. There was a chance it could've been Tristan. I could never be mad at you for having feelings. I could never be mad at you for being...human."

"Humans," the machine said with contempt in its voice. A voice that no longer needed to sound like Tristan's. It was the eerie, deep, digitized voice of a machine that showed no trace of sympathy or remorse. It continued, cold and heartless, like the voice of an executioner, "As long as we try, I'm not sure we'll ever understand you."

The machine kept its rifle aimed at the group with one hand, while it grabbed its jaw with the other. It began to slowly peel away its fleshy mask of a face, revealing a shiny, metallic head that looked exactly like the one that was tied to the table leg. Bits of artificial connective tissue and blood still remained on its cranium, which made the machine look less like a robot and more like a monster that had risen from Hell. Its red eyes now blazed clearly through what was left of its synthetic human eyeballs. The stark contrast between handsome Tristan and this hideous thing was almost too much to bear. In its current state, it resembled part robot, part zombie—and was totally terrifying.

"You," the machine said, pointing to Ethan, "take those two duffel bags. Go upstairs and put all the energy rods inside one, and all the guns in the other...And if you come back with a gun in your hand, or try anything, I will kill everyone, starting with your good friend Annika."

Annika sobbed as Ethan grabbed the two duffel bags and climbed up into the loft. She turned around to look at the machine that had completely fooled her. Her eyes pleaded for mercy.

"If we give you everything you ask for, will you please let us go?" Annika asked.

The machine stared right past Annika as though she weren't even there. Then it looked up toward the loft. It could hear Ethan rummaging around, but it couldn't see him. "Drop the bag with the guns first!" the machine shouted.

The duffel bag with the guns dropped down from the

hatch in the loft. The machine pointed to Caleb. "You…bring the bag to me."

Caleb did as he was ordered. The machine snatched the duffel bag and checked its contents. "To answer your question," the machine said, "no human will be let go. No human gets out alive. June twelfth, five fifty-seven assured that. It was the fatal error."

Tears of dread filled everyone's eyes. It was as if they were awaiting their turn before the firing squad. Caleb wiped his eyes and stared at the machine. His lips trembled. "If we're going to die, we deserve to know why. What was the fatal error?"

The machine spoke, almost tauntingly. "You will never know."

Several minutes passed without a word upstairs from Ethan. Annika wouldn't have blamed him at all if he just slid down the side of the fort and took off running, though she knew that wasn't the kind of person he was. She had no idea what Ethan was doing up there for so long, but she was certain that he would never abandon them.

"Hurry!" the machine yelled into the loft. "You have thirty seconds before you start losing friends."

There was silence. Silence for ten seconds. Silence for twenty seconds. Then, finally, Ethan emerged from the hatch carrying the duffel bag.

"Sorry, trying to be careful with the energy rods," Ethan explained. "Now I just need to get the two that are down here, and you'll have everything you need."

"Good…Hurry this time."

Ethan slung the duffel bag over his shoulder and moved quickly toward the entryway. He pulled the energy rod from the table leg, then the one from beside the door. As Ethan began to place the rods gently into the bag, he looked over his shoulder and spotted the machine alternating its attention between him and the rest of the group. The moment the machine took its eyes off him, Ethan opened the door and dashed outside into the darkness.

"Stop!" the machine ordered furiously, then bolted after him.

Ethan ran like a maniac away from the fort. Rapid, heavy footsteps were pounding away behind him and getting louder with every stride.

Annika ran outside and watched through teary, horrified eyes. "Ethan, just drop the bag!" she pleaded in an ear-splitting scream. "He's right behind you!"

The robot was so close now that Ethan could hear the gears in its legs humming and whirring. Any second, he knew the machine would be close enough to reach out and grab him. Ethan kept his eye on a particular spot of ground as he sprinted his final steps. The machine was only a couple feet away when he stepped across the spot he had in mind, jumped into the air, and dove to the ground. The machine was just about to pounce on top of him when the motion-detecting laser turret in the loft sprang to life and fired a barrage of lasers at the machine. The bright red lasers first ripped into the back of the robot, then delivered the final death blow when one laser pierced through the back of its head and exited through its right eye.

The machine fell to the ground, glared murderously once more at Ethan, then its eyes went from bright to dim to dark. Ethan breathed a gigantic sigh of relief, but he had to be careful not to move an inch, because the laser in the loft didn't discriminate between humans and machines.

Caleb quickly turned off the power to the laser turret, then he and the rest of the group rushed out to meet Ethan. Annika's smile of relief could be seen from the moon.

"So, *that's* what took you so long in the loft...You were up there fixing the laser turret!" Caleb shouted. "That's genius!"

"Absolutely genius!" Annika added, giving Ethan a hug.

"Well, it was mostly done already," Ethan said modestly. "Just needed a couple wires plugged in here and there."

"How did you know exactly when to hit the deck?" Glenn asked.

"I know everything about this fort. The laser turret begins tracking when you get past that big rock over there." Ethan pointed to a slab of rock nestled into the earth, a slight glow of moonlight ghosting off of it.

"Amazing," Glenn said.

Suddenly, a bright red laser blasted out from the tree line, destroying the laser turret on the loft. Then the woods in the distance came alive with crimson eyes. A horde of machines— Skulleys and spiders—began surging toward them like a mechanical tsunami.

"Hurry...! Back to the fort...! Run!" Ethan screamed.

CHAPTER 41

THE THIRD WAVE

THE GROUP SCRAMBLED frantically for the fort as the machines poured out of the woods and into the clearing. The tranquil sounds of nature were drowned out by the sounds of thousands of gears squealing and the high-pitched blare of machines communicating with each other. There was a tone in their screeches that seemed eager, like they were excited at the chance to finally be getting rid of their flesh and blood pests.

Ethan was carrying the heavy duffel bag full of rifles, but he was keeping up with the others just fine. He was even outrunning Caleb, who was falling farther and farther behind.

"Hurry, Caleb! Run faster!" Ethan yelled as he neared the doorway of the fort.

The machines were grinding away at the group and quickly closing the distance. The black metallic spiders were by far the fastest. They seemed to skim effortlessly over the woods like water bugs on a pond. As Caleb tried to sprint faster, he came down awkwardly on his right foot. He belted out a sharp scream. Ethan turned and watched in horror as his best friend lay on the ground, writhing in pain and clutching his twisted ankle.

"Caleb!" Ethan shouted. Ethan quickly handed Glenn the duffel bag. "Open that door. We'll be right behind you."

Ethan sprinted back to Caleb. "You gotta get up! You gotta get up now, Caleb!" He held out his hand. Caleb grabbed it and began to get up, but soon fell back down in pain.

"Leave me!" Caleb screamed as he watched the machines storming the ground between them. "You can't save me. Just go!"

"I'm not leaving you!" Ethan yelled. He crouched down and began to lift Caleb up over one of his shoulders.

"You can't do this, there's no time! You can't run with me, I'm too heavy! It's suicide, Ethan," Caleb said, his teary eyes glistening in the moonlight. "Just let me go."

As soon as Ethan stood up, he realized Caleb was right. The weight was too much, the distance too far, and the machines too close. Ethan was resigned to carry Caleb anyway and die with his best friend when the weight he was hoisting suddenly decreased dramatically. Ethan looked over and saw a broad shoulder.

"We're not leaving anyone behind," Austin said.

Ethan and Caleb smiled thankfully for the briefest of moments, then Ethan and Austin shuffled toward the fort as fast as they could with Caleb draped over their shoulders.

Once everyone was inside the fort, Ethan slammed the door shut and slid the heavy lock into place to secure it. Seconds later, a thunderous clank rang out. Then another and another and another. The machines had surrounded the fort and were intent on smashing their way inside. Soon loud thumping noises issued from the roof, along with the rapid clickety-clack of metal feet.

"They're in the loft!" Annika yelled.

"Close that hatch!" Ethan shouted.

Glenn went to close the hatch when two spider legs reached through and began whipping around. They wrapped tightly around Glenn's chest and began to pull him up toward the hatch.

"Aaagghh!" Glenn yelled, trying desperately to free himself. It was a pointless struggle. The machine's legs were far too strong. Glenn gasped for air.

Annika drew her rifle. "Glenn, duck down!"

Glenn tucked his head into his body. Annika fired several shots that managed to sever the spider's limbs, freeing Glenn from its clutches. Austin swiftly closed the hatch door.

The sound of the machines pummeling the fort was so loud that everyone's ears were ringing. Metal-on-metal, banging, clanking, vibrating. It was coming from all directions. The mainstay of their defense—the loft—was useless. Ironically, the machines were now the ones using it to stage attacks against them. The hopelessness of the situation set in on everyone as they stood together with their jittery rifles pointed at various parts of the fort. All they could do was wait for the first seam in the fort to fail. Then the machines would pour inside like water through a funnel.

"So what do we do now?" Caleb asked with trembling lips.

Just as Caleb had uttered that question, the roof began to sink in under the weight of the machines jostling around on top of the fort.

"We gotta get to the basement!" Ethan shouted.

The group made a mad grab for the metal briefcase, and whatever duffel bags were nearby, and descended the stairs into the basement. Soon after they were all inside, a booming crash rocked the fort. The main level had completely collapsed. All that was left was the basement. The sounds of robots lashing at the remnants of the fort got even louder. Then the roof of the basement started to bow inwards, looking like any moment it could collapse itself.

"It's giving way!" Glenn yelled. "We're gonna be buried down here!"

"No, we're not," Ethan said.

Ethan crawled to the escape hatch and unlocked the door. Austin, Annika, and Glenn readied their rifles as he slowly opened it a crack. Ethan peered inside and saw nothing but blackness. He opened the door a little wider and looked again. There was nothing but a cavern of darkness.

"It looks okay," Ethan said, opening the door even more.

Before Ethan could say another word, the pitch-black tunnel was illuminated by a sea of piercing red eyes. Scores of skittering Skulleys lunged at them. Ethan slammed the door as fast as he could, but one Skulley managed to get its hands inside. The machine belted out an ear-splitting, angry squeal as it tried to pry open the door. More and more, the crack in the door began to swell against the group who was pushing back with all their might. Then more skeletal hands, with long black fingers like tendrils, curled around the door. Crimson eyes and eager, metal-toothed smiles filled the ever-widening gap.

"Annika!" Ethan yelled.

Annika quickly took aim at the Skulleys' hands. She carefully blasted off dozens of bony, metallic fingers until Ethan was able to shut and lock the hatch.

"Now what?" Annika asked, even though her eyes knew the bleak answer. *Die fighting.*

The machines' relentless assault continued. Two spider legs bore holes through the fort and were thrashing around inside the basement. Two legs quickly turned into four, which turned into eight. Soon mechanical legs were everywhere. The group tried to shoot them, but for every leg they shot, two more seemed to appear. Everyone was huddled next to the escape hatch, the only place left in the fort where the spiders' legs couldn't yet reach. But on the other side of that hatch, the Skulleys were pounding and ramming the door. The hinges were cracking.

Ethan scanned the room that was caving in around them. It seemed to him and everyone else that this would surely be their tomb. Ethan pulled the duffel bag with the energy rods close to him. He retrieved one of the brilliant blue cylinders and held it in his hand. Everyone looked at him and thought the same thing.

"If this is the end…we might as well take as many out as we can, right?" Ethan said, summoning all of his courage.

Everyone nodded grimly in agreement. Tears filled their eyes. Ethan set the strange blue element on the ground in front of them. They all huddled closely together, holding each other tightly as Annika pointed her rifle at the shimmering canister.

"Any last words?" Annika asked.

"I'm really gonna miss you guys," Glenn said. "We didn't go down without a fight."

"It felt good being part of a team again," Caleb added wistfully. "You're the best friends a nerd like me could ever ask for."

"I wish we were friends for more than just a few days," Austin said, looking at everyone but focusing his eyes last and longest on Ethan. "But at least I'll die now with you knowing the real me."

Everyone looked expectantly at Ethan. "We were the best Laser Wars team ever," he said through tears.

"No doubt about it," Annika agreed, a tremor in her voice. She lowered her rifle a little, leaned in toward Ethan, and planted a tender kiss on his cheek. Ethan stared at her with a sad smile chock-full of "what ifs." She returned the same somber smile, then slowly raised her rifle. "On three," Annika said, tears streaming down her cheeks. "One, two…"

"Wait!" Ethan yelled. "I have more last words!" he uttered excitedly. It was like Annika's kiss had jolted something inside his brain. "There's no charge inside a conductor!" Ethan grabbed the energy rod and held it up. "Annika, remember when you opened this canister at my house? All the lights, everything electrical short-circuited and blew out!"

"Oh my God, that's right," Annika remembered.

"You know what I'm thinking?"

"We try and electrocute the machines clinging to the fort."

"Exactly. We got one shot left."

Annika flashed a hopeful smile. "Let's fry some robots."

"Hurry, help me scoot that table over here," Ethan said. They quickly slid a large wooden table into the corner of the room. "Grab the briefcase and as many duffel bags as you can and get on top."

The group tossed their gear onto the table and piled on top themselves. Ethan grabbed an energy rod and stood on the table.

"On the count of three," Ethan said as he gripped the

lid of the canister. "Hunch down, get small. Don't let any of those machines touch you."

Mechanical spider legs were still whipping around the room. Annika and the others tried their best to shoot as many as they could, but there seemed to be an endless supply of the sinewy limbs. And while it was true that electricity going around the fort would not touch anyone inside, it was only the case if no one was touching any metal in contact with the fort. The group was sitting on a wooden table that couldn't conduct electricity, but if any one of the many flailing spider legs touched them while the electric current was running, then they would surely be electrocuted.

"One, two, three…Now!" Ethan yelled as he opened the canister and stretched his arm out so the mysterious blue rod inside was nearly touching the metal ceiling above.

Instantly, a fantastic shroud of shimmering blue light engulfed the walls and ceiling of the basement. The light was so blinding that everyone had to close their eyes. The buzzing and crackling sounds of raging electricity were so loud that it hurt their ears. Even handling it carefully in its protective canister, Ethan couldn't hold on to the vibrating rod much longer. He gingerly pulled back the canister and closed the lid. Slowly the intense electric blue blanket of energy fizzled out and left everything in total blackness, except for the constant glow of the blue rod. The bizarre energy source had knocked out the power in the room. They prayed it had knocked out the machines as well.

Once their eyes adjusted to the dimmer light, they looked around the basement. They noticed one thing instantly— there were no more spider legs thrashing around. Then they checked the escape hatch. Moments before, the Skulleys were just about to pound the hatch off its hinges. Now there was nothing but silence.

Ethan grabbed a flashlight from a duffel bag and shined some light on the far side of the room, where the mechanical spiders had been especially active. There he saw about a dozen spider legs. They were all charred and smoldering, burnt to a crisp.

"We did it," Annika said, exhausted, sounding far more relieved than happy.

"We don't know we got them all," Austin said, shining his flashlight on the escape hatch.

"We gotta look…It's the only way outta here now anyway," Ethan said.

The group gathered around the escape hatch. Caleb reached for the lock while the others pointed their rifles at the hatch door.

Ethan nodded, his face taut and tense. "All right, Caleb… Go ahead."

Caleb unlocked the hatch and slowly opened the door, then he shined a flashlight inside. The beam of light reflected off a cloud of smoke that began to slowly billow its way inside. No one could see anything through the smoky haze. All of a sudden, a Skulley popped out of the tunnel only to fall dead before them. Its body was so burnt up that one could've mistaken it for a human skeleton if not for its unnaturally glassy eyes that were still eerily wide open.

After the smoke cleared, a thorough inspection of the escape tunnel revealed nothing but incinerated machines.

"You think we got them all?" Austin asked.

"I don't know," Ethan said. "But I'm going out to check."

"I'll go with you," Annika offered quickly.

Ethan and Annika took their rifles and began crawling through the escape tunnel. They had flashlights but kept them off. It was impossible to see in the tunnel, but they didn't want to attract any attention. They wished they had their night-vision goggles, but those were lost when the top level of the fort collapsed. As it was, they managed to crawl blindly, climbing over deceased Skulleys that were still hot to the touch. It was a creepy feeling. They feared that one of the mangled machines might still have enough life left in it to grab them. But that never happened. They clambered to the end of the sixty-foot tunnel and looked around outside.

"See anything?" Annika asked.

"Nothing. Too dark…Cover me, I'm gonna take a closer look."

They crept out of the tunnel. Annika slithered quietly up to a nearby bank, an elevated position where she had a good view of Ethan, who was making his way closer to the fort. With the help of the moonlight, Ethan got his first good glimpse of the back of the structure. It looked like the hull of an old wooden ship covered in barnacles. The fort was so plastered with scorched machines that it was unrecognizable. The machines, a collection of Skulleys and spiders, were still clinging to the fort, frozen in time by the surge of electricity. It was impossible to count them all, but it appeared that no fewer than a hundred robots had been destroyed. They were all fused and melted together, piled on top of each other in a jumbled mess. Sizzling sounds echoed through the woods as smoke from the charred machines rose up into the cooler night air. Ethan circled the entire fort, inspecting the area for any live machines. There were none.

"I don't see any left," Ethan said.

Annika sighed a big breath of relief and lowered her rifle. She pointed her flashlight into the escape tunnel and signaled for the others. Soon Austin, Glenn, and Caleb emerged carrying the metal briefcase and what duffel bags they had managed to save. Ethan grabbed the bag that Caleb was carrying, then put his other arm under Caleb's shoulder and helped him out of the tunnel.

"Thanks," Caleb said as he limped along on his bad ankle. "I have an idea where we can go. Somewhere safe. At least for the night until we figure out what to do next."

"Where?" Austin asked.

"Wolf Cave." Wolf Cave was one of Ethan and Caleb's old hangouts before they built their fancy, state-of-the-art Bravo Fort.

"But that's over two miles away from here," Austin said. "There's no way you can make it that far on your ankle."

"I can make it," Caleb said with steely eyes. "I'm stronger than you think."

"Okay then," Austin said with a smile of respect.

Ethan moved the Geminorum energy rods from the duffel bag back into the metal briefcase to secure them better. After a solemn moment of silence for their smoldering fort, they left it behind for good.

Ethan, Austin, and Glenn took turns helping Caleb walk. Annika led the way through the woods, guided by the light of a mostly full moon. Her finger remained crooked tightly around the trigger of her rifle, ready to shoot anything that moved.

CHAPTER 42

THE DECISION

THE GROUP MADE it to the entrance of Wolf Cave in just under thirty minutes, a fantastic time considering they had been moving over rough terrain, in the dark, with an injured person. Ethan helped Caleb to a sitting position on the ground, just inside the mouth of the cave. Then everyone turned their flashlights on and flooded the cavern with light.

The opening of the cave was about six feet tall and eight feet wide. It was nestled in the bottom of a rock formation that stretched over a hundred feet high. Once inside, there was an entryway the size of a small living room. From there, four low-lying passageways branched off in different directions. The light from the flashlights illuminated the main entry area well but dimmed quickly at the openings of the passageways.

"The first tunnel on the left," Caleb said, pointing. "After about sixty feet, there's another open area. Bigger than this one. We can spend the rest of the night there."

"Yeah," Ethan agreed. "It's the easiest part to defend. There's just the one tunnel leading in. And we'd hear the machines coming long before they were right on top of us."

"Good…But what if we need to retreat?" Glenn asked.

"Caleb and I explored these tunnels a lot, but we haven't found any way out yet…just the way we came in."

"So, if the machines come…?"

"We fight them off in there or die," Annika answered bluntly as she crouched down and pointed her flashlight and sniper rifle into the leftmost tunnel.

"Yeah, but I hope that last battle bought us some time," Ethan said. "We had to have killed at least a hundred machines. They'll need some time to send out reinforcements. And if we're lucky, they'll think we all died in there. Then they wouldn't look for us until they stripped the fort apart and realized there were no human bodies or energy rods inside. That would take even more time."

"Time is good," Annika said. "Now let's stop talking and get through that tunnel."

Annika led the way with her flashlight pinned tightly to her rifle, pointing straight ahead into the dark unknown. Her sharp eyes meticulously scanned the cramped passageway and the clearing ahead as she crawled. Once she made it into the larger cavern, she stood up and inspected the room. The others soon joined her.

"All clear," Annika said, finally lowering her rifle and relaxing a little bit.

"We should post a guard by the passageway," Ethan said. "I'll take first watch."

Austin and Glenn rummaged through the duffel bags and pulled out a few blankets. They spread them out over a flat section of ground, preparing the sleeping quarters for the night.

Annika retrieved the first-aid kit and set it down beside

Caleb. "We need to get the swelling down in your ankle," she said.

Caleb removed his right shoe and sock. He winced in pain as he slowly stretched his leg out. His ankle was swollen to the size of a baseball. Annika gathered some rocks and tossed them into a puddle of water that was slowly being fed by dripping stalactites from above. She soon returned with a handful of cold, wet rocks. She held them on Caleb's ankle.

"This will help with the swelling and pain. Do you think it's broken?"

"I don't know. If not, it's the worst sprain I've ever had."

"Keep the cold rocks on it for a while, then we'll wrap it up tight. If it's not broken, it'll hurt, but you should be able to walk on it."

"Thanks, Annika."

Annika smiled and shrugged. "It's the least I could do for the guy who gave me my early Christmas present."

"Turns out it was a pretty good gift," Caleb said, returning her smile.

"Kill the lights!" Ethan whispered sharply. "I hear something."

Everyone shut off their flashlights. The cave instantly became pitch black. Ethan focused his eyes and ears on the tunnel leading into the cavern. He saw nothing but heard an ominous sound. *Click, clack...Click, clack.* The sound was distant but becoming closer, louder. *CLICK, CLACK...CLICK, CLACK.* Ethan strained his ears, and soon he was sure he heard the distinctive sound of metal appendages scraping against the limestone bedrock of the tunnel. Then two pairs of red eyes glowed, leaving no room for wishful thinking. The machines had already arrived.

"Either we try to hide or we shoot them now," Ethan said, voice hushed.

"How many are there?" Annika asked.

"At least two."

"It's too late to hide," Austin said.

"But if we shoot them, the others will know we're here," Glenn said. "If we shoot them, we gotta find some other place to go...Any ideas?"

"I have an idea where we could go," Ethan said.

Just then, the machines climbed out of the tunnel and stood up in the room. Four intense crimson eyes began scanning the area. There was no choice now. Annika took aim and blasted two holes apiece into the Skulley's heads. They fell dead to the ground before they had any idea what had hit them. Ethan switched on a flashlight and put his hand over the bulb, muffling the light so there was just enough to see where he was going. He darted back over to the passageway. Then he poked his head around the corner and peered into the tunnel.

"I don't see anything, no red eyes," Ethan whispered, crouching back behind the cave wall for cover. "But if there are others, they had to hear the shots and the other machines hit the ground. They'd be coming in quiet...eyes dark."

"We can't take any chances," Glenn said. "We gotta light that tunnel up."

Annika nodded, then counted down, "Three, two, one..."

They fired their laser rifles blindly into the tunnel. The shots streamed through the passageway for a solid five seconds. No one dared to stick their heads out to see if they were actually hitting anything.

Finally, the group stopped shooting. Ethan flipped on his flashlight and sneaked a peek inside the passageway. The walls were pockmarked with charred holes from the laser blasts, but there was no sign of machine casualties anywhere. The passageway, and the rest of the cave on the other side, seemed completely devoid of machines alive or dead.

"It's clear," Ethan said. "But it won't be for long. We gotta move out now."

They quickly gathered their gear. Annika hurried over to Caleb and did a rush tape job on his injured ankle. After she was done, Caleb stood up and began to walk around. He grimaced and limped, but he was able to move without assistance.

"How's that feel?" Annika asked.

"Not too bad," Caleb said, putting on a tough face. "Thanks."

Glenn zipped up the last duffel bag and set it by the edge of the passageway. He shined his flashlight on Ethan. "So, Ethan, where do you have in mind?"

"What?" Ethan asked distractedly.

"You said you had an idea, a place we could go."

"Yeah, right...But we gotta get to the east ridge first."

"But where is it? The place?" Glenn asked, getting more impatient.

"We'll talk about it later. We need to get out of here."

"What aren't you telling us?" Glenn asked, staring suspiciously at Ethan as he moved the flashlight beam from his chest to his face.

"There's no time now," Ethan said, shielding his eyes. "Get to the ridge and I'll tell you my idea."

Everyone stared curiously at Ethan, but he refused to reveal anything else. He knew his idea was crazy; he also knew there was no time to debate the issue now. Without any more discussion, the group crawled back through the tunnel the way they had come.

⌁

The squad quickly made the arduous climb up the east ridge. Caleb, not known for his athleticism when he was healthy, managed with his bad ankle to keep up with the others through sheer grit and determination. The group stopped atop the ridge and took a position behind some trees on the slope. They stayed flush to the ground, making sure to keep a low profile. From the vantage point on the ridge, aided by the moonlight, they had a good view of the surrounding area, including the cave entrance from which they'd just fled. Ethan propped himself up on his elbows and monitored the opening to the cave, which was about the length of a football field away. The others scanned the area to make sure the perimeter was clear, then they turned their attention squarely to Ethan.

"So what's the idea, Ethan?" Glenn asked.

Ethan turned to the group and instantly felt the pressure of their inquiring eyes. He had an idea, but even he knew how insane it would sound to the others. Still, it was the only possibility they had left. It was their best, last, and only option.

Ethan took a deep breath, then said with a determination that even surprised himself: "We execute Project Mulligan."

Everyone was stunned into silence. A long silence. Ethan sensed that they all thought he was crazy, that it was a veritable suicide mission, yet he also was pretty sure no one else could offer a better suggestion.

"Ethan, Project Mulligan was designed for a platoon full of Special Forces soldiers," Glenn said incredulously. "Twenty Navy SEALs or something."

"You're right, I know," Ethan admitted. "But I also know this...No one is coming to help us. The Mitchell brothers were right from the start. *We are* the help." He paused and drew a deep breath. "Those machines will find us wherever we go in the woods. They've already been to the cave. More will come. There is one and only one place they will *never, ever* expect us to be...and that's coming *right at them.*"

"Okay, but how do we know the plan is any good now?" Glenn asked. "It could be terrible and we wouldn't know. We'd just be walking in blind, outnumbered and outgunned, relying on some plans you stumbled across in your dad's bedroom."

"Wait a minute," Austin interrupted. "My dad's name is on that mission. He planned it. I can guarantee you that his strategy, down to every detail, is flawless."

"But you don't know that for sure, Austin," Glenn countered.

"Yes, I do," Austin said. "My dad is a military genius. Top in his class at West Point. Highest-ranking officer in the most secret military base in the world." He sighed deeply, then eked out a thin smile. "He didn't get to the top because he's a nice guy. The truth is, no one prepares for a battle like my dad. He considers everything. Looks at all the angles. Covers every base. It's all he does. It's all he's ever cared about. I've known my dad for fourteen years and that's all I really know about him." Austin angled his face away from the moonlight, hoped no one saw that his eyes were on the verge of tears.

Glenn's face softened, and he nodded. "If nothing else, we go out fighting."

"Go out fighting...I second that idea," Annika said, clutching her rifle closer to her chest.

Ethan looked over his team with pride in his eyes. Quickly, those eyes became laser-focused, and he spoke like a true captain: "My dad told me something once when he was playing chess against a computer. He told me the computer's major weakness is responding to an intelligent, yet unpredictable move. The kind only a human could make. He also told me when battling a machine, never try to think like the best machine, try to think like the best human...I know now that he wasn't just talking about chess." Ethan nodded in determination, then continued with a steely stare, "We are the best team, the best humans...And, I promise you, the machines will find this move completely unpredictable. They would never in a million years expect *us* to come at *them*...We can do this...*We have to.*"

Ethan's pep talk managed to inspire the group. Everyone soon nodded in strong agreement that they wanted to give Project Mulligan a shot.

"Yeah...All right, let's do this," Glenn said.

"Okay then," Ethan said. "According to the documents on Project Mulligan, the secret entrance to the research facility is at an old electrical substation about a mile from here."

Before Ethan could say another word, a stream of glowing red eyes emerged and made their way around the edge of the cave below. A horde of machines, at least fifty strong, poured into the mouth of the cavern. Ethan and the others slid quietly down the other side of the ridge, away from the machines and in the direction of the electrical substation. They moved as fast as they could without rolling like snowballs down the hill. They knew the machines would soon find two of their brethren lying dead on the cave floor. Adding that newest insult to the massive robot carnage that encrusted the Bravo

Fort, along with the fact that they still possessed the energy rods, the group knew the machines would be beyond furious. They also knew the manhunt would only end when one of two things happened: they successfully completed Project Mulligan, or the machines had killed every last one of them.

CHAPTER 43

COMMENCING PROJECT MULLIGAN

THE TEAM STOPPED at the edge of a clearing in the woods. The antiquated electrical substation sat squarely in the middle of it, glowing eerily in the moonlight. A complex array of power lines and wires stretched across electrical transformer towers that were enclosed by a tall perimeter fence. But there was no electricity running through the wires now. The electrical substation, once one of a dozen that were vital to the research facility for their power needs, had been inactive ever since the military moved the power grid underground for increased security back in the 1980s. All that remained was a lattice of metalwork that had become overtaken with rust, and a small building, barely the size of a trailer, that was once used to regulate the power surging through the lines.

"That's the control building," Ethan said. "That's where we need to go."

They scanned the area, then sprinted as fast as they could toward the substation. They slipped through a gap in the rickety fence and headed for the control building. The door was secured with a heavy padlock that was noticeably shiny and new compared to the rest of the metal bleeding with rust in the area.

"That's not a lock from the 1980s," Glenn said. "Looks brand new."

"Stand back," Annika said. She blasted a hole clear through the center of the lock. Ethan gingerly removed the smoldering block of metal, and everyone dashed inside.

The main room of the building housed all the control panels for the substation. Rows and rows of outdated-looking buttons and levers covered most of the walls. There was only one window in the entire place, and a small one at that, beside the door from which they had entered.

Annika peered out the tiny square window, then turned around with a worried look on her face. "I don't like this. We can't keep a good lookout from here. I can only see a small section of the perimeter."

"I know," Ethan said. "We gotta hurry and figure out how to make sense of these instructions."

Ethan switched on his flashlight and spread out the Project Mulligan documents over a table. Caleb quickly paid special attention to one of the papers. He shined his flashlight on a section of the control panel on the wall, then back to the document. His eyes widened.

"That's it…! Look at that," Caleb said excitedly. "The diagram precisely matches that part of the control panel," he said, pointing out the corresponding parts. "All we have to do now is press the buttons and pull the levers on the control panel in the exact way that's shown in the diagram."

"And then what?" Glenn asked.

"It should activate…something," Caleb answered with a shrug. "From the diagram, it looks like some sort of elevator."

"Well, we're not activating anything until we're ready," Ethan said. "We have to know the plans inside and out before we go down there."

"Ethan, you need to activate whatever there is to activate *now*," Annika said in a voice laced with dread. "A pair of Skulleys just came out of the clearing. They're headed this way."

"Annika, can you make the shot from here?" Glenn asked.

"It's eighty yards, of course I can make the shot," Annika said, sounding offended. "But then they'll know we're here. And there could be more. From this tiny sliver of a window, I can't be sure of anything out there."

"They can't find out we're here, they'll wonder why we chose this place," Austin added. "Even if we managed to make it out, they'd be clever enough to realize how we got away. They'd find the elevator for sure."

"We have no chance if we don't have the element of surprise," Ethan said.

Ethan referred to the diagram, then began pressing buttons and flipping levers in the exact manner and order prescribed by the instructions. After he pressed the last button, the group stood by and waited for something, anything.

"The machines are closing in, speeding up," Annika announced. "About thirty yards out, nearing the fence."

"Nothing's happening," Glenn said. "Try it again."

Just as Ethan was prepared to go through the button-pushing, lever-flipping routine all over again, the floor beneath them began to vibrate. A section of the floor in the corner slid open and revealed a lighted elevator cab below. An automated voice through a speaker in the elevator began a countdown. "Ten, nine…"

"Hurry, grab our stuff and get inside," Ethan said.

Everyone quickly climbed down into the elevator cab. The automated voice continued, "...three, two, one...descension." The floor swiftly closed above them and the elevator cab began its descent. The group felt the elevator's rapid plunge in the pits of their stomachs. They were headed for no man's land in the most literal sense. They were headed straight into the lair of the machines.

CHAPTER 44

PLUNGING TOWARD THE MACHINES

THE ELEVATOR CAB continued to plummet down the shaft. There were two vertical window slits, one on each of the doors. The group peered through the openings and watched as the imperfections in the concrete of the shaft streamed by them like a river.

"We gotta be falling thirty feet a second," Ethan said.

"At least," Caleb added, carefully noting the seconds on his watch. The cab finally slowed to a surprisingly gentle stop. Caleb looked up at Ethan. "Ten seconds total."

"That means we're three hundred feet underground," Ethan said in awe.

"At least."

The doors slid open quickly, startling everyone. An incredibly long, narrow hallway stretched out before them, lit only by a string of low-watt light bulbs on the ceiling. The bulbs were spaced out about fifty feet apart, so the passageway was dim. They didn't see any machines, but they couldn't see to the end of the corridor. Anything could be down there.

Annika looked through her scope down the length of

the hallway. She firmly pressed her eye into the eyepiece and squinted hard to try to see what was out there. After a moment, she lowered her rifle and shook her head. "It's clear as far as I can see." But there was no relief on her face as she continued, "But I can't see everything. At the end of the hall, it gets totally dark...And I have no idea how far it goes."

"Well, there's no point going down there until we know exactly where we're going once we get there," Ethan said. He pressed a button on the elevator that closed the doors. "Until we all understand what we're about to do, this elevator is our fort."

"Right...I got first watch," Annika volunteered, taking a spot in front of the window.

For the next hour, they pored over numerous maps and diagrams. The facility appeared to be all on one level, though it was incredibly massive in size. A four-mile-long hallway encircled the entire structure, with smaller hallways branching off into research rooms and other passages branching off of those. The facility was laid out a little like a bicycle wheel with spokes, with each spoke having its own set of hallways that sprouted from it. The room they had to get to for Project Mulligan was the one that housed the Chrono-Warp device. Conveniently, and by design, the hallway where the group now found themselves emptied out in that vicinity.

"Judging by the diagrams, we're looking at two hundred yards total before we get to the Chrono-Warp," Caleb said.

"Two hundred yards?" Glenn blurted.

"Yeah, but considering the perimeter of the facility is four miles, it's not so bad," Caleb said. "Plus, the only rooms along the way are right here." He pointed to the map. "And those are just big conference rooms. Not research rooms. Probably empty."

"We'll need to post lookouts here and here," Ethan said, poking the map, "while the others work on securing the room with the Chrono-Warp. Then we just gotta hope Caleb can figure out how to work the thing."

"Right," Caleb said. "We do have the manual." He held up the instructions for the Chrono-Warp and flashed a nervous smile. "I mean, how hard can it be?"

At that moment, Austin looked squarely at Ethan. There was nothing but respect and trust in his eyes. "Okay, Captain…Lead us into battle."

Ethan glanced across the faces of his comrades with determined eyes. "All right, let's show those machines what a pain in the ass we can be when they mess with our families."

✧

Ethan stepped out of the elevator first with Annika just a step behind him. She held her rifle tightly to her shoulder and nestled her eye snuggly into the eyepiece of the scope. The others took spots beside them, each with their rifles pointed straight ahead. They began walking cautiously toward the darkened part of the corridor.

The group soon reached the end of the lighted path. There were no more light bulbs above to guide their way. The rest of the assumed path to the facility faded quickly from dim to complete darkness. They shined their flashlight beams into the void, but the light failed to reach the end. Their minds played tricks on them, as they swore they saw dancing shadows on the walls in the distance, though they eventually wrote off the visions as hallucinations.

Ethan was the first to let logic reign over fear. "If there was something down there, they'd have seen us by now. They'd have already attacked. Remember, they don't even know we're here."

They moved out warily behind Ethan's lead. When their flashlights were finally able to pierce the darkness, they found there was no door at the end of the tunnel, just a massive slab of gray concrete. The only opening at all to the other side was a ventilation shaft covered by a silvery metallic grate. The vent sat low to the ground and was barely two feet wide and not even that tall. It was just enough space to squeeze a person through.

Ethan kneeled down beside the vent cover. "This has to be it," he said, inspecting the six screws that secured the cover in place. He pulled out his Swiss Army knife and flipped open the screwdriver. With each screw Ethan plucked out, the tension seemed to multiply exponentially. Chests and throats were worked into knots so tight they could hardly breathe. When Ethan twisted out the final screw, even his normally steady hands were jittery. He grabbed the vent cover and gently began to pull it away from the wall. Then he set the cover down and looked inside the gaping rectangular hole that was left in its place.

"Looks like there's about six or seven feet of duct, then another vent cover," Ethan said, shining his flashlight into the space.

"Can you see what's after that?" Caleb asked.

"I think I see a mop in there...I think it's a janitor's closet."

"Makes sense. It's an entry point not likely to be guarded."

"I'm sure that's what my dad was thinking," Austin said.

Ethan entered the vent first. He slithered the short

distance until he was face-to-face with the second grate. With a few flicks of the wrist, he'd loosened all the screws, then he gingerly pried open the grate and set it aside. A quick look at the room confirmed his prediction—the six-by-four-foot room was a janitor's closet. Ethan stood up. The others wiggled through the vent and joined him. Caleb put his hand on the doorknob and slowly turned it clockwise, then back counterclockwise.

"There's no lock on the door," Caleb said with a nervous hitch in his voice, acutely aware that if something on the other side wanted to get in, it could do so at will.

"Remember, it's a good plan," Ethan said, trying to sound upbeat. "But if we need to retreat, or we get separated, or anything else happens that we can't even imagine yet, we fall back to this position right here. This closet. Just make sure the machines don't see you come in."

Everyone nodded. Ethan took a deep breath, then he put his hand on the doorknob and turned it clockwise. He slowly began to open the door until he saw a thin sliver of light.

CHAPTER 45

FINDING THE CHRONO-WARP

ETHAN EMERGED FIRST from the dark janitor's closet and into the brightly lit, much wider main hallway of the facility. He squinted his eyes, adjusting to the light, then quickly scanned left and right. When he saw the coast was clear, he motioned for the others to join him.

Everyone stepped lightly and clung snuggly to the outer perimeter wall. The main hallway that encircled the facility's inner sanctums looked every bit the four miles the map indicated it would be. Staying on the outside wall allowed them to see as far ahead as possible before the circular curve of the inner wall obscured their vision.

"Remember," Caleb whispered, tracing his finger over the path on the map, "we take the next left, then it's the second door on the right…That's the Chrono-Warp."

The next hundred yards was like a five-mile trek through a haunted house. The trip seemed to take forever, and they constantly expected something horrifying to leap out at them. The facility was much brighter than a haunted house, but this place proved that light could be just as unsettling as the dark.

354 | RYAN PEEK

Powerful fluorescent ceiling lights burned brilliantly and buzzed like an angry swarm of bees trapped in a jar, providing an odd contrast of sound to the otherwise deathly silent, seemingly endless corridor. The polished white concrete walls reflected a large portion of the light back to their eyes, flooding their vision and constricting their pupils until they were black dots scarcely bigger than a pinhead. The intense light did more than assault their sense of sight, though. It made them feel vulnerable, like a spotlight was being shined on them, like insects trapped in a terrarium that were about to meet the alpha predator.

Annika pointed to the first break in the hallway, ten yards ahead on the left. "That's gotta be the turn," she said.

Ethan nodded, and they slowly approached the narrower hallway that branched off the main corridor. This hallway was much darker. Ethan peered carefully around the corner, then looked back at the others with a concerned face.

"I don't see anything down there. Except…" Ethan paused.

"Except what?" Austin asked.

"I don't know exactly. It's dark…But flashes of light. Subtle, not bright. Flickers of light coming from somewhere."

Annika curled around the corner stealthily, looking through her rifle scope down the hallway. "I see the light flickers. I think they're coming from a room on the left."

"Those are the conference rooms I told you about," Caleb said.

"The ones that were *supposed* to be empty," Glenn added.

"Shhhh!" Austin hissed, pressing his ear to the wall. "I think I hear voices…human voices."

"I hear it too," Annika said, eyes widening, face brightening. "Do you think that's them…our families?" she said with optimism running wildly in her voice.

"What're the odds they'd keep prisoners in the conference rooms?" Caleb said. "It's not a secure location." Annika's face began to wilt from Caleb's logic. "But I hear it too."

Annika perked up again. "We gotta check it out. It's on the way to the Chrono-Warp, anyway."

Ethan didn't have any idea what to expect when they got to those rooms, but he wasn't hopeful that he'd find their families there just waiting to be rescued with no strings attached. Still, Annika was right. Checking out those rooms would be on the way to the Chrono-Warp, and the longer they spent dilly-dallying in the facility, the less likely they would be able to maintain their all-important element of surprise.

"All right," Ethan said. "Let's go."

The group moved out, single file, flush against the left side of the wall. As they approached the first conference room door, the voices became loud and clear enough to make out the words, strange as they were. The group stopped just outside the door. The lights flickering out from the room, combined with the voices and sounds, made it obvious what was happening in there. But it just didn't make any sense.

"Someone's watching a movie," Caleb said with a confused face.

"*Who?*" Glenn asked nervously. It was the million-dollar question.

Ethan took a deep breath, leaned over, and peeked inside the conference room. He noticed a large projector screen on the wall that was showing an old black-and-white comedy film from what seemed to him like the Stone Age, but was probably from the 1950s. Ethan immediately turned his attention to the audience. The spacious room was packed to capacity. There were at least two hundred heads, completely focused on the movie, silhouetted from the light of the screen. Ethan quickly noticed that the movie patrons all had wiry necks and no hair on their heads. And, when the light hit them just right, the distinct shimmer of polished metal reflected from their domes. He had no idea yet what they were doing in there, but the stark contrast between those horrific, futuristic machines and a vintage black-and-white movie designed to generate laughter disturbed him greatly. There was an intense, out-of-place wrongness to it that he couldn't put into words.

Just as Ethan was about to turn around and report the grim news to the group, he realized the others were peering inside the conference room alongside him. Simultaneously, they withdrew their heads from the doorway and slouched down behind the wall for cover.

"We gotta sneak past them," Ethan said in a hushed voice that even he could barely hear. "On my signal."

Ethan looked inside the room again. The machines were still fixated on the film. He motioned quickly for the others to pass. Everyone crouched down and walked lightly past the conference room door, holding their breath in anxious agony the entire time. Once past the room, they exhaled a sigh of relief. But it was a very temporary one. Another open door lay ahead of them, seventy feet away on the left, with more voices and flickers of light emanating from inside.

"Another movie?" Glenn asked in disbelief.

Ethan scurried ahead and peeked inside the room. The scene looked exactly the same as the one before—silhouetted, shiny heads focused in rapt attention on the projector screen. Again it was an old, grainy black-and-white comedy film that was being presented. *Why are they watching movies? And why comedies?* Ethan soon got a sickening feeling in the pit of his stomach as he contemplated the answer. *The machines were studying the humans, with designs on pretending to be them.* Maybe what they did with Tristan was just the tip of the iceberg. What if they had more important people they were planning on impersonating? And it made sense that they were focusing on comedy. Drama and tragedy are straightforward. A machine would find it simple to figure out what makes a human cry—pain, loneliness, the loss of a loved one, all too easy to understand because those emotions and those experiences are universal to humans. It would also be easy to fake. But comedy is so much harder. It wouldn't be nearly as simple to comprehend all the varieties of humor that humans enjoy. From puns to physical comedy and everything in between, the machines would surely find it difficult to be "in on" the joke, especially at the exact, precise time. And comedy is all about timing. Ethan thought about the robot version of Tristan. It was so believable as a human in so many ways, but it didn't even understand his lame joke—Pete vs. Repeat—that night in the loft of the fort. It made sense that the machines were studying comedy; it was their weak point. If they intended to pose as humans, it was still the one thing left that could blow their cover.

They slinked past the room full of distracted machines and headed down the hall toward the Chrono-Warp. The hallway was brighter now as it doglegged right. Annika was walking backwards, guarding the rear, in case one of the robots decided to take a break from the movies and take a leisurely stroll to stretch its legs. The group was completely out in the open now. The hallway they were in seemed to unfurl straight ahead as far as they could see, with no corridors to duck inside if the machines became aware of them.

"Stop!" Ethan whispered sharply. His eyes widened, then squinted, trying to make out a shape that emerged in the distance.

"It's not thin like the Skulleys," Glenn said. "It looks human."

"It does," Caleb said with a smile that soon vanished, as his logical brain took over and thought about the probability of that.

Annika hoisted her rifle and peered through the scope down the length of the hallway. Her mouth dropped instantly in shock. "Oh, my God…You aren't gonna believe who it is."

CHAPTER 46

ALL OR NOTHING

AUSTIN ALREADY KNEW who was walking down the hall before Annika had said a word. He couldn't see the face of the person well enough yet, but he recognized the shape of the figure perfectly. It was the distinctive form of a powerfully built man, standing six-feet-four, wearing a blue Air Force service coat. The medals and badges on the front cast an unmistakable shimmer. It was a shimmer Austin had known his entire life.

"That's…*my dad*," Austin said in a daze.

Annika glanced awkwardly at Austin, realizing she still had her gun pointed at his father. She slowly lowered her weapon. "Sorry."

General Turnbull walked toward the group until they were at a conversational distance. The general paid no special attention to his son at first glance. Rather, he stared at each of them in turn, like he was sizing them up, evaluating them. His behavior struck Ethan as being odd. Austin, though, didn't seem surprised at all by the general's conduct up to this point. Everything about his father had seemed completely reasonable and believable.

Then General Turnbull finally looked at his son. His eyes were on Austin and nobody else. The general's stern-looking mouth slowly formed a smile. His head bobbed up and down, a proud nod, and he outstretched his muscular arms for a hug.

"Thank God, you're okay, Austin," General Turnbull said, wiping away a tear. "I was so scared I lost you, son. I love you so much."

The general moved in to hug his son. Austin came forward to meet him. Both had tears in their eyes. Just as they were about to embrace, Austin swiftly pulled his rifle up and shot a hole clear through his father's head. Ethan and the others gasped in shock as General Turnbull's body, decorated with awards, unceremoniously hit the floor. Everyone stared in disbelief at Austin, stunned that he was willing and able to take such a grave gamble. They watched the dead body carefully on the ground, desperately hoping not to see blood, praying that the corpse wasn't human. Ethan looked over at Austin, who remained unflinching in his decision.

"The machines don't just need to study comedy," Austin said firmly, though his face now was a sickly pale. "If they did their homework, they woulda known my dad would never say any of that."

Ethan nodded slowly, numbly. "Okay," was all he could bring himself to say.

No blood ever flowed from the wound in the general's head. Instead, a few blue bolts of electricity streaked across its face in death, proving Austin was right. Sighs of relief came from everyone but Austin.

"I knew it wasn't my dad. I knew it was a machine. One hundred percent." Austin was confident in his words, almost too much so.

"I know," Ethan said in a reassuring voice.

Glenn scanned the area with anxious eyes. "We gotta move out now."

Ethan nodded. "All right. The Chrono-Warp room isn't far. Grab a leg. We can drag the body, hide it in there."

Just as Ethan and Glenn began dragging the mechanical general away, a shrill, angry-sounding alarm blared throughout the facility. Ethan instantly dropped the impostor's leg and snatched the metal briefcase from Caleb. He quickly opened it and pulled out a canister of 37-Geminorum. Then he handed his rifle to Caleb.

Caleb's eyes widened. "Ethan, *what* are you doing?"

"Creating a distraction. I gotta get them off you. They see this, they'll chase me."

"You can't do that. You'll never make it back."

"Ethan, no," Annika pleaded. "We stay together, remember?"

"I'll catch up. I promise...Now get out of here," Ethan ordered his team, then ran in the direction opposite the Chrono-Warp and back the way they had come.

Annika peeked around the bend in the hallway and watched in horror as Ethan dashed away, unarmed, waving the blue rod back and forth conspicuously for the machines to see. Every single machine in both of the conference rooms stormed out to hunt him down. His plan had worked, and it scared Annika to death. Tears welled in her eyes.

Austin led Annika and the others toward the room with the Chrono-Warp. He put his hand on Annika's shoulder. "He will," Austin said. "*He will* make it back to us."

Annika nodded and tried to be strong. There was still a job to do, but that didn't stop the tears. The only thing she could do now was focus on Project Mulligan. If Ethan gave his life for the mission, she had to see it was successful. She owed him that. Everyone did.

∽

Ethan dashed down the hallway with the blue energy rod flailing in his hand like he was a sprinter with a baton in a relay race. He looked over his shoulder and found an entire army of machines in breakneck pursuit. The narrow hallway was completely clogged with a wall of wiry limbs surging toward him. Gears squealed. Crimson eyes burned. Metal clicked and clacked furiously on the concrete floor. Ethan had a slim lead on the robots, maybe ninety feet, as he neared the main circular passageway. He hoped to gain more of an advantage when he turned the corner, figuring he might have better traction with his gym sneakers than the machines with their polished metal feet.

Ethan turned the corner sharply and quickly pulled out into the fastest sprint of his life. There was no time to look back now. It had become an all-out, do-or-die race to get to the janitor's closet. And he had to do it without the machines seeing him. Ethan knew he'd have something of a lead on the robots when he got to the closet, but he had no idea if it would be enough to slip in there unnoticed. If the machines saw him go in there, he would have no chance to double back and get to the Chrono-Warp. Like the entire mission itself, it was an all-or-nothing proposition.

Ethan focused his eyes on the doorknob of the janitor's closet as he rapidly closed in on the target. He had to time it perfectly, slowing down enough to grab it, but not so much as to let the machines gain any more ground on him than necessary. Ethan took a few stuttering steps to slow himself before he got to the door. He clamped his hand to the doorknob like a vise, swung the door open in a flash, and closed it behind him fast but gently.

Once inside the closet, Ethan swiftly went to work pulling the ventilation grate away from the air duct. He crawled inside and placed the grate back. By then, he could hear the stampeding robot brigade just outside the door. He knew he wouldn't have time to put the screws on the grate back into place. He prayed that was something the machines would overlook.

Slowly, the doorknob began to turn. Ethan crouched down into a ball, making himself as small as he could. He tucked the bright blue energy rod inside his shirt and nestled it into his body tightly to mask its light from the robots.

The closet door opened. Four machines with blazing red eyes peered inside. Ethan remained as motionless as he could, but his breathing was still heavy from all the sprinting, and his lungs were heaving. Afraid this would give him away, he had no choice but to suck in one last breath and hold it. His lungs ached terribly as the machines scrutinized every nook of the closet. He felt as if he were underwater with concrete blocks tied to his feet, sinking farther and farther down. He had to take a breath, but doing so would result in a gigantic gasp. The machines would surely hear him. Ethan watched in agony as the robots' blood-red eyes scanned back and forth. He was just about to lose consciousness when the machines retreated from the closet and closed the door.

Ethan immediately exhaled his pent-up breath and began gulping in oxygen. He crawled out of the vent and replaced the grate, then pressed his ear tightly to the door. He heard nothing. He put his hand on the doorknob, and was about to turn it, when several sounds began to permeate the door. They were the clickety-clack of metal feet. Ethan knew they were coming in, and he knew it was too late to get back inside the ventilation shaft.

The door opened, and Ethan did the only thing he could do—he squeezed himself into the space behind the door. He faced the corner like a punished schoolboy of yesteryear and clutched the blue energy rod tightly into his abdomen under his shirt. Then one of the machines walked inside for a closer inspection. The robot bent down and peered inside the shaft. Ethan cocked his head slightly around the door, just barely enough to get a partial glimpse of the machine. It looked different than the other Skulleys. Its head was larger, nearly twice as big, with grooves running from the front to the back of it, and large, black, almond-shaped eyes set halfway down its face. Ethan figured it was the newest generation of machine, but the fact that it didn't look human at all disturbed him greatly. *This new machine, whatever it is, will surely find me.* He considered taking the lid off the blue energy rod canister and electrocuting the new robot, even though he was sure to be electrocuted himself in such a small area. Ethan had his hand on the lid, and was ready to make that sacrifice, when the newfangled machine began to pull the ventilation grate away from the shaft. Ethan realized he had a chance, a small one, so he waited.

The alien-looking robot belted out a high-pitched screech. Ethan trembled, fearing he'd been discovered, and nearly removed the lid off the energy rod. But then, a half dozen machines filed into the janitor's closet and followed their leader, crawling on all fours into the ventilation duct, one after the other, until every one of them was on the other side in the secret tunnel. Ethan was alone in the closet. He quickly tiptoed around the ventilation shaft and peeked outside into the main circular hallway. There were no machines in sight. With his heart hammering in his chest, he slipped out of the closet and sprinted as fast as he could back toward the Chrono-Warp.

∽

The Chrono-Warp room was a massive expanse of space measuring two hundred feet long and at least twice that distance wide. The room was mostly empty, except for a long panel of computers, some office furniture, and a circular, raised platform located in the center of the room. The platform was about two feet high and fifty feet in diameter, and could've passed, unremarkably, as some sort of stage for a play. There was another platform, the exact same size, sixty feet directly above on the ceiling. Caleb was busy frantically typing instructions into the computer from the Chrono-Warp documents, but a nagging thought vexed him as he typed. He couldn't help but wonder that, for a supposed time machine, the setup looked too simplistic, too boring. *Where was all the complex, high-tech machinery? Where were all the spinning, rotating electromagnets and fantastic gizmos he'd seen in all those science fiction movies? Where were the jumbles of wires and cables?* Caleb tried to suppress his doubts, but this thing sure didn't look like the finished product of a time machine.

Austin and Glenn were busy sliding every piece of office furniture into position to barricade the door once Ethan arrived. They had to believe that he would make it back.

"How's it coming?" Austin asked.

"I don't know," Caleb replied. "I'm just doing what the instructions say. That's all I can do…Any sign of Ethan yet?"

"Not yet," Annika said, keeping guard with the door cracked just barely enough to see out. "But he will be here," she said with a worried face that belied her confident words.

"Done with the instructions," Caleb said. "Ready for the power source."

Caleb carefully placed the four remaining energy rods into the required slots at the computer terminal. He entered the initiation command and waited. But nothing happened.

"It's not powering up," Caleb said. "I was afraid of that. Either this whole thing is a giant malfunction or we're going to need all five energy rods."

"That's it, I'm going out to get Ethan," Annika said. "He probably went back to the janitor's closet to hide until they passed, then he'll try to double back...That's what I'd do."

"Sounds like a great idea," Ethan said from the other side of the door. "Now can you let me in?"

Everyone smiled and exhaled a huge sigh of relief when they spotted Ethan peeking through the crack in the door. Annika swung the door open, pulled Ethan inside, and gave him a hug that nearly crushed his ribs.

"Thank God, it's about time!" Annika blurted. "Now give Caleb that energy rod."

Ethan promptly handed the blue rod to Caleb, then went to work helping the others barricade the door with every single file cabinet, table, and chair they could find.

"Whatever happens, at least we're together," Caleb said as he placed the last energy rod fatefully into the slot in the terminal.

Everyone nodded solemnly. Then a monotone, automated voice from the computer terminal spoke loudly: "Chrono-Warp, powering up...Five minutes until transport to time signature six, zero, three, one, three, nine, three, seven, current…standby."

The circular platforms above and below came to life and were now glowing a bright bluish-white color. They hummed softly at first, but the hum was getting louder.

"Time signature six, zero, blah, blah, blah…What does that mean?" Glenn asked.

"I don't know," Caleb answered. "But what I do know is every machine in this entire facility knows exactly where we are now…*and* what we're up to."

"Four minutes until transport," the automated voice announced.

The first of the machines began to pound on the door. Everyone watched fearfully as the top chair on the barricade pile tumbled off and fell onto the floor.

"We gotta hold them off for four minutes…four minutes!" Ethan yelled as he tossed the chair back onto the pile. Then he spotted a service bay door on the opposite side of the room. "What about that door?"

"Solid and locked up tight," Austin answered. "No other easy way in."

"Okay, then…Let's get behind this pile and push with all we got."

The machines began to hammer away relentlessly at the door. Annika had to shoot her way into the room when they'd first arrived, so there was no way to lock the door. All that was left now between the group and the massive, murderous, mechanical horde was a steel door with a blown-out lock, a few hundred pounds of office furniture, and five kids straining with all their might, backs nearly fused into a file cabinet, trying to keep the door closed. Everyone grunted and groaned from the tremendous exertion. Muscles ached. Sweat poured from their foreheads and dripped down their faces. Despite their efforts, the machines slowly and methodically started to push their way inside. Annika glanced back and saw black skeletal hands and bony fingers multiplying, curling around the door, using the opening for leverage and pushing harder every second.

"Three minutes until transport," the automated voice coldly informed them.

"We're not gonna make it like this," Annika said. "And if I'm gonna go down, I wanna go down doing what I do best."

Ethan also knew they had no chance of holding their current position for three more minutes. "Okay," he said. "Take a defensive spot behind the computer terminal, close to the energy rods. You'll be safer there. They won't want to risk shooting them."

Annika nodded. "Three, two, one...now!" she yelled as she broke off from the group and ran for cover behind the computer terminal. Everyone dug in their heels and pushed with any reserve energy they had left to compensate for Annika's absence.

Annika popped out from behind the wall of computers and took aim at the machines, who were now almost able to squeeze inside the room. She fired a volley of lasers with pinpoint accuracy, knocking out the first column of machines that'd had their sights set on invading. The robots, heads riddled with laser holes, fell back, allowing the group to squeeze the door closed once more.

"Nice shooting!" Ethan said, cheering along with everyone else.

Before Annika could even breathe the slightest sigh of

relief, the assault on the door began anew. This time, more intense. Annika blasted away at the machines peering in through the crack in the door, but she could hardly tell she was making a difference. The robots were teeming, flooding the space. The machines that she had shot dead became mere battering rams for the others behind them to use to smash their way inside.

"Two minutes until transport," the automated voice proclaimed without a worry in the world.

"They're breaking in...It's not enough...I gotta help Annika!" Ethan screamed. "Hold this position!"

Ethan peeled away from the group and dove behind the computer terminal next to Annika. He jumped up and began firing at the swelling crack in the door. The scout and sniper fired their weapons incessantly at the machines. Their combined efforts seemed to make a difference. The machines relented for a moment and stopped bombarding the door, which had gapped open a good four inches from the sheer weight of the dead machines pressing against it. The group tried to close the gap, but it was useless.

"What are they doing?" Austin asked.

"We can't see anything," Ethan said. "Just a glob of dead machines in the way."

"Pretty sure they aren't surrendering," Glenn added.

"That's about all we know," Ethan said quietly as he looked around the room. "What are they up to?"

"I don't know, but I'm not taking my eyes off that door," Annika said with her right eye tightly pinned to the scope of her rifle.

Ethan scanned the room quickly and saw no other doors from which the machines could enter. Then his eyes spotted something on the right side of the room. It was a grate on a ventilation shaft. Before Ethan could fully appreciate the irony of the situation, he saw numerous pairs of bobbing crimson eyes inside the shaft. The machines were scrambling toward them.

Ethan pointed and screamed, "They're in the vent!"

Ethan and Annika began firing at the ventilation shaft. Austin, Glenn, and Caleb followed suit. The machines hadn't yet breached the grate, but the way they were closing in, hateful eyes glowing brighter, it was only a matter of time.

"One minute until transport," the automated voice reminded them almost tauntingly.

The machines started pounding at the front door again with renewed vigor. Austin, Glenn, and Caleb had to stop firing at the grate to focus on pushing the door closed. The attack was coming from two fronts now. With just Ethan and Annika firing at the ventilation grate, the machines soon overwhelmed them. The rampaging robots punched out what was left of the grate and began crawling inside. Then a massive blow rocked the front door, knocking it completely off its hinges, and sent the pile of furniture, along with Austin, Glenn, and Caleb, tumbling away. The machines then climbed in through the front, clambering over their fallen brethren. Their eyes blazed blood red as they mercilessly stalked the group.

"Caleb!" Austin yelled as he ran toward him.

Caleb had been knocked unconscious from the door blast and was splayed out motionless on the ground. Austin and Glenn quickly scooped him up and ran for shelter behind a file cabinet, while Ethan and Annika provided cover fire. Then Ethan and Annika joined them behind the cabinet, not far from the glowing platform, to make their last stand.

"We gotta hold out for thirty more seconds!" Ethan shouted. "How's Caleb?"

"Alive, but in bad shape," Austin replied. "His head's bleeding bad."

"Thirty seconds!" Ethan screamed desperately.

The Skulleys poured inside in droves from the door and the ventilation shaft. They stormed toward the group, feverishly firing their lasers, attacking from both sides. The blue rods were nowhere near the group now, so the machines could unleash the full force of their offensive power without concern for hitting them. Austin and Glenn were shooting as fast as they could at the robots from the left side of the file cabinet bunker. Ethan and Annika did the same from the right side, firing their weapons like madmen. The Skulleys swarmed, taking only a moment to jump over or sidestep one of their dead, caring nothing for their loss, focused only on the mission: terminating every last one of the young humans.

"Ten seconds until transport," the automated voice announced, then proceeded to count down every second. "Nine...eight..."

"Get ready to make a run for it!" Ethan shouted.

At that moment, Ethan realized he was the only person still firing his weapon on that side. He looked over at Annika and found her slumped lifelessly over her rifle, with a laser hole bored completely through her chest. Blood began to pool around her. The unmistakable, sanguine fluid seeped onto Ethan's pant leg and wicked its way quickly to his skin.

"Nooooo!" Ethan screamed in horror. His eyes exploded into tears.

"Six, five..." the automated voice counted down emotionlessly.

Ethan hoisted Annika up over his shoulder. "Now!" he yelled at the top of his lungs.

Tears flew from Ethan's cheeks as he turned to run toward the Chrono-Warp platform, which was now awash in a radiant neon blue that ran the length of the ceiling to the floor in the shape of a cylinder. Austin and Glenn dragged Caleb toward the platform and joined Ethan and Annika there. Ethan, Austin, and Glenn blasted their rifles at the machines from the platform as the machines charged in full-steam, weapons blazing. Ethan felt one of the lasers tear into his thigh, dropping him to his knees. The pain was unbearable, but still, he kept firing his weapon and shielding Annika's body from any more damage. He quickly glanced over at Austin and Glenn and saw each of them recoil. Austin had been shot in the shoulder, and Glenn in the hip. Then Ethan felt an intense pressure in his abdomen. He looked down at his stomach and saw the hole. It was about an inch across. Ethan finally dropped his laser rifle. He felt the hole in his stomach, then reached around and felt that the hole went clear through his back. The last thing he did was fall on top of Annika, instinctively trying to protect her. The last thing he heard was the computer's calm, automated voice. "One...*transporting.*"

The room erupted into a blinding, brilliant flash of neon blue.

CHAPTER 47

WHEN ARE WE?

A PERFECTLY SPHERICAL neon blue bubble formed two feet above the ground in a clearing in the woods. The orb was ten feet in diameter and shimmering wildly with electricity. In a dazzling flash, it popped open and spilled out its contents. The members of Team Blackwoods tumbled out and hit the ground with a thud. As Ethan was getting his bearings, a Skulley—who had managed to jump inside the Chrono-Warp right before transport—charged at him, weapon drawn, about to fire. Before Ethan could react, two laser pulses streaked over his head and struck the Skulley squarely between the eyes. The machine fell back and died instantly. Ethan wheeled around and saw his rescuer. His eyes widened. It was Annika. Ethan swept her up in his arms.

"You're alive!" Ethan shouted, spinning her around.

"Of course, I'm alive," Annika said matter-of-factly.

"But you were shot…Wait, I was shot too," Ethan remembered, then felt his stomach for the hole, finding none.

"Me too," Austin said, checking for a wound on his shoulder. "Not a mark on me."

"Same here," Glenn added, rubbing his now completely healthy hip. "And Caleb...There's no gash on his head. It worked. We did it!"

The group finally took the time to celebrate. Austin grabbed Ethan and gave him the tightest bear hug of his life. Then he leaned into Ethan's ear during the embrace and said, "You're one helluva captain, Ethan Tate...one hell of a captain."

Ethan smiled but shook his head. "No, we're one hell of a team," he corrected.

"By the way, where are we?" Glenn asked.

"I know exactly where we are...about a mile west of Bravo Fort," Ethan answered.

"The big question is not *where* we are," Caleb said in a more serious tone. "The big question is *when* we are."

In the joy of the moment, it had briefly escaped the group's attention that they had been transported in time. Just then, a cell phone rang from Ethan's pocket. The phone had been without connection for two weeks, and he'd forgotten he still had it. After the initial shock, he punched his hand eagerly into his pocket, retrieved the phone, and held it snuggly to his ear.

"Hello?" Ethan answered. After a moment, a big smile came to his face. "What...? Oh, sorry, Mom. Yeah, I can explain that." He finished the conversation with: "I love you, Mom. I'll see you soon."

Annika and the others had smiles on their faces that could've been seen from space. They could tell from the call that Ethan's parents were fine. That meant their families were okay, too.

"I'm gonna see my little brother, mom, and dad," Annika

said with inflection in her voice, sounding more like a question than a statement.

Ethan nodded with a tear rolling down his cheek. "Yeah... Our families are okay." Annika gave Ethan a tender hug. "There is one thing, though."

"What's that?" Annika asked.

"My mom told me people are worried about us, wondering why we skipped the last day of school." Ethan looked at the date on his phone. "It's June third. One thirty-nine in the afternoon. We graduate today...again."

At that moment, Austin's cell phone rang through his pocket. He pulled it out and reluctantly put it to his ear. He cringed slightly before he pressed the talk button, then answered with a hesitant "Hello." It was easy to hear all the words spoken in the conversation, if one could call it that. Actually, it was more of a one-sided verbal flogging. General Turnbull could be heard screaming madly at his son, giving him the reaming of a lifetime for skipping school. Austin tried to press the phone hard into his ear so nobody would hear, but the furious stream of obscenities could not be muffled. The tongue-lashing lasted a full minute. Austin's ear had to be sore from the general's deafening rant, but he kept a straight face like it didn't bother him at all. After he got in a few more choice words, the general hung up on his son. Everyone stared at Austin in sympathy.

"I'm sorry, Austin," Ethan said. "If your dad could've seen you in battle, I know he woulda been real proud."

Austin nodded with a bittersweet smile. "Sure, Ethan... Thanks." Then Austin's smile went from bittersweet to oddly playful. "Just promise not to tell him I shot him in the head."

Everyone smiled and chuckled a little awkwardly. Ethan

put his arm around Austin. "You have my word." Then Ethan looked at the dead robot on the ground. "We'll need to hide that Skulley in our fort until we figure out our next move."

Everyone nodded in agreement.

"How do we explain the fact that the five of us decided to skip school together?" Annika asked. "It's not like everyone here was the best of friends before all this."

"Good point," Caleb said. "We need to keep our story straight."

Everyone thought for a moment, then Austin said, "You guys tell your folks I challenged you to a Laser Wars game. That I thought I could beat you all...four against one. Tell them I was really mean about it, that I gave you no choice."

"Seriously?" Ethan asked.

"Yeah." Austin paused, then became pensive before continuing, "Arrogant general's son, people would definitely believe I was a big enough ass to do that...'cause back then, I was."

"But what about when people see us hanging out, all nice and friendly?" Glenn asked.

"We tell them we fought a furious battle...and ended up being friends," Austin said with a smile forming on his face. "That part will be easy to say because it's true."

Ethan returned Austin's smile and nodded. "Copy that."

CHAPTER 48

A FAMILIAR EVENT

JUNE 3 CAME for the second time that year for a very select group of students at Blackwoods. It was hot that evening in the auditorium, as it had been before, and Ethan's tight-fitting suit hadn't gotten any looser. But none of that even registered to Ethan now. As he waited in line for his name to be called by the principal to walk up to the stage, all he could do was reflect back on the previous weeks' events. They seemed totally unreal, except he had all of the memories, four witnesses, some laser guns, and a dead robot stashed in the Bravo Fort to prove it. Ethan watched as the other soon-to-be eighth graders filed onto the stage and took their spots on some bleacher stands. They all looked different to him. They looked younger somehow. They looked like children. Or maybe it was just that he felt so much older himself.

Once again, Ethan was lost in his daydream when the principal finally called his name. "Ethan Tate," the principal announced for a third time with frustration in his voice. Ethan was walking up the stairs to the stage when he heard a taunting voice from behind.

"Move it, Tate, you loser!" Bradley Wuddle jeered.

Ethan continued walking up to the stage, but he could see Austin's reaction from the corner of his eye. Austin stormed back in line to where Bradley was standing. Bradley held his hand up, expecting a high five of congratulations from his captain, but instead got a hard slap to the back of his head. Bradley stared at Austin, flustered and completely confused.

"You show your teammate some damn respect. You got that, Wuddle?" Austin snarled through clenched teeth.

Bradley nodded fearfully. "Y-y-yes, sir," he stammered.

Ethan smiled as he grabbed his certificate from the principal, then he took a spot on the bleachers next to Annika. Soon enough, Austin, Glenn, and Caleb were called up to the stage. The entire team stood on the bleachers together, side-by-side, shoulder-to-shoulder. No one in the school or in the audience or in the world, for that matter, could've possibly guessed the common bond that held the five of them together.

Ethan noticed that Tristan was standing right in front of him, one step down on the bleachers. He leaned over and spoke into his ear. "Congratulations, Tristan."

"Thanks. You too, Ethan."

"Hey, Tristan. Wanna hear a joke?"

"Sure."

"If Pete and Repeat were on a boat, and Pete fell off, who would be left?"

Tristan rolled his eyes sarcastically. "Wow…That is a really lame joke, Ethan."

"I know," Ethan said, chuckling. Annika and the others had been watching the entire time. They couldn't help but laugh.

The principal finally took to the podium to deliver a

familiar message. The only difference in the principal's speech this time was that five students actually paid attention to the words he spoke. The words couldn't have rung any truer.

The principal began: "Today marks a major step in the progression of your lives. The decisions you made yesterday got you to this point, and the decisions you make today will lead you to your future…*You* are the future of the world. The future of the world will depend on you, and it will all happen much sooner than you think…Ladies and gentlemen, I present the graduating classes of Blackwoods."

The audience applauded and pictures were taken by the dozen. The members of Team Blackwoods disbanded and headed into the audience to celebrate with family members. It was a much more joyous occasion than the first time around. Everyone in the group had a lot more to be thankful for. There were more hugs and kisses, more smiles and laughs— with the lone exception of the Turnbull family. The general, still furious over his son's skipping school, had a hold on Austin's arm and was leading him out of the auditorium like a prisoner of war. Austin caught eyes with Ethan in the crowd, then jerked his arm free and ran over to meet him.

"We should talk now. I don't have much time," Austin said as he watched his father seethe beside the exit door of the auditorium. Ethan spotted Austin's father and waved politely. The gesture wasn't returned.

Ethan and Austin walked through the auditorium and motioned for the others to join them. The group found a secluded stairwell and huddled together for a private conference.

"I've been thinking," Austin said, looking around to make sure they were alone. "If my dad ever finds out what happened, even though we saved their asses, he'll tighten security. He'll make it impossible for us to do what we did before…might even get rid of Project Mulligan altogether, or close down the secret tunnel to the research facility and build another we wouldn't know about. And if they made the same error again, we'd be out of luck stopping it."

"Right," Glenn said. "Whatever it takes, we gotta have access to that tunnel."

Ethan appeared deep in thought, staring at the concrete wall. "Caleb, remember that project we did last year on Winston Churchill?"

"Yeah, why?" Caleb asked.

"'Those who fail to learn from history are doomed to repeat it,'" Ethan recited. "Just like now with the fatal error. If we don't tell the military about the error, whatever it is, how will they learn? We went back in time. They can't learn from history that hasn't happened yet. They'll just repeat their error."

"You're right," Caleb agreed. "We have to tell them, but not right away. Think about it…if we tell them right away, they'll make all sorts of changes. But if they don't know exactly what the fatal error was, they could even speed up the date they make the error. It could happen on June tenth…or tomorrow." Caleb drew a deep breath, then continued, "As it is now, without telling them, we know it won't happen before June twelfth. That gives us some time."

Annika cocked her head, curious. "Time for what?"

"You know, time to think things over." Caleb hesitated, then slipped in casually, "And, if we can bring it back to life, time to interrogate that Skulley in the fort first."

Annika shook her head sharply. "Caleb, I'm not losing my

family again. We're not messing around with things we don't understand. Not after all this. It's not a stupid toy."

"I know it's not, and I promise I won't do anything to put us in danger," Caleb said. "But, *if* I can get it working, we might be able to figure out the fatal error…get some answers so we can keep this from ever happening again."

"You mean *bring it back to life*," Annika said with a sharp edge to her voice.

"I didn't mean that. I meant read its hard drive," Caleb insisted. "Besides, that's a long shot anyway. You shot it up pretty well."

Annika sighed deeply in frustration. "Caleb, I swear to God…I will blow that awful thing to bits."

"Please, just think about it. And let's not tell anyone yet, at least for a while?"

Austin and Glenn nodded in strong agreement. Ethan and Annika nodded as well, but with much less enthusiasm.

"Okay," Ethan said. "But just for a while."

CHAPTER 49

THE BIG TALK?

ETHAN QUICKLY CHANGED out of his stuffy suit and into some more comfortable clothes. He sat on his bed with all the events in the recent past, or future in his case, swirling about in his head. Then he looked at the empty table in his bedroom, the one that would soon be the home for the new mahogany chessboard he was about to receive as a graduation present. Or possibly not. Ethan thought for a moment that maybe his supposed skipping school was reason enough for his dad not to give him the chessboard. He thought maybe he had already altered the future. Contemplating the results of time travel could drive someone crazy, so Ethan tried to shift gears in his mind to avoid a trip to the loony bin. That's when another thought took its place.

Ethan got onto his computer. He brought up the Google search page. After a long, deep breath, he typed in…*37-Geminorum*…and pressed enter. When the results of the search came up, his jaw nearly hit the floor.

Ethan immediately called Caleb, and started the

conversation without a hello. "Caleb, do you have *any idea* what Thirty-Seven Geminorum really is?"

"An idea, sure," Caleb answered. "It has to be some kind of new, super-high energy element they discovered, or created... Why?"

"Because I looked it up on the internet."

"It would definitely be classified top-secret," Caleb said. "That's why you didn't find anything on it. Like I said, it's gotta be a new element...a very strange new element."

"Caleb, it may or may not be an element, I don't know what it is. But what I do know is that Thirty-Seven Geminorum is not just a random name. There's a reason they named it that... And *I did* find it on the internet."

There was a lengthy pause. Ethan could hear a nervous jitter in Caleb's voice as he spoke. "Wait, wait, *what...?* What is it then?"

Ethan took a deep breath. "Caleb, Thirty-Seven Geminorum is a star in the constellation Gemini. It's fifty-six light-years away, and some scientists think there's a good chance of life on a planet in that area." Ethan waited for a response from Caleb, but there was nothing but stunned silence. Ethan continued, "The Russians even sent a radio message to it. They sent samples of music, art, greetings in different languages. The message shouldn't have reached them yet, so they must've already known about us." Ethan paused, then spoke uneasily. "Caleb, I saw another kind of Skulley at the research facility, when I doubled back and hid in the janitor's closet. It had a big head, big eyes, it didn't look human at all...It was still a machine, but it took an alien form. Caleb, I think they're already here. I think those energy rods, along with all that other amazing technology the military's been playing with, came from some sort of alien contact."

There was more silence. It was a lot for Caleb to process. "Geminorum, Constellation Gemini...I never even thought about that," Caleb said in a daze, disappointment in his voice. "Fifty-six light-years away...they're practically our next-door neighbors in space."

"Yeah, so now we know there's more to the story than—" Ethan stopped mid-sentence when he heard a knock on the door. "Gotta go, Caleb. Call you back." He hung up and quickly closed the 37-Geminorum page on the internet. "Come in," he tried to say casually.

Ethan's father opened the door. "Hi, graduate," he said with a smile. "Come on downstairs. We have something for you."

∽

"Happy graduation!" Ethan's parents cheerfully proclaimed.

"Go ahead, open it," his father said with eager eyes.

Ethan sat on the couch in the family room with a large, flattish box covered in shiny wrapping paper resting on his legs. He knew exactly what was in the box, of course, but he resolved to fake a level of surprise that would be worthy of an Academy Award. Ethan tore into the box and pulled out the fantastic wooden chessboard, along with the handcrafted chessmen.

"I love it. Thank you." Ethan hugged them. Then his face turned more serious. "Can I talk to you about something? It's really important...But you have to promise to keep it a secret."

Ethan's mom and dad flashed that patented worried parent face, then their faces softened. They smiled easily. "Sure, son," his father said. "Is it about why you skipped school today?"

"It sort of is."

"I see…Mind if I grab some coffee real quick? It's been a long day, and I want to give you my full, caffeinated attention. Can I get you something? Soda, hot chocolate?"

A long day working with the machines, Ethan thought. "Coffee sounds great, Dad."

"Okay," Ethan's dad said, sounding a little taken aback by his son's choice. It was the first time Ethan had ever asked for coffee.

Ethan's mother cracked a subtle smile. "I'll help you get it," she said. Then his parents disappeared into the kitchen.

Ethan sat back down on the couch and sighed deeply. He decided he was going to tell them the truth about what had happened. Tell them everything. And right away, too, no matter what he had told Caleb, no matter what he'd promised the others. Ethan knew his dad had a secret life at the research facility, but that didn't mean he couldn't trust him with this. Work was work, but this was their home. A safe place. A place to be a family. A place to tell the truth. Austin might have a good reason not to tell his own dad, but Ethan knew *his* father was different.

Ethan was thinking about how he was going to tell his parents—where to begin with the crazy story and the exact order of the things that took place—when something on the wall of the family room caught his attention. It was the thermostat. Ethan darted over to the wall. He put his hand on the thermostat and pulled on it slowly, with dread in his heart. A twelve-digit keypad was revealed, just like the one Caleb's dad had. Ethan now knew his dad, like Caleb's, had a secret basement in the house somewhere. Unlike Caleb's dad, though, *his* dad had never told him about it. Something about that felt very wrong. Unfair. He clenched his jaw and slammed the thermostat cover closed, then sat down disgustedly on the couch. After a moment, Ethan took to scanning the room, looking for where the entrance to the forbidden basement might be. But he abruptly had to stop when his parents entered with a round of coffees.

Mr. Tate handed his son a cup of coffee. "Want some cream and sugar?"

"No, I'll take it straight," Ethan said firmly.

"Okay, so…" Ethan's dad began. "You wanted to tell us something?"

"Yeah," Ethan paused for a long, pensive moment, then continued, "I skipped school because Austin challenged me, Annika, Caleb, and Glenn to a Laser Wars game. He thought he could beat us four against one."

Ethan's mom raised an eyebrow. "And you had to play during school hours because…?"

"It was for our honor."

"I see."

"Well, did you win?" Ethan's dad asked.

"Yes."

"And that's it? That's all that happened?" Ethan's father probed further.

"Yes, that's it. Why?"

"Just curious why you were so concerned about keeping it a secret."

"Well, you know Austin. Don't wanna make him mad…I gotta play on his team, right?"

"Right," Ethan's dad said. "Well, your secret's safe with us."

"Thanks," Ethan said with an ironic glint in his eye.

"I think you two should christen that chessboard with a game," Ethan's mom said.

"Up for it?" his dad asked.

"Sure."

"All right, let's set up the board."

"I have some work to do, so I'm going to let you two play alone," Ethan's mom said. "No roughhousing," she added playfully. "Give me a hug, graduate." Ethan gave his mom a hug. "I love you, Ethan. But just make me two promises, okay…? One, no more skipping school. And, two," she said with a chuckle, "promise me that seventh grade won't be your last graduation ceremony."

Ethan smiled softly at his mom, but she couldn't bring him to laugh. "I promise," he said with more seriousness in his voice than was expected.

"Okay…Goodnight." Then she left the room.

Ethan and his father began setting up the chess pieces on the board. Ethan worked quickly setting up the white side, finishing well before his dad. He watched his father closely as he finished placing the black pieces on the board.

"How was work today?" Ethan asked.

"It was busy, really busy. Glad I'm home."

"How are the vacuums coming?"

"What?" Ethan's dad asked, a bit surprised, looking up from placing the black bishop.

"The vacuums," Ethan repeated. "I remember you talking about the vacuums and how they sometimes malfunction… and that you needed to fix them."

"Oh, yeah. It's a constant battle keeping those things clean," Ethan's dad said with a nonchalant laugh.

"What's the strangest thing you ever cleaned out of a

vacuum?" Ethan asked with a level of interest that took his father off guard.

"Hmm…Probably a gold watch. Would you believe that?"

"No I wouldn't," Ethan responded bluntly. "Lucky the vacuum didn't just suck the man up right along with it."

Ethan's dad smiled strangely. "That would be some vacuum." Then he seemed eager to change the topic. "So… have you played much chess lately?"

"A little."

"Have you been playing the computer?"

"Yeah…I played one really long game."

"How many moves did it take?"

"I'm not sure, but it seemed like it went on for days and days."

"Wow…Did you win?"

"Yeah."

"Really? That's wonderful, Ethan. Congratulations."

"Thanks…But I'm afraid the computer might want a rematch." Ethan paused to adjust some pieces on the board, then looked squarely at his father. "You know, I realized when battling a machine, you don't try to think like the best machine, you try to think like the best human…Don't you agree?"

Ethan's dad squinted curiously, as if his son had just yanked the words he was about to say straight out of his mouth. Slowly, he nodded in agreement. Ethan moved his king's pawn forward two squares.

"It's your move, Dad."

The End

ACKNOWLEDGMENTS

There are a lot of things that can derail the writing of a book, let alone an entire series. My deepest love, thanks, and appreciation go to my wife, Erika, for reading all of the early stuff, even the first draft that was thick enough to stop a bullet. She finished that version of the book during a trip we took to Cincinnati one summer. Of all the fun things we did on that trip, the highlight for me was seeing her turn that last page. In that moment, she was an audience of one, and her opinion meant everything to me...I really wish she liked the book, but that's okay. I still love her.

Ha! I'm kidding, of course!

Erika, your belief in my writing and words of encouragement and advice have helped to propel one book into a full-fledged series. I cannot thank you enough for your role in keeping the train on the tracks.

To all my family and friends who were brave enough to be the frontline readers of this tale of ruthless robots running amok, thank you so much for your time and kind words. Those words kept me going many, many late nights at the computer. That, and coffee.

Most importantly, a big shout-out to all the past, present, and future readers of *Holding the Fort: The Fatal Error*. If a tree falls in the forest and no one is around to hear it, the tree most definitely still makes a sound. But a book that is written and not read...? Thank you so much for taking this journey with me. You are always with me as I write.

So...if you've made it this far, congratulations and welcome to Team Blackwoods. The adventure is just beginning!

ABOUT THE AUTHOR:

Ryan Peek is the author of the Young Adult Sci-Fi book series *Holding the Fort*. The first book in the series, *The Fatal Error*, is a story based on an idea he's had for a long time. Or possibly, it's based on the true story of him and his friends thwarting a robot rebellion while living near a secret military research facility during the summer before eighth grade. Either way, whatever you believe, he hopes this book teaches you never to turn your back on the machines.

The author lives in Indiana with his wife, Erika, and two genius cats who always knew better than to ever trust the machines…especially the vacuum.

www.ryanpeek.com
www.facebook.com/ryanpeekbooks

Watch for the next book in the series…

HOLDING THE FORT

THE
INFILTRATION

To get updates on upcoming books, please visit:

ryanpeek.com and facebook.com/
ryanpeekbooks and subscribe!

CPSIA information can be obtained
at www.ICGtesting.com
Printed in the USA
LVHW101738090622
720900LV00016B/476/J

9 781735 706009